A Tramp Abroad

'One day it occurred to me that it had been many years since the world had been afforded the spectacle of a man adventurous enough to undertake a journey through Europe on foot. After much thought, I decided that I was a person fitted to furnish to mankind this spectacle. So I determined to do it. This was in March, 1878.'

Thus Mark Twain begins his irreverent and witty account of how he and his companion, Harris, walked around Germany, Switzerland and Italy. His travels are as delightfully adventurous as anything he dreamed up for his fictional heroes, Tom Sawyer and Huckleberry Finn, and it is fitting that this edition of *A Tramp Abroad* should be introduced by Norman Lewis, the distinguished author of *A Dragon Apparent*.

D1331811

A Tramp Abroad

Mark Twain

Introduction by Norman Lewis

Century
London Melbourne Auckland Johannesburg

First published by Chatto & Windus in 1898

© Introduction Norman Lewis 1982

This edition first published in 1982
Reprinted in 1985, 1986 by Century,
an imprint of Century Hutchinson Ltd,
Brookmount House, 62–65 Chandos Place, London WC2N 4NW

Century Hutchinson South Africa (Pty) Ltd
PO Box 337, Berglvei, 2012 South Africa

Century Hutchinson Australia Pty Ltd
PO Box 496, 16–22 Church Street, Hawthorn, Victoria 3122, Australia

Century Hutchinson New Zealand Ltd
PO Box 40–086, Glenfield, Auckland 10, New Zealand

ISBN 0 7126 0033 7 (cased)
     0 7126 0034 5 (paper)

Reprinted in Great Britain by
Richard Clay (The Chaucer Press) Ltd,
Bungay, Suffolk

CONTENTS

Introduction by Norman Lewis

Contents

CHAPTER 8

CHAPTER 9

CHAPTER 10

CHAPTER 11

Contents

Contents

Contents

Contents

Contents

Contents

CHAPTER 48

CHAPTER 49

CHAPTER 50

APPENDIX

INTRODUCTION

Mark Twain began and ended his life a joker. Born in 1835, he was apprenticed at the age of thirteen to a printer, but soon abandoned the tedium of this employment for the free and easy life of a deck-hand then pilot on a Mississippi river steamer. The cry most frequently heard in this environment was 'mark twain', announcing when soundings were taken, that a minimum depth of two fathoms had been reached, and the young Samuel Lenghorne, as he was then, was inspired to change his name to this. The reborn Mark Twain eventually abandoned the river to become a lecturer on humerous topics, and thereafter a writer. *The Adventures of Tom Sawyer* and *The Adventures of Huckleberry Finn* made him world famous, but his travel books were equally renowned in their day. *Innocents Abroad* and *A Tramp Abroad* sold prodigiously, and have remained classics of their kind.

Mark Twain founded a recognizably American school of humerous writing, strongly influencing most of the practitioners of the genre that followed him. He was the first of the debunkers, complaining in *A Tramp Abroad* that the superbly turned-out ladies at the opera harboured fleas, that Rhine wine was only vinegar under another label, and that the much esteemed flower of the eidelweiss was the colour of bad cigar ash. Mark Twain fathered the wisecrack, and many of the irreverent comments abounding in the pages of this book are pure Groucho Marx. Some of the early critics found this brand of humour 'wild and exaggerated' but a taste for it soon grew and spread. The sallies come unexpectedly like thunderclaps out of a clear sky. Describing in deadpan style the miseries of rising at three am to watch one of the long succession of sunrises, the author mentions, as if in passing, that he yawned so widely that his top teeth were caught on a nail in the wall. Later, crossing a rickety bridge in a storm, he notes that this is shaken by the largest of raindrops. One seems to be reading S.J. Perelman, and it is no accident that the doyen of modern American humour should have been a devoted student of the Master's writings. Sometimes it is hard to decide whether or not we are being spoofed. Mark Twain, thorough in all his doings, studied painting in order to be able to illustrate his books. He tells us that the first of his oils, hung in an exhibition in Heidelberg, was taken for a Turner. It is a claim we may be inclined to accept at the beginning of the book, but remembering it when we have reached its end, doubt encroaches upon belief.

A Tramp Abroad appeared at a time when Americans had discovered picturesque Europe, and they went there in their tens of thousands to undertake peregrinations committed as much to obligation as pleasure. It was the mind-broadening process that mattered, and every traveller carried, slung over the shoulder, a guide book case stuffed with all the available literature. No recommended sight was left unseen, and every fact assiduously checked. It was a serious business, and the tourists dressed for these outings with the formality of the students Mark Twain saw at Heidelberg preparing themselves for their duels. The author followed suit, describing his appearance with characteristic self-mockery. The final touch was an idea brought back from the Orient. 'Around our hats were many folds of soft white muslin, with the ends hanging and flapping down our backs.' He drew on a cornucopeia of such experiences, much of them grotesque, as when he is trodden on by a seven-foot-tall woman, but the mockery was stiffened with the keenest observation and a self-driving relish for hard work.

In this lies the difference between *A Tramp Abroad* and the majority of travel books that poured in a spate from the publishers at this time, which were little better than insipid and amateurish impressions, and devoid of the solid information Mark Twain so painstakingly collected. Alpenstock in one hand, and a sun umberella in the other, his binoculars hanging from his neck and a pedometer totting up his paces, he covered enormous distances on foot. He crossed all the passes, spent nights embattled with bed-bugs in deplorable inns, collected legends wherever he went. The slower the travel the better. 'The dusty and deafening railroad rush' of a train that could reach forty-five mph was naturally to be avoided, but he occasionally consented to ride in a diligence, although his happiest experience was clearly a long trip by raft. In these journeyings he saw and described in fresh and readable prose all that was most remarkable in Alpine Europe of his day.

A Tramp Abroad is full of wit, but there is much poetry too, and for us nostalgia. It is a zestful and beguiling account of travel and adventures in romantic places before their taming by mass tourism and the deadening affluence it produced.

Norman Lewis
1982

CHAPTER 1

One day it occurred to me that it had been many years since the world had been afforded the spectacle of a man adventurous enough to undertake a journey through Europe on foot. After much thought, I decided that I was a person fitted to furnish to mankind this spectacle. So I determined to do it. This was in March, 1878.

I looked about me for the right sort of person to accompany me in the capacity of agent, and finally hired a Mr. Harris for this service.

It was also my purpose to study art while in Europe. Mr. Harris was in sympathy with me in this. He was as much of an enthusiast in art as I was, and not less anxious to learn to paint. I desired to learn the German language; so did Harris.

Towards the middle of April we sailed in the 'Holsatia,' Captain Brandt, and had a very pleasant trip indeed.

After a brief rest at Hamburg, we made preparations for a long pedestrian trip southward in the soft spring weather, but at the last moment we changed the programme, for private reasons, and took the express train.

We made a short halt at Frankfort-on-the-Main, and found it an interesting city. I would have liked to visit the birth-place of Gutenberg, but it could not be done, as no memorandum of the site of the house has been kept. So we spent an hour in the Goethe mansion instead. The city permits this house to belong to private parties, instead of gracing and dignifying herself with the honour of possessing and protecting it.

Frankfort is one of the sixteen cities which have the distinction of being the place where the following incident occurred. Charlemagne, while chasing the Saxons (as *he* said), or being chased by them (as *they* said), arrived at the bank of the river at dawn, in a fog. The enemy were either before him or behind him; but in any case he wanted to get across, very badly. He would have given anything for a guide, but none was to be had. Presently he saw a deer, followed by her young, approach the water. He watched her, judging that she would seek a ford, and he was right. She waded over, and the army followed. So a great Frankish victory or defeat was gained or avoided; and in order to commemorate the episode, Charlemagne commanded a city to be built there, which he named Frankfort—the ford of the Franks. None of the other cities where this event happened were named from it. This is good evidence that Frankfort was the first place it occurred at.

Frankfort has another distinction—it is the birthplace of the German alphabet: or at least of the German word for alphabet—*Buchstaben*. They say that the first movable types were made on birch sticks—*Buchstabe*—hence the name.

I was taught a lesson in political economy in Frankfort. I had brought from home a box containing a thousand very cheap cigars. By way of experiment I stepped into a little shop in a queer old back street, took four gaily decorated boxes of wax matches and three cigars, and laid down a silver piece worth 48 cents. The man gave me 43 cents change.

In Frankfort everybody wears clean clothes, and I think we noticed that this strange thing was the case in Hamburg too, and in the villages along the road. Even in the narrowest and poorest and most ancient quarters of Frankfort neat and clean clothes were the rule. The little children of both sexes were nearly always nice enough to take into a body's lap. And as for the uniforms of the soldiers, they were newness and brightness carried to perfection. One could never detect a smirch or a grain of dust upon them. The street car conductors and drivers wore pretty uniforms, which seemed to be just out of the bandbox, and their manners were as fine as their clothes.

In one of the shops I had the luck to stumble upon a book which has charmed me nearly to death. It is entitled 'The Legends of the Rhine from Basle to Rotterdam,' by F.J. Kiefer; translated by L.W. Garnham, B.A.

All tourists *mention* the Rhine legends—in that sort of way which quietly pretends that the mentioner has been familiar with them all his life, and that the reader cannot possibly be ignorant of them—but no tourist ever *tells* them. So this little book fed me in a very hungry place; and I, in my turn, intend to feed my reader, with one or two little lunches from the same larder. I shall not mar Garnham's translation by meddling with its English; for the most toothsome thing about it is its quaint fashion of building English sentences on the German plan,—and punctuating them according to no plan at all.

In the chapter devoted to 'Legends of Frankfort' I find the following.

The Knave of Bergen

'In Frankfort at the Romer was a great mask-ball, at the coronation festival, and in the illuminated saloon, the clanging music invited to dance, and splendidly appeared the rich toilets and charms of the ladies, and the festively costumed Princes and Knights. All seemed pleasure, joy, and roguish gayety, only one of the numerous guests had a gloomy exterior, but exactly the black armour in which he walked about excited general attention, and his tall figure, as well as the noble propriety of his movements, attracted especially the regards of the ladies. Who the Knight was? Nobody could guess, for his Vizier was well closed, and nothing made him recognisable. Proud and yet modest he advanced to the Empress; bowed on one knee before her seat, and begged for the favour of a waltz with the Queen of the festival. And she allowed his request. With light and graceful steps he danced through the long saloon, with the sovereign who thought never to have found a more dexterous and excellent dancer. But also by the grace of his manner, and fine conversation he knew to win the Queen, and she graciously accorded him a second dance for which he begged, a third, and a fourth, as well as others were not refused him. How all regarded the happy dancer, how many envied him the high favour; how increased curiosity, who the masked knight could be.

'Also the Emperor became more and more excited with curiosity, and with great suspense one awaited the hour, when according to mask-law, each masked guest must make himself known. This moment came; but although all others had unmasked, the secret knight still refused to allow his features to be seen, till at last the Queen, driven by curiosity, and vexed at the obstinate refusal, commanded him to open his Vizier. He opened it, and none of the high ladies and knights knew him. But from the crowded spectators, 2 officials advanced, who recognised the black dancer, and horror and terror spread in the saloon, as they said who the supposed knight was. It was the executioner of Bergen. But glowing with rage, the King commanded to seize the criminal and lead him to death, who had ventured to dance, with the Queen; so disgraced the Empress, and insulted the crown. The culpable threw himself at the feet of the Emperor, and said,—

' "Indeed I have heavily sinned against all noble guests assembled here, but most heavily against you my sovereign and my queen. The Queen is insulted by my haughtiness equal to treason, but no punishment, even blood, will not be able to wash out the disgrace, which you have suffered by me. Therefore, oh King! allow me to propose a remedy, to efface the shame, and to render it as if not done. Draw your sword and knight me, then I will throw down my gauntlet, to every one who dares speak disrespectfully of my king."

'The Emperor was surprised at this bold proposal, however it appeared the wisest to him; "You are a brave knave," he replied after a moment's consideration, "however your advice is good, and displays prudence, as your offence shows adventurous courage. Well then"—and gave him the knight-stroke—"so I raise you to nobility, who begged for grace for your offence now kneels before me, rise as knight; knavish you have acted, and Knave of Bergen shall you be called henceforth," and gladly the Black knight rose; three cheers were given in honour of the Emperor, and loud cries of joy testified the approbation with which the Queen danced still once with the Knave of Bergen.

CHAPTER 2

Heidelberg

We stopped at an hotel by the railway station. Next morning, as we sat in my room waiting for breakfast to come up, we got a good deal interested in something which was going on over the way in front of another hotel. First, the personage who is called the *portier* (who is not the porter, but is a sort of first-mate of an hotel)[1] appeared at the door in a spick and span new blue cloth uniform, decorated with shining brass buttons, and with bands of gold lace around his cap and wristbands; and he wore white gloves, too. He shed an official glance upon the situation, and then began to give orders. Two women-servants came out with pails and brooms and brushes, and gave the side-walk a thorough scrubbing; meanwhile two others scrubbed the four marble steps which led up to the door; beyond these we could see some men-servants taking up the carpet of the grand staircase. This carpet was carried away and the last grain of dust beaten and banged and swept out of it; then brought back and put down again. The brass stair rods received an exhaustive polishing and were returned to their places. Now a troop of servants brought pots and tubs of blooming plants and formed them into a beautiful jungle about the door and the base of the staircase. Other servants adorned all the balconies of the various stories with flowers and banners; others ascended to the roof

[1] See Appendix A.

and hoisted a great flag on a staff there. Now came some more chambermaids and retouched the sidewalk, and afterwards wiped the marble steps with damp cloths, and finished by dusting them off with feather brushes. Now a broad black carpet was brought out and laid down the marble steps and out across the side-walk to the kerbstone. The *portier* cast his eye along it, and found it was not absolutely straight; he commanded it to be straightened; the servants made the effort—made several efforts, in fact—but the *portier* was not satisfied. He finally had it taken up, and then he put it down himself and got it right.

At this stage of the proceedings a narrow, bright red carpet was unrolled and stretched from the top of the marble steps to the kerbstone, along the centre of the black carpet. This red path cost the *portier* more trouble than even the black one had done. But he patiently fixed and refixed it until it was exactly right and lay precisely in the middle of the black carpet. In New York these performances would have gathered a mighty crowd of curious and intensely interested spectators; but here it only captured an audience of half-a-dozen little boys, who stood in a row across the pavement, some with their school knapsacks on their backs and their hands in their pockets, others with arms full of bundles, and all absorbed in the show. Occasionally one of them skipped irreverently over the carpet and took up a position on the other side. This always visibly annoyed the *portier*.

Now came a waiting interval. The landlord, in plain clothes, and bareheaded, placed himself on the bottom marble step, abreast the *portier*, who stood on the other end of the same step; six or eight waiters, gloved, bareheaded, and wearing their whitest linen, their whitest cravats, and their finest swallow-tails, grouped themselves about these chiefs, but leaving the carpet-way clear. Nobody moved or spoke any more, but only waited.

In a short time the shrill piping of a coming train was heard and immediately groups of people began to gather in the street. Two or three open carriages arrived, and deposited some maids-of-honour and some male officials at the hotel. Presently another open carriage brought the Grand-Duke of Baden, a stately man in uniform, who wore the handsome brass-mounted, steel-spiked helmet of the army on his head. Last came the Empress of Germany and the Grand Duchess of Baden in a close carriage; these passed through the low bowing groups of servants and disappeared in the hotel, exhibiting to us only the backs of their heads, and then the show was over.

It appears to be as difficult to land a monarch as it is to launch a ship.

But as to Heidelberg. The weather was growing pretty warm—very warm, in fact. So we left the valley and took quarters at the Schloss Hotel, on the hill, above the Castle.

Heidelberg lies at the mouth of a narrow gorge—a gorge the shape of a shepherd's crook; if one looks up it he perceives that it is about straight for a mile and a half, then makes a sharp curve to the right and disappears. This gorge—along whose bottom pours the swift Neckar—is confined between (or cloven through) a couple of long, steep ridges, a thousand feet high and densely wooded clear to their summits, with the exception of one section which has been shaved and put under cultivation. These ridges are chopped off at the mouth of the gorge, and form two bold and conspicuous headlands, with Heidelberg nestling between them; from their bases spreads away the vast dim expanse of the Rhine valley, and into this expanse the Neckar goes wandering in shining curves, and is presently lost to view.

Now, if one turns and looks up the gorge once more, he will see the Schloss Hotel on the right, perched on a precipice overlooking the Neckar,—a precipice which is so sumptuously cushioned and draped with foliage that no glimpse of the rock appears. The building seems very airily situated. It has the appearance of being on a shelf halfway up the wooded mountain side; and as it is remote and isolated, and very white, it makes a strong mark against the lofty leafy rampart at its back.

This hotel had a feature which was a decided novelty; and one which might be adopted with advantage by any house which is perched in a commanding situation. This feature may be described as a series of glass-enclosed parlours *clinging to the outside of the house*, one against each and every bedchamber and drawing-room. They are like long, narrow, high-ceiled bird-cages hung against the building. My room was a corner room, and had two of these things, a north one and a west one.

From the north cage one looks up the Neckar gorge; from the west one he looks down it. This last affords the most extensive view, and it is one of the loveliest that can be imagined, too. Out of a billowy upheaval of vivid green foliage, a rifle-shot removed, rises the huge ruin of Heidelberg Castle,[1] with empty window arches, ivy-mailed battlements, mouldering towers—the Lear of inanimate nature,—deserted, discrowned, beaten by the storms, but royal still, and beautiful. It is a fine sight to see the evening sunlight suddenly strike the leafy declivity at the Castle's base and dash up it and drench it as with a luminous spray, while the adjacent groves are in deep shadow.

Behind the Castle swells a great dome-shaped hill, forest-clad, and beyond that a nobler and loftier one. The Castle looks down upon the compact brown-roofed town; and from the town two picturesque old bridges span the river. Now the view broadens; through the gateway of the sentinel headlands you gaze out over the wide Rhine plain, which stretches away, softly and richly-tinted, grows gradually and dreamily indistinct, and finally melts imperceptibly into the remote horizon.

I have never enjoyed a view which had such a serene and satisfying charm about it as this one gives.

The first night we were there, we went to bed and to sleep early, but I awoke at the end of two or three hours, and lay a comfortable while listening to the soothing patter of the rain against the balcony windows. I took it to be rain, but it turned out to be only the murmur of the restless Neckar, tumbling over her dykes and dams far below, in the gorge. I got up and went into the west balcony and saw a wonderful sight. Away down on the level, under the black mass of the Castle, the town lay, stretched along the river, its intricate cobweb of streets jewelled with twinkling light upon the water, in the black shadows of the arches; and away at the extremity of all this fairy spectacle blinked and glowed a massed multitude of gas jets which seemed to cover acres of ground; it was as if all the diamonds in the world had been spread out there. I did not know before, that a half mile of sextuple railways tracks could be made such an

[1] See Appendix B.

adornment.

One thinks Heidelberg by day—with surroundings—is the last possibility of the beautiful; but when he sees Heidelberg by night, a fallen Milky Way, with that glittering railway constellation pinned to the border, he requires time to consider upon the verdict.

One never tires of poking about in the dense woods that clothe all these lofty Neckar hills to their tops. The great deeps of a boundless forest have a beguiling and impressive charm in any country; but German legends and fairy tales have given these an added charm. They have peopled all that region with gnomes, and dwarfs, and all sorts of mysterious and uncanny creatures. At the time I am writing of, I had been reading so much of this literature that sometimes I was not sure but I was beginning to believe in the gnomes and fairies as realities.

One afternoon I got lost in the woods about a mile from the hotel, and presently fell into a train of dreamy thought about animals which talk, and kobolds, and enchanted folk, and the rest of the pleasant legendary stuff; and so, by stimulating my fancy, I finally got to imagining I glimpsed small flitting shapes here and there down the columned aisles of the forest. It was a place which was peculiarly meet for the occasion. It was a pine wood, with so thick and soft a carpet of brown needles that one's footfall made no more sound than if he was treading on wool; the tree-trunks were as round and straight and smooth as pillars, and stood close together; they were bare of branches to a point about twenty-five feet above ground, and from there upward so thick with boughs that not a ray of sunlight could pierce through. The world was bright with sunshine outside, but a deep and mellow twilight reigned in there, and also a silence so profound that I seemed to hear my own breathings.

When I had stood ten minutes, thinking and imagining, and getting my spirit in tune with the place, and in the right mood to enjoy the supernatural, a raven suddenly uttered a hoarse croak over my head. It made me start; and then I was angry because I started. I looked up, and the creature was sitting on a limb right over me, looking down at me. I felt something of the same sense of humiliation and injury which one feels when he finds that a human stranger has been clandestinely inspecting him in his privacy and mentally commenting upon him. I eyed the raven, and the raven eyed me. Nothing was said during some seconds. Then the bird stepped a little way along his limb to get a better point of observation, lifted his wings, stuck his head far down below his shoulders toward me, and croaked again—a croak with a distinctly insulting expression about it. If he had spoken in English he could not have said any more plainly than he did say in raven, 'Well, what do *you* want here?' I felt as foolish as if I had been caught in some mean act by a responsible being, and reproved for it. However, I made no reply; I would not bandy words with a raven. The adversary waited a while, with his shoulders still lifted, his head thrust down between them, and his keen bright eye fixed on me; then he threw out two or three more insults, which I could not understand, further than that I knew a portion of them consisted of language not used in church.

I still made no reply. Now the adversary raised his head and called. There was an answering croak from a little distance in the wood—evidently a croak of inquiry. The adversary explained with enthusiasm, and the other raven dropped everything and came. The two sat side by side on the limb and discussed me as freely and offensively as two great naturalists might discuss a new kind of bug. The thing became more and more embarrassing. They called in another friend. This was too much. I saw that they had the advantage of me, and so I concluded to get out of the scrape by walking out of it. They enjoyed my defeat as much as any low white people could have done. They craned their necks and laughed at me (for a raven *can* laugh, just like a man), they squalled insulting remarks after me as long as they could see me. They were nothing but ravens—I knew that—what they thought about me could be a matter of no consequence—and yet when even a raven shouts after you: 'What a hat!' 'O, pull down your vest!' and that sort of thing, it hurts you and humiliates you, and there is no getting around it with fine reasoning and pretty arguments.

Animals talk to each other, of course. There can be no question about that; but I suppose there are very few people who can understand them. I never knew but one man who could. I knew he could, however, because he told me so himself. He was a middle-aged, simple-hearted miner who had lived in a lonely corner of California, among the woods and mountains, a good many years, and had studied the ways of his only neighbours, the beasts and the birds, until he believed he could accurately translate any remark which they made. This was Jim Baker. According to Jim Baker, some animals have only a limited education, and use only very simple words, and scarcely ever a comparison or a flowery figure; whereas, certain other animals have a large vocabulary, a fine command of language and a ready and fluent delivery; consequently these latter talk a great deal; they like it; they are conscious of their talent, and they enjoy 'showing off.' Baker said that, after long and careful observation, he had come to the conclusion that the blue-jays were the best talkers he had found among birds and beasts. Said he:—

'There's more *to* a blue-jay than any other creature. He has got more moods, and more different kinds of feelings than other creatures; and mind you, whatever a blue-jay feels, he can put into language. And no mere commonplace language either, but rattling, out-and-out book-talk—and bristling with metaphor, too—just bristling! And as for command of language—why *you* never see a blue-jay get stuck for a word. No man ever did. They just boil out of him! And another thing: I've noticed a good deal, and there's no bird, or cow, or anything that uses as good grammar as a blue-jay. You may say a cat uses good grammar. Well, a cat does—but you let a cat get excited, once; you let a cat get to pulling fur with another cat on a shed, nights, and you'll hear grammer that will give you the lockjaw. Ignorant people think it's the *noise* which fighting cats make that is so aggravating, but it ain't so; it's the sickening grammar they use. Now I've never heard a jay use bad grammar but very seldom; and when they do, they are as ashamed as a human; they shut right down and leave.

'You may call a jay a bird. Well, so he is, in a measure—because he's got feathers on him, and don't belong to no church, perhaps; but otherwise he is just as much a human as you be. And I'll tell you for why. A jay's gifts, and instincts, and

feelings, and interests, cover the whole ground. A jay hasn't got
any more principle than a Congressman. A jay will lie, a jay will
steal, a jay will deceive, a jay will betray; and four times out of
five, a jay will go back on his solemnest promise. The sacredness
of an obligation is a thing which you can't cram into no blue-
jay's head. Now, on top of all this, there's another thing; a jay
can outswear any gentleman in the mines. You think a cat can
swear. Well, a cat can; but you give a blue-jay a subject that
calls for his reserve powers, and where is your cat? Don't talk to
me—I know too much about this thing. And there's yet another
thing: in the one little particular of scolding—just good, clean,
out-and-out scolding—a blue-jay can lay over anything, human
or divine. Yes, sir, a jay is everything that a man is. A jay can
cry, a jay can laugh, a jay can feel shame, a jay can reason and
plan and discuss, a jay likes gossip and scandal, a jay has got a
sense of humour, a jay knows when he is an ass just as well as
you do—may be better. If a jay ain't human, he'd better take in
his sign, that's all. Now I'm going to tell you a perfectly true fact
about some blue-jays.'

CHAPTER 3

Baker's Blue-Jay Yarn

'When I first begun to understand jay language correctly, there was a little incident happened here. Seven years ago, the last man in this region but me, moved away. There stands his house,—been empty ever since; a log house, with a plank roof—just one big room, and no more; no ceiling—nothing between the rafters and the floor. Well, one Sunday morning I was sitting out here in front of my cabin, with my cat, taking the sun, and looking at the blue hills, and listening to the leaves rustling so lonely in the trees, and thinking of the home away yonder in the States, that I hadn't heard from in thirteen years, when a blue-jay lit on that house, with an acorn in his mouth, and says, "Hello, I reckon I have struck something." When he spoke, the acorn dropped out of his mouth and rolled down the roof, of course, but he didn't care; his mind was all on the thing he had struck. It was a knot-hole in the roof. He cocked his head to one side, shut one eye, and put the other one to the hole, like a 'possum looking down a jug; then he glanced up with his bright eyes, gave a wink or two with his wings—which signifies gratification, you understand,—and says, "It looks like a hole, it's located like a hole,—blamed if I don't believe it *is* a hole!"

'Then he cocked his head down and took another look; he glances up perfectly joyful, this time; winks his wings and his tail both, and says, "O, no, this ain't no fat thing, I reckon! If I ain't in luck!—why it's a perfectly elegant hole!" So he flew down and got that acorn, and fetched it up and dropped it in, and was just tilting his head back, with the heavenliest smile on his face, when all of a sudden he was paralysed into a listening attitude, and that smile faded gradually out of his countenance like breath off'n a razor, and the queerest look of surprise took its place. Then he says, "Why, I didn't hear it fall!" He cocked his eye at the hole again, and took a long look; raised up and shook his head; stepped around to the other side of the hole, and took another look from that side; shook his head again. He studied a while, then he just went into the *de*tails—walked round and round the hole, and spied into it from every point of the compass. No use. Now he took a thinking attitude on the comb of the roof, and scratched the back of his head with his right foot a minute, and finally says, "Well, it's too many for *me*, that's certain; must be a mighty long hole; however, I ain't got no time to fool around here, I got to 'tend to business; I reckon it's all right—chance it, anyway."

'So he flew off and fetched another acorn and dropped it in, and tried to flirt his eye to the hole quick enough to see what become of it, but he was too late. He held his eye there as much as a minute; then he raised up and sighed, and says, "Confound it, I don't seem to understand this thing, no way; however, I'll tackle her again." He fetched another acorn, and done his level best to see what become of it, but he couldn't. He says, "Well, *I* never struck no such a hole as this, before; I'm of the opinion it's a totally new kind of a hole." Then he begun to get mad. He held in for a spell, walking up and down the comb of the roof and shaking his head and muttering to himself; but his feelings got the upper hand of him, presently, and he broke loose and cussed himself black in the face. I never see a bird take on so about a little thing. When he got through he walks to the hole and looks in again for half a minute; then he says, "Well, you're a long hole, and a deep hole, and a mighty singular hole altogether—but I've started in to fill you, and I'm d——d if I *don't* fill you, if it takes a hundred years!"

'And with that, away he went. You never see a bird work so since you was born. He laid into his work like a nigger, and the way he hove acorns into that hole for about two hours and a half was one of the most exciting and astonishing spectacles I ever struck. He never stopped to take a look any more—he just hove 'em in and went for more. Well, at last he could hardly flop his wings, he was so tuckered out. He comes adrooping down, once more, sweating like an ice-pitcher, drops his acorn in and says, "*Now* I guess I've got the bulge on you by this time!" So he bent down for a look. If you'll believe me, when his head come up again he was just pale with rage. He says, "I've shovelled acorns enough in there to keep the family thirty years, and if I can see a sign of one of 'em I wish I may land in a museum with a belly full of sawdust in two minutes!"

'He just had strength enough to crawl up on to the comb, and lean his back agin the chimbly, and then he collected his impressions, and begun to free his mind. I see in a second that what I had mistook for profanity in the mines was only just the rudiments, as you may say.

'Another jay was going by, and heard him doing his devotions, and stops to inquire what was up. The sufferer told him the whole circumstance, and says, "Now yonder's the hole, and if you don't believe me go and look for yourself." So this fellow went and looked, and comes back and says, "How many did you say you put in there?" "Not any less than two tons," says the sufferer. The other jay went and looked again. He couldn't seem to make it out, so he raised a yell, and three more jays come. They all examined the hole, they all made the sufferer tell it over again, then they all discussed it, and got off as many leather-headed opinions about it as an average crowd of humans could have done.

'They called in more jays; then more and more, till pretty soon this whole region 'peared to have a blue flush about it. There must have been five thousand of them; and such another jawing and disputing and ripping and cussing, you never heard. Every jay in the whole lot put his eye to the hole and delivered a more chuckle-headed opinion about the mystery than the jay that went there before him. They examined the house all over, too. The door was standing half open, and at last one old jay happened to go and light on it and look in. Of course that knocked the mystery galley-west in a second. There lay the acorns, scattered all over the floor. He flopped his wings and raised a whoop. "Come here!" he says, "come here, everybody; hang'd if this fool hasn't been trying to fill up a house with acorns!" They all came a-swooping down like a blue cloud, and as each fellow lit on the door and took a glance, the whole absurdity of the contract that that first jay had tackled hit him home, and he fell over backwards, and the next jay took his place and done the same.

'Well, sir, they roosted around here on the house-top and the trees for an hour, and guffawed over that thing like human beings. It ain't any use to tell me a blue-jay hasn't got a sense of humour, because I know better. And memory, too. They brought jays here from all over the United States to look down that hole, every summer for three years. Other birds too. And they could all see the point, except an owl that come from Nova Scotia to visit the Yo Semite, and he took this thing in on his way back. He said he couldn't see anything funny in it. But then he was a good deal disappointed about Yo Semite, too.'

CHAPTER 4

Student Life

The summer semester was in full tide; consequently the most frequent figure in and about Heidelberg was the student. Most of the students were Germans, of course, but the representatives of foreign lands were very numerous. They hailed from every corner of the globe,—for instruction is cheap in Heidelberg, and so is living, too. The Anglo-American Club, composed of British and American students, had twenty-five members, and there was still much material left to draw from.

Nine-tenths of the Heidelberg students wore no badge or uniform; the other tenth wore caps of various colours, and belonged to social organisations called 'corps.' There were five corps, each with a colour of its own; there were white caps, blue caps, and red, yellow, and green ones. The famous duel-fighting is confined to the 'corps' boys. The '*Kneip*' seems to be a speciality of theirs, too. Kneips are held, now and then, to celebrate great occasions,—like the election of a beer-king, for instance. The solemnity is simple; the five corps assemble at night, and at a signal they all fall loading themselves with beer, out of pint mugs, as fast as possible, and each man keeps his own count,—usually by laying aside a lucifer match for each mug he empties. The election is soon decided. When the candidates can hold no more, a count is instituted, and the one who has drunk the greatest number of pints is proclaimed king. I was told that the last beer-king elected by the corps,—or by his own capabilities,—emptied his mug seventy-five times. No stomach could hold all that quantity at one time, of course,—but there are ways of frequently creating a vacuum, which those who have been much at sea will understand.

One sees so many students abroad at all hours, that he presently begins to wonder if they ever have any working hours. Some of them have, some of them haven't. Each can choose for himself whether he will work or play; for German university life is a very free life; it seems to have no restraints. The student does not live in the college buildings, but hires his own lodgings, in any locality he prefers, and he takes his meals when and where he pleases. He goes to bed when it suits him, and does not get up at all unless he wants to. He is not entered at the university for any particular length of time; so he is likely to change about. He passes no examination upon entering college. He merely pays a trifling fee of five or ten dollars, receives a card entitling him to the privileges of the university, and that is the end of it. He is now ready for business,—or play, as he shall prefer. If he elects to work, he finds a large list of lectures to choose from. He selects the subjects which he will study, and enters his name for these studies; but he can skip attendance.

The result of this system is, that lecture-courses upon specialities of an unusual nature are often delivered to very slim audiences, while those upon more practical and every-day matters of education are delivered to very large ones. I heard of one case where, day after day, the lecturer's audience consisted of three students,—and always the same three. But one day two of them remained away. The lecturer began as usual—

'Gentlemen,'—

—then, without a smile, he corrected himself, saying,—

'Sir,'—

—and went on with his discourse.

It is said that the vast majority of the Heidelberg students are hard workers, and make the most of their opportunities; that they have no surplus means to spend in dissipation, and no time to spare for frolicking. One lecture follows right on the heels of another, with very little time for the student to get out of one hall and into the next; but the industrious ones manage it by going on a trot. The professors assist them in the saving of their time by being promptly in their little boxed-up pulpits when the hours strike, and as promptly out again when the hour finishes. I entered an empty lecture-room one day just before the clock struck. The place had simple, unpainted pine desks and benches for about 200 persons.

About a minute before the clock struck, a hundred and fifty students swarmed in, rushed to their seats, immediately spread open their note-books and dipped their pens in the ink. When the clock began to strike, a burly professor entered, was received with a round of applause, moved swiftly down the centre aisle, said 'Gentlemen,' and began to talk as he climbed his pulpit steps; and by the time he had arrived in his box and faced his audience, his lecture was well under way and all the pens were going. He had no notes, he talked with prodigious rapidity and energy for an hour,—then the students began to remind him in certain well-understood ways that his time was up; he seized his hat, still talking, proceeded swiftly down his pulpit steps, got out the last word of his discourse as he struck the floor; everybody rose respectfully, and he swept rapidly down the aisle and disappeared. An instant rush for some other lecture room followed, and in a minute I was alone with the empty benches once more.

Yes, without doubt, idle students are not the rule. Out of eight hundred in the town, I knew the faces of only about fifty; but these I saw everywhere and daily. They walked about the streets and the wooded hills, they drove in cabs, they boated on the river, they sipped beer and coffee, afternoons, in the Schloss gardens. A good many of them wore the coloured caps of the corps. They were finely and fashionably dressed, their manners were quite superb, and they led an easy, careless, comfortable life. If a dozen of them sat together, and a lady or a gentleman passed whom one of them knew and saluted, they all rose to their feet and took off their caps. The members of a corps always received a fellow-member in this way, too; but they paid no attention to members of other corps; they did not seem to see them. This was not a discourtesy; it was only a part of the elaborate and rigid corps etiquette.

There seems to be no chilly distance existing between the German students and the professor; but, on the contrary, a companionable intercourse, the opposite of chilliness and reserve. When the professor enters a beer hall in the evening where students are gathered together, these rise up and take off their caps, and invite the old gentleman to sit with them and partake. He accepts, and the pleasant talk and the beer flow for an hour or two, and by-and-by the professor, properly charged and comfortable, gives a cordial good-night, while the students stand bowing and uncovered; and then he moves on his happy way homeward with all his vast cargo of learning afloat in his hold. Nobody finds fault or feels outraged; no harm has been done.

It seemed to be a part of corps etiquette to keep a dog or so, too. I mean a corps dog,—the common property of the organisation, like the corps steward or head servant; then there are other dogs, owned by individuals.

On a summer afternoon in the Castle gardens, I have seen six students march solemnly into the grounds, in single file, each carrying a bright Chinese parasol and leading a prodigious dog by a string. It was a very imposing spectacle. Sometimes there would be about as many dogs around the pavilion as students; and of all breeds and of all degrees of beauty and ugliness. These dogs had a rather dry time of it: for they were tied to the benches and had no amusement for an hour or two at a time, except what they could get out of pawing at the gnats, or trying to sleep and not succeeding. However, they got a lump of sugar occasionally—they were fond of that.

It seemed right and proper that students should indulge in dogs; but everybody else had them, too,—old men and young ones, old women and nice young ladies. If there is one spectacle that is unpleasanter than another, it is that of an elegantly

dressed young lady towing a dog by a string. It is said to be the
sign and symbol of blighted love. It seems to me that some other
way of advertising it might be devised, which would be just as
conspicuous and yet not so trying to the proprieties.

It would be a mistake to suppose that the easy-going,
pleasure-seeking student carries an empty head. Just the
contrary. He has spent nine years in the gymnasium, under a
system which allowed him no freedom, but rigorously compelled
him to work like a slave. Consequently he has left the
gymnasium with an education which is so extensive and
complete, that the most a university can do for it is to perfect
some of its profounder specialities. It is said that when a pupil
leaves the gymnasium, he not only has a comprehensive
education, but he *knows* what he knows,—it is not befogged
with uncertainty, it is burnt into him so that it will stay. For
instance, he does not merely read and write Greek, but speaks it;
the same with the Latin. Foreign youth steer clear of the
gymnasium; its rules are too severe. They go to the university to
put a mansard roof on their whole general education; but the
German student already has his mansard roof, so he goes there
to add a steeple in the nature of some speciality, such as a
particular branch of law, or medicine, or philology—like
international law, or diseases of the eye, or special study of the
ancient Gothic tongues. So this German attends only the
lectures which belong to the chosen branch, and drinks his beer
and tows his dog around, and has a general good time the rest of
the day. He has been in rigid bondage so long that the large
liberty of university life is just what he needs and likes and
thoroughly appreciates; and as it cannot last for ever, he makes
the most of it while it does last, and so lays up a good rest
against the day that must see him put on the chains once more
and enter the slavery of official or professional life.

CHAPTER 5

At the Students' Duelling-Ground

One day in the interest of science my agent obtained permission to bring me to the students' duelling-place. We crossed the river and drove up the bank a few hundred yards, then turned to the left, entered a narrow alley, followed it a hundred yards, and arrived at a two-story public-house; we were acquainted with its outside aspect, for it was visible from the hotel. We went upstairs and passed into a large whitewashed apartment, which was perhaps fifty feet long, by thirty feet wide and twenty or twenty-five high. It was a well-lighted place. There was no carpet. Across one end and down both sides of the room extended a row of tables, and at these tables some fifty or seventy-five students[1] were sitting.

Some of them were sipping wine, others were playing cards, others chess, other groups were chatting together, and many were smoking cigarettes while they waited for the coming duels. Nearly all of them wore coloured caps; there were white caps, green caps, blue caps, red caps, and bright yellow ones; so, all the five corps were present in strong force. In the windows at the vacant end of the room stood six or eight long, narrow-bladed swords with large protecting guards for the hand, and outside was a man at work sharpening others on a grindstone. He understood his business; for when a sword left his hand one

[1] See Appendix C.

could shave himself with it.

It was observable that the young gentlemen neither bowed to nor spoke with students whose caps differed in colour from their own. This did not mean hostility, but only an armed neutrality. It was considered that a person could strike harder in the duel, and with a more earnest interest, if he had never been in a condition of comradeship with his antagonist; therefore, comradeship between the corps was not permitted. At intervals the presidents of the five corps have a cold official intercourse with each other, but nothing further. For example, when the regular duelling day of one of the corps approaches, its president calls for volunteers from among the membership to offer battle; three or more respond,—but there must not be less than three; the president lays their names before the other presidents, with the request that they furnish antagonists for these challengers from among their corps. This is promptly done. It chanced that the present occasion was the battle-day of the Red Cap Corps. They were the challengers, and certain caps of other colours had volunteered to meet them. The students fight duels in the room which I have described, *two days in every week during seven and a half or eight months in every year.* This custom has continued in Germany two hundred and fifty years.

To return to my narrative. A student in a white cap met us and introduced us to six or eight friends of his who also wore white caps, and while we stood conversing, two strange-looking figures were led in from another room. They were students panoplied for the duel. They were bare-headed; their eyes were protected by iron goggles which projected an inch or more, the leather straps of which bound their ears flat against their heads; their necks were wound around and around with thick wrappings which a sword could not cut through; from chin to ankle they were padded thoroughly against injury; their arms were bandaged and re-bandaged, layer upon layer, until they looked like solid black logs. These weird apparitions had been handsome youths, clad in fashionable attire fifteen minutes before, but now they did not resemble any beings one ever sees unless in nightmares. They strode along, with their arms projecting straight out from their bodies; they did not hold them out themselves, but fellow-students walked beside them and gave the needed support.

There was a rush for the vacant end of the room now, and we followed and got good places. The combatants were placed face to face, each with several members of his own corps about him to assist; two seconds, well padded, and with swords in their hands, took near stations; a student belonging to neither of the opposing corps placed himself in a good position to umpire the combat; another student stood by with a watch and a memorandum-book to keep record of the time and the number and nature of the wounds; a grey-haired surgeon was present with his lint, his bandages, and his instruments. After a moment's pause the duellists saluted the umpire respectfully, then one after another the several officials stepped forward, gracefully removed their caps and saluted him also, and returned to their places. Everything was ready now; students stood crowded together in the foreground, and others stood behind them on chairs and tables. Every face was turned towards the centre of attraction.

The combatants were watching each other with alert eyes; a perfect stillness, a breathless interest reigned. I felt that I was going to see some wary work. But not so. The instant the word was given, the two apparitions sprang forward and began to rain blows down upon each other with such lightning rapidity that I could not quite tell whether I saw the swords or only the flashes they made in the air; the rattling din of these blows, as they struck steel or paddings, was something wonderfully stirring, and they were struck with such terrific force that I could not understand why the opposing sword was not beaten down under the assault. Presently, in the midst of the sword-flashes, I saw a handful of hair skip into the air as if it had lain loose on the victim's head and a breath of wind had puffed it suddenly away.

The seconds cried 'Halt!' and knocked up the combatants' swords with their own. The duellists sat down; a student official stepped forward, examined the wounded head, and touched the place with a sponge once or twice; the surgeon came and turned back the hair from the wound, and revealed a crimson gash two or three inches long, and proceeded to bind an oval piece of leather and a bunch of lint over it; the tallykeeper stepped up and tallied one for the opposition in his book.

Then the duellists took position again; a small stream of blood was flowing down the side of the injured man's head, and over his shoulder, and down his body to the floor, but he did not seem to mind this. The word was given, and they plunged at each other as fiercely as before; once more the blows rained, and rattled, and flashed; every few moments the quick-eyed seconds would notice that a word was bent—then they called 'Halt!' struck up the contending weapons, and an assisting student straightened the bent one.

The wonderful turmoil went on—presently a bright spark sprang from a blade, and that blade, broken in several pieces, sent one of its fragments flying to the ceiling. A new sword was provided, and the fight proceeded. The exercise was tremendous, of course, and in time the fighters began to show great fatigue. They were allowed to rest a moment, every little while; they got other rests by wounding each other, for then they could sit down while the doctor applied the lint and bandages. The law is that the battle must continue fifteen minutes if the men can hold out; and as the pauses do not count, this duel was protracted to twenty or thirty minutes, I judged. At last it was decided that the men were too much wearied to do battle longer. They were led away drenched with crimson from head to foot. That was a good fight, but it could not count, partly because it did not last the lawful fifteen minutes (of actual fighting), and partly because neither man was disabled by his wounds. It was a drawn battle, and corps-law requires that drawn battles shall be re-fought as soon as the adversaries are well of their hurts.

During the conflict, I had talked a little, now and then, with a young gentleman of the white cap corps, and he had mentioned that he was to fight next—and had also pointed out his challenger, a young gentleman who was leaning against the opposite wall smoking a cigarette, and restfully observing the duel then in progress.

My acquaintanceship with a party to the coming contest had the effect of giving me a kind of personal interest in it; I naturally wished he might win, and it was the reverse of pleasant to learn that he probably would not, because, although he was a notable swordsman, the challenger was held to be his superior.

The duel presently began, and in the same furious way which had marked the previous one. I stood close by, but could not tell which blows told and which did not, they fell and vanished so like flashes of light. They all seemed to tell; the swords always bent over the opponents' heads, from the forehead back over the crown, and seemed to touch, all the way; but it was not so—a protecting blade, invisible to me, was always interposed between. At the end of ten seconds each man had struck twelve or fifteen blows, and warded off twelve or fifteen, and no harm done; then a sword became disabled, and a short rest followed whilst a new one was brought. Early in the next round the white corps student got an ugly wound on the side of his head, and gave his opponent one like it. In the third round the latter received another bad wound in the head, and the former had his under lip divided. After that, the white corps student gave many severe wounds, but got none of consequence in return. At the end of five minutes, from the beginning of the duel, the surgeon stopped it; the challenging party had suffered such injuries that any addition to them might be dangerous. These injuries were a fearful spectacle, but are better left undescribed. So, against expectation, my acquaintance was the victor.

CHAPTER 6

The third duel was brief and bloody. The surgeon stopped it when he saw that one of the men had received such bad wounds that he could not fight longer without endangering his life.

The fourth duel was a tremendous encounter; but at the end of five or six minutes the surgeon interfered once more: another man so severely hurt as to render it unsafe to add to his harms. I watched this engagement as I had watched the others—with rapt interest and strong excitement, and with a shrink and a shudder for every blow that laid open a cheek or a forehead; and a conscious paling of my face when I occasionally saw a wound of a yet more shocking nature inflicted. My eyes were upon the loser of this duel when he got his last and vanquishing wound—it was in his face, and it carried away his—but no matter, I must not enter into details. I had but a glance, and then turned quickly away, but I would not have been looking at all if I had known what was coming. No, that is probably not true; one thinks he would not look if he knew what was coming, but the interest and the excitement are so powerful that they would doubtless conquer all other feelings; and so, under the fierce exhilaration of the clashing steel, he would yield and look, after all. Sometimes spectators of these duels faint, and it does seem a very reasonable thing to do, too.

Both parties to this fourth duel were badly hurt; so much so that the surgeon was at work upon them nearly or quite an hour—a fact which is suggestive. But this waiting interval was not wasted in idleness by the assembled students. It was past noon; therefore they ordered their landlord, downstairs, to send up hot beefsteaks, chickens, and such things, and these they ate. sitting comfortably at the several tables, whilst they chatted, disputed, and laughed. The door to the surgeon's room stood open, meantime, but the cutting, sewing, splicing, and bandaging going on in there in plain view, did not seem to disturb anyone's appetite. I went in and saw the surgeon labour awhile, but could not enjoy it; it was much less trying to see the wounds given and received than to see them mended; the stir and turmoil, and the music of the steel were wanting here—one's nerves were wrung by this grisly spectacle, whilst the duel's compensating pleasurable thrill was lacking.

Finally the doctor finished, and the men who were to fight the closing battle of the day came forth. A good many dinners were not completed yet, but no matter, they could be eaten cold after the battle; therefore everybody crowded forward to see. This was not a love duel, but a 'satisfaction' affair. These did not belong to any of the corps, but they were furnished with weapons and armour, and permitted to fight here by the five corps as a courtesy. Evidently these two young men were unfamiliar with the duelling ceremonies, though they were not unfamiliar with the sword. When they were placed in position, they thought it was time to begin—and they did begin, too, and with a most impetuous energy, without waiting for anybody to give the word. This vastly amused the spectators, and even broke down their studied and courtly gravity, and surprised them into laughter. Of course the seconds struck up the swords and started the duel over again. At the word, the deluge of blows began, but before long the surgeon once more interfered—for the only reason which ever permits him to interfere—and the day's war was over. It was now two in the afternoon, and I had been present since half-past nine in the morning. The field of battle was indeed a red one by this time; but some sawdust soon righted that. There had been one duel before I arrived. In it one of the men received many injuries, while the other one escaped without a scratch.

I had seen the heads and faces of ten youths gashed in every direction by the keen two-edged blades, and yet had not seen a victim wince, nor heard a moan, or detected any fleeting expression which confessed the sharp pain the hurts were inflicting. This was good fortitude indeed. Such endurance is to be expected in savages and prize-fighters, for they are born and educated to it; but to find it in such perfection in these gently bred and kindly nurtured young fellows is matter for surprise. It was not merely under the excitement of the sword play that this fortitude was shown; it was shown in the surgeon's room, where an uninspiring quiet reigned, and where there was no audience. The doctor's manipulations brought out neither grimaces nor moans; and in the fights it was observable that these lads hacked and slashed with the same tremendous spirit, after they were covered with streaming wounds, which they had shown in the beginning.

The world in general looks upon the college duels as very farcical affairs; true, but considering that the college duel is fought by boys, that the swords are real swords, and that the head and face are exposed, it seems to me that it is a farce which has quite a grave side to it. People laugh at it mainly because they think the student is so covered up with armour that he cannot be hurt. But it is not so; his eyes and ears are protected, but the rest of his face is in danger, and he would sometimes lose it but for the interference of the surgeon. It is not intended that his life shall be endangered. Fatal accidents are possible, however. For instance, the student's sword may break, and the end of it fly up behind his antagonist's ear and cut an artery which could not be reached if the sword remained whole. This has happened sometimes, and death has resulted on the spot. Formerly the student's armpits were not protected—and at that time the swords were pointed, whereas they are blunt now—so an artery in the armpit was sometimes cut, and death followed. Then, in the days of sharp-pointed swords, a spectator was an occasional victim; the end of a broken sword flew five or ten feet and buried itself in his neck or his heart. and death ensued instantly. The student duels in Germany occasion two or three deaths every year now, but this arises only from the carelessness of the wounded men; they eat or drink imprudently, or commit excesses in the way of over-exertion; inflammation sets in, and gets such a headway that it cannot be arrested. Indeed there is blood and pain and danger enough about the college duel to entitle it to a considerable degree of respect.

All the customs, all the laws, all the details pertaining to the student duel are quaint and naïve. The grave, precise, and courtly ceremony with which the thing is conducted, invests it with a sort of antique charm.

This dignity and these knightly graces suggest the tournament, not the prize-fight. The laws are as curious as they are strict. For instance, the duellist may step forward from the line he is placed upon, if he chooses, but never back of it. If he steps back of it, or even leans back, it is considered that he did it to avoid a blow or contrive an advantage, so he is dismissed from his corps in disgrace. It would seem but natural to step from under a descending sword unconsciously, and against one's will and intent, yet this unconsciousness is not allowed. Again, if, under the sudden anguish of a wound, the received of it makes a grimace, he falls some degrees in the estimation of his fellows; his corps are ashamed of him, they call him 'hare-foot,' which is the German equivalent for chicken-hearted.

CHAPTER 7

In addition to the corps laws, there are some corps usages which have the force of laws.

Perhaps the president of a corps notices that one of the membership who is no longer an exempt—that is, a freshman—has remained a sophomore some little time without volunteering to fight; some day, the president, instead of calling for volunteers, will *appoint* this sophomore to measure swords with a student of another corps; he is free to decline—everybody says so—there is no compulsion. This is all true—but I have not heard of any student who *did* decline. He would naturally rather retire from the corps than decline; to decline, and still remain in the corps, would make him unpleasantly conspicuous, and properly so, since he knew, when he joined, that his main business, as a member, would be to fight. No, there is no law against declining—except the law of custom, which is confessedly stronger than written law, everywhere.

The ten men whose duels I had witnessed did not go away when their hurts were dressed, as I had supposed they would, but came back, one after another, as soon as they were free of the surgeon, and mingled with the assemblage of the duelling room. The white cap student who won the second fight witnessed the remaining three, and talked with us during the intermissions. He could not talk very well, because his opponent's sword had cut his under lip in two, and then the surgeon had sewed it together and overlaid it with a profusion of white plaister patches; neither could he eat easily, still he contrived to accomplish a slow and troublesome luncheon while the last duel was preparing. The man who was the worst hurt of all played chess while waiting to see this engagement. A good part of his face was covered with patches and bandages, and all the rest of his head was covered and concealed by them. It is said that the student likes to appear on the street and in other public places in this kind of array, and that this predilection often keeps him out when exposure to rain or sun is a positive danger for him. Newly bandaged students are a very common spectacle in the public gardens of Heidelberg. It is also said that the student is glad to get wounds in the face, because the scars they leave will show so well there; and it is also said that these face wounds are so prized that youths have even been known to pull them apart from time to time and put red wine in them, to make them heal badly and leave as ugly a scar as possible. It does not look reasonable, but it is roundly asserted and maintained nevertheless. I am sure of one thing—scars are plenty enough in Germany among the young men; and very grim ones they are, too. They criss-cross the face in angry red welts, and are permanent and ineffaceable. Some of these scars are of a very strange and dreadful aspect; and the effect is striking when several such accent the milder ones, which form a city map on a man's face; they suggest the 'burned district' then.

We had often noticed that many of the students wore a coloured silk band or riband diagonally across their breasts.[1] It transpired that this signifies that the wearer has fought three

---

[1] FROM MY DIARY.—Dined in an hotel a few miles up the Neckar, in a room whose walls were hung all over with framed portrait-groups of the Five Corps; some were recent, but many antedated photography, and were pictured in lithography—the dates ranged back to forty or fifty years ago. Nearly every individual wore the riband across his breast. In one portrait-group, representing (as each of these pictures did) an entire Corps, I took pains to count the ribands: there were twenty-seven members, and twenty-one of them wore that significant badge.

duels in which a decision was reached—duels in which he was either whipped or was whipped—for drawn battles do not count. After a student has received his riband, he is 'free;' he can cease from fighting, without reproach—except some one insult him; his president cannot appoint him to fight; he can volunteer if he wants to, or remain quiescent if he prefers to do so. Statistics show that he does *not* prefer to remain quiescent. They show that the duel has a singular fascination about it somewhere, for these free men, so far from resting upon the privilege of the badge, are always volunteering. A corps student told me it was on record that Prince Bismarck fought thirty-two of these duels in a single summer term when he was in college. So he fought twenty-nine after his badge had given him the right to retire from the field.

The statistics may be found to possess interest in several particulars. Two days in every week are devoted to duelling. The rule is rigid that there must be three duels on each of these days; there are generally more, but there cannot be fewer. There were six the day I was present; sometimes there are seven or eight. It is insisted that eight duels a week—four for each of the two days—is too low an average to draw a calculation from, but I will reckon from that basis, preferring an under-statement to an over-statement of the case. This requires about 480 or 500 duellists in a year—for in summer the college term is about three and a half months, and in winter it is four months and sometimes longer. Of the 750 students in the university at the time I am writing of, only eighty belonged to the five corps, and it is only these corps that do the duelling; occasionally other students borrow the arms and battle-ground of the five corps in order to settle a quarrel, but this does not happen every duelling day.[1] Consequently eighty youths furnish the material for some 250 duels a year. This average gives six fights a year to each of the eighty. This large work could not be accomplished if the

---

[1] They have to borrow the arms because they could not get them elsewhere or otherwise. As I understand it, the public authorities, all over Germany, allow the five corps to keep swords, but *do not allow them to use them*. This law is rigid; it is only the execution of it that is lax.

badge-holders stood upon their privilege and ceased to volunteer.

Of course, where there is so much fighting, the students make it a point to keep themselves in constant practice with the foil. One often sees them, at the tables in the Castle grounds, using their whips or canes to illustrate some new sword trick which they have heard about; and between the duels, on the day whose history I have been writing, the swords were not always idle; every now and then we heard a succession of the keen hissing sounds which the sword makes when it is being put through its paces in the air, and this informed us that a student was practising. Necessarily this unceasing attention to the art develops an expert occasionally. He becomes famous in his own university, his renown spreads to other universities. He is invited to Göttingen, to fight with a Göttingen expert; if he is victorious, he will be invited to other colleges, or those colleges will send their experts to him. Americans and Englishmen often join one or another of the five corps. A year or two ago, the principal Heidelberg expert was a big Kentuckian; he was invited to the various universities, and left a wake of victory behind him all about Germany; but at last a little student in Strasburg defeated him. There was formerly a student in Heidelberg who had picked up somewhere and mastered a peculiar trick of cutting up under instead of cleaving down from above. While the trick lasted he won in sixteen successive duels in his own university; but by that time observers had discovered what his charm was, and how to break it, therefore his championship ceased.

The rule which forbids social intercourse between members of duelling corps is strict. In the dwelling house, in the parks on the street, and anywhere and everywhere that students go, caps of colour group themselves together. If all the tables in a public garden were crowded but one, and that one had two red-cap students at it and ten vacant places, the yellow caps, the blue caps, the white caps, and the green caps, seeking seats, would go by that table and not seem to see it, nor seem to be aware that there was such a table in the grounds. The student by whose courtesy we had been enabled to visit the duelling place wore the white cap—Prussian Corps. He introduced us to many white caps, but to none of another colour. The corps etiquette extended even to us, who were strangers, and required us to group with the white corps only, and speak only with the white corps, while we were their guests, and keep aloof from caps of the other colours. Once I wished to examine some of the swords, but an American student said, 'It would not be quite polite; these now in the windows all have red hilts or blue; they will bring in some with white hilts presently, and those you can handle freely.' When a sword was broken in the first duel, I wanted a piece of it; but its hilt was the wrong colour, so it was considered best and politest to await a proper season. It was brought to me after the room was cleared. The length of these swords is about three feet, and they are quite heavy. One's disposition to cheer, during the course of the duels or at their close, was naturally strong, but corps etiquette forbade any demonstrations of this sort. However brilliant a contest or a victory might be, no sign or sound betrayed that anyone was moved. A dignified gravity and repression were maintained at all times.

When the duelling was finished and we were ready to go, the gentlemen of the Prussian Corps to whom we had been introduced took off their caps in the courteous German way, and also shook hands; their brethren of the same order took off their caps and bowed, but without shaking hands; the gentlemen of the other corps treated us just as they would have treated white caps—they fell apart, apparently unconsciously, and left us an unobstructed pathway, but did not seem to see us or how we were there. If we had gone thither the following week as guests of another corps, the white caps, without meaning any offence, would have observed the etiquette of their order, and ignored our presence.[1]

---

[1] How strangely are comedy and tragedy blended in this life! I had not been home a full-hour after witnessing those playful sham-duels, when circumstances made it necessary for me to get ready immediately to assist personally at a real one—a duel with no effeminate limitations in the matter of results, but a battle to the death. An account of it, in the next chapter, will show the reader that duels between boys for fun and duels between men in earnest are very different affairs.

CHAPTER 8

The Great French Duel

Much as the modern French duel is ridiculed by certain smart people, it is in reality one of the most dangerous institutions of our day. Since it is always fought in the open air, the combatants are nearly sure to catch cold. M. Paul de Cassagnac, the most inveterate of the French duellists, has suffered so often in this way that he is at last a confirmed invalid; and the best physician in Paris has expressed the opinion that if he goes on duelling for fifteen or twenty years more—unless he forms the habit of fighting in a comfortable room where damps and draughts cannot intrude—he will eventually endanger his life. This ought to moderate the talk of those people who are so stubborn in maintaining that the French duel is the most health-giving of recreations because of the open-air exercise it affords. And it ought also to moderate that foolish talk about French duellists and socialist-hated monarchs being the only people who are immortal.

But it is time to get at my subject. As soon as I heard of the late fiery outbreak between M. Gambetta and M. Fourtou in the French Assembly, I knew that trouble must follow. I knew it because a long personal friendship with M. Gambetta had revealed to me the desperate and implacable nature of the man. Vast as are his physical proportions, I knew that the thirst for revenge would penetrate to the remotest frontiers of his person.

I did not wait for him to call on me, but went at once to him.

As I expected, I found the brave fellow steeped in a profound French calm. I say French calm, because French calmness and English calmness have points of difference. He was moving swiftly back and forth among the *débris* of his furniture, now and then staving chance fragments of it across the room with his foot; grinding a constant grist of curses through his set teeth; and halting every little while to deposit another handful of his hair on the pile which he had been building of it on the table.

He threw his arms around my neck, bent me over his stomach to his breast, kissed me on both cheeks, hugged me four or five times, and then placed me in his own arm-chair. As soon as I had got well again, we began business at once.

I said I supposed he would wish me to act as his second, and he said, 'Of course.' I said I must be allowed to act under a French name, so that I might be shielded from obloquy in my country, in case of fatal results. He winced here, probably at the suggestion that duelling was not regarded with respect in America. However, he agreed to my requirement. This accounts for the fact that in all the newspaper reports M. Gambetta's second was apparently a Frenchman.

First, we drew up my principal's will. I insisted upon this, and stuck to my point. I said I had never heard of a man in his right mind going out to fight a duel without first making his will. He said he had never heard of a man in his right mind doing anything of the kind. When he had finished the will, he wished to proceed to a choice of his 'last words.' He wanted to know how the following words, as a dying exclamation, struck me:—

'I die for my God, for my country, for freedom of speech, for progress, and the universal brotherhood of man!'

I objected that this would require too lingering a death; it was a good speech for a consumptive, but not suited to the exigencies of the field of honour. We wrangled over a good many ante-mortem outbursts, but I finally got him to cut his obituary down to this, which he copied into his memorandum book, purposing to get it by heart:—

'I DIE THAT FRANCE MAY LIVE.'

I said that this remark seemed to lack relevancy; but he said relevancy was a matter of no consequence in last words—what you wanted was thrill.

The next thing in order was the choice of weapons. My principal said he was not feeling well, and would leave that and the other details of the proposed meeting to me. Therefore I wrote the following note and carried it to M. Fourtou's friend:—

'Sir,—M. Gambetta accepts M. Fourtou's challenge, and authorises me to propose Plessis-Piquet as the place of meeting; to-morrow morning at daybreak as the time; and axes as the weapons. I am, sir, with great respect,   MARK TWAIN.'

M. Fourtou's friend read this note, and shuddered. Then he turned to me, and said, with a suggestion of severity in his tone—

'Have you considered, sir, what would be the inevitable result of such a meeting as this?'

'Well, for instance, what *would* it be?'

'Bloodshed!'

'That's about the size of it,' I said. 'Now, if it is a fair question, what was your side proposing to shed?'

I had him there. He saw he had made a blunder, so he hastened to explain it away. He said he had spoken jestingly. Then he added that he and his principal would enjoy axes, and indeed prefer them, but such weapons were barred by the French code, and so I must change my proposal.

I walked the floor, turning the thing over in my mind, and finally it occurred to me that Gatling guns at fifteen paces would be a likely way to get a verdict on the field of honour. So I framed this idea into a proposition.

But it was not accepted. The code was in the way again. I proposed rifles; then double-barrelled shot-guns; then Colt's navy revolvers. These being all rejected, I reflected a while, and sarcastically suggested brick-bats at three-quarters of a mile. I always hate to fool away a humorous thing on a person who has no perception of humour; and it filled me with bitterness when this man went soberly away to submit the last proposition to his principal.

He came back presently and said his principal was charmed with the idea of brick-bats at three-quarters of a mile, but must decline on account of the danger to disinterested parties passing between. Then I said—

'Well, I am at the end of my string now. Perhaps *you* would
be good enough to suggest a weapon? Perhaps you have even
had one in your mind all the time?'

His countenance brightened, and he said with alacrity—

'Oh, without doubt, monsieur!'

So he fell to hunting in his pockets—pocket after pocket, and
he had plenty of them—muttering all the while, 'Now, what
could I have done with them?'

At last he was successful. He fished out of his vest pocket a
couple of little things which I carried to the light and ascertained
to be pistols. They were single-barrelled and silver-mounted, and
very dainty and pretty. I was not able to speak for emotion. I
silently hung one of them on my watch-chain, and returned the
other. My companion in crime now unrolled a postage-stamp
containing several cartridges, and gave me one of them. I asked
if he meant to signify by this that our men were to be allowed
but one shot apiece. He replied that the French code permitted
no more. I then begged him to go on and suggest a distance, for
my mind was growing weak and confused under the strain
which had been put upon it. He named sixty-five yards. I nearly
lost my patience. I said—

'Sixty-five yards, with these instruments? Squirt-guns would
be deadlier at fifty. Consider, my friend, you and I are banded
together to destroy life, not make it eternal.'

But with all my persuasions, all my arguments, I was only
able to get him to reduce the distance to thirty-five yards; and
even this concession he made with reluctance, and said with a
sigh—

'I wash my hands of this slaughter; on your head be it.'

There was nothing for me but to go home to my old lion-heart
and tell my humiliating story. When I entered, M. Gambetta,
was laying his last lock of hair upon the altar. He sprang
towards me, exclaiming—

'You have made the fatal arrangements—I see it in your eye!'

'I have.'

His face paled a trifle, and he leaned upon the table for
support. He breathed thick and heavily for a moment or two, so

tumultuous were his feelings; then he hoarsely whispered—

'The weapon, the weapon! Quick! what is the weapon?'

'This!' and I displayed that silver-mounted thing. He cast but one glance at it, then swooned ponderously to the floor.

When he came to, he said mournfully—

'The unnatural calm to which I have subjected myself has told upon my nerves. But away with weakness! I will confront my fate like a man and a Frenchman.'

He rose to his feet, and assumed an attitude which for sublimity has never been approached by man, and has seldom been surpassed by statues. Then he said, in his deep bass tones—

'Behold, I am calm, I am ready, reveal to me the distance.'

'Thirty-five yards'...

I could not lift him up, of course; but I rolled him over, and poured water down his back. He presently came to, and said—

'Thirty-five yards—without a rest? But why ask? Since murder was that man's intention, why should he palter with small details? But mark you one thing: in my fall the world shall see how the chivalry of France meets death.'

After a long silence he asked—

'Was nothing said about that man's family standing up with him, as an offset to my bulk? But no matter; I would not stoop to make such a suggestion; if he is not noble enough to suggest it himself, he is welcome to this advantage, which no honourable man would take.'

He now sank into a sort of stupor of reflection, which lasted some minutes; after which he broke silence with—

'The hour—what is the hour fixed for the collision?'

'Dawn, to-morrow.'

He seemed greatly surprised, and immediately said—

'Insanity! I never heard of such a thing. Nobody is abroad at such an hour.'

'That is the reason I named it. Do you mean to say you want an audience?'

'It is no time to bandy words. I am astonished that M. Fourtou should ever have agreed to so strange an innovation. Go at once and require a later hour.'

I ran downstairs, threw open the front door, and almost plunged into the arms of M. Fourtou's second. He said—

'I have the honour to say that my principal strenuously objects to the hour chosen, and begs you will consent to change it to half-past nine.'

'Any courtesy, sir, which it is in our power to extend is at the service of your excellent principal. We agree to the proposed change of time.'

'I beg you to accept the thanks of my client.' Then he turned to a person behind him, and said, 'You hear, M. Noir, the hour is altered to half-past nine.' Whereupon M. Noir bowed, expressed his thanks, and went away. My accomplice continued—

'If agreeable to you, your chief surgeons and ours shall proceed to the field in the same carriage, as is customary.'

'It is entirely agreeable to me, and I am obliged to you for mentioning the surgeons, for I am afraid I should not have thought of them. How many shall I want? I suppose two or three will be enough.'

'Two is the customary number for each party. I refer to "chief" surgeons; but considering the exalted positions occupied by our clients, it will be well and decorous that each of us appoint several consulting surgeons, from among the highest in the profession. These will come in their own private carriages. Have you engaged a hearse?'

'Bless my stupidity, I never thought of it! I will attend to it right away. I must seem very ignorant to you; but you must try to overlook that, because I have never had any experience of such a swell duel as this before. I have had a good deal to do with duels on the Pacific coast, but I see now that they were crude affairs. A hearse—sho! we used to leave the elected lying around loose, and let anybody cord them up and cart them off that wanted to. Have you anything further to suggest?'

'Nothing, except that the head undertakers shall ride together, as is usual. The subordinates and mutes will go on foot, as is also usual. I will see you at eight o'clock in the morning, and we will then arrange the order of the procession. I have the honour to bid you a good day.'

I returned to my client, who said, 'Very well; at what hour is the engagement to begin?'

'Half-past nine.'

'Very good indeed. Have you sent the fact to the newspapers?'

'*Sir*! If after our long and intimate friendship you can for a moment deem me capable of so base a treachery—'

'Tut, tut! What words are these, my dear friend? Have I wounded you? Ah, forgive me; I am overloading you with labour. Therefore go on with the other details, and drop this one from your list. The bloody-minded Fourtou will be sure to attend to it. Or I myself—yes, to make certain, I will drop a note to my journalistic friend, M. Noir.'

'Oh, come to think, you may save yourself the trouble; that other second has informed M. Noir.'

'H'm! I might have known it. It is just like that Fourtou, who always wants to make a display.'

At half-past nine in the morning the procession approached the field of Plessis-Piquet in the following order: first came our carriage—nobody in it but M. Gambetta and myself; then a carriage containing M. Fourtou and his second; then a carriage containing two poet-orators who did not believe in God, and these had MS. funeral orations projecting from their breast-pockets; then a carriage containing the head surgeons and their cases of instruments; then eight private carriages containing consulting surgeons; then a hack containing a coroner; then the two hearses; then a carriage containing the head undertakers; then a train of assistants and mutes on foot; and after these came plodding through the fog a long procession of camp followers, police, and citizens generally. It was a noble turn-out, and would have made a fine display if we had had thinner weather.

There was no conversation. I spoke several times to my principal, but I judge he was not aware of it, for he always referred to his note-book and muttered absently, 'I die that France may live.'

Arrived on the field, my fellow-second and I paced off the thirty-five yards, and then drew lots for choice of position. This latter was but an ornamental ceremony, for all choices were alike in such weather. These preliminaries being ended, I went to my principal and asked him if he was ready. He spread himself out to his full width, and said in a stern voice, 'Ready! Let the batteries be charged.'

The loading was done in the presence of duly constituted witnesses. We considered it best to perform this delicate service with the assistance of a lantern, on account of the state of the weather. We now placed our men.

At this point the police noticed that the public had massed themselves together on the right and left of the field; they therefore begged a delay, while they should put these poor people in a place of safety. The request was granted.

The police having ordered the two multitudes to take positions behind the duellists, we were once more ready. The weather growing still more opaque, it was agreed between myself and the other second that before giving the fatal signal we should each deliver a loud whoop to enable the combatants to ascertain each other's whereabouts.

I now returned to my principal, and was distressed to observe that he had lost a good deal of his spirit. I tried my best to hearten him. I said, 'Indeed, sir, things are not as bad as they seem. Considering the character of the weapons, the limited number of shots allowed, the generous distance, the impenetrable solidity of the fog, and the added fact that one of the combatants is one-eyed and the other cross-eyed and near-sighted, it seems to me that this conflict need not necessarily be fatal. There are chances that both of you may survive. Therefore cheer up; do not be down-hearted.'

This speech had so good an effect that my principal immediately stretched forth his hand and said, 'I am myself again; give me the weapon.'

I laid it, all lonely and forlorn, in the centre of the vast solitude of his palm. He gazed at it and shuddered. And still mournfully contemplating it, he murmured, in a broken voice—

'Alas, it is not death I dread, but mutilation.'

I heartened him once more, and with such success that he presently said, 'Let the tragedy begin. Stand at my back; do not desert me in this solemn hour, my friend.'

I gave him my promise. I now assisted him to point his pistol towards the spot where I judged his adversary to be standing, and cautioned him to listen well and further guide himself by my fellow-second's whoop. Then I propped myself against M. Gambetta's back, and raised a rousing 'Whoop-ee!' This was answered from out the far distances of the fog, and I immediately shouted—

'One,—two,—three,—*fire!*'

Two little sounds like *spit! spit!* broke upon my ear, and in the same instant I was crushed to the earth under a mountain of flesh. Bruised as I was, I was still able to catch a faint accent from above, to this effect—

'I die for...for...perdition take it, what *is* it I die for?... oh, yes,—FRANCE! I die that France may live!'

The surgeons swarmed around with their probes in their hands, and applied their microscopes to the whole area of M. Gambetta's person, with the happy result of finding nothing in the nature of a wound. Then a scene ensued which was in every way gratifying and inspiriting.

The two gladiators fell upon each other's necks, with floods of proud and happy tears; that other second embraced me; the surgeons, the orators, the undertakers, the police, everybody embraced, everybody congratulated, everybody cried, and the whole atmosphere was filled with praise and with joy unspeakable.

It seemed to me then that I would rather be a hero of a French duel than a crowned and sceptred monarch.

When the commotion had somewhat subsided, the body of surgeons held a consultation, and after a good deal of debate decided that with proper care and nursing there was reason to believe that I would survive my injuries. My internal hurts were deemed the most serious, since it was apparent that a broken rib had penetrated my left lung, and that many of my organs had been pressed out so far to one side or the other of where they belonged, that it was doubtful if they would ever learn to perform their functions in such remote and unaccustomed localities. They then set my left arm in two places, pulled my right hip into its socket again, and re-elevated my nose. I was an object of great interest, and even admiration; and many sincere and warm-hearted persons had themselves introduced to me, and said they were proud to know the only man who had been hurt in a French duel in forty years.

I was placed in an ambulance at the very head of the procession; and thus with gratifying *éclat* I was marched into Paris, the most conspicuous figure in that great spectacle, and deposited at the hospital.

The Cross of the Legion of Honour has been conferred upon me. However, few escape that distinction.

Such is the true version of the most memorable private conflict of the age.

I have no complaints to make against anyone. I acted for myself, and I can stand the consequences. Without boasting, I think I may say I am not afraid to stand before a modern French duellist, but as long as I keep in my right mind I will never consent to stand behind one again.

CHAPTER 9

One day we took the train and went down to Mannheim to see 'King Lear' played in German. It was a mistake. We sat in our seats three whole hours, and never understood anything but the thunder and lightning; and even that was reversed to suit German ideas, for the thunder came first and the lightning followed after.

The behaviour of the audience was perfect. There were no rustlings, or whisperings, or other little disturbances; each act was listened to in silence, and the applauding was done after the curtain was down. The doors opened at half-past four, the play began promptly at half-past five, and within two minutes afterwards all who were coming were in their seats, and quiet reigned. A German gentleman in the train had said that a Shakespearian play was an appreciated treat in Germany, and that we should find the house filled. It was true; all the six tiers were filled, and remained so to the end—which suggested that it is not only balcony people who like Shakespeare in Germany, but those of the pit and the gallery too.

Another time, we went to Mannheim and attended a shivaree—otherwise an opera—the one called 'Lohengrin.' The banging and slamming and booming and crashing were something beyond belief. The racking and pitiless pain of it remains stored up in my memory alongside the memory of the time that I had my teeth fixed. There were circumstances which made it necessary for me to stay through the four hours to the end, and I stayed; but the recollection of that long, dragging, relentless season of suffering is indestructible. To have to endure it in silence, and sitting still, made it all the harder. I was in a railed compartment with eight or ten strangers, of the two sexes, and this compelled repression; yet at times the pain was so exquisite that I could hardly keep the tears back. At those times, as the howlings and wailings and shriekings of the singers, and the ragings and roarings and explosions of the vast orchestra, rose higher and higher, and wilder and wilder, and fiercer and fiercer, I could have cried if I had been alone. Those strangers would not have been surprised to see a man do such a thing who was being gradually skinned, but they would have marvelled at it here, and made remarks about it no doubt, whereas there was nothing in the present case which was an advantage over being skinned. There was a wait of half an hour at the end of the first act, and I could have gone out and rested during that time, but I could not trust myself to do it, for I felt that I should desert and stay out. There was another wait of half an hour towards nine o'clock, but I had gone through so much by that time that I had no spirit left, and so had no desire but to be let alone.

I do not wish to suggest that the rest of the people there were like me, for indeed they were not. Whether it was that they naturally liked that noise, or whether it was that they had learned to like it by getting used to it, I did not at that time know; but they did like it,—this was plain enough. While it was going on they sat and looked as rapt and grateful as cats do when one strokes their backs; and whenever the curtain fell they rose to their feet, in one solid mighty multitude, and the air was snowed thick with waving handkerchiefs, and hurricanes of applause swept the place. This was not comprehensible to me. Of course there were many people there who were not under compulsion to stay; yet the tiers were as full at the close as they had been at the beginning. This showed that the people liked it.

It was a curious sort of play. In the matter of costumes and scenery it was fine and showy enough; but there was not much action. That is to say, there was not much really done, it was only talked about; and always violently. It was what one might call a narrative play. Everybody had a narrative and a grievance, and none were reasonable about it, but all in an offensive and ungovernable state. There was little of that sort of customary thing where the tenor and the soprano stand down by the footlights, warbling, with blended voices, and keep holding out their arms towards each other and drawing them back and spreading both hands over first one breast and then the other with a shake and a pressure—no, it was every rioter for himself and no blending. Each sang his indictive narrative in turn, accompanied by the whole orchestra of sixty instruments; and when this had continued for some time, and one was hoping they might come to an understanding and modify the noise, a great chorus composed entirely of maniacs would suddenly break forth, and then during two minutes, and sometimes three, I lived over again all that I had suffered the time the orphan asylum burned down.

We only had one brief little season of heaven and heaven's sweet ecstasy and peace during all this long and diligent and acrimonious reproduction of the other place. This was while a gorgeous procession of people marched around and around, in the third act, and sang the Wedding Chorus. To my untutored ear that was music—almost divine music. While my seared soul was steeped in the healing balm of those gracious sounds, it seemed to me that I could almost re-suffer the torments which had gone before, in order to be so healed again. There is where the deep ingenuity of the operatic idea is betrayed. It deals so largely in pain that its scattered delights are prodigiously augmented by the contrasts. A pretty air in an opera is prettier there than it could be anywhere else, I suppose, just as an honest man in politics shines more than he would elsewhere.

I have since found out that there is nothing the Germans like so much as an opera. They like it, not in a mild and moderate way, but with their whole hearts. This is a legitimate result of habit and education. Our nation will like the opera, too, by-and-by, no doubt. One in fifty of those who attend our operas likes it already, perhaps, but I think a good many of the other forty-nine go in order to learn to like it, and the rest in order to be able to talk knowingly about it. The latter usually hum the airs while

they are being sung, so that their neighbours may perceive that
they have been to operas before. The funerals of these do not
occur often enough.

A gentle, old-maidish person and a sweet young girl of
seventeen sat right in front of us that night at the Mannheim
opera. These people talked between the acts, and I understood
them, though I understood nothing that was uttered on the
distant stage. At first they were guarded in their talk, but after
they had heard my agent and me conversing in English they
dropped their reserve, and I picked up many of their
little confidences; no, I mean many of *her* little
confidences—meaning the elder party—for the young girl only
listened, and gave assenting nods, but never said a word. How
pretty she was, and how sweet she was! I wished she would
speak. But evidently she was absorbed in her own thoughts, her
own young-girl dreams, and found a dearer pleasure in silence.
But she was not dreaming sleepy dreams—no, she was awake,
alive, alert; she could not sit still a moment. She was an
enchanting study. Her gown was of a soft white silky stuff that
clung to her round young figure like a fish's skin, and it was
rippled over with the gracefullest little fringy films of lace; she
had deep, tender eyes, with long, curved lashes; and she had
peachy cheeks, and a dimpled chin, and such a dear little dewy
rosebud of a mouth; and she was so dove-like, so pure, and so
gracious, so sweet and bewitching. For long hours I did mightily
wish she would speak. And at last she did; the red lips parted,
and out leaped her thought, and with such a guileless and pretty
enthusiasm too: 'Auntie, I just *know* I've got five hundred fleas
on me!'

That was probably over the average. Yes, it must have been
very much over the average. The average at that time in the
Grand Duchy of Baden was forty-five to a young person (when
alone), according to the official estimate of the Home Secretary
for that year; the average for older people was shifty and
indeterminable, for whenever a wholesome young girl came into
the presence of her elders she immediately lowered their average
and raised her own. She became a sort of contribution-box. This
dear young thing in the theatre had been sitting there

unconsciously taking up a collection. Many a skinny old being in our neighbourhood was the happier and the restfuller for her coming.

In that audience, that night, there were eight very conspicuous people. These were ladies who had their hats or bonnets on. What a blessed thing it would be if a lady could make herself conspicuous in our theatres by wearing her hat! It is not usual in Europe to allow ladies and gentlemen to take bonnets, hats, overcoats, canes, or umbrellas into the auditorium, but in Mannheim this rule was not enforced because the audiences were largely made up of people from a distance, and among these were always a few timid ladies who were afraid that if they had to go into an ante-room to get their things when the play was over, they would miss their train. But the great mass of those who came a distance always ran the risk and took the chances, preferring the loss of the train to a breach of good manners and the discomfort of being unpleasantly conspicuous during a stretch of three or four hours.

CHAPTER 10

Three or four hours! That is a long time to sit in one place, whether one be conspicuous or not, yet some of Wagner's operas bang along for six whole hours on a stretch! But the people sit there and enjoy it all, and wish it would last longer. A German lady in Munich told me that a person could not like Wagner's music at first, but must go through the deliberate process of learning to like it—then he would have his sure reward; for when he had learned to like it he would hunger for it and never be able to get enough of it. She said that six hours of Wagner was by no means too much. She said that this composer had made a complete revolution in music, and was burying the old masters one by one. And she said that Wagner's operas differed from all others in one notable respect, and that was that they were not merely spotted with music here and there, but were *all* music, from the first strain to the last. This surprised me. I said I had attended one of his insurrections, and found hardly *any* music in it except the Wedding Chorus. She said 'Lohengrin' was noisier than Wagner's other operas, but that if I would keep on going to see it I would find by-and-by that it was all music, and therefore would then enjoy it. I *could* have said, 'But would you advise a person to deliberately practise having the toothache in the pit of his stomach for a couple of years in order that he might then come to enjoy it?' But I reserved that remark.

This lady was full of the praises of the head-tenor who had performed in a Wagner opera the night before, and went on to enlarge upon his old and prodigious fame, and how many honours had been lavished upon him by the princely houses of Germany. Here was another surprise. I had attended that very opera, in the person of my agent, and had made close and accurate observations. So I said—

'Why, madam, *my* experience warrants me in stating that that tenor's voice is not a voice at all, but only a shriek—the shriek of a hyena.'

'That is very true,' she said; 'he cannot sing now, it is already many years that he has lost his voice, but in other times he sang, yes, divinely! So whenever he comes, now, you shall see, yes, that the theatre will not hold the people. *Jawohl bei Gott!* his voice is *wunderschön* in that past time.'

I said she was discovering to me a kindly trait in the Germans which was worth emulating. I said that over the water we were not quite so generous; that with us, when a singer had lost his voice and a jumper had lost its legs, these parties ceased to draw. I said I had been to the opera in Hanover once, and in Mannheim once, and in Munich (through my authorised agent) once, and this large experience had nearly persuaded me that the Germans *preferred* singers who couldn't sing. This was not such a very extravagant speech either, for that burly Mannheim tenor's praises had been the talk of all Heidelberg for a week before his performance took place, yet his voice was like the distressing noise which a nail makes when you scratch it across a window-pane. I said so to Heidelberg friends the next day, and they said, in the calmest and simplest way, that that was very true, but that in earlier times his voice *had* been wonderfully fine. And the tenor in Hanover was just another example of this sort. The English-speaking German gentleman who went with me to the opera there was brimming with enthusiasm over that tenor. He said—

'*Ach Gott!* a great man! You shall see him. He is so celebrate in all Germany; and he has a pension, yes, from the Government. He not obliged to sing now, only twice every year; but if he not sing twice each year they take him his pension away.'

Very well, we went. When the renowned old tenor appeared, I got a nudge and an excited whisper—

'Now you see him!'

But the 'celebrate' was an astonishing disappointment to me. If he had been behind a screen I should have supposed they were performing a surgical operation on him. I looked at my friend. To my great surprise he seemed intoxicated with pleasure, his eyes were dancing with eager delight. When the curtain at last fell, he burst into the stormiest applause, and kept it up—as did the whole house—until the afflictive tenor had come three times before the curtain to make his bow. While the glowing enthusiast was swabbing the perspiration from his face, I said—

'I don't mean the least harm, but really, now, do you think he can sing?'

'Him! *No! Gott im Himmel, aber,* how he has been able to sing twenty-five years ago!' [Then pensively.] '*Ach*, no, *now* he not sing any more, he only cry. When he think he sing, now, he not sing at all, no; he only makes like a cat which is unwell.'

Where and how did we get the idea that the Germans are a stolid, phlegmatic race? In truth, they are widely removed from that. They are warm-hearted, emotional, impulsive, enthusiastic, their tears come at the mildest touch, and it is not hard to move them to laughter. They are the very children of impulse. We are cold and self-contained, compared with the Germans. They hug and kiss and cry and shout and dance and sing; and where we use one loving, petting expression, they pour out a score. Their language is full of endearing diminutives; nothing that they love escapes the application of a petting diminutive—neither the house, nor the dog, nor the horse, nor the grandmother, nor any other creature, animate or inanimate.

In the theatres at Hanover, Hamburg, and Mannheim, they had a wise custom. The moment the curtain went up, the lights in the body of the house went down. The audience sat in the cool gloom of a deep twilight, which greatly enhanced the glowing splendours of the stage. It saved gas, too, and people were not sweated to death.

When I saw 'King Lear' played, nobody was allowed to see a scene shifted; if there was nothing to be done but slide a forest out of the way and expose a temple beyond, one did not see that forest split itself in the middle and go shrieking away, with the accompanying disenchanting spectacle of the hands and heels of the impelling impulse—no, the curtain was always dropped for an instant—one heard not the least movement behind it—but when it went up, the next instant, the forest was gone. Even when the stage was being entirely re-set, one heard no noise. During the whole time that 'King Lear' was playing, the curtain was never down two minutes at any one time. The orchestra played until the curtain was ready to go up for the first time, then they departed for the evening. Where the stage-waits never reach two minutes, there is no occasion for music. I had never seen this two-minute business between acts but once before, and that was when the 'Shaughran' was played at Wallack's.

I was at a concert in Munich one night, the people were streaming in, the clock-hand pointed to seven, the music struck up, and instantly all movement in the body of the house ceased—nobody was standing, or walking up the aisles, or fumbling with a seat, the stream of incomers had suddenly dried up at its source. I listened undisturbed to a piece of music that was fifteen minutes long—always expecting some tardy ticket-holders to come crowding past my knees, and being continuously and pleasantly disappointed—but when the last note was struck, here came the stream again. You see, they had made those late comers wait in the comfortable waiting-parlour from the time the music had begun until it was ended.

It was the first time I had ever seen this sort of criminals denied the privilege of destroying the comfort of a house full of their betters. Some of these were pretty fine birds, but no matter, they had to tarry outside in the long parlour under the inspection of a double rank of liveried footmen and waiting-maids who supported the two walls with their backs and held the wraps and traps of their masters and mistresses on their arms.

We had no footmen to hold our things, and it was not permissible to take them into the concert room; but there were some men and women to take charge of them for us. They gave us checks for them and charged a fixed price, payable in advance—five cents.

In Germany they always hear one thing at an opera which has never yet been heard in America, perhaps—I mean the closing strain of a fine solo or duet. We always smash into it with an earthquake of applause. The result is that we rob ourselves of the sweetest part of the treat; we get the whisky, but we don't get the sugar in the bottom of the glass.

Our way of scattering applause along through an act seems to me to be better than the Mannheim way of saving it all up till the act is ended. I do not see how an actor can forget himself and portray hot passion before a cold still audience. I should think he would feel foolish. It is a pain to me to this day, to remember how that old German Lear raged and wept and howled around the stage, with never a response from that hushed house, never a single outburst till the act was ended. To me there was something unspeakably uncomfortable in the solemn dead silence that always followed this old person's tremendous outpourings of his feelings. I could not help putting myself in his place—I thought I knew how sick and flat he felt during those silences, because I remembered a case which came under my observation once, and which—but I will tell the incident.

One evening on board a Mississippi steamboat, a boy of ten years lay asleep in a berth—a long, slim-legged boy; he was encased in quite a short shirt; it was the first time he had ever made a trip on a steamboat, and so he was troubled, and scared, and had gone to bed, with his head filled with impending snaggings, and explosions, and conflagrations, and sudden death. About ten o'clock some twenty ladies were sitting around about the ladies' saloon, quietly reading, sewing, embroidering, and so on, and among them sat a sweet, benignant old dame with round spectacles on her nose and her busy knitting-needles in her hands. Now all of a sudden, into the midst of this peaceful scene burst that slim-shanked boy in the brief shirt, wild-eyed, erect-haired, and shouting, 'Fire, fire! *jump and run, the boat's afire, and there ain't a minute to lose!*' All those ladies looked sweetly up and smiled, nobody stirred, the old lady pulled her spectacles down, looked over them, and said, gently—

'But you mustn't catch cold, child. Run and put on your breast-pin, and then come and tell us all about it.'

It was a cruel chill to give to a poor little devil's gushing vehemence. He was expecting to be a sort of hero—the creator of a wild panic—and here everybody sat and smiled a mocking smile, and an old woman made fun of his bugbear. I turned and crept humbly away—for I was that boy—and never even cared to discover whether I had dreamed the fire or actually seen it.

I am told that in a German concert or opera they hardly ever encore a song; that though they may be dying to hear it again, their good breeding usually preserves them against requiring the repetition.

Kings may encore; that is quite another matter; it delights everybody to see that the King is pleased; and as to the actor encored, his pride and gratification are simply boundless. Still, there are circumstances in which even a royal encore—

But it is better to illustrate. The King of Bavaria is a poet, and has a poet's eccentricities—with the advantage over all other poets of being able to gratify them, no matter what form they may take. He is fond of the opera, but not fond of sitting in the presence of an audience; therefore, it has sometimes occurred, in Munich, that when an opera has been concluded and the players were getting off their paint and finery, a command has come to them to get their paint and finery on again. Presently the King would arrive, solitary and alone, and the players would begin at the beginning and do the entire opera over again with only that one individual in the vast solemn theatre for audience. Once he took an odd freak into his head. High up and out of sight, over the prodigious stage of the court theatre is a maze of interlacing water-pipes, so pierced that, in case of fire, innumerable little thread-like streams of water can be caused to descend; and in case of need, this discharge can be augmented to a pouring flood. American managers might make a note of that. The king was sole audience. The opera proceeded, it was a piece with a storm in it; the mimic thunder began to mutter, the mimic wind began to wail and sough, and the mimic rain to patter. The King's interest rose higher and higher: it developed into enthusiasm. He cried out—

'It is good, very good indeed! But I will have real rain! turn on the water!'

The manager pleaded for a reversal of the command; said it would ruin the costly scenery and the splendid costumes, but the King cried—

'No matter, no matter, I will have real rain! Turn on the water!'

So the real rain was turned on and began to descend in gossamer lances to the mimic flower beds and gravel walks of the stage. The richly dressed actresses and actors tripped about singing bravely and pretending not to mind it. The King was delighted—his enthusiasm grew higher. He cried out—

'Bravo, bravo! More thunder! more lightning! turn on more rain!'

The thunder boomed, the lightning glared, the storm-winds raged, the deluge poured down. The mimic royalty on the stage, with their soaked satins clinging to their bodies, slopped around ankle-deep in water, warbling their sweetest and best, the fiddlers under the eaves of the stage sawed away for dear life, with the cold overflow spouting down the backs of their necks, and the dry and happy King sat in his lofty box, and wore his gloves to ribbons applauding.

'More yet!' cried the King; 'more yet—let loose all the thunder, turn on all the water! I will hang the man that raises an umbrella!'

When this most tremendous and effective storm that had ever been produced in any theatre was at last over, the King's approbation was measureless. He cried—

'Magnificent, magnificent! *Encore!* Do it again!'

But the manager succeeded in persuading him to recall the encore, and said the company would feel sufficiently rewarded and complimented in the mere fact that the encore was desired by his Majesty, without fatiguing him with a repetition to gratify their own vanity.

During the remainder of the act the lucky performers were those whose parts required changes of dress; the others were a soaked, bedraggled, and uncomfortable lot, but in the last degree picturesque. The stage scenery was ruined, trap-doors were so swollen that they wouldn't work for a week afterwards, the fine costumes were spoiled, and no end of minor damages were done by that remarkable storm.

It was a royal idea—that storm—and royally carried out. But observe the moderation of the King: he did not insist upon his encore. If he had been a gladsome, unreflecting American opera audience, he probably would have had his storm repeated and repeated until he drowned all those people.

CHAPTER 11

The summer days passed pleasantly in Heidelberg. We had a skilled trainer, and under his instructions we were getting our legs in the right condition for the contemplated pedestrian tours; we were well satisfied with the progress which we had made in the German language,[1] and more than satisfied with what we had accomplished in Art. We had had the best instructors in drawing and painting in Germany—Hämmerling, Vogel, Müller, Dietz, and Schumann. Hämmerling taught us landscape painting, Vogel taught us figure drawing, Müller taught us to do still-life, and Dietz and Schumann gave us a finishing course in two specialties—battlepieces and shipwrecks. Whatever I am in Art I owe to these men. I have something of the manner of each and all of them; but they all said that I had also a manner of my own, and that it was conspicuous. They said there was a marked individuality about my style, insomuch that if I ever painted the commonest type of a dog, I should be sure to throw a something into the aspect of that dog which would keep him from being mistaken for the creation of any other artist. Secretly I wanted to believe all these kind sayings, but I could not; I was afraid that my masters' partiality for me, and pride in me, biassed their judgment. So I resolved to make a test. Privately, and unknown to anyone, I painted my great picture, 'Heidelberg Castle

[1] See Appendix D for information concerning this fearful tongue.

Illuminated'—my first really important work in oils—and had it hung up in the midst of a wilderness of oil pictures in the Art Exhibition, with no name attached to it. To my great gratification it was instantly recognised as mine. All the town flocked to see it, and people even came from neighbouring localities to visit it. It made more stir than any other work in the Exhibition. But the most gratifying thing of all was that chance strangers, passing through, who had not heard of my picture, were not only drawn to it, as by a loadstone, the moment they entered the gallery, but always took it for a 'Turner.'

Mr. Harris was graduated in Art about the same time with myself, and we took a studio together. We waited awhile for some orders; then as time began to drag a little, we concluded to make a pedestrian tour. After much consideration we determined on a trip up the shores of the beautiful Neckar to Heilbronn. Apparently nobody had ever done that. There were ruined castles on the overhanging cliffs and crags all the way; these were said to have their legends, like those on the Rhine, and, what was better still, they had never been in print. There was nothing in the books about that lovely region, it had been neglected by the tourist, it was virgin soil for the literary pioneer.

Meantime the knapsacks, the rough walking-suits, and the stout walking-shoes which we had ordered, were finished and brought to us. A Mr. X. and a young Mr. Z. had agreed to go with us. We went around one evening and bade good-bye to our friends, and afterwards had a little farewell banquet at the hotel. We got to bed early, for we wanted to make an early start, so as to take advantage of the cool of the morning.

We were out of bed at break of day, feeling fresh and vigorous, and took a hearty breakfast, then plunged down through the leafy arcades of the Castle grounds, towards the town. What a glorious summer morning it was, and how the flowers did pour out their fragrance, and how the birds did sing! It was just the time for a tramp through the woods and mountains.

We were all dressed alike: broad slouch hats, to keep the sun off; grey knapsacks; blue army shirts; blue overalls; leathern gaiters buttoned tight from knee down to ankle; high-quarter coarse shoes snugly laced. Each man had an opera-glass, a canteen, and a guide-book case slung over his shoulder, and carried an alpenstock in one hand and a sun umbrella in the other. Around our hats were wound many folds of soft white muslin, with the ends hanging and flapping down our backs—an idea brought from the Orient and used by tourists all over Europe. Harris carried the little watch-like machine called a 'pedometer,' whose office is to keep count of a man's steps and tell how far he has walked. Everybody stopped to admire our costumes and give us a hearty 'Pleasant march to you!'

When we got down town I found that we could go by rail to within five miles of Heilbronn. The train was just starting, so we jumped aboard and went tearing away in splendid spirits. It was agreed all around that we had done wisely, because it would be just as enjoyable to walk *down* the Neckar as up it, and it could not be needful to walk both ways. There were some nice German people in our compartment. I got to talking some pretty private matters presently, and Harris became nervous; so he nudged me and said—

'Speak in German—these Germans may understand English.'

I did so, and it was well I did; for it turned out that there was not a German in that party who did not understand English perfectly. It is curious how widespread our language is in Germany. After a while some of those folks got out, and a German gentleman and his two young daughters got in. I spoke in German to one of the latter several times, but without result. Finally she said—

'Ich verstehe nur Deutsch und Englisch'— or words to that effect. That is, 'I don't understand any language but German and English.'

And sure enough, not only she but her father and sister spoke English. So after that we had all the talk we wanted; and we wanted a good deal, for they were very agreeable people. They were greatly interested in our costumes; especially the alpenstocks, for they had not seen any before. They said that the Neckar road was perfectly level, so we must be going to Switzerland or some other rugged country; and asked us if we did not find the walking pretty fatiguing in such warm weather.

But we said No.

We reached Wimpfen—I think it was Wimpfen—in about three hours, and got out, not the least tired; found a good hotel and ordered beer and dinner; then took a stroll through the venerable old village. It was very picturesque and tumble-down, and dirty and interesting. It had queer houses five hundred years old in it, and a military tower, 115 feet high, which had stood there more than ten centuries. I made a little sketch of it. I kept a copy, but gave the original to the Burgomaster. I think the original was better than the copy, because it had more windows in it, and the grass stood up better and had a brisker look. There was none around the tower, though; I composed the grass myself, from studies I made in a field by Heidelberg in Hämmerling's time. The man on top, looking at the view, is apparently too large, but I found he could not be made smaller conveniently. I wanted him there, and I wanted him visible, so I thought out a way to manage it; I composed the picture from two points of view; the spectator is to observe the man from about where that flag is, and he must observe the tower itself from the ground. This harmonises the seeming discrepancy.

Near an old cathedral, under a shed, were three crosses of stone—mouldy and damaged things, bearing life-size stone figures. The two thieves were dressed in the fanciful court costumes of the middle of the sixteenth century, while the Saviour was nude, with the exception of a cloth around the loins.

We had dinner under the green trees in a garden belonging to the hotel and overlooking the Neckar; then, after a smoke, we went to bed. We had a refreshing nap, then got up about three in the afternoon and put on our panoply. As we tramped gaily out at the gate of the town, we overtook a peasant's cart, partly laden with odds and ends of cabbages and similar vegetable rubbish, and drawn by a small cow and a smaller donkey yoked together. It was a pretty slow concern, but it got us into Heilbronn before dark—five miles, or possibly it was seven.

We stopped at the very same inn which the famous old robber knight and rough fighter, Götz von Berlichingen, abode in after he got out of captivity in the Square Tower of Heilbronn between three hundred and fifty and four hundred years ago.

Harris and I occupied the same room which he had occupied, and the same paper had not all peeled off the walls yet. The furniture was quaint old carved stuff, full four hundred years old, and some of the smells were over a thousand. There was a hook in the wall, which the landlord said the terrific old Götz used to hang his iron hand on when he took it off to go to bed. This room was very large—it might be called immense—and it was on the first floor; which means it was in the second story, for in Europe the houses are so high that they do not count the first story, else they would get tired climbing before they got to the top. The wall paper was a fiery red, with huge gold figures in it, well smirched by time, and it covered all the doors. These doors fitted so snugly and continued the figures of the paper so unbrokenly that when they were closed one had to go feeling and searching along the wall to find them. There was a stove in the corner—one of those tall, square, stately white porcelain things that looks like a monument, and keeps you thinking of death when you ought to be enjoying your travels. The windows looked out on a little alley, and over that into a stable and some poultry and pig yards in the rear of some tenement houses. There were the customary two beds in the room, one in one end of it, the other in the other, about an old-fashioned brass-mounted single-barrelled pistol-shot apart. They were fully as narrow as the usual German bed, too, and had the German bed's ineradicable habit of spilling the blankets on the floor every time you forgot yourself and went to sleep.

A round table as large as King Arthur's stood in the centre of the room; while the waiters were getting ready to serve our dinner on it we all went out to see the renowned clock on the front of the municipal buildings.

CHAPTER 12

The *Rathhaus*, or municipal building, is of the quaintest and most picturesque Middle-Age architecture. It has a massive portico and steps before it, heavily balustraded, and adorned with life-size rusty iron knights in complete armour. The clock-face on the front of the building is very large, and of curious pattern. Ordinarily a gilded angel strikes the hour on a big bell with a hammer; as the striking ceases, a life-size figure of Time raises its hour-glass and turns it; two golden rams advance and butt each other; a gilded cock lifts its wings; but the main features are two great angels, who stand on each side of the dial with long horns at their lips: it was said that they blew melodious blasts on these horns every hour; but they blew only at night when the town was still.

Within the *Rathhaus* were a number of huge wild boars' heads, preserved and mounted on brackets along the wall; they bore inscriptions telling who killed them, and how many hundred years ago it was done. One room in the building was devoted to the preservation of ancient archives. There they showed us no end of aged documents; some were signed by Popes, some by Tilley and other great generals, and one was a letter written and subscribed by Götz von Berlichingen in Heilbronn in 1519, just after his release from the Square Tower.

This fine old robber-knight was a devoutly and sincerely religious man, hospitable, charitable to the poor, fearless in fight, active, enterprising, and possessed of a large and generous nature. He had in him a quality which was rare in that rough time—the quality of being able to overlook moderate injuries, and of being able to forgive and forget mortal ones as soon as he had soundly trounced the authors of them, He was prompt to take up any poor devil's quarrel and risk his neck to right him. The common folk held him dear, and his memory is still green in ballad and tradition. He used to go on the highway and rob rich wayfarers; and other times he would swoop down from his high castle on the hills of the Neckar and capture passing cargoes of merchandise. In his Memoirs he piously thanks the Giver of all Good for remembering him in his needs and delivering sundry such cargoes into his hands at times when only special providences could have relieved him. He was a doughty warrior, and found a deep joy in battle. In an assault upon a stronghold in Bavaria, when he was only twenty-three years old, his right hand was shot away, but he was so interested in the fight that he did not observe it for a while. He said that the iron hand which was made for him afterward, and which he wore for more than half a century, was nearly as clever a member as the fleshy one had been. I was glad to get a *fac-simile* of the letter written by this fine old German Robin Hood, though I was not able to read it. He was a better artist with his sword than with his pen.

We went down by the river and saw the Square Tower. It was a very venerable structure, very strong, and very unornamental. There was no opening near the ground. They had to use a ladder to get into it, no doubt.

We visited the principal church, also, a curious old structure, with a tower-like spire adorned with all sorts of grotesque images. The inner walls of the church were placarded with large mural tablets of copper, bearing engraved inscriptions celebrating the merits of old Heilbronn worthies of two or three centuries ago, and also bearing rudely-painted effigies of themselves and their families tricked out in the queer costumes of those days. The head of the family sat in the foreground, and beyond him extended a sharply receding and diminishing row of sons; facing him sat his wife, and beyond her extended a long row of diminishing daughters. The family was usually large, but the perspective bad.

Then we hired the hack and the horse which Götz von Berlichingen used to use, and drove several miles into the country to visit the place called *Weibertreu*—Wife's Fidelity, I suppose it means. It was a feudal castle of the Middle Ages. When we reached its neighbourhood we found it was beautifully situated, but on top of a mound, or hill, round and tolerably steep, and about two hundred feet high. Therefore, as the sun was blazing hot, we did not climb up there, but took the place on trust, and observed it from a distance, while the horse leaned up against a fence and rested. The place has no interest except that which is lent it by its legend, which is a very pretty one—to this effect.

The Legend

In the Middle Ages a couple of young dukes, brothers, took opposite sides in one of the wars, the one fighting for the Emperor, the other against him. One of them owned the castle and village on top of the mound which I have been speaking of, and in his absence his brother came with his knights and soldiers and began a siege. It was a long and tedious business; for the people made a stubborn and faithful defence. But at last their supplies ran out, and starvation began its work; more fell by hunger than by the missiles of the enemy. They by-and-by surrendered, and begged for charitable terms. But the beleaguering prince was so incensed against them for their long resistance that he said he would spare none but the women and children—all the men should be put to the sword without exception, and all their goods destroyed. Then the women came and fell on their knees and begged for the lives of their husbands.

'No,' said the prince, 'not a man of them shall escape alive; you yourselves shall go with your children into houseless and friendless banishment; but that you may not starve I grant you this one grace, that each woman may bear with her from this place as much of her most valuable property as she is able to carry.'

Very well, presently the gates swung open and out filed those women carrying their *husbands* on their shoulders. The besiegers, furious at the trick, rushed forward to slaughter the men, but the Duke stepped between and said—

'No, put up your swords—a prince's word is inviolable.'

When we got back to the hotel, King Arthur's Round Table was ready for us in its white drapery, and the head waiter and his first assistant, in swallow-tails and white cravats, brought in the soup and the hot plates at once.

Mr. X. had ordered the dinner, and when the wine came on, he picked up a bottle, glanced at the label, and then turned to the grave, the melancholy, the sepulchral head waiter, and said it was not the sort of wine he had asked for. The head waiter picked up the bottle, cast his undertaker-eye on it, and said—

'It is true; I beg pardon.' Then he turned on his subordinate and calmly said, 'Bring another label.'

At the same time he slid the present label off with his hand and laid it aside; it had been newly put on, its paste was still wet. When the new label came, he put it on; our French wine being now turned into German wine, according to desire, the head waiter went blandly about his other duties, as if the working of this sort of miracle was a common and easy thing to him.

Mr. X. said he had not known before that there were people honest enough to do this miracle in public, but he was aware that thousands upon thousands of labels were imported into America from Europe every year, to enable dealers to furnish to their customers, in a quiet and inexpensive way, all the different kinds of foreign wines they might require.

We took a turn around the town, after dinner, and found it fully as interesting in the moonlight as it had been in the day time. The streets were narrow and roughly paved, and there was not a sidewalk or a street lamp anywhere. The dwellings were centuries old, and vast enough for hotels. They widened all the way up; the stories projected further and further forward and aside as they ascended, and the long rows of lighted windows, filled with little bits of panes, curtained with figured white muslin and adorned outside with boxes of flowers, made a pretty effect. The moon was bright, and the light and shadow very strong; and nothing could be more picturesque than those curving streets, with their rows of huge high gables leaning far over toward each other in a friendly gossiping way, and the crowds below drifting through the alternating blots of gloom and mellow bars of moonlight. Nearly everybody was abroad, chatting, singing, romping, or massed in lazy comfortable attitudes in the doorways.

In one place there was a public building which was fenced about with a thick, rusty chain, which sagged from post to post in a succession of low swings. The pavement here was made of heavy blocks of stone. In the glare of the moon a party of barefooted children were swinging on those chains and having a noisy good time. They were not the first ones who had done that; even their great-great-grandfathers had not been the first to do it when they were children. The strokes of the bare feet had worn grooves inches deep in the stone flags; it had taken many generations of swinging children to accomplish that. Everywhere in the town were the mould and decay that go with antiquity, and evidence it; but I do not know that anything else gave us so vivid a sense of the old age of Heilbronn as those foot-worn grooves in the paving stones.

CHAPTER 13

When we got back to the hotel I wound and set the pedometer and put it in my pocket, for I was to carry it next day and keep record of the miles we made. The work which we had given the instrument to do during the day which had just closed, had not fatigued it perceptibly.

We were in bed by ten, for we wanted to be up and away on our tramp homeward with the dawn. I hung fire, but Harris went to sleep at once. I hate a man who goes to sleep at once; there is a sort of indefinable something about it which is not exactly an insult, and yet is an insolence; and one which is hard to bear, too. I lay there fretting over this injury, and trying to go to sleep; but the harder I tried the wider awake I grew. I got to feeling very lonely in the dark, with no company but an undigested dinner. My mind got a start by-and-by, and began to consider the beginning of every subject which has ever been thought of; but it never went further than the beginning; it was touch and go; it fled from topic to topic with a frantic speed. At the end of an hour my head was in a perfect whirl, and I was dead tired, fagged out.

The fatigue was so great that it presently began to make some head against the nervous excitement; while imagining myself wide awake, I would really doze into momentary unconsciousnesses, and come suddenly out of them with a physical jerk which nearly wrenched my joints apart—the delusion of the instant being that I was tumbling backwards over a precipice. After I had fallen over eight or nine precipices and thus found out that one half of my brain had been asleep eight or nine times without the wide-awake, hard-working other half suspecting it, the periodical unconsciousnesses began to extend their spell gradually over more of my brain-territory, and at last I sank into a drowse which grew deeper and deeper and was doubtless just on the very point of becoming a solid, blessed, dreamless stupor, when—what was that?

My dulled faculties dragged themselves partly back to life, and took a receptive attitude. Now out of an immense, a limitless distance, came a something which grew and grew, and approached, and presently was recognisable as a sound—it had rather seemed to be a feeling, before. This sound was a mile away, now—perhaps it was the murmur of a storm; and now it was nearer—not a quarter of a mile away; was it the muffled rasping and grinding of distant machinery? No, it came still nearer; was it the measured tramp of a marching troop? But it came nearer still, and still nearer—and at last it was right in the room: it was merely a mouse gnawing the woodwork. So I had held my breath all that time for such a trifle.

Well, what was done could not be helped; I would go to sleep at once and make up the lost time. That was a thoughtless thought. Without intending it—hardly knowing it—I fell to listening intently to that sound, and even unconsciously counting the strokes of the mouse's nutmeg-grater. Presently I was deriving exquisite suffering from this employment, yet maybe I could have endured it if the mouse had attended steadily to his work; but he did not do that; he stopped every now and then, and I suffered more while waiting and listening for him to begin again than I did while he was gnawing. Along at first I was mentally offering a reward of five,—six,—seven,—ten dollars for that mouse; but towards the last I was offering rewards which were entirely beyond my means. I close-reefed my ears,—that is to say, I bent the flaps of them down, and furled them into five or six folds, and pressed them against the hearing-orifice,—but it did no good: the faculty was so sharpened by nervous excitement that it was become a microphone, and could hear through the overlays without trouble.

My anger grew to a frenzy. I finally did what all persons before me have done, clear back to Adam—resolved to throw something. I reached down and got my walking-shoes, then sat up in bed and listened, in order to exactly locate the noise. But I couldn't do it; it was as unlocatable as a cricket's noise; and where one thinks that that is, is always the very place where it isn't. So I presently hurled a shoe at random, and with a vicious vigour. It struck the wall over Harris's head and fell down on him; I had not imagined I could throw so far. It woke Harris, and I was glad of it until I found he was not angry; then I was sorry. He soon went to sleep again, which pleased me; but straightway the mouse began again, which roused my temper once more. I did not want to wake Harris a second time, but the gnawing continued until I was compelled to throw the other shoe. This time I broke a mirror—there were two in the room—I got the largest one of course. Harris woke again, but did not complain, and I was sorrier than ever. I resolved that I would suffer all possible torture before I would disturb him a third time.

The mouse eventually retired, and by-and-by I was sinking to sleep, when a clock began to strike; I counted till it was done, and was about to drowse again when another clock began; I counted; then the two great Rathhaus clock angels began to send forth soft, rich, melodious blasts from their long trumpets. I had never heard anything that was so lovely, or weird, or mysterious—but when they got to blowing the quarter-hours, they seemed to me to be overdoing the thing. Every time I dropped off for a moment, a new noise woke me. Each time I woke, I missed my coverlet, and had to reach down to the floor and get it again.

At last all sleepiness forsook me. I recognised the fact that I was hopelessly and permanently wide awake. Wide awake, and feverish and thirsty. When I had lain tossing there as long as I could endure it, it occurred to me that it would be a good idea to dress and go out in the great square and take a refreshing wash in the fountain, and smoke and reflect there until the remnant of the night was gone.

I believed I could dress in the dark without waking Harris. I had banished my shoes after the mouse, but my slippers would do for a summer night. So I rose softly, and gradually got on everything—down to one sock. I couldn't seem to get on the track of that sock, any way I could fix it. But I had to have it; so I went down on my hands and knees with one slipper on and the other in my hand, and began to paw gently around and rake the floor, but with no success. I enlarged my circle, and went on pawing and raking. With every pressure of my knee, how the floor creaked! and every time I chanced to rake against any article, it seemed to give out thirty-five or thirty-six times more noise than it would have done in the day time. In those cases I always stopped and held my breath till I was sure Harris had not awakened—then I crept along again. I moved on and on, but I could not find the sock; I could not seem to find anything but furniture. I could not remember that there was much furniture in the room when I went to bed, but the place was alive with it now—especially chairs—chairs everywhere—had a couple of families moved in, in the meantime? And I never could seem to *glance* on one of those chairs, but always struck it full and square with my head. My temper rose, by steady and sure degrees, and as I pawed on and on, I fell to making vicious comments under my breath.

Finally, with a venomous access of irritation, I said I would leave without the sock; so I rose up and made straight for the door—as I supposed—and suddenly confronted my dim spectral image in the unbroken mirror. It startled the breath out of me, for an instant; it also showed me that I was lost, and had no sort of idea where I was. When I realised this, I was so angry that I had to sit down on the floor and take hold of something to keep from lifting the roof off with an explosion of opinion. If there had been only one mirror, it might possibly have helped to locate me; but there were two, and two were as bad as a thousand; besides, these were on opposite sides of the room. I could see the dim blur of the windows, but in my turned-around condition they were exactly where they ought not to be, and so they only confused me instead of helping me.

I started to get up, and knocked down an umbrella; it made a noise like a pistol-shot when it struck that hard, slick carpetless floor; I grated my teeth, and held my breath—Harris did not stir. I set the umbrella slowly and carefully on the end against the wall, but as soon as I took my hand away, its heel slipped from under it, and down it came again with another bang. I shrunk together and listened a moment in silent fury—no harm done, everything quiet. With the most painstaking care and nicety I stood the umbrella up once more, took my hand away, and down it came again.

I have been strictly reared, but if it had not been so dark and solemn and awful there in that lonely vast room, I do believe I should have said something then which could not be put into a Sunday-school book without injuring the sale of it. If my reasoning powers had not been already sapped dry by my harassments, I would have known better than to try to set an umbrella on end on one of those glassy German floors in the dark; it can't be done in the daytime without four failures to one success. I had one comfort, though—Harris was yet still and silent—he had not stirred.

The umbrella could not locate me—there were four standing around the room, and all alike. I thought I would feel along the wall and find the door in that way. I rose up and began this operation, but raked down a picture. It was not a large one, but it made noise enough for a panorama. Harris gave out no sound, but I felt that if I experimented any further with the pictures I should be sure to wake him. Better give up trying to get out. Yes, I would find King Arthur's Round Table once more—I had already found it several times—and use it for a base of departure on an exploring tour for my bed; if I could find my bed I could then find my water pitcher; I would quench my raging thirst and turn in. So I started on my hands and knees, because I could go faster that way, and with more confidence, too, and not knock down things. By-and-by I found the table—with my head—rubbed the bruise a little, then rose up and started, with hands abroad and fingers spread, to balance myself. I found a chair; then the wall; then another chair; then a sofa; then an alpenstock, then another sofa; this confounded me, for I had thought there was only one sofa. I hunted up the table again and took a fresh start; found some more chairs.

It occurred to me, now, as it ought to have done before, that as the table was round, it was therefore of no value as a base to aim from; so I moved off once more, and at random among the wilderness of chairs and sofas—wandered off into unfamiliar regions, and presently knocked a candlestick off a mantelpiece; grabbed at the candlestick and knocked off a lamp; grabbed at the lamp and knocked off a water-pitcher with a rattling crash, and thought to myself, 'I've found you at last—I judged I was close upon you.' Harris shouted 'murder,' and 'thieves,' and finished with 'I'm absolutely drowned.'

The crash had roused the house. Mr. X. pranced in in his long night garment with a candle, young Z. after him with another candle; a procession swept in at another door with candles and lanterns, landlord and two German guests in their nightgowns, and a chambermaid in hers.

I looked around; I was at Harris's bed, a Sabbath day's journey from my own. There was only one sofa, it was against the wall; there was only one chair where a body could get at it—I had been revolving around it like a planet, and colliding with it like a comet half the night.

I explained how I had been employing myself, and why. Then the landlord's party left, and the rest of us set about our preparations for breakfast, for the dawn was ready to break. I glanced furtively at my pedometer, and found I had made forty-seven miles. But I did not care, for I had come out for a pedestrian tour anyway.

CHAPTER 14

When the landlord learned that I and my agent were artists, our party rose perceptibly in his esteem; we rose still higher when he learned that we were making a pedestrian tour of Europe.

He told us all about the Heidelberg road, and which were the best places to avoid, and which the best ones to tarry at; he charged me less than cost for the things I broke in the night; he put up a fine luncheon for us, and added to it a quantity of great light-green plums, the pleasantest fruit in Germany; he was so anxious to do us honour that he would not allow us to walk out of Heilbronn, but called up Götz von Berlichingen's horse and cab and made us ride.

I made a sketch of the turn-out. It is not a Work, it is only what artists call a 'study'—a thing to make a finished picture from. This sketch has several blemishes in it; for instance, the waggon is not travelling as fast as the horse is. This is wrong. Again, the person trying to get out of the way is too small; he is out of perspective, as we say. The two upper lines are not the horse's back, they are the reins; there seems to be a wheel missing—this would be corrected in a finished Work, of course. That thing flying out behind is not a flag, it is a curtain. That other thing up there is the sun, but I didn't get enough distance on it. I do not remember, now, what that thing is that is in front of the man who is running, but I think it is a haystack or a woman. This study was exhibited in the Paris Salon of 1879, but did not take any medal; they do not give medals for studies.

We discharged the carriage at the bridge. The river was full of logs—long, slender, barkless pine logs—and we leaned on the rails of the bridge and watched the men put them together into rafts. These rafts were of a shape and construction to suit the crookedness and extreme narrowness of the Neckar. They were from 50 to 100 yards long, and they gradually tapered from a 9-log breadth at their sterns, to a 3-log breadth at their bow-ends. The main part of the steering is done at the bow, with a pole; the 3-log breadth there furnishes room for only the steersman, for these little logs are not larger around than an average young lady's waist. The connections of the several sections of the raft are slack and pliant, so that the raft may be readily bent into any sort of curve required by the shape of the river.

The Neckar is in many places so narrow that a person can throw a dog across it, if he has one; when it is also sharply curved in such places, the raftsman has to do some pretty nice snug piloting to make the turns. The river is not always allowed to spread over its whole bed—which is as much as thirty, and sometimes forty yards wide—but is split into three equal bodies of water, by stone dykes which throw the main volume, depth, and current, into the central one. In low water these neat narrow-edged dykes project four or five inches above the surface, like the comb of a submerged roof; but in high water they are overflowed. A hatful of rain makes high water in the Neckar, and a basketful produces an overflow.

There are dykes abreast the Schloss Hotel, and the current is violently swift at that point. I used to sit for hours in my glass cage, watching the long narrow rafts slip along through the central channel, grazing the right-bank dyke, and aiming carefully for the middle arch of the stone bridge below; I watched them in this way, and lost all this time hoping to see one of them hit the bridge-pier and wreck itself some time or other, but was always disappointed. One was smashed there one morning, but I had just stepped into my room a moment to light a pipe, so I lost it.

While I was looking down upon the rafts that morning in Heilbronn, the dare-devil spirit of adventure came suddenly upon me, and I said to my comrades—

'*I* am going to Heidelberg on a raft. Will you venture with me?'

Their faces paled a little, but they assented with as good a grace as they could. Harris wanted to cable his mother—thought it his duty to do that, as he was all she had in this world—so, while he attended to this, I went down to the longest and finest raft and hailed the captain with a hearty 'Ahoy, shipmate!' which put us upon pleasant terms at once, and we entered upon business. I said we were on a pedestrian tour to Heidelberg, and would like to take passage with him. I said this partly through young Z., who spoke German very well, and partly through Mr. X., who spoke it peculiarly. I can *understand* German as well as the maniac that invented it, but I *talk* it best through an interpreter.

The captain hitched up his trousers, then shifted his quid thoughtfully. Presently he said just what I was expecting he would say, that he had no licence to carry passengers, and therefore was afraid the law would be after him in case the matter got noised about or any accident happened. So I *chartered* the raft and the crew, and took all the responsibility on myself.

With a rattling song the starboard watch bent to their work and hove the cable short, then got the anchor home, and our bark moved off with a stately stride, and soon was bowling along at about two knots an hour.

Our party were grouped amidships. At first the talk was a little gloomy, and ran mainly upon the shortness of life, the uncertainty of it, the perils which beset it, and the need and wisdom of being always prepared for the worst; this shaded off into low-voiced references to the dangers of the deep, and kindred matters; but as the grey east began to redden, and the mysterious solemnity and silence of the dawn to give place to the joy-songs of the birds, the talk took a cheerier tone, and our spirits began to rise steadily.

Germany, in the summer, is the perfection of the beautiful, but nobody has understood, and realised, and enjoyed the utmost possibilities of this soft and peaceful beauty unless he has voyaged down the Neckar on a raft. The motion of a raft is the needful motion; it is gentle, and gliding, and smooth, and noiseless; it calms down all feverish activities, it soothes to sleep all nervous hurry and impatience; under its restful influence all the troubles and vexations and sorrows that harass the mind vanish away, and existence becomes a dream, a charm, a deep and tranquil ecstasy. How it contrasts with hot and perspiring pedestrianism and dusty and deafening railroad rush, and tedious jolting behind tired horses over blinding white roads!

We went slipping silently along, between the green and fragrant banks, with a sense of pleasure and contentment that grew and grew all the time. Sometimes the banks were overhung with thick masses of willows that wholly hid the ground behind; sometimes we had noble hills on one hand, clothed densely with foliage to their tops, and on the other hand open levels blazing with poppies, or clothed in the rich blue of the corn-flower; sometimes we drifted in the shadow of forests, and sometimes along the margin of long stretches of velvety grass, fresh and green and bright, a tireless charm to the eye. And the birds!—they were everywhere; they swept back and forth across the river constantly, and their jubilant music was never stilled.

It was a deep and satisfying pleasure to see the sun create the new morning, and gradually, patiently, lovingly, clothe it on with splendour after splendour, and glory after glory, till the miracle was complete. How different is this marvel observed from a raft, from what it is when one observes it through the dingy windows of a railway station in some wretched village, while he munches a petrified sandwich and waits for the train.

CHAPTER 15

Down The River

Men and women and cattle were at work in the dewy fields by this time. The people often stepped aboard the raft, as we glided along the grassy shores, and gossiped with us and with the crew for a hundred yards or so, then stepped ashore again, refreshed by the ride.

Only the men did this, the women were too busy. The women do all kinds of work on the Continent. They dig, they hoe, they reap, they sow, they bear monstrous burdens on their backs, they shove similar ones long distances on wheelbarrows, they drag the cart when there is no dog or lean cow to drag it, and when there is, they assist the dog or cow. Age is no matter: the older the woman, the stronger she is, apparently. On the farm a woman's duties are not defined, she does a little of everything; but in the towns it is different, there she only does certain things, the men do the rest. For instance, an hotel chambermaid has nothing to do but make beds and fires in fifty or sixty rooms, bring towels and candles, and fetch several tons of water up several flights of stairs, a hundred pounds at a time, in prodigious metal pitchers. She does not have to work more than eighteen or twenty hours a day, and she can always get down on her knees and scrub the floors of halls and closets when she is tired and needs a rest.

As the morning advanced and the weather grew hot, we took off our outside clothing, and sat in a row along the edge of the raft and enjoyed the scenery, with our sun umbrellas over our heads and our legs dangling in the water. Every now and then we plunged in and had a swim. Every projecting grassy cape had its joyous group of naked children, the boys to themselves and the girls to themselves, the latter usually in care of some motherly dame who sat in the shade of a tree with her knitting. The little boys swam out to us sometimes, but the little maids stood knee-deep in the water, and stopped their splashing and frolicking to inspect the raft with their innocent eyes as it drifted by. Once we turned a corner suddenly, and surprised a slender girl of twelve years or upwards, just stepping into the water. She had no time to run, but she did what answered just as well; she promptly drew a lithe young willow bough athwart her white body with one hand, and then contemplated us with a simple and untroubled interest. Thus she stood while we glided by. She was a pretty creature, and she and her willow bough made a very pretty picture, and one which could not offend the modesty of the most fastidious spectator. Her white skin had a low bank of fresh green willows for background and effective contrast—for she stood against them—and above and out of them projected the eager faces and white shoulders of two smaller girls.

Towards noon we heard the inspiriting cry—

'Sail ho!'

'Where away?' shouted the captain.

'Three points off the weather bow!'

We ran forward to see the vessel. It proved to be a steamboat—for they had begun to run a steamer up the Neckar, for the first time in May. She was a tug, and one of very peculiar build and aspect. I had often watched her from the hotel, and wondered how she propelled herself, for apparently she had no propeller or paddles. She came churning along, now, making a deal of noise of one kind and another, and aggravating it every now and then by blowing a hoarse whistle. She had nine keel-boats hitched on behind and following after her in a long, slender rank. We met her in a narrow place, between dykes, and there was hardly room for us both in the cramped passage. As she went grinding and groaning by, we perceived the secret of her moving impulse. She did not drive herself up the river with paddles or propeller, she pulled herself by hauling on a great chain. This chain is laid in the bed of the river, and is only fastened at the two ends. It is seventy miles long. It comes in over the boat's bow, passes around a drum, and is paid out astern. She pulls on that chain, and so drags herself up the river or down it. She has neither bow nor stern, strictly speaking, for she has a long-bladed rudder on each end, and she never turns around. She uses both rudders all the time, and they are powerful enough to enable her to turn to the right or the left, and steer around curves in spite of the strong resistance of the chain. I would not have believed that that impossible thing could be done; but I saw it done, and therefore I know that there is one impossible thing which *can* be done. What miracle will man attempt next?

We met many big keel boats on their way up, using sails, mule power, and profanity—a tedious and laborious business. A wire rope led from the foretop mast to the file of mules on the towpath a hundred yards ahead, and by dint of much banging and swearing and urging, the detachment of drivers managed to get a speed of two or three miles an hour out of the mules against the stiff current. The Neckar has always been used as a canal, and thus has given employment to a great many men and animals; but now that this steamboat is able, with a small crew and a bushel or so of coal, to take nine keel boats farther up the river in one hour than thirty men and thirty mules can do it in two, it is believed that the old-fashioned towing industry is on its deathbed. A second steamboat began work in the Neckar three months after the first one was put in service.

At noon we stepped ashore and bought some bottled beer, and got some chickens cooked while the raft waited; then we immediately put to sea again, and had our dinner while the beer was cold and the chickens hot. There is no pleasanter place for such a meal than a raft that is gliding down the winding Neckar, past green meadows and wooded hills, and slumbering villages, and craggy heights graced with crumbling towers and battlements.

In one place we saw a nicely dressed German gentleman

without any spectacles. Before I could come to anchor he had got away. It was a great pity. I so wanted to make a sketch of him. The captain comforted me for my loss, however, by saying that the man was without any doubt a fraud who had spectacles, but kept them in his pocket in order to make himself conspicuous.

Below Hassmersheim we passed Hornberg, Götz von Berlichingen's old castle. It stands on a bold elevation 200 feet above the surface of the river; it has high vine-clad walls inclosing trees, and a peaked tower about 75 feet high. The steep hillside, from the castle clear down to the water's edge, is terraced and clothed thick with grape vines. This is like farming a mansard roof. All the steeps along that part of the river which furnish the proper exposure, are given up to the grape. That region is a great producer of Rhine wines. The Germans are exceedingly fond of Rhine wines; they are put up in tall, slender bottles, and are considered a pleasant beverage. One tells them from vinegar by the label.

The Hornberg hill is to be tunnelled, and the new railway will pass under the castle.

The Cave of The Spectre

Two miles below Hornberg castle is a cave in a low cliff, which the captain of the raft said had once been occupied by a beautiful heiress of Hornberg—the Lady Gertrude—in the old times. It was seven hundred years ago. She had a number of rich and noble lovers and one poor and obscure one, Sir Wendel Lobenfeld. With the native chuckleheadedness of the heroine of romance, she preferred the poor and obscure lover. With the native sound judgment of the father of a heroine of romance, the Von Berlichingen of that day shut his daughter up in his donjon keep, or his oubliette, or his culverine, or some such place, and resolved that she should stay there until she selected a husband from among her rich and noble lovers. The latter visited her and persecuted her with their supplications, but without effect, for her heart was true to her poor despised Crusader, who was fighting in the Holy Land. Finally she resolved that she would endure the attentions of the rich lovers no longer; so one stormy night she escaped and went down the river and hid herself in the cave on the other side. Her father ransacked the country for her, but found not a trace of her. As the days went by, and still no tidings of her came, his conscience began to torture him, and he caused proclamation to be made that if she were yet living and would return, he would oppose her no longer, she might marry whom she would. The months dragged on, all hope forsook the old man, he ceased from his customary pursuits and pleasures, he devoted himself to pious works, and longed for the deliverance of death.

Now just at midnight, every night, the lost heiress stood in the mouth of her cave, arrayed in white robes, and sang a little love ballad which her Crusader had made for her. She judged that if he came home alive the superstitious peasants would tell him about the ghost that sang in the cave, and that as soon as they described the ballad he would know that none but he and she knew that song, therefore he would suspect that she was alive, and would come and find her. As time went on, the people of the region became sorely distressed about the Spectre of the Haunted Cave. It was said that ill-luck of one kind or another always overtook anyone who had the misfortune to hear that song. Eventually, every calamity that happened thereabouts was laid at the door of that music. Consequently no boatman would consent to pass the cave at night; the peasants shunned the place, even in the daytime.

But the faithful girl sang on, night after night, month after month, and patiently waited; her reward must come at last. Five years dragged by, and still, every night at midnight, the plaintive tones floated out over the silent land, while the distant boatmen and peasants thrust their fingers into their ears and shuddered out a prayer.

And now came the Crusader home, bronzed and battle-scarred, but bringing a great and splendid fame to lay at the feet of his bride. The old lord of Hornberg received him as a son, and wanted him to stay by him and be the comfort and blessing of his age; but the tale of that young girl's devotion to him and its pathetic consequences made a changed man of the knight. He could not enjoy his well-earned rest. He said his heart was broken, he would give the remnant of his life to high deeds in the cause of humanity, and so find a worthy death and a blessed reunion with the brave true heart whose love had more honoured him than all his victories in war.

When the people heard this resolve of his they came and told him there was a pitiless dragon in human disguise in the Haunted Cave, a dread creature which no knight had yet been bold enough to face, and begged him to rid the land of its desolating presence. He said he would do it. They told him about the song, and when he asked what song it was, they said the memory of it was gone, for nobody had been hardy enough to listen to it for the past four years and more.

Towards midnight the Crusader came floating down the river in a boat, with his rusty cross-bow in his hands. He drifted silently through the dim reflections of the crags and trees, with his intent eyes fixed upon the low cliff which he was approaching. As he drew nearer he discerned the black mouth of the cave. Now,—is that a white figure? Yes. The plaintive song begins to well forth and float away over meadow and river,—the crossbow is slowly raised to position, a steady aim is taken, the bolt flies straight to the mark, the figure sinks down, still singing, the knight takes the wool out of his ears, and recognises the old ballad,—too late! Ah, if he had only not put the wool in his ears!

The Crusader went away to the wars again, and presently fell in battle, fighting for the Cross. Tradition says that during several centuries the spirit of the unfortunate girl sang nightly from the cave at midnight, but the music carried no curse with it; and although many listened for the mysterious sounds few were favoured, since only those could hear them who had never failed in a trust. It is believed that the singing still continues, but it is known that nobody has heard it during the present century.

CHAPTER 16

An Ancient Legend Of The Rhine

The last legend reminds one of the 'Lorelei'—a legend of the Rhine. There is a song called 'The Lorelei.'

Germany is rich in folk-songs, and the words and airs of several of them are peculiarly beautiful—but 'The Lorelei' is the people's favourite. I could not endure it at first, but by-and-by it began to take hold of me, and now there is no tune which I like so well.

It is not possible that it is much known in America, else I should have heard it there. The fact that I never heard it there is evidence that there are others in my country who have fared likewise; therefore, for the sake of these, I mean to print the words and the music in this chapter. And I will refresh the reader's memory by printing the legend of the Lorelei too. I have it by me in the 'Legends of the Rhine,' done into English by the wildly gifted Garnham, Bachelor of Arts, I print the legend partly to refresh my own memory, too, for I have never read it before.

The Legend

Lore (two syllables) was a water nymph who used to sit on a high rock called Ley or Lei (pronounced like our word *lie*) in the Rhine, and lure boatmen to destruction in a furious rapid which marred the channel at that spot. She so bewitched them with her plaintive songs and her wonderful beauty, that they forgot everything else to gaze up at her, and so they presently drifted among the broken reefs and were lost.

In those old, old times the Count Bruno lived in a great castle near there with his son the Count Hermann, a youth of twenty. Hermann had heard a great deal about the beautiful Lore, and had finally fallen very deeply in love with her without having yet seen her. So he used to wander to the neighbourhood of the Lei, evenings, with his zither and 'Express his Longing in low Singing,' as Garnham says. On one of these occasions, 'suddenly there hovered around the top of the rock a brightness of unequalled clearness and colour, which, in increasing smaller circles thickened, was the enchanting figure of the beautiful Lore.

'An unintentional cry of Joy escaped the Youth, he let his Zither fall, and with extended arms he called out the name of the enigmatical Being, who seemed to stoop lovingly to him and beckon to him in a friendly manner; indeed, if his ear did not deceive him, she called his name with unutterable sweet Whispers, proper to love. Beside himself with delight, the youth lost his senses and sank senseless to the earth.'

After that he was a changed person. He went dreaming about, thinking only of his fairy and caring for nought else in the world. 'The old Count saw with affliction this changement in his son,' whose cause he could not divine, and tried to divert his mind into cheerful channels, but to no purpose. Then the old Count used authority. He commanded the youth to betake himself to the camp. Obedience was promised. Garnham says:—

'It was on the evening before his departure, as he wished still once to visit the Lei and offer to the Nymph of the Rhine his Sighs, the tones of his Zither, and his Songs. He went, in his boat, this time accompanied by a faithful squire, down the stream. The moon shed her silvery light over the whole Country; the steep bank mountains appeared in the most fantastical shapes, and the high oaks on either side bowed their Branches on Hermann's passing. As soon as he approached the Lei, and was aware of the surf-waves, his attendant was seized with an inexpressible Anxiety, and he begged permission to land; but the

Knight swept the strings of his Guitar and sang:

'Once I saw thee in dark night,
In supernatural Beauty bright;
Of Light-rays was the Figure wove,
To share its light, locked-hair strove.

'Thy Garment colour wave-dove,
By thy hand the sign of love,
Thy eyes' sweet enchantment,
Raying to me, oh! entrancement.

'Oh, wert thou but my sweetheart,
How willingly thy love to part!
With delight I should be bound
To thy rocky house in deep ground.'

That Hermann should have gone to that place at all, was not wise; that he should have gone with such a song as that in his mouth was a most serious mistake. The Lorelei did not 'call his name in unutterable sweet Whispers' this time. No, that song naturally worked an instant and thorough 'changement' in her; and not only that, but it stirred the bowels of the whole afflicted region round about there—for

'Scarcely had these tones sounded, everywhere there began tumult and sound, as if voices above and below the water. On the Lei rose flames, the Fairy stood above, as that time, and beckoned with her right hand clearly and urgently to the infatuated Knight, while with a staff in her left she called the waves to her service. They began to mount heavenward; the boat was upset, mocking every exertion; the waves rose to the gunwale, and splitting on the hard stones, the Boat broke into Pieces. The youth sank into the depths, but the squire was thrown on shore by a powerful wave.'

The bitterest things have been said about the Lorelei during many centuries, but surely her conduct upon this occasion entitles her to our respect. One feels tenderly toward her and is moved to forget her many crimes and remember only the good deed that crowned and closed her career.

LORELEI.

Andante.

1. Ich weiss nicht, was soll es be - deu - ten, dass ich so trau-rig bin; ein
2. Die schön - . ste Jung - frau sit - zet dort o - ben wun-der-bar, ihr
3. Den Schif-fer im klei - nen Schif - fe er-greift es mit wil-dem Weh: er

Mär-chen aus al - ten Zei - ten, das kommt mir nicht aus dem Sinn. Die
gold - nes Ge - schmeide blit - zet, sie kämmt ihr gol-de-nes Haar, sie
schaut nicht die Fel - sen-rif - fe, er schaut nur hin - auf in die Höh. Ich

1. Luft ist kühl und es dun - kelt, und ru - hig fliesst der Rhein; der
2. kümmt es mit gol - de - nem Kam - me, und singt ein Lied da - bei; das
3. glau - be, die Wel - len ver - schlin - gen, am En - de Schif-fer und Kahn; und

cres.
Gi - pfel des Ber - ges fun - kelt im A - bend son - nen - schein,
hat ei ne wun - der - sa - me, ge - wal - ti - ge Me - lo - dei.
das hat mit ih - rem Sin - gen die Lo - re - lei ge - than.
cres.

'The Fairy was never more seen; but her enchanting tones have often been heard. In the beautiful, refreshing, still nights of spring, when the moon pours her silver light over the Country, the listening shipper hears from the rushing of the waves, the echoing Clang of a wonderfully charming voice, which sings a song from the crystal castle, and with sorrow and fear he thinks on the young Count Hermann, seduced by the Nymph.'

Here is the music and the German words by Heinrich Heine. This song has been a favourite in Germany for forty years, and will remain a favourite always, maybe.

I have a prejudice against people who print things in a foreign language and add no translation. When I am the reader, and the author considers me able to do the translating myself, he pays me quite a nice compliment—but if he would do the translating for me I would try to get along without the compliment.

If I were at home, no doubt I could get a translation of this poem, but I am abroad and can't; therefore I will make a translation myself. It may not be a good one, for poetry is out of my line, but it will serve my purpose—which is, to give the un-German young girl a jingle of words to hang the tune on until she can get hold of a good version, made by some who is a poet and knows how to convey a poetical thought from one language to another.

The Lorelei

I cannot divine what it meaneth,
　This haunting nameless pain:
A tale of the bygone ages
　Keeps brooding through my brain:

The faint air cools in the gloaming,
　And peaceful flows the Rhine,
The thirsty summits are drinking
　The sunset's flooding wine;

The loveliest maiden is sitting
　High-throned in yon blue air,

Her golden jewels are shining,
  She combs her golden hair;

She combs with a comb that is golden,
  And sings a weird refrain
That steeps in a deadly enchantment
  The listener's ravished brain:

The doomed in his drifting shallop,
  Is tranced with the sad sweet tone,
He sees not the yawning breakers,
  He sees but the maid alone:

The pitiless billows engulf him!—
  So perish sailor and bark;
And this, with her baleful singing,
  Is the Lorelei's gruesome work.

I have a translation by Garnham, Bachelor of Arts, in the 'Legends of the Rhine,' but it would not answer the purpose I mentioned above, because the measure is too nobly irregular; it don't fit the tune snugly enough; in places it hangs over at the ends too far, and in other places one runs out of words before he gets to the end of a bar. Still, Garnham's translation has high merits, and I am not dreaming of leaving it out of my book. I believe this poet is wholly unknown in America and England; I take peculiar pleasure in bringing him forward because I consider that I discovered him:

The Lorelei

Translated by L.W. Garnham, B.A.

I do not know what it signifies
  That I am so sorrowful:
A fable of old times so terrifies,
  Leaves my heart so thoughtful.

The air is cool and it darkens,
  And calmly flows the Rhine;
The summit of the mountain hearkens
  In evening sunshine line.

The most beautiful Maiden entrances
  Above wonderfully there,
Her beautiful golden attire glances,
  She combs her golden hair.

With golden comb so lustrous,
  And thereby a song sings,
It has a tone so wondrous,
  That powerful melody rings.

The shipper in the little ship
  It affects with woe's sad might;
He does not see the rocky clip,
  He only regards dreaded height.

I believe the turbulent waves
  Swallow at last shipper and boat;
She with her singing craves
  All to visit her magic moat.

No translation could be closer. He has got in all the facts; and in their regular order too. There is not a statistic wanting. It is as succinct as an invoice. That is what a translation ought to be; it should exactly reflect the thought of the original. You can't *sing* 'Above wonderfully there,' because it simply won't go to the tune, without damaging the singer; but it is a most clingingly exact translation of *Dort oben wunderbar*—fits it like a blister. Mr. Garnham's reproduction has other merits—a hundred of them—but it is not necessary to point them out. They will be detected.

No one with a specialty can hope to have a monopoly of it. Even Garnham has a rival. Mr. X. had a small pamphlet with him which he had bought while on a visit to Munich. It was entitled 'A Catalogue of Pictures in the Old Pinacotek,' and was written in a peculiar kind of English. Here are a few extracts:

'It is not permitted to make use of the work in question to a publication of the same contents as well as to the pirated edition of it.'

'An evening landscape. In the foreground near a pond and a group of white beeches is leading a footpath animated by travellers.'

'A learned man in a cynical and torn dress holding an open book in his hand.'

'St. Bartholomew and the Executioner with the knite to fulfil the martyr.'

'Portrait of a young man. A long while this picture was thought to be Bindi Altoviti's portrait; now somebody will again have it to be the self-portrait of Raphael.'

'Susan bathing, surprised by the two old men. In the background the lapidation of the condemned.'

('Lapidation' is good; it is much more elegant than 'stoning.')

'St. Rochus sitting in a landscape with an angel who looks at his plague-sore, while the dog the bread in his mouth attents him.'

'Spring; The Goddess Flora, sitting. Behind her a fertile valley perfused by a river.'

'A beautiful bouquet animated by May-bugs, &c.'

'A warrior in armour with a gypseous pipe in his hand leans against the table and blows the smoke far away of himself.'

'A Dutch landscape along a navigable river which perfuses it till to the background.'

'Some peasants singing in a cottage. A woman lets drink a child out of a cup.'

'St. John's head as a boy—painted in fresco on a brick.' (Meaning a tile.)

'A young man of the Riccio family, his hair cut off right at the end, dressed in black with the same cap. Attributed to Raphael, but the signation is false.'

'The Virgin holding the Infant. Is very painted in the manner of Sassoferrato.'

'A Larder with greens and dead game animated by a cook-maid and two kitchen-boys.'

However, the English of this catalogue is at least as happy as that which distinguishes an inscription upon a certain picture in Rome—to wit:—

'Revelations-View. St. John in Patterson's Island.'

But meantime the raft is moving on.

CHAPTER 17

A mile or two above Eberbach we saw a peculiar ruin projecting above the foliage which clothed the peak of a high and very steep hill. This ruin consisted of merely a couple of crumbling masses of masonry which bore a rude resemblance to human faces; they leaned forward and touched foreheads, and had the look of being absorbed in conversation. This ruin had nothing very imposing or picturesque about it, and there was no great deal of it, yet it was called the 'Spectacular Ruin.'

Legend Of The 'Spectacular Ruin'

The captain of the raft, who was as full of history as he could stick, said that in the Middle Ages a most prodigious fire-breathing dragon used to live in that region, and made more trouble than a tax collector. He was as long as a railway train, and had the customary impenetrable green scales all over him. His breath bred pestilence and conflagration, and his appetite bred famine. He ate men and cattle impartially, and was exceedingly unpopular. The German emperor of that day made the usual offer; he would grant to the destroyer of the dragon any one solitary thing he might ask for; for he had a surplusage of daughters, and it was customary for dragon-killers to take a daughter for pay.

So the most renowned knights came from the four corners of

the earth and retired down the dragon's throat one after the other. A panic arose and spread. Heroes grew cautious. The procession ceased. The dragon became more destructive than ever. The people lost all hope of succour, and fled to the mountains for refuge.

At last Sir Wissenschaft, a poor and obscure knight, out of a far country, arrived to do battle with the monster. A pitiable object he was, with his armour hanging in rags about him, and his strange-shaped knapsack strapped upon his back. Everybody turned up their noses at him, and some openly jeered him. But he was calm. He simply inquired if the emperor's offer was still in force. The emperor said it was—but charitably advised him to go and hunt hares, and not endanger so precious a life as his in an attempt which had brought death to so many of the world's most illustrious heroes.

But this tramp only asked—'Were any of these heroes men of science?' This raised a laugh, of course, for science was despised in those days. But the tramp was not in the least ruffled. He said he might be a little in advance of his age, but no matter—science would come to be honoured, some time or other. He said he would march against the dragon in the morning. Out of compassion, then, a decent spear was offered him, but he declined, and said, 'spears were useless to men of science.' They allowed him to sup in the servants' hall, and gave him a bed in the stables.

When he started forth in the morning, thousands were gathered to see. The emperor said—

'Do not be rash; take a spear, and leave off your knapsack.'

But the tramp said—

'It is not a knapsack,' and moved straight on.

The dragon was waiting and ready. He was breathing forth vast volumes of sulphurous smoke and lurid blasts of flame. The ragged knight stole warily to a good position, then he unslung his cylindrical knapsack—which was simply the common fire-extinguisher known to modern times—and the first chance he got he turned on his hose and shot the dragon square in the centre of his cavernous mouth. Out went the fires in an instant, and the dragon curled up and died.

This man had brought brains to his aid. He had reared dragons from the egg, in his laboratory; he had watched over them like a mother, and patiently studied them and experimented upon them while they grew. Thus he had found out that fire was the life principle of a dragon; put out the dragon's fires and it could make steam no longer, and must die. He could not put out a fire with a spear, therefore he invented the extinguisher. The dragon being dead, the emperor fell on the hero's neck and said—

'Deliverer, name your request,' at the same time beckoning out behind with his heel for a detachment of his daughters to form and advance. But the tramp gave them no observance. He simply said—

'My request is, that upon me be conferred the monopoly of the manufacture and sale of spectacles in Germany.'

The emperor sprang aside, and exclaimed—

'This transcends all the impudence I ever heard! A modest demand, by my halidome! Why didn't you ask for the imperial revenues at once, and be done with it?'

But the monarch had given his word, and he kept it. To everybody's surprise, the unselfish monopolist immediately reduced the price of spectacles to such a degree that a great and crushing burden was removed from the nation. The emperor, to commemorate this generous act, and to testify his appreciation of it, issued a decree commanding everybody to buy this benefactor's spectacles and wear them, whether they needed them or not.

So originated the widespread custom of wearing spectacles in Germany; and as a custom once established in these old lands is imperishable, this one remains universal in the empire to this day. Such is the legend of the monopolist's once stately and sumptuous castle, now called the 'Spectacular Ruin.'

On the right bank, two or three miles below the Spectacular Ruin, we passed by a noble pile of castellated buildings overlooking the water from the crest of a lofty elevation. A stretch of two hundred yards of the high front wall was heavily draped with ivy, and out of the mass of buildings within rose three picturesque old towers. The place was in fine order, and was inhabited by a family of princely rank. This castle had its legend, too, but I should not feel justified in repeating it, because I doubted the truth of some of its minor details.

Along in this region a multitude of Italian labourers were blasting away the frontage of the hills to make room for the new railway. They were fifty or a hundred feet above the river. As we turned a sharp corner they began to wave signals and shout warnings to us to look out for the explosions. It was all very well to warn us, but what could *we* do? You can't back a raft up stream, you can't hurry it down stream, you can't scatter out to one side when you haven't any room to speak of, you won't take to the perpendicular cliffs on the other shore when they appear to be blasting there too. Your resources are limited, you see. There is simply nothing for it but to watch and pray.

For some hours we had been making three and a half or four miles an hour, and we were still making that. We had been dancing right along until these men began to shout, then for the next ten minutes it seemed to me that I had never seen a raft go so slowly. When the first blast went off we raised our sun-umbrellas and waited for the result. No harm done; none of the stones fell in the water. Another blast followed, and another, and another. Some of the rubbish fell in the water just astern of us.

We ran that whole battery of nine blasts in a row, and it was certainly one of the most exciting and uncomfortable weeks I ever spent, either aship or ashore. Of course we frequently manned the poles and shoved earnestly for a second or so, but every time one of those spurts of dust and *débris* shot aloft every man dropped his pole and looked up to get the bearings of his share of it. It was very busy times along there for a while. It appeared certain that we must perish, but even that was not the bitterest thought; no, the abjectly unheroic nature of the death—that was the sting—that and the bizarre wording of the resulting obituary—'*Shot with a rock on a raft.*' There would be no poetry written about it. None *could* be written about it. Example:—

> *Not* by war's shock, or war's shaft—
> *Shot*, with a rock, on a raft.

No poet who valued his reputation would touch such a theme as that. I should be distinguished as the only 'distinguished dead' who went down to the grave unsonnetted in 1878.

But we escaped, and I have never regretted it. The last blast was a peculiarly strong one, and after the small rubbish was done raining around us and we were just going to shake hands over our deliverance, a later and larger stone came down amongst our little group of pedestrians and wrecked an umbrella. It did no other harm, but we took to the water just the same.

It seems that the heavy work in the quarries and the new railway gradings is done mainly by Italians. That was a revelation. We have the notion in our country that Italians never do heavy work at all, but confine themselves to the lighter arts, like organ-grinding, operatic singing, and assassination. We have blundered, that is plain.

All along the river, near every village, we saw little station houses for the future railway. They were finished and waiting for the rails and business. They were as trim and snug and pretty as they could be. They were always of brick or stone; they were of graceful shape; they had vines and flowers about them already, and around them the grass was bright and green, and showed that it was carefully looked after. They were a decoration to the beautiful landscape, not an offence. Wherever one saw a pile of gravel or a pile of broken stone, it was always heaped as trimly and exactly as a new grave or a stack of cannon-balls; nothing about those stations, or along the railroad or the waggon road was allowed to look shabby or be un-ornamental. The keeping a country in such beautiful order as Germany exhibits, has a wise practical side to it, for it keeps thousands of people in work and bread who would otherwise be idle and mischievous.

As the night shut down, the captain wanted to tie up, but I thought maybe we might make Hirschhorn, so we went on. Presently the sky became overcast, and the captain came aft looking uneasy. He cast his eye aloft, then shook his head, and said it was coming on to blow. My party wanted to land at once, therefore I wanted to go on. The captain said we ought to shorten sail, anyway, out of common prudence. Consequently

the larboard watch was ordered to lay in his pole. It grew quite
dark now, and the wind began to rise. It wailed through the
swaying branches of the trees and swept our decks in fitful gusts.
Things were taking on an ugly look. The captain shouted to the
steersman on the forward log—

'How's she heading?'

The answer came faint and hoarse from far forward—

'Nor'-east-and-by-nor'—east-by-east, half-east, sir.'

'Let her go off a point!'

'Ay-ay, sir!'

'What water have you got?'

'Shoal, sir. Two foot large, on the stabboard, two and a half
scant on the labboard!'

'Let her go off another point!'

'Ay-ay, sir!'

'Forward, men, all of you! Lively, now! Stand by to crowd
her round the weather corner!'

'Ay-ay, sir!'

Then followed a wild running and trampling and hoarse
shouting, but the forms of the men were lost in the darkness, and
the sounds were distorted and confused by the roaring of the
wind through the shingle bundles. By this time the sea was
running inches high, and threatening every moment to engulf the
frail bark. Now came the mate hurrying aft, and said, close to
the captain's ear, in a low, agitated voice—

'Prepare for the worst, sir—we have sprung a leak.'

'Heavens! where?'

'Right aft the second row of logs.'

'Nothing but a miracle can save us. Don't let the men know,
or there will be a panic and mutiny! Lay her in shore, and stand
by to jump with the stern-line the moment she touches.
Gentlemen, I must look to you to second my endeavours in this
hour of peril. You have hats—go forrard and bail for your lives!'

Down swept another mighty blast of wind, clothed in spray
and thick darkness. At such a moment as this, came from away
forward that most appalling of all cries that are ever heard at
sea—

'*Man overboard!*'

The captain shouted—

'Hard a-port! Never mind the man! Let him climb aboard or wade ashore!'

Another cry came down the wind—

'Breakers ahead!'

'Where away?'

'Not a log's length off her port fore-foot!'

We had groped our slippery way forward, and were now bailing with the frenzy of despair, when we heard the mate's terrified cry, from far aft—

'Stop that dashed bailing, or we shall be aground!'

But this was immediately followed by the glad shout—

'Land aboard the starboard transom!'

'Saved!' cried the captain. 'Jump ashore and take a turn around a tree, and pass the bight aboard!'

The next moment we were all on shore weeping and embracing for joy, while the rain poured down in torrents. The captain said he had been a mariner for forty years on the Neckar, and in that time had seen storms to make a man's cheek blanch and his pulses stop, but he had never, never seen a storm that even approached this one. How familiar that sounded! For I have been at sea a good deal, and have heard that remark from captains with a frequency accordingly.

We framed in our minds the usual resolution of thanks and admiration and gratitude, and took the first opportunity to vote it, and put it in writing and present it to the captain, with the customary speech.

We tramped through the darkness and the drenching summer rain full three miles, and reached 'The Naturalist Tavern,' in the village of Hirschhorn, just an hour before midnight, almost exhausted from hardship, fatigue, and terror. I can never forget that night.

The landlord was rich, and therefore could afford to be crusty and disobliging; he did not at all like being turned out of his warm bed to open his house for us. But no matter, his household got up and cooked a quick supper for us, and we brewed a hot punch for ourselves, to keep off consumption. After supper and punch we had an hour's soothing smoke while we fought the

naval battle over again, and voted the resolutions; then we
retired to exceedingly neat and pretty chambers upstairs that
had clean, comfortable beds in them with heirloom pillow-cases
most elaborately and tastefully embroidered by hand.

Such rooms and beds and embroidered linen are as frequent
in German village inns as they are rare in ours. Our villages are
superior to German villages in more merits, excellences,
conveniences and privileges than I can enumerate, but the hotels
do not belong in the list.

'The Naturalist Tavern' was not a meaningless name; for all
the halls and all the rooms were lined with large glass cases
which were filled with all sorts of birds and animals, glass-eyed,
ably stuffed, and set up in the most natural and eloquent and
dramatic attitudes. The moment we were a-bed the rain cleared
away, and the moon came out. I dozed off to sleep while
contemplating a great white stuffed owl which was looking
intently down on me from a high perch with the air of a person
who thought he had met me before, but could not make out for
certain.

But young Z. did not get off so easily. He said that as he was
sinking deliciously to sleep, the moon lifted away the shadows,
and developed a huge cat, on a bracket, dead and stuffed, but
crouching, with every muscle tense, for a spring, and with its
glittering eyes aimed straight at him. It made Z. uncomfortable.
He tried closing his own eyes, but that did not answer, for a
natural instinct kept making him open them again to see if the
cat was still getting ready to launch at him, which she always
was. He tried turning his back, but that was a failure; he knew
the sinister eyes were on him still. So at last he had to get up,
after an hour or two of worry and experiment, and set the cat
out in the hall. So he won, that time.

CHAPTER 18

In the morning we took breakfast in the garden, under the trees, in the delightful German summer fashion. The air was filled with the fragrance of flowers and wild animals; the living portion of the menagerie of the 'Naturalist Tavern' was all about us. There were great cages populous with fluttering and chattering foreign birds, and other great cages and greater wire pens, populous with quadrupeds, both native and foreign. There were some free creatures, too, and quite sociable ones they were. White rabbits went loping about the place, and occasionally came and sniffed at our shoes and shins; a fawn, with a red ribbon on its neck, walked up, and examined us fearlessly; rare breeds of chickens and doves begged for crumbs, and a poor old tailless raven hopped about with an humble, shame-faced mien, which said, 'Please do not notice my exposure—think how you would feel in my circumstances, and be charitable.' If he was observed too much he would retire behind something, and stay there until he judged the party's interest had found another object. I never have seen another dumb creature that was so morbidly sensitive. Bayard Taylor, who could interpret the dim reasonings of animals, and understood their moral natures better than most men, would have found some way to make this poor old chap forget his troubles for a while, but we had not his kindly art, and so had to leave the raven to his griefs.

After breakfast we climbed the hill and visited the ancient

castle of Hirschhorn, and the ruined church near it. There were
some curious old bas-reliefs leaning against the inner walls of the
church—sculptured lords of Hirschhorn in complete armour,
and ladies of Hirschhorn in the picturesque court costumes of
the Middle Ages. These things are suffering damage and passing
to decay; for the last Hirschhorn has been dead for two hundred
years, and there is nobody now who cares to preserve the family
relics. In the chancel was a twisted stone column, and the
captain told us a legend about it, of course, for in the matter of
legends he could not seem to restrain himself; but I do not repeat
his tale, because there was nothing plausible about it, except that
the Hero wrenched this column into its present screw-shape with
his hands—just one single wrench. All the rest of the legend was
doubtful.

But Hirschhorn is best seen from a distance, down the river.
Then the clustered brown towers perched on the green hilltop,
and the old battlemented stone wall stretching up and over the
grassy ridge and disappearing in the leafy sea beyond, make a
picture whose grace and beauty entirely satisfy the eye.

We descended from the church by steep stone stairways
which curved this way and that down narrow alleys between the
packed and dirty tenements of the village. It was a quarter well
stocked with deformed, leering, unkempt and uncombed idiots,
who held out hands or caps and begged piteously. The people of
the quarter were not all idiots, of course, but all that begged
seemed to be, and were said to be

I was thinking of going by skiff to the next town,
Neckarsteinach; so I ran to the riverside in advance of the party,
and asked a man there if he had a boat to hire. I suppose I must
have spoken High German,—Court German,—I intended it for
that, anyway,—so he did not understand me. I turned and
twisted my question around and about, trying to strike that
man's average, but failed. He could not make out what I wanted.
Now Mr. X. arrived, faced this same man, looked him in the
eye, and emptied this sentence on him, in the most glib and
confident way:—

'Can man boat get here?'

The mariner promptly understood and promptly answered. I

can comprehend why he was able to understand that particular
sentence, because by mere accident all the words in it except
'get' have the same sound and the same meaning in German that
they have in English; but how he managed to understand Mr.
X.'s next remark puzzled me. I will insert it presently. X. turned
away a moment, and I asked the mariner if he could not find a
board, and so construct an additional seat. I spoke in the purest
German; but I might as well have spoken in the purest Choctaw
for all the good it did. The man tried his best to understand me;
he tried, and kept on trying, harder and harder, until I saw it was
really of no use, and said—

'There, don't strain yourself; it is of no consequence.'

Then X. turned to him and crisply said—

'Machen Sie a flat board.'

I wish my epitaph may tell the truth about me if the man did
not answer up at once, and say he would go and borrow a board
as soon as he had lit the pipe which he was filling.

We changed our mind about taking a boat, so we did not have
to go. I have given Mr. X.'s two remarks just as he made them.
Four of the five words in the first one were English, and that
they were also German was only accidental, not intentional;
three out of the five words in the second remark were English,
and English only, and the two German ones did not mean
anything in particular, in such a connection.

X. always spoke English to Germans, but his plan was to turn
the sentence wrong end first and upside down, according to
German construction, and sprinkle in a German word without
any essential meaning to it, here and there, by way of flavour.
Yet he always made himself understood. He could make those
dialect-speaking raftsmen understand him, sometimes, when
even young Z. had failed with them; and young Z. was a pretty
good German scholar. For one thing, X. always spoke with such
confidence—perhaps that helped. And possibly the raftsmen's
dialect was what is called *platt-Deutsch*, and so they found his
English more familiar to their ears than another man's German.
Quite indifferent students of German can read Fritz Reuter's
charming platt-Deutsch tales with some little facility because
many of the words are English. I suppose this is the tongue

which our Saxon ancestors carried to England with them. By-and-by I will inquire of some other philologist.

However, in the meantime, it had transpired that the men employed to caulk the raft had found that the leak was not a leak at all, but only a crack between the logs—a crack which belonged there, and was not dangerous, but had been magnified into a leak by the disordered imagination of the mate. Therefore we went aboard again with a good degree of confidence, and presently got to sea without accident. As we swam smoothly along between the enchanting shores, we fell to swapping notes about manners and customs in Germany and elsewhere.

As I write, now, many months later, I perceive that each of us, by observing and noting and inquiring diligently and day by day, had managed to lay in a most varied and opulent stock of misinformation. But this is not surprising; it is very difficult to get accurate details in any country.

For example, I had the idea once, in Heidelberg, to find out all about those five student corps. I started with the White Cap Corps. I began to inquire of this and that and the other citizen, and here is what I found out:—

1. It is called the Prussian Corps, because none but Prussians are admitted to it.

2. It is called the Prussian Corps for no particular reason. It has simply pleased each corps to name itself after some German State.

3. It is not named the Prussian Corps at all, but only the White Cap Corps.

4. Any student can belong to it who is a German by birth.

5. Any student can belong to it who is European by birth.

6. Any European-born student can belong to it, except he be a Frenchman.

7. Any student can belong to it, no matter where he was born.

8. No student can belong to it who is not of noble blood.

9. No student can belong to it who cannot show three full generations of noble descent.

10. Nobility is not a necessary qualification.

11. No moneyless student can belong to it.

12. Money qualification is nonsense—such a thing has never been thought of.

I got some of this information from the students themselves—students who did not belong to the corps. I finally went to headquarters—to the White Caps—where I would have gone in the first place if I had been acquainted. But even at headquarters I found difficulties; I perceived that there were things about the White Cap Corps which one member knew and another one didn't. It was natural; for very few members of any organisation know *all* that can be known about it. I doubt if there is a man or a woman in Heidelberg who would not answer promptly and confidently three out of every five questions about the White Cap Corps which a stranger might ask; yet it is a very safe bet that two of the three answers would be incorrect every time.

There is one German custom which is universal—the bowing courteously to strangers when sitting down at table or rising up from it. This bow startles a stranger out of his self-possession, the first time it occurs, and he is likely to fall over a chair or something, in his embarrassment, but it pleases him nevertheless. One soon learns to expect this bow and be on the look-out and ready to return it; but to learn to lead off and make the initial bow one's self is a difficult matter for a diffident man. One thinks, 'If I rise to go, and tender my bow and these ladies and gentlemen take it into their heads to ignore the custom of their nation, and not return it, how shall I feel in case I survive to feel anything?' Therefore he is afraid to venture. He sits out the dinner, and makes the strangers rise first and originate the bowing. A *table d'hôte* dinner is a tedious affair for a man who seldom touches anything after the three first courses; therefore I used to do some pretty dreary waiting because of my fears. It took me months to assure myself that those fears were groundless, but I did assure myself at last by experimenting diligently through my agent. I made Harris get up and bow and leave: invariably his bow was returned, then I got up and bowed myself and retired.

Thus my education proceeded easily and comfortably for me, but not for Harris. Three courses of a *table d'hôte* dinner were enough for me, but Harris preferred thirteen.

Even after I had acquired full confidence, and no longer needed the agent's help, I sometimes encountered difficulties. Once at Baden-Baden I nearly lost a train because I could not be sure that three young ladies opposite me at table were Germans, since I had not heard them speak; they might be American, they might be English, it was not safe to venture a bow; but just as I had got that far with my thought, one of them began a German remark, to my great relief and gratitude; and before she had got out her third word, our bows had been delivered and graciously returned, and we were off.

There is a friendly something about the German character which is very winning. When Harris and I were making a pedestrian tour through the Black Forest, we stopped at a little country inn for dinner one day; two young ladies and a young gentleman entered and sat down opposite us. They were pedestrians too. Our knapsacks were strapped upon our backs, but they had a sturdy youth along to carry theirs for them. All parties were hungry, so there was no talking. By-and-by the usual bows were exchanged, and we separated.

As we sat at a late breakfast in the hotel at Allerheiligen, next morning, these young people entered and took places near us without observing us; but presently they saw us and at once bowed and smiled; not ceremoniously, but with the gratified look of people who have found acquaintances where they were expecting strangers. Then they spoke of the weather and the roads. We also spoke of the weather and the roads. Next, they said they had had an enjoyable walk, notwithstanding the weather. We said that that had been our case, too. Then they said they had walked thirty English miles the day before, and asked how many we had walked. I could not lie, so I told Harris to do it. Harris told them we had made thirty English miles, too. That was true; we had 'made' them, though we had had a little assistance here and there.

After breakfast they found us trying to blast some information out of the dumb hotel clerk about routes, and observing that we were not succeeding pretty well, they went and got their maps and things, and pointed out and explained our course so clearly that even a New York detective could have followed it. And when we started they spoke out a hearty good-bye and wished us a pleasant journey. Perhaps they were more generous with us than they might have been with native wayfarers because we were a forlorn lot and in a strange land; I don't know; I only know it was lovely to be treated so.

Very well, I took an American young lady to one of the fine balls in Baden-Baden, one night, and at the entrance-door upstairs we were halted by an official—something about Miss Jones's dress was not according to rule; I don't remember what it was, now: something was wanting—her back hair, or a shawl, or a fan, or a shovel, or something. The official was ever so polite, and ever so sorry, but the rule was strict, and he could not let us in. It was very embarrassing, for many eyes were on us. But now a richly dressed girl stepped out of the ball-room, inquired into our trouble, and said she could fix it in a moment. She took Miss Jones to the robing-room, and soon brought her back in regulation trim, and then we entered the ball-room with this benefactress unchallenged.

Being safe now, I began to puzzle through my sincere but ungrammatical thanks, when there was a sudden mutual recognition—the benefactress and I had met at Allerheiligen. Two weeks had not altered her good face, and plainly her heart was in the right place yet, but there was such a difference between these clothes and the clothes I had seen her in before, when she was walking thirty miles a day in the Black Forest, that it was quite natural that I had failed to recognise her sooner. I had on *my* other suit, too, but my German would betray me to a person who had heard it once, anyway. She brought her brother and sister, and they made our way smooth for that evening.

Well, months afterwards. I was driving through the streets of Munich in a cab with a German lady, one day, when she said—

'There, that is Prince Ludwig and his wife, walking along there.'

Everybody was bowing to them—cabmen, little children, and everybody else—and they were returning all the bows and overlooking nobody, when a young lady met them and made a deep curtsey.

'That is probably one of the ladies of the court,' said my German friend.

I said—

'She is an honour to it, then. I know her. I don't know her name, but I know *her*. I have known her at Allerheiligen and Baden-Baden. She ought to be an Empress, but she may be only a Duchess; it is the way things go in this world.'

If one asks a German a civil question, he will be quite sure to get a civil answer. If you stop a German in the street and ask him to direct you to a certain place, he shows no sign of feeling offended. If the place be difficult to find, ten to one the man will drop his own matters and go with you and show you. In London, too, many a time, strangers have walked several blocks with me to show me the way. There is something very real about this sort of politeness. Quite often, in Germany, shopkeepers who could not furnish me the article I wanted, have sent one of their employés with me to show me a place where it could be had.

CHAPTER 19

However, I wander from the raft. We made the port of Neckarsteinach in good season, and went to the hotel and ordered a trout dinner, the same to be ready against our return from a two-hour pedestrian excursion to the village and castle of Dilsberg, a mile distant, on the other side of the river. I do not mean that we proposed to be two hours making two miles—no, we meant to employ most of the time in inspecting Dilsberg.

For Dilsberg is a quaint place. It is most quaintly and picturesquely situated, too. Imagine the beautiful river before you; then a few rods of brilliant green sward on its opposite shore; then a sudden hill—no preparatory gently-rising slopes, but a sort of instantaneous hill—a hill two hundred and fifty or three hundred feet high, as round as a bowl, with the same taper upward that an inverted bowl has, and with about the same relation of height to diameter that distinguishes a bowl of good honest depth—a hill which is thickly clothed with green bushes—a comely, shapely hill, rising abruptly out of the dead level of the surrounding green plains, visible from a great distance down the bends of the river, and with just exactly room on the top of its head for its steepled and turreted and roof-clustered cap of architecture, which same is tightly jammed and compacted within the perfectly round hoop of the ancient village wall.

There is no house outside the wall on the whole hill, or any vestige of a former house; all the houses are inside the wall, but there isn't room for another one. It is really a finished town, and has been finished a very long time. There is no space between the wall and the first circle of buildings; no, the village wall is itself the rear wall of the first circle of buildings, and the roofs jut a little over the wall and thus furnish it with eaves. The general level of the massed roofs is gracefully broken and relieved by the dominating towers of the ruined castle and the tall spires of a couple of churches; so, from a distance, Dilsberg has rather more the look of a king's crown than a cap. That lofty green eminence and its quaint coronet form quite a striking picture, you may be sure, in the flush of the evening sun.

We crossed over in a boat and began the ascent by a narrow, steep path, which plunged us at once into the leafy deeps of the bushes. But they were not cool deeps by any means, for the sun's rays were weltering hot, and there was little or no breeze to temper them. As we panted up the sharp ascent, we met brown, bare-headed and bare-footed boys and girls, occasionally, and sometimes men; they came upon us without warning, they gave us good-day, flashed out of sight in the bushes, and were gone as suddenly and mysteriously as they had come. They were bound for the other side of the river to work. This path had been travelled by many generations of these people. They have always gone down to the valley to earn their bread, but they have always climbed their hill again to eat it, and to sleep in their snug town.

It is said that the Dilsbergers do not emigrate much; they find that living up there above the world, in their peaceful nest, is pleasanter than living down in the troublous world. The seven hundred inhabitants are all blood-kin to each other, too; they have always been blood-kin to each other for fifteen hundred years; they are simply one large family, and they like the home folks better than they like strangers, hence they persistently stay at home. It has been said that for ages Dilsberg has been merely a thriving and diligent idiot-factory. I saw no idiots there, but the captain said, 'Because of late years the government has taken to lugging them off to asylums and other-wheres; and government wants to cripple the factory, too, and is trying to get these

Dilsbergers to marry out of the family, but they don't like to.'

The captain probably imagined all this, as modern science denies that the intermarrying of relatives deteriorates the stock.

Arrived within the wall, we found the usual village sights and life. We moved along a narrow, crooked lane which had been paved in the Middle Ages. A strapping, ruddy girl was beating flax or some such stuff in a little bit of a goods-box of a barn, and she swung her flail with a will—if it was a flail; I was not farmer enough to know what she was at; a frowsy, barelegged girl was herding half a dozen geese with a stick—driving them along the lane and keeping them out of the dwellings; a cooper was at work in a shop which I know he did not make so large a thing as a hogshead in, for there was not room. In the front rooms of dwellings girls and women were cooking or spinning, and ducks and chickens were waddling in and out, over the threshold, picking up chance crumbs and holding pleasant converse; a very old and wrinkled man sat asleep before his door, with his chin upon his breast, and his extinguished pipe in his lap; soiled children were playing in the dirt everywhere along the lane, unmindful of the sun.

Except the sleeping old man, everybody was at work, but the place was very still and peaceful, nevertheless; so still that the distant cackle of the successful hen smote upon the ear but little dulled by intervening sounds. That commonest of village sights was lacking here—the public pump, with its great stone tank or trough of limpid water, and its group of gossiping pitcher-bearers; for there is no well or fountain or spring on this tall hill; cisterns of rain water are used.

Our alpenstocks and muslin tails compelled attention, and as we moved through the village we gathered a considerable procession of little boys and girls, and so went in some state to the castle. It proved to be an extensive pile of crumbling walls, arches and towers, massive, properly grouped for picturesque effect, weedy, grass-grown, and satisfactory. The children acted as guides; they walked us along the top of the highest wall, then took us up into a high tower and showed us a wide and beautiful landscape, made up of wavy distances of woody hills, and a nearer prospect of undulating expanses of green lowlands on the

one hand, and castle-graced crags and ridges on the other, with
the shining curves of the Neckar flowing between. But the
principal show, the chief pride of the children, was the ancient
and empty well in the grass-grown court of the castle. Its
massive stone curb stands up three or four feet above ground,
and is whole and uninjured. The children said that in the Middle
Ages this well was four hundred feet deep, and furnished all the
village with an abundant supply of water, in war and peace.
They said that in that old day its bottom was below the level of the
Neckar, hence the water supply was inexhaustible.

But there were some who believed it had never been a well at
all, and was never deeper than it is now—eighty feet; that at that
depth a subterranean passage branched from it and descended
gradually to a remote place in the valley, where it opened into
somebody's cellar or other hidden recess, and that the secret of
this locality is now lost. Those who hold this belief say that
herein lies the explanation that Dilsberg, besieged by Tilley and
many a soldier before him, was never taken: after the longest
and closest sieges the besiegers were astonished to perceive that
the besieged were as fat and hearty as ever, and as well furnished
with munitions of war—therefore it must be that the Dilsbergers
had been bringing these things in through the subterranean
passage all the time.

The children said that there was in truth a subterranean outlet
down there, and they would prove it. So they set a great truss of
straw on fire and threw it down the well, while we leaned on the
curb and watched the glowing mass descend. It struck bottom
and gradually burned out. No smoke came up. The children
clapped their hands and said—

'You see! Nothing makes so much smoke as burning
straw—now where did the smoke go to, if there is no
subterranean outlet?'

So it seemed quite evident that the subterranean outlet indeed
existed. But the finest thing within the ruin's limits was a noble
linden, which the children said was four hundred years old, and
no doubt it was. It had a mighty trunk and a mighty spread of
limb and foliage. The limbs near the ground were nearly the
thickness of a barrel.

That tree had witnessed the assaults of men in mail—how remote such a time seems, and how ungraspable is the fact that real men ever did fight in real armour!—and it had seen the time when these broken arches and crumbling battlements were a trim and strong and stately fortress, fluttering its gay banners in the sun, and peopled with vigorous humanity,—how impossibly long ago that seems!—and here it stands yet, and possibly may still be standing here, sunning itself and dreaming its historical dreams, when to-day shall have been joined to the days called 'ancient.'

Well, we sat down under the tree to smoke, and the captain delivered himself of his legend.

The Legend Of Dilsberg Castle

It was to this effect. In the old time there was once a great company assembled at the castle, and festivity ran high. Of course there was a haunted chamber in the castle, and one day the talk fell upon that. It was said that whoever slept in it would not wake again for fifty years. Now when a young knight named Conrad von Geisberg heard this, he said that if the castle were his he would destroy that chamber, so that no foolish person might have the chance to bring so dreadful a misfortune upon himself and afflict such as loved him with the memory of it. Straightway the company privately laid their heads together to contrive some way to get this superstitious young man to sleep in that chamber. And they succeeded—in this way. They persuaded his betrothed, a lovely mischievous young creature, niece of the lord of the castle, to help them in their plot. She presently took him aside and had speech with him. She used all her persuasions, but could not shake him; he said his belief was firm that if he should sleep there he would wake no more for fifty years, and it made him shudder to think of it. Catharina began to weep. This was a better argument; Conrad could not hold out against it. He yielded, and said she should have her wish if she would only smile and be happy again. She flung her arms about his neck, and the kisses she gave him showed that her thankfulness and her pleasure were very real. Then she flew to tell the company her success, and the applause she received made her glad and proud she had undertaken her mission, since all alone she had accomplished what the multitude had failed in.

At midnight, that night, after the usual feasting, Conrad was taken to the haunted chamber and left there. He fell asleep, by-and-by.

When he awoke again and looked about him, his heart stood still with horror! The whole aspect of the chamber was changed. The walls were mouldy and hung with ancient cobwebs; the curtains and beddings were rotten; the furniture was rickety and ready to fall to pieces. He sprang out of bed, but his quaking knees sank under him and he fell to the floor.

'This is the weakness of age,' he said.

He rose and sought his clothing. It was clothing no longer. The colours were gone, the garments gave way in many places while he was putting them on. He fled, shuddering, into the corridor, and along it to the great hall. Here he was met by a middle-aged stranger of a kind countenance, who stopped and gazed at him with surprise. Conrad said—

'Good sir, will you send hither the lord Ulrich?'

The stranger looked puzzled a moment, then said—

'The lord Ulrich?'

'Yes—if you will be so good.'

The stranger called—'Wilhelm!' A young serving man came, and the stranger said to him—

'Is there a lord Ulrich among the guests?'

'I know none of the name, so please your honour.'

Conrad said, hesitatingly—

'I did not mean a guest, but the lord of the castle, sir.'

The stranger and the servant exchanged wondering glances. Then the former said—

'I am the lord of the castle.'

'Since when, sir?'

'Since the death of my father, the good lord Ulrich, more than forty years ago.'

Conrad sank upon a bench and covered his face with his hands while he rocked his body to and fro and moaned. The stranger said in a low voice to the servant—

'I fear me this poor old creature is mad. Call someone.'

In a moment several people came, and grouped themselves about talking in whispers. Conrad looked up and scanned the faces about him wistfully. Then he shook his head and said in a grieved voice—

'No, there is none among ye that I know. I am old and alone in the world. They are dead and gone these many years that cared for me, But sure, some of these aged ones I see about me can tell me some little word or two concerning them.'

Several bent and tottering men and women came nearer and answered his questions about each former friend as he mentioned the names. This one they said had been dead ten years, that one twenty, another thirty. Each succeeding blow struck heavier and heavier. At last the sufferer said—

'There is one more, but I have not the courage to—O my lost Catharina!'

One of the old dames said—

'Ah, I knew her well, poor soul! A misfortune overtook her lover, and she died of sorrow nearly fifty years ago. She lieth under the linden tree without the court.'

Conrad bowed his head and said—

'Ah, why did I ever wake! And so she died of grief for me, poor child. So young, so sweet, so good. She never wittingly did a hurtful thing in all the little summer of her life. Her loving debt shall be repaid—for I will die of grief for her.'

His head drooped upon his breast. In a moment there was a wild burst of joyous laughter, a pair of round young arms were flung about Conrad's neck, and a sweet voice cried—

'There, Conrad mine, thy kind words kill me—the farce shall go no further! Look up, and laugh with us—'twas all a jest!'

And he did look up, and gazed, in a dazed wonderment—for the disguises were stripped away, and the aged men and women were bright and young and gay again. Catharina's happy tongue ran on—

' 'Twas a marvellous jest, and bravely carried out. They gave you a heavy sleeping draught before you went to bed, and in the night they bore you to a ruined chamber where all had fallen to decay, and placed these rags of clothing by you. And when your sleep was spent and you came forth, two strangers, well instructed in their parts, were here to meet you; and all we, your friends, in our disguises, were close at hand, to see and hear, you may be sure. Ah, 'twas a gallant jest! Come, now, and make thee ready for the pleasures of the day. How real was thy misery for the moment, thou poor lad! Look up and have thy laugh, now!'

He looked up, and searched the merry faces about him in a dreamy way, then sighed and said—

'I am a-weary, good strangers; I pray you lead me to her grave.'

All the smiles vanished away, every cheek blanched, Catharina sank to the ground in a swoon.

All day the people went about the castle with troubled faces, and communed together in under-tones. A painful hush pervaded the place which had lately been so full of cheery life. Each in his turn tried to arouse Conrad out of his hallucination and bring him to himself; but all the answer any got was a meek, bewildered stare, and then the words,—

'Good stranger, I have no friends, all are at rest these many years; ye speak me fair, ye mean me well, but I know ye not; I am alone and forlorn in the world—prithee lead me to her grave.'

During two years Conrad spent his days, from the early morning till the night, under the linden tree, mourning over the imaginary grave of his Catharina. Catharina was the only company of the harmless madman. He was very friendly toward her because, as he said, in some ways she reminded him of his Catharina whom he had lost 'fifty years ago.' He often said—

'She was so gay, so happy-hearted—but you never smile; and always when you think I am not looking, you cry.'

When Conrad died, they buried him under the linden, according to his directions, so that he might rest 'near his poor Catharina.' Then Catharina sat under the linden alone, every day and all day long, a great many years, speaking to no one, and never smiling; and at last her long repentance was rewarded with death, and she was buried by Conrad's side.

Harris pleased the captain by saying it was a good legend; and pleased him further by adding—

'Now that I have seen this mighty tree, vigorous with its four hundred years, I feel a desire to believe the legend for *its* sake; so I will humour the desire, and consider that the tree really watches over those poor hearts and feels a sort of human tenderness for them.'

We returned to Neckarsteinach, plunged our hot heads into the trough at the town pump, and then went to the hotel and ate our trout dinner in leisurely comfort, in the garden, with the beautiful Neckar flowing at our feet, the quaint Dilsberg looming beyond, and the graceful towers and battlements of a couple of mediaeval castles (called the 'Swallow's Nest'[1] and 'The Brothers') assisting the rugged scenery of a bend of the river down to our right. We got to sea in season to make the eight-mile run to Heidelberg before the night shut down. We sailed by the hotel in the mellow glow of sunset, and came slashing down with the mad current into the narrow passage between the dykes. I believed I could shoot the bridge myself, so I went to the forward triplet of logs and relieved the pilot of his pole and his responsibility.

We went tearing along in a most exhilarating way, and I performed the delicate duties of my office very well indeed for a first attempt; but perceiving, presently, that I really was going to shoot the bridge itself instead of the archway under it, I judiciously stepped ashore. The next moment I had my long coveted desire: I saw a raft wrecked. It hit the pier in the centre and went all to smash and scatteration like a box of matches struck by lightning.

I was the only one of our party who saw this grand sight; the others were attitudinising, for the benefit of the long rank of young ladies who were promenading on the bank, and so they lost it. But I helped to fish them out of the river, down below the bridge, and then described it to them as well as I could. They were not interested, though. They said they were wet and felt ridiculous, and did not care anything for descriptions of scenery. The young ladies, and other people, crowded around and

---

[1] The seeker after information is referred to Appendix E for our Captain's Legend of the 'Swallow's Nest' and 'The Brothers.'

showed a great deal of sympathy, but that did not help matters; for my friends said they did not want sympathy, they wanted a back alley and solitude.

CHAPTER 20

Next morning brought good news—our trunks had arrived from Hamburg at last. Let this be a warning to the reader. The Germans are very conscientious, and this trait makes them very particular. Therefore if you tell a German you want a thing done immediately, he takes you at your word; he thinks you mean what you say; so he does that thing immediately—according to his idea of immediately—which is about a week; that is, it is a week if it refers to the building of a garment, or it is an hour and a half if it refers to the cooking of a trout. Very well; if you tell a German to send your truck to you by 'slow freight,' he takes you at your word; he sends it by 'slow freight,' and you cannot imagine how long you will go on enlarging your admiration of the expressiveness of that phrase in the German tongue, before you get that trunk. The hair on my trunk was soft and thick and useful, when I got it ready for shipment in Hamburg; it was baldheaded when it reached Heidelberg. However, it was still sound, that was a comfort, it was not battered in the least; the baggagemen seemed to be conscientiously careful, in Germany, of the baggage entrusted to their hands. There was nothing now in the way of our departure, therefore we set about our preparations.

Naturally my chief solicitude was about my collection of

Keramics. Of course I could not take it with me; that would be inconvenient, and dangerous besides. I took advice, but the best bric-à-brackers were divided as to the wisest course to pursue: some said, pack the collection and warehouse it; others said, try to get it into the Grand Ducal Museum at Mannheim for safe keeping. So I divided the collection, and followed the advice of both parties. I set aside for the Museum those articles which were the most frail and precious.

Among these was my Etruscan tear-jug. I bought this tear-jug of a dealer in antiquities for four hundred and fifty dollars. It is very rare. The man said the Etruscans used to keep tears or something in these things, and that it was very hard to get hold of a broken one now. I also set aside my Henri II plate. This is very fine and rare; the shape is exceedingly beautiful and unusual. It has wonderful decorations on it. It cost more than the tear-jug, as the dealer said there was not another plate just like it in the world. He said there was much false Henri II ware around, but that the genuineness of this piece was unquestionable. He showed me its pedigree, or its history if you please; it was a document which traced this plate's movements all the way down from its birth—showed who bought it, from whom, and what he paid for it—from the first buyer down to me, whereby I saw that it had gone steadily up from thirty-five cents to seven hundred dollars. he said that whole Keramic world would be informed that it was now in my possession and would make a note of it, with the price paid.

I also set apart my exquisite specimen of Old Blue China. This is considered to be the finest example of Chinese art now in existence. I do not refer to the bastard Chinese art of modern times, but that noble and pure and genuine art which flourished under the fostering and appreciative care of the Emperors of the Chung-a-Lung-Fung dynasty.

There were Masters in those days; but alas! it is not so now. Of course the main preciousness of this piece lies in its colour; it is that old sensuous, pervading, ramifying, interpolating, transboreal blue which is the despair of modern art.

However, I must not be frittering away the reader's time with these details. I did not intend to go into any detail at all, at first, but it is the failing of the true keramiker, or the true devotee in any department of bric-à-brackery, that once he gets his tongue or his pen started on his darling theme, he cannot well stop until he drops from exhaustion. He has no more sense of the flight of time than has any other lover when talking of his sweetheart. The very 'marks' on the bottom of a piece of rare crockery are able to throw me into a gibbering ecstasy; and I could forsake a drowning relative to help dispute about whether the stopple of a departed Buon Retiro scent-bottle was genuine or spurious.

Many people say that for a male person, bric-à-brac hunting is about as robust a business as making doll-clothes, or decorating Japanese pots with decalcomanie butterflies would be, and these people fling mud at that elegant Englishman, Byng, who wrote a book called 'The Bric-à-Brac Hunter,' and make fun of him for chasing around after what they choose to call 'his despicable trifles'; and for 'gushing' over these trifles; and for exhibiting his 'deep infantile delight' in what they call his 'tuppeny collection of beggarly triviality'; and for beginning his book with a picture of himself, seated, in a 'sappy, self-complacent attitude, in the midst of his poor little ridiculous bric-à-brac junk shop'.

It is easy to say these things; it is easy to revile us, easy to despise us; therefore, let these people rail on; they cannot feel as Byng and I feel—it is their loss, not ours. For my part I am content to be a bric-à-bracker and a keramiker—more, I am proud to be so named. I am proud to know that I lose my reason as immediately in the presence of a rare jug with an illustrious mark on the bottom of it, as if I had just emptied that jug. Very well; I packed and stored a part of my collection, and the rest of it I placed in the care of the Grand Ducal Museum in Mannheim, by permission. My Old Blue China Cat remains there yet. I presented it to that excellent institution.

I had but one misfortune with my things. An egg which I had kept back from breakfast that morning was broken in packing. It was a great pity. I had shown it to the best connoisseurs in Heidelberg, and they all said it was an antique. We spent a day or two in farewell visits, and then left for Baden-Baden. We had a pleasant trip of it, for the Rhine valley is always lovely. The only trouble was that the trip was too short. If I remember rightly, it only occupied a couple of hours; therefore I judge that the distance was very little, if any, over fifty miles. We quitted the train at Oos, and walked the entire remaining distance to Baden-Baden, with the exception of a lift of less than an hour which we got on a passing waggon, the weather being exhaustingly warm. We came into town on foot.

One of the first persons we encountered, as we walked up the street, was the Rev. Mr.——, an old friend from America—a lucky encounter, indeed, for his is a most gentle, refined and sensitive nature, and his company and companionship are a genuine refreshment. We knew he had been in Europe some time, but were not at all expecting to run across him. Both parties burst forth into loving enthusiasms, and Rev. Mr.——said—

'I have got a brimful reservoir of talk to pour out on you, and an empty one ready and thirsting to receive what you have got; we will sit up till midnight and have a good satisfying interchange, for I leave here early in the morning.' We agreed to that, of course.

I had been vaguely conscious, for a while, of a person who was walking in the street abreast of us. I had glanced furtively at him once or twice, and noticed that he was a fine, large, vigorous young fellow, with an open, independent countenance, faintly shaded with a pale and even almost imperceptible crop of early down, and that he was clothed from head to heel in cool and enviable snow-white linen. I thought I had also noticed that his head had a sort of listening tilt to it. Now about this time the Rev. Mr.——said—

'The side-walk is hardly wide enough for three, so I will walk behind; but keep the talk going, keep the talk going, there's no time to lose, and you may be sure I will do my share.' He ranged himself behind us, and straightway that stately snow-white young fellow closed up the side-walk alongside him, fetched him a cordial slap on the shoulder with his broad palm, and sung out with a hearty cheeriness—

'*Americans*, for two-and-a-half and the money up! *Hey*?'

'The Reverend winced, but said mildly,—

'Yes—we are Americans.'

'Lord love you, you can just bet that's what I am, every time! Put it there!'

He held out his Sahara of a palm, and the Reverend laid his diminutive hand in it, and got so cordial a shake that we heard his glove burst under it.

'Say, didn't I put you up right?'

'O yes.'

'Sho! I spotted you for *my* kind the minute I heard your clack. You been over here long?'

'About four months. Have you been over long?'

'*Long*? Well, I should say so! Going on two *years*, by geeminy! Say, are you homesick?'

'No, I can't say that I am. Are you?'

'Oh, *hell*, yes!' This with immense enthusiasm.

The Reverend shrunk a little, in his clothes, and we were aware, rather by instinct than otherwise, that he was throwing out signals of distress to us; but we did not interfere or try to succour him, for we were quite happy.

The young fellow hooked his arm into the Reverend's now, with the confiding and grateful air of a waif who has been longing for a friend, and a sympathetic ear, and a chance to lisp once more the sweet accents of the mother tongue—and then he limbered up the muscles of his mouth and turned himself loose—and with such a relish! Some of his words were not Sunday-school words, so I am obliged to put blanks where they occur.

'Yes indeedy! If *I* ain't an American there *ain't* any Americans, that's all. And when I heard you fellows gassing away in the good old American language, I'm —— if it wasn't all I could do to keep from hugging you! My tongue's all warped with trying to curl it around these —— forsaken wind-galled nine-jointed German words here; now I *tell* you it's awful good to lay it over a Christian word once more and kind of let the old taste soak in. I'm from Western New York. My name is Cholley Adams. I'm a student, you know. Been here going on two years. I'm learning to be a horse-doctor. I *like* that part of it, you know, but —— these people, they won't learn a fellow in his own language, they make him learn in German; so before I could tackle the horse-doctoring I had to tackle this miserable language.

'First-off, I thought it would certainly give me the botts, but I don't mind it now. I've got it where the hair's short, I think; and dontchuknow, they made me learn Latin, too. Now between you and me, I wouldn't give a —— for all the Latin that was ever jabbered; and the first thing *I* calculate to do when I get through, is to just sit down and forget it. 'Twont take me long, and I don't mind the time, anyway. And I tell you what! the difference between school-teaching over yonder and school-teaching over here—sho! *We* don't know anything about it! Here you've got to peg and peg and peg, and there just ain't any let-up—and what you learn here, you've got to *know*, dontchuknow—or else you'll have one of these —— spavined, spectacled, ring-boned, knock-kneed old professors in your hair. I've been here long *enough*, and I'm getting blessed tired of it, mind I *tell* you. The old man wrote me that he was coming over in June, and said he'd take me home in August, whether I was done with my education or not, but durn him, he didn't come; never said why; just sent me a hamper of Sunday-school books, and told me to be good, and hold on a while. I don't take to Sunday-school books, dontchuknow—I don't hanker after them when I can get pie—but I *read* them, anyway, because whatever the old man tells me to do, that's the thing that I'm a-going to *do*, or tear something you know. I buckled in and read all of those books, because he wanted me to; but that kind of thing don't excite *me*; I like something *hearty*. But I'm awful homesick. I'm homesick from ear-socket to crupper, and from crupper to hock joint; but it ain't any use, I've got to stay here, till the old man drops the rag and gives the word—yes, *sir*, right here in this —— country I've got to linger till the old man says *Come*!—and you bet your bottom dollar, Johnny, it *ain't* just as easy as it is for a cat to have twins!'

At the end of this profane and cordial explosion he fetched a prodigious '*Whoosh*!' to relieve his lungs and make recognition of the heat, and then he straightway dived into his narrative again for 'Johnny's' benefit, beginning, 'Well, —— it ain't any use talking, some of those old American words *do* have a kind of a bully swing to them; a man can *express* himself with 'em—a man can get at what he wants to *say*, dontchuknow.'

When we reached our hotel and it seemed that he was about to lose the Reverend, he showed so much sorrow, and begged so hard and so earnestly, that the Reverend's heart was not hard enough to hold out against the pleadings—so he went away with the parent-honouring student, like a right Christian, and took supper with him in his lodgings and sat in the surf-beat of his slang and profanity till near midnight, and then left him—left him pretty well talked out, but grateful 'clear down to his frogs,' as he expressed it. The Reverend said it had transpired during the interview that 'Cholley' Adams's father was an extensive dealer in horses in Western New York; this accounted for Cholley's choice of a profession. The Reverend brought away a pretty high opinion of Cholley as a manly young fellow, with stuff in him for a useful citizen; he considered him rather a rough gem, but a gem, nevertheless.

CHAPTER 21

Baden-Baden sits in the lap of the hills, and the natural and artificial beauties of the surroundings are combined effectively and charmingly. The level strip of ground which stretches through and beyond the town is laid out in handsome pleasure grounds, shaded by noble trees and adorned at intervals with lofty and sparkling fountain-jets. Thrice a day a fine band makes music in the public promenade before the Conversation-House, and in the afternoons and evenings that locality is populous with fashionably dressed people of both sexes, who march back and forth past the great music stand and look very much bored, though they make a show of feeling otherwise. It seems like a rather aimless and stupid existence. A good many of these people are there for a real purpose, however; they are racked with rheumatism, and they are there to stew it out in the hot baths. These invalids looked melancholy enough, limping about on their canes and crutches, and apparently brooding over all sorts of cheerless things. People say that Germany, with her damp stone houses, is the home of rheumatism. If that is so, Providence must have foreseen that it would be so, and therefore filled the land with these healing baths. Perhaps no other country is so generously supplied with medicinal springs as Germany. Some of these baths are good for one ailment, some for another; and again, peculiar ailments are conquered by combining the individual virtues of several different baths. For instance, for some forms of disease the patient drinks the native hot water of Baden-Baden, with a spoonful of salt from Carlsbad springs dissolved in it. That is not a dose to be forgotten right away.

They don't *sell* this hot water; no, you go into the great Trinkhalle, and stand around, first on one foot and then on the other, while two or three young girls sit pottering at some sort of lady-like sewing work in your neighbourhood and can't seem to see you—polite as three-dollar clerks in government offices.

By-and-by one of these rises painfully, and 'stretches'; —stretches fists and body heavenward till she raises her heels from the floor, at the same time refreshing herself with a yawn of such comprehensiveness that the bulk of her face disappears behind her upper lip, and one is able to see how she is constructed inside—then she slowly closes her cavern, brings down her fists and her heels, comes languidly forward, contemplates you contemptuously, draws you a glass of hot water and sets it down where you can get it by reaching for it. You take it and say—

'How much?'—and she returns you, with elaborate indifference, a beggar's answer—

'*Nach Beliebe* (what you please).'

This thing of using the common beggar's trick and the common beggar's shibboleth to put you on your liberality when you were expecting a simple straightforward commercial transaction, adds a little to your prospering sense of irritation. You ignore her reply, and ask again—

'How much?'

And she calmly, indifferently, repeats—

'*Nach Beliebe.*'

You are getting angry, but you are trying not to show it; you resolve to keep on asking your question till she changes her answer, or at least her annoyingly indifferent manner. Therefore, if your case be like mine, you two fools stand there, and without perceptible emotion of any kind, or any emphasis on any syllable, you look blandly into each other's eyes, and hold the following idiotic conversation—

'How much?'

'Nach Beliebe.'

'How much?'
'Nach Beliebe.'
'How much?'
'Nach Beliebe.'
'How much?'
'Nach Beliebe.'
'How much?'
'Nach Beliebe.'
'How much?'
'Nach Beliebe.'

I do not know what another person would have done, but at this point I gave it up; that cast-iron indifference, that tranquil contemptuousness, conquered me, and I struck my colours. Now I knew she was used to receiving about a penny from many people who care nothing about the opinions of scullery maids, and about tuppence from moral cowards; but I laid a silver twenty-five-cent piece within her reach and tried to shrivel her up with this sarcastic speech—

'If it isn't enough, will you stoop sufficiently from your official dignity to say so?'

She did not shrivel. Without deigning to look at me at all, she languidly lifted the coin and bit it!—to see if it was good. Then she turned her back and placidly waddled to her former roost again, tossing the money into an open till as she went along. She was victor to the last, you see.

I have enlarged upon the ways of this girl because they are typical; her manners are the manners of a goodly number of the Baden-Baden shopkeepers. The shopkeeper there swindles you if he can, and insults you whether he succeeds in swindling you or not. The keepers of baths also take great and patient pains to insult you. The frowsy woman who sat at the desk in the lobby of the great Friederichsbad and sold bath tickets, not only insulted me twice every day, with rigid fidelity to her great trust, but she took trouble enough to cheat me out of a shilling, one day, to have fairly entitled her to ten. Baden-Baden's splendid gamblers are gone, only her microscopic knaves remain.

An English gentleman who had been living there several years said—

'If you could disguise your nationality, you would not find any insolence here. These shopkeepers detest the English and despise the Americans; they are rude to both, more especially to ladies of your nationality and mine. If these go shopping without a gentleman or a man servant, they are tolerably sure to be subjected to petty insolences—insolences of manner and tone rather than word, though words that are hard to bear are not always wanting. I know of an instance where a shopkeeper tossed a coin back to an American lady with the remark, snappishly uttered, "We don't take French money here."—And I know of a case where an English lady said to one of these shopkeepers, "Don't you think you ask too much for this article?" and he replied with the question, "Do you think you are obliged to buy it?" However, these people are not impolite to Russians or Germans. And as to rank, they worship that, for they have long been used to generals and nobles. If you wish to see to what abysses servility can descend, present yourself before a Baden-Baden shopkeeper in the character of a Russian prince.'

It is an inane town, filled with sham, and petty fraud, and snobbery, but the baths are good. I spoke with many people, and they were all agreed in that. I had had twinges of rheumatism unceasingly during three years, but the last one departed after a fortnight's bathing there, and I have never had one since. I fully believe I left my rheumatism in Baden-Baden. Baden-Baden is welcome to it. It was little, but it was all I had to give. I would have preferred to leave something that was catching, but it was not in my power.

There are several hot springs there, and during two thousand years they have poured forth a never-diminishing abundance of the healing water. This water is conducted in pipes to the numerous bath-houses, and is reduced to an endurable temperature by the addition of cold water. The new Friederichsbad is a very large and beautiful building, and in it one may have any sort of bath that has ever been invented, and with all the additions of herbs and drugs that his ailment may need or that the physician of the establishment may consider a useful thing to put into the water. You go there, enter the great

door, get a bow graduated to your style and clothes from the
gorgeous portier, and a bath-ticket and an insult from the frowsy
woman for a quarter, she strikes a bell, and a serving-man
conducts you down a long hall and shuts you into a
commodious room which has a washstand, a mirror, a bootjack,
and a sofa in it, and there you undress at your leisure.

The room is divided by a great curtain. You draw this curtain
aside, and find a large white marble bath-tub, with its rim sunk
to the level of the floor, and with three white marble steps
leading down into it. This tub is full of water, which is as clear as
crystal, and is tempered to 28° Réaumur (about 95° Fahrenheit).
Sunk into the floor, by the tub, is a covered copper box which
contains some warm towels and a sheet. You look fully as white
as an angel when you are stretched out in that limpid bath. You
remain in it ten minutes the first time, and afterwards increase
the duration from day to day, till you reach twenty-five or thirty
minutes. There you stop. The appointments of the place are so
luxurious, the benefit so marked, the price so moderate, and the
insults so sure, that you very soon find yourself adoring the
Friederichsbad and infesting it.

We had a plain, simple, unpretending, good hotel in Baden-
Baden—the Hôtel de France—and alongside my room I had a
giggling, cackling, chattering family who always went to bed
just two hours after me and always got up just two hours ahead
of me. But that is common in German hotels; the people
generally go to bed long after eleven and get up long before
eight. The partitions convey sound like a drumhead, and
everybody knows it; but no matter, a German family who are all
kindness and consideration in the daytime make apparently no
effort to moderate their noises for your benefit at night. They
will sing, laugh, and talk loudly, and bang furniture around in
the most pitiless way. If you knock on your wall appealingly,
they will quiet down and discuss the matter softly amongst
themselves for a moment—then, like the mice, they fall to
persecuting you again, and as vigorously as before. They keep
cruelly late and early hours, for such noisy folk.

Of course when one begins to find fault with foreign people's
ways, he is very likely to get a reminder to look nearer home,

before he gets far with it. I open my note-book to see if I can find some more information of a valuable nature about Baden-Baden, and the first thing I fall upon is this:

Baden-Baden (no date).—Lot of vociferous Americans at breakfast this morning. Talking *at* everybody, while pretending to talk among themselves. On their first travels, manifestly. Showing off. The usual signs—airy, easy-going references to grand distances and foreign places. 'Well *good*-bye, old fellow, if I don't run across you in Italy, you hunt me up in London before you sail.'

The next item which I find in my note-book is this one:

'The fact that a band of 6,000 Indians are now murdering our frontiersmen at their impudent leisure, and that we are only able to send 1,200 soldiers against them, is utilised here to discourage emigration to America. The common people think the Indians are in New Jersey.'

This is a new and peculiar argument against keeping our army down to a ridiculous figure in the matter of numbers. It is rather a striking one, too. I have not distorted the truth in saying that the facts in the above item, about the army and the Indians, are made use of to discourage emigration to America. That the common people should be rather foggy in their geography, and foggy as to the location of the Indians, is matter for amusement, maybe, but not of surprise.

There is an interesting old cemetery in Baden-Baden, and we spent several pleasant hours in wandering through it and spelling out the inscriptions on the aged tombstones. Apparently after a man has lain there a century or two, and has had a good many people buried on top of him, it is considered that his tombstone is not needed by him any longer. I judge so from the fact that hundreds of old gravestones have been removed from the graves and placed against the inner walls of the cemetery. What artists they had in the old times! They chiselled angels and cherubs and devils and skeletons on the tombstones in the most lavish and generous way—as to supply—but curiously grotesque and outlandish as to form. It is not always easy to tell which of the figures belong among the blest, and which of them among the opposite party. But there was an inscription, in French, on one

of these old stones which was quaint and pretty, and was plainly
not the work of any other than a poet. It was to this effect:—

HERE
REPOSES IN GOD,
CAROLINE DE CLÉRY,
A RELIGIEUSE OF ST. DENIS,
AGED 83 YEARS—AND BLIND.
THE LIGHT WAS RESTORED TO HER
IN BADEN, THE 5TH OF JANUARY,
1839.

We made several excursions on foot to the neighbouring
villages, over winding and beautiful roads, and through
enchanting woodland scenery. The woods and roads were
similar to those at Heidelberg, but not so bewitching. I suppose
that roads and woods which are up to the Heidelberg mark are
rare in the world.

Once we wandered clear away to La Favorita Palace, which
is several miles from Baden-Baden. The grounds about the
palace were fine; the palace was a curiosity. It was built by a
Margravine in 1725, and remains as she left it at her death. We
wandered through a great many of its rooms, and they all had
striking peculiarities of decoration. For instance, the walls of one
room were pretty completely covered with small pictures of the
Margravine in all conceivable varieties of fanciful costumes,
some of them male.

The walls of another room were covered with grotesquely and
elaborately figured hand-wrought tapestry. The musty ancient
beds remained in the chambers, and their quilts and curtains and
canopies were decorated with curious hand-work, and the walls
and ceilings frescoed with historical and mythological scenes in
glaring colours. There was enough crazy and rotten rubbish in
the building to make the true brick-à-bracker green with envy. A
painting in the dining-hall verged upon the indelicate—but then
the Magravine was herself a trifle indelicate.

It is in every way a wildly and picturesquely decorated house,
and brimful of interest as a reflection of the character and tastes

of that rude bygone time.

In the grounds, a few rods from the palace, stands the Magravine's chapel, just as she left it—a coarse wooden structure, wholly barren of ornament. It is said that the Margravine would give herself up to debauchery and exceedingly fast living for several months at a time, and then retire to this miserable wooden den and spend a few months in repenting and getting ready for another good time. She was a devoted Catholic, and was perhaps quite a model sort of a Christian as Christians went then, in high life.

Tradition says she spent the last two years of her life in the strange den I have been speaking of, after having indulged herself in one final, triumphant and satisfying spree. She shut herself up there, without company, and without even a servant, and so abjured and forsook the world. In her little bit of a kitchen she did her own cooking; she wore a hair shirt next the skin, and castigated herself with whips—these aids to grace are exhibited there yet. She prayed and told her beads, in another little room before a waxen Virgin niched in a little box against the wall; she bedded herself like a slave.

In another small room is an unpainted wooden table, and behind it sit half-life-size waxen figures of the Holy Family, made by the very worst artist that ever lived, perhaps, and clothed in gaudy, flimsy drapery.[1] The Margravine used to bring her meals to this table and *dine with the Holy Family*. What an idea that was! What a grisly spectacle it must have been! Imagine it! Those rigid, shock headed figures, with corpsy complexions and fishy glass eyes, occupying one side of the table in the constrained attitudes and dead fixedness that distinguish all men that are born of wax, and this wrinkled, smouldering old fire-eater occupying the other side, mumbling her prayers and munching her sausages in the ghostly stillness and shadowy indistinctness of a winter twilight. It makes one feel crawly even to think of it.

In this sordid place, and clothed, bedded, and fed like a

[1] The Saviour was represented as a lad of about fifteen years of age. This figure had lost one eye.

pauper, this strange princess lived and worshipped during two years, and in it she died. Two or three hundred years ago, this would have made the poor den holy ground; and the church would have set up a miracle-factory there and made plenty of money out of it. The den could be moved into some portions of France and made a good property even now.

CHAPTER 22

From Baden-Baden we made the customary trip into the Black Forest. We were on foot most of the time. One cannot describe those noble woods, nor the feeling with which they inspire him. A feature of the feeling, however, is a deep sense of contentment; another feature of it is a buoyant, boyish gladness; and a third and very conspicuous feature of it is one's sense of the remoteness of the work-day world and his entire emancipation from it and its affairs.

Those woods stretch unbroken over a vast region; and everywhere they are such dense woods, and so still, and so piney and fragrant. The stems of the trees are trim and straight, and in many places all the ground is hidden for miles under a thick cushion of moss of a vivid green colour, with not a decayed or ragged spot in its surface, and not a fallen leaf or twig to mar its immaculate tidiness. A rich cathedral gloom pervades the pillared aisles; so the stray flecks of sunlight that strike a trunk here and a bough yonder are strongly accented, and when they strike the moss they fairly seem to burn. But the weirdest effect, and the most enchanting, is that produced by the diffused light of the low afternoon sun; no single ray is able to pierce its way in, then, but the diffused light takes colour from moss and foliage, and pervades the place like a faint, green-tinted mist, the theatrical fire of fairyland. The suggestion of mystery and the supernatural which haunts the forest at all times is intensified by this unearthly glow.

We found the Black Forest farmhouses and villages all that the Black Forest stories have pictured them. The first genuine specimen which we came upon was the mansion of a rich farmer and member of the Common Council of the parish or district. He was an important personage in the land, and so was his wife also, of course. His daughter was the 'catch' of the region, and she may be already entering into immortality as the heroine of one of Auerbach's novels for all I know. We shall see, for if he puts her in I shall recognise her by her Black Forest clothes, and her burned complexion, her plump figure, her fat hands, her dull expression, her gentle spirit, her generous feet, her bonnetless head, and the plaited tails of hemp-coloured hair hanging down her back.

The house was big enough for an hotel; it was a hundred feet long and fifty wide, and ten feet high, from ground to eaves; but from the eaves to the comb of the mighty roof was as much as forty feet, or maybe even more. This roof was of ancient mud-coloured straw thatch a foot thick, and was covered all over, except in a few trifling spots, with a thriving and luxurious growth of green vegetation, mainly moss. The mossless spots were places where repairs had been made by the insertion of bright new masses of yellow straw. The eaves projected far down, like sheltering, hospitable wings. Across the gable that fronted the road, and about ten feet above the ground, ran a narrow porch, with a wooden railing; a row of small windows filled with very small panes looked upon the porch. Above were two or three other little windows, one clear up under the sharp apex of the roof. Before the ground-floor door was a huge pile of manure. The door of a second-story room on the side of the house was open, and occupied by the rear elevation of a cow. Was this probably the drawing-room? All of the front half of the house from the ground up seemed to be occupied by the people, the cows, and the chickens, and all the rear half by draught animals and hay. But the chief feature all around this house was the big heaps of manure.

We became very familiar with the fertiliser in the Forest. We fell unconsciously into the habit of judging of a man's station in life by this outward and eloquent sign. Sometimes we said, 'Here is a poor devil, this is manifest.' When we saw a stately accumulation, we said, 'Here is a banker.' When we encountered a country seat surrounded by an Alpine pomp of manure, we said, 'Doubtless a duke lives here.'

The importance of this feature has not been properly magnified in the Black Forest stories. Manure is evidently the Black Forester's main treasure—his coin, his jewel, his pride, his Old Master, his keramics, his bric-à-brac, his darling, his title to public consideration, envy, veneration, and his first solicitude when he gets ready to make his will. The true Black Forest novel, if it is ever written, will be skeletoned somewhat in this way:—

Skeleton For Black Forest Novel

Rich old farmer, named Huss. Has inherited great wealth of manure, and by diligence has added to it. It is double-starred in 'Baedeker.'[1] The Black Forest artist paints it—his masterpiece. The King comes to see it. Gretchen Huss, daughter and heiress. Paul Hoch, young neighbour, suitor for Gretchen's hand—ostensibly; he really wants the manure. Hoch has a good many cart-loads of the Black Forest currency himself, and therefore is a good catch; but he is sordid, mean, and without sentiment, whereas Gretchen is all sentiment and poetry. Hans Schmidt, young neighbour, full of sentiment, full of poetry, loves Gretchen; Gretchen loves him. But he has no manure. Old Huss forbids him the house. His heart breaks, he goes away to die in the woods, far from the cruel world—for he says, bitterly, 'What is man, without manure?'

[Interval of six months.]

Paul Hoch comes to old Huss and says, 'I am at last as rich as you required—come and view the pile.' Old Huss views it, and says, 'It is sufficient—take her and be happy'—meaning Gretchen.

[Interval of two weeks.]

[1] When Baedeker's guide-books mention a thing and put two stars ** after it, it means 'well worth visiting.'—M.T.

Wedding party assembled in old Huss's drawing-room; Hoch placid and content, Gretchen weeping over her hard fate. Enter old Huss's head book-keeper. Huss says fiercely, 'I gave you three weeks to find out why your books don't balance, and to prove that you are not a defaulter; the time is up—find me the missing property or you go to prison as a thief.' Book-keeper: 'I have found it.' 'Where?' Book-keeper (sternly—tragically): 'In the bridegroom's pile!'—behold the thief—see him blench and tremble!' [Sensation.] Paul Hoch: 'Lost, lost!'—falls over the cow in a swoon and is hand-cuffed. Gretchen: 'Saved!' Falls over the calf in a swoon of joy, but is caught in the arms of Hans Schmidt, who springs in at that moment. Old Huss: 'What, you here, varlet? unhand the maid and quit the place.' Hans (still supporting the insensible girl!): 'Never! Cruel old man, know that I come with claims which even you cannot despise.'

Huss: 'What, *you*? Name them.'

Hans: 'Then listen. The world had forsaken me, I forsook the world. I wandered in the solitude of the forest, longing for death, but finding none. I fed upon roots, and in my bitterness I dug for the bitterest, loathing the sweeter kind. Digging, three days agone, I struck a manure mine!—A Golconda, a limitless Bonanza of solid manure! I can buy you *all*, and have mountain ranges of manure left! Ha ha! *now* thou smilest a smile!' [Immense sensation.] Exhibition of specimens from the mine. Old Huss, enthusiastically: 'Wake her up, shake her up, noble young man, she is yours!' Wedding takes place on the spot; book-keeper restored to his office and emoluments; Paul Hoch led off to gaol. The Bonanza King of the Black Forest lives to a good old age, blessed with the love of his wife and of his twenty-seven children, and the still sweeter envy of everybody around.

We took our noon meal of fried trout one day at the Plow Inn, in a very pretty village (Ottenhöfen), and then went into the public room to rest and smoke. There we found nine or ten Black Forest grandees assembled around a table. They were the Common Council of the parish. They had gathered there at eight o'clock that morning to elect a new member, and they had now been drinking beer four hours at the new member's expense. They were men of fifty or sixty years of age, with grave, good-

natured faces, and were all dressed in the costume made familiar
to us by the Black Forest stories: broad, round-topped, black
felt hats, with the brims curled up all around; long red
waistcoats with large metal buttons, black alpaca coats with the
waists up between the shoulders. There were no speeches, there
was but little talk, there were no frivolities; the Council filled
themselves gradually, steadily, but surely, with beer, and
conducted themselves with sedate decorum, as became men of
position, men of influence, men of manure.

We had a hot afternoon tramp up the valley, along the grassy
bank of a rushing stream of clear water, past farmhouses, water-
mills, and no end of wayside crucifixes, and saints, and Virgins.
These crucifixes, etc., are set up in memory of departed friends
by survivors, and are almost as frequent as telegraph poles are
in other lands.

We followed the carriage road, and had our usual luck; we
travelled under a beating sun, and always saw the shade leave
the shady places before we could get to them. In all our
wanderings we seldom managed to strike a piece of road at its
time for being shady. We had a particularly hot time of it on that
particular afternoon, and with no comfort but what we could get
out of the fact that the peasants at work away up on the steep
mountain sides above our heads were even worse off than we
were. By-and-by it became impossible to endure the intolerable
glare and heat any longer; so we struck across the ravine and
entered the deep cool twilight of the forest, to hunt for what the
guide-book called the 'old road.'

We found an old road, and it proved eventually to be the right
one, though we followed it at the time with the conviction that it
was the wrong one. If it was the wrong one there could be no use
in hurrying, therefore we did not hurry, but sat down frequently
on the soft moss, and enjoyed the restful quiet and shade of the
forest solitudes. There had been distractions in the carriage
road—school children, peasants, wagons, troops of
pedestrianising students from all over Germany—but we had
the old road all to ourselves.

Now and then, while we rested, we watched the laborious ant
at his work. I found nothing new in him—certainly nothing to

change my opinion of him. It seems to me that in the matter of intellect the ant must be a strangely overrated bird. During many summers now I have watched him, when I ought to have been in better business, and I have not yet come across a living ant that seemed to have any more sense than a dead one. I refer to the ordinary ant, of course; I have had no experience of those wonderful Swiss and African ones which vote, keep drilled armies, hold slaves, and dispute about religion. Those particular ants may be all that the naturalist paints them, but I am persuaded that the average ant is a sham. I admit his industry, of course; he is the hardest-working creature in the world—when anybody is looking—but his leather-headedness is the point I make against him. He goes out foraging, he makes a capture, and then what does he do? Go home? No; he goes anywhere but home. He doesn't know where home is. His home may be only three feet away; no matter, he can't find it. He makes his capture, as I have said; it is generally something which can be of no sort of use to himself or anybody else; it is usually seven times bigger than it ought to be; he hunts out the awkwardest place to take hold of it; he lifts it bodily up in the air by main force, and starts—not towards home, but in the opposite direction; not calmly and wisely, but with a frantic haste which is wasteful of his strength; he fetches up against a pebble, and, instead of going around it, he climbs over it backwards, dragging his booty after him, tumbles down on the other side, jumps up in a passion, kicks the dust off his clothes, moistens his hands, grabs his property viciously, yanks it this way, then that, shoves it ahead of him a moment, turns tail and lugs it after him another moment, gets madder and madder, then presently hoists it into the air and goes tearing away in an entirely new direction; comes to a weed; it never occurs to him to go around it. No; he must climb it, and he does climb it, dragging his worthless property to the top—which is as bright a thing to do as it would be for me to carry a sack of flour from Heidelberg to Paris by way of Strasburg steeple. When he gets up there he finds that that is not the place; takes a cursory glance at the scenery, and either climbs down again or tumbles down, and starts off once more—as usual, in a new direction. At the end of half an hour he fetches up within six inches of the place he started from, and lays his burden down. Meantime, he has been over all the ground for two yards around, and climbed all the weeds and pebbles he came across. Now he wipes the sweat from his brow, strokes his limbs, and then marches aimlessly off, in as violent a hurry as ever. He traverses a good deal of zigzag country, and by-and-by stumbles on his same booty again. He does not remember to have ever seen it before; he looks around to see which is not the way home, grabs his bundle, and starts. He goes through the same adventures he had before; finally stops to rest, and a friend comes along. Evidently the friend remarks that a last year's grasshopper leg is a very noble acquisition, and inquires where he got it. Evidently the proprietor does not remember exactly where he did get it, but thinks he got it 'around here somewhere.' Evidently the friend contracts to help him freight it home. Then, with a judgment peculiarly antic (pun not intentional), they take hold of opposite ends of that grasshopper leg and begin to tug with all their might in opposite directions. Presently they take a rest, and confer together. They decide that something is wrong, they can't make out what. Then they go at it again, just as before. Same result. Mutual recriminations. They warm up, and the dispute ends in a fight. They lock themselves together and chew each other's jaws for a while; then they roll and tumble on the ground till one loses a horn or a leg and has to haul off for repairs. They make up and go to work again in the same old insane way, but the crippled ant is at a disadvantage; tug as he may, the other one drags off the booty and him at the end of it. Instead of giving up, he hangs on, and gets his shins bruised against every obstruction that comes in the way. By-and-by, when that grasshopper leg has been dragged all over the same old ground once more, it is finally dumped at about the spot where it originally lay. The two perspiring ants inspect it thoughtfully and decide that dried grasshopper legs are a poor sort of property after all, and then each starts off in a different direction to see if he can't find an old nail or something else that is heavy enough to afford entertainment and at the same time valueless enough to make an ant want to own it.

There in the Black Forest, on the mountain side, I saw an ant go through with such a performance as this with a dead spider of fully ten times his own weight. The spider was not quite dead, but too far gone to resist. He had a round body the size of a pea. The little ant—observing that I was noticing—turned him on his back, sunk his fangs into his throat, lifted him into the air, and started vigorously off with him, stumbling over little pebbles, stepping on the spider's legs and tripping himself up, dragging him backwards, shoving him bodily ahead, dragging him up stones six inches high instead of going around them, climbing weeds twenty times his own height and jumping from their summits—and finally leaving him in the middle of the road to be confiscated by any other fool of an ant that wanted him. I measured the ground which this ass traversed, and arrived at the conclusion that what he had accomplished inside of twenty minutes would constitute some such job as this—relatively speaking—for a man; to wit: to strap two eight hundred pound horses together, carry them eighteen hundred feet, mainly over (not around) boulders averaging six feet high, and in the course of the journey climb up and jump from the top of one precipice like Niagara, and three steeples, each a hundred and twenty feet high; and then put the horses down, in an exposed place, without anybody to watch them, and go off to indulge in some other idiotic miracle for vanity's sake.

Science has recently discovered that the ant does not lay up anything for winter. This will knock him out of literature to some extent. He does not work, except when people are looking, and only then when the observer has a green, naturalistic look, and seems to be taking notes. This amounts to deception, and will injure him for the Sunday schools. He has not judgment enough to know what is good to eat from what isn't. This amounts to ignorance, and will impair the world's respect for him. He cannot stroll around a stump and find his way home again. This amounts to idiocy, and once the damaging fact is established, thoughtful people will cease to look up to him, the sentimental will cease to fondle him. His vaunted industry is but a vanity and of no effect, since he never gets home with anything he starts with. This disposes of the last remnant of his reputation, and wholly destroys his main usefulness as a moral agent, since it will make the sluggard hesitate to go to him any more. It is strange beyond comprehension that so manifest a humbug as the ant has been able to fool so many nations and keep it up so many ages without being found out.

The ant is strong, but we saw another strong thing, where we had not suspected the presence of much muscular power before. A toadstool—that vegetable which springs to full growth in a single night—had torn loose and lifted a matted mass of pine needles and dirt of twice its own bulk into the air, and supported it there, like a column supporting a shed. Ten thousand toadstools, with the right purchase, could lift a man, I suppose. But what good would it do?

All our afternoon's progress had been up hill. About five or half-past we reached the summit, and all of a sudden the dense curtain of the forest parted, and we looked down into a deep and beautiful gorge and out over a wide panorama of wooded mountains with their summits shining in the sun and their glade-furrowed sides dimmed with purple shade. The gorge under our feet—called Allerheiligen—afforded room in the grassy level at its head for a cosy and delightful human nest, shut away from the world and its botherations, and consequently the monks of the old times had not failed to spy it out; and here were the brown and comely ruins of their church and convent to prove that priests had as fine an instinct seven hundred years ago in ferreting out the choicest nooks and corners in a land as priests have to-day.

A big hotel crowds the ruins a little now, and drives a brisk trade with summer tourists. We descended into the gorge and had a supper which would have been very satisfactory if the trout had not been boiled. The Germans are pretty sure to boil a trout or anything else if left to their own devices. This is an argument of some value in support of the theory that they were the original colonists of the wild islands off the coast of Scotland. A schooner laden with oranges was wrecked upon one of those islands a few years ago, and the gentle savages rendered the captain such willing assistance that he gave them as many oranges as they wanted. Next day he asked them how they liked them. They shook their heads and said—

'Baked, they were tough; and even boiled, they warn't things for a hungry man to hanker after.'

We went down the glen after supper. It is beautiful—a mixture of sylvan loveliness and craggy wildness. A limpid torrent goes whistling down the glen, and towards the foot of it winds through a narrow cleft between lofty precipices and hurls itself over a succession of falls. After one passes the last of these he has a backward glimpse of the falls which is very pleasing—they rise in a seven-stepped stairway of foamy and glittering cascades, and make a picture which is as charming as it is unusual.

CHAPTER 23

We were satisfied that we could walk to Oppenau in one day, now that we were in practice, so we set out next morning after breakfast determined to do it. It was all the way down hill, and we had the loveliest summer weather for it. So we set the pedometer, and then stretched away on an easy, regular stride, down through the cloven forest, drawing in the fragrant breath of the morning in deep refreshing draughts, and wishing we might never have anything to do for ever but walk to Oppenau, and keep on doing it, and then doing it over again.

Now the true charm of pedestrianism does not lie in the walking, or in the scenery, but in the talking. The walking is good to time the movement of the tongue by, and to keep the blood and the brain stirred up and active; the scenery and the woodsy smells are good to bear in upon a man as unconscious and unobtrusive charm and solace to eye and soul and sense; but the supreme pleasure comes from the talk. It is no matter whether one talks wisdom or nonsense, the case is the same; the bulk of the enjoyment lies in the wagging of the gladsome jaw and the flapping of the sympathetic ear.

And what a motley variety of subjects a couple of people will casually rake over in the course of a day's tramp! There being no constraint, a change of subject is always in order, and so a body is not likely to keep pegging at a single topic until it grows tiresome. We discussed everything we knew, during the first fifteen or twenty minutes, that morning, and then branched out into the glad, free boundless realm of the things we were not certain about.

Harris said that if the best writer in the world once got the slovenly habit of doubling up his 'have's' he could never get rid of it while he lived. That is to say, if a man gets the habit of saying, 'I should have liked to have known more about it,' instead of saying simply and sensibly, 'I should have liked to know more about it,' that man's disease is incurable. Harris said that this sort of lapse is to be found in every copy of every newspaper that has ever been printed in English, and in almost all of our books. He said he had observed it in Kirkham's grammar and in Macaulay. Harris believed that milk-teeth are commoner in men's mouths than those 'doubled-up have's.'[1]

That changed the subject to dentistry. I said I believed the average man dreaded tooth-pulling more than amputation, and that he would yell quicker under the former operation than he would under the latter. The philosopher Harris said that the average man would not yell in either case if he had an audience. Then he continued:—

'When our brigade first went into camp on the Potomac we used to be brought up standing, occasionally, by an ear-splitting howl of anguish. That meant that a soldier was getting a tooth pulled in a tent. But the surgeons soon changed that; they instituted open-air dentistry. There never was a howl afterwards—that is, from the man who was having the tooth pulled. At the daily dental hour there would always be about 500 soldiers gathered together in the neighbourhood of that dental chair waiting to see the performance—and help; and the moment the surgeon took a grip on the candidate's tooth, and began to lift, every one of those 500 rascals would clap his hand to his jaw and begin to hop around on one leg and howl with all the lungs he had! It was enough to raise your hair to hear that variegated and enormous unanimous caterwaul burst out! With so

[1] I do not know that there have not been moments in the course of the present session when I should have been very glad to have accepted the proposal of my noble friend, and to have exchanged parts in some of our evenings of work.'—From a speech of the English Chancellor of the Exchequer, August 1879.

big and so derisive an audience as that, a sufferer wouldn't emit a sound though you pulled his head off. The surgeons said that pretty often a patient was compelled to laugh, in the midst of his pangs, but that they had never caught one crying out, after the open-air exhibition was instituted.'

Dental surgeons suggested doctors, doctors suggested death, death suggested skeletons—and so, by a logical process, the conversation melted out of one of these subjects and into the next, until the topic of skeletons raised up Nicodemus Dodge out of the deep grave in my memory where he had lain buried and forgotten for twenty-five years. When I was a boy in a printing office in Missouri, a loose-jointed, long-legged, tow-headed, jeans-clad, countrified cub of about sixteen lounged in one day, and without removing his hands from the depths of his trousers pockets, or taking off his faded ruin of a slouch hat, whose broken brim hung limp and ragged about his eyes and ears like a bug-eaten cabbage leaf, stared indifferently around, then leaned his hip against the editor's table, crossed his mighty brogans, aimed at a distant fly from a crevice in his upper teeth, laid him low, and said with composure—

'Whar's the boss?'

'I am the boss,' said the editor, following this curious bit of architecture wonderingly along up to its clock-face with his eye.

'Don't want anybody fur to learn the business, 't aint likely?'

'Well, I don't know. Would you like to learn it?'

'Pap's so po' he cain't run me no mo', so want to git a show somers if I kin, 'tain't no diffunce what—I'm strong and hearty, and I don't turn my back on no kind of work, hard nur soft.'

'Do you think you would like to learn the printing business?'

'Well, I don't re'ly k'yer a durn what I *do* learn, so's I git a chance fur to make my way. I'd just as soon learn print'n 's anything.'

'Can you read?'

'Yes—middlin'.'

'Write?'

'Well, I've seed people could lay over me thar.'

'Cipher?'

'Not good enough to keep store, I don't reckon, but up as fur

as twelve-times-twelve I ain't no slouch. 'Tother side of that is
what gits me.'

'Where is your home?'

'I'm f'm old Shelby.'

'What's your father's religious denomination?'

'Him? O, he's a blacksmith.'

'No, no—I don't mean his trade. What's his *religious*
denomination?'

'O—I didn't understand you befo'. He's a Freemason.'

'No, no—you don't get my meaning yet. What I mean is,
does he belong to any *church*?'

'*Now* you're talkin'! Couldn't make out what you was a tryin'
to get through yo' head no way. B'long to a *church*! Why, boss,
he's ben the pizenest kind of a Free-will Babtis' for forty year.
They ain't no pizener ones 'n' what *he* is. Mighty good man, pap
is. Everybody says that. If they said any diffrunt they wouldn't
say it whar *I* wuz—not *much* they wouldn't.'

'What is your own religion?'

'Well, boss, you've kind o' got me thar—and yit you hain't
got me so mighty much, nuther. I think 't if a feller he'ps another
feller when he's in trouble, and don't cuss, and don't do no mean
things, nur noth'n' he ain' no business to do, and don't spell the
Saviour's name with a little g, he ain't runnin' no resks—he's
about as saift as if he b'longed to a church.'

'But suppose he did spell it with a little g—what then?'

'Well, if he done it a-purpose, I reckon he wouldn't stand no
chance—he *oughtn't* to have no chance, anyway, I'm most
rotten certain 'bout that.'

'What is your name?'

'Nicodemus Dodge.'

'I think maybe you'll do, Nicodemus. We'll give you a trial,
anyway.'

'All right.'

'When would you like to begin?'

'Now.'

So within ten minutes after we had first glimpsed this
nondescript he was one of us, and with his coat off and hard at
it.

Beyond that end of our establishment which was furthest from the street was a deserted garden, pathless, and thickly grown with the bloomy and villainous 'jimpson' weed and its common friend the stately sunflower. In the midst of this mournful spot was a decayed and aged little 'frame' house, with but one room, one window, and no ceiling—it had been a smoke-house a generation before. Nicodemus was given this lonely and ghostly den as a bedchamber.

The village smarties recognised a treasure in Nicodemus, right away—a butt to play jokes on. It was easy to see that he was inconceivably green and confiding. George Jones had the glory of perpetrating the first joke on him; he gave him a cigar with a fire-cracker in it and winked to the crowd to come; the thing exploded presently and swept away the bulk of Nicodemus's eyebrows and eyelashes. He simply said—

'I consider them kind of seeg'yars dangersome'—and seemed to suspect nothing. The next evening Nicodemus waylaid George and poured a bucket of ice-water over him.

One day, while Nicodemus was in swimming, Tom McElroy 'tied' his clothes. Nicodemus made a bonfire of Tom's, by way of retaliation.

A third joke was played upon Nicodemus, a day or two later—he walked up the middle aisle of the village church, Sunday night, with a staring handbill pinned between his shoulders. The joker spent the remainder of the night, after church, in the cellar of a deserted house, and Nicodemus sat on the cellar door till toward breakfast time to make sure that the prisoner remembered that if any noise was made some rough treatment would be the consequence. The cellar had two feet of stagnant water in it, and was bottomed with six inches of soft mud.

But I wander from the point. It was the subject of skeletons that brought this boy back to my recollection. Before a very long time had elapsed, the village smarties began to feel an uncomfortable consciousness of not having made a very shining success out of their attempts on the simpleton from 'old Shelby.' Experimenters grew scarce and chary. Now the young doctor came to the rescue. There was delight and applause when he proposed to scare Nicodemus to death, and explained how he was going to do it. He had a noble new skeleton—the skeleton of the late and only local celebrity, Jimmy Finn, the village drunkard—a grisly piece of property which he had bought of Jimmy Finn himself, at auction, for fifty dollars, under great competition, when Jimmy lay very sick in the tan-yard a fortnight before his death. The fifty dollars had gone promptly for whisky, and had considerably hurried up the change of ownership in the skeleton. The doctor would put Jimmy Finn's skeleton in Nicodemus's bed!

This was done—about half-past ten in the evening. About Nicodemus's usual bedtime—midnight—the village jokers came creeping stealthily through the jimpson weeds and sunflowers toward the lonely frame den. They reached the window and peeped in. There sat the long-legged pauper, on his bed, in a very short shirt, and nothing more; he was dangling his legs contentedly back and forth, and wheezing the music of 'Camptown Races' out of a paper-overlaid comb which he was pressing against his mouth; by him lay a new jewsharp, a new top, a solid india-rubber ball, a handful of painted marbles, five pounds of 'store' candy, and a well-gnawed slab of gingerbread as big and as thick as a volume of sheet music. He had sold the skeleton to a travelling quack for three dollars, and was enjoying the result!

Just as we had finished talking about skeletons and were drifting into the subject of fossils, Harris and I heard a shout, and glanced up the steep hillside. We saw men and women standing away up there looking frightened, and there was a bulky object tumbling and floundering down the steep slope toward us. We got out of the way, and when the object landed in the road it proved to be a boy. He had tripped and fallen, and there was nothing for him to do but trust to luck and take what might come.

When one starts to roll down a place like that there is no stopping till the bottom is reached. Think of people *farming* on a slant which is so steep that the best you can say of it—if you want to be fastidiously accurate—is, that it is a little steeper than a ladder and not quite so steep as a mansard roof. But that is what they do. Some of the little farms on the hillside opposite Heidelberg were stood up 'edgeways.' The boy was wonderfully jolted up, and his head was bleeding from cuts which it had got from small stones on the way.

Harris and I gathered him up and set him on a stone, and by that time the men and women had scampered down and brought his cap.

Men, women, and children flocked out from neighbouring cottages and joined the crowd; the pale boy was petted, and stared at, and commiserated, and water was brought for him to drink, and bathe his bruises in. And such another clatter of tongues! All who had seen the catastrophe were describing it at once, and each trying to talk louder than his neighbour; and one youth of a superior genius ran a little way up the hill, called attention, tripped, fell, rolled down among us, and thus triumphantly showed exactly how the thing had been done.

Harris and I were included in all the descriptions: how we were coming along; how Hans Gross shouted; how we looked up startled; how we saw Peter coming like a cannon-shot; how judiciously we got out of the way, and let him come; and with what presence of mind we picked him up and brushed him off, and set him on a rock when the performance was over. We were as much heroes as anybody else except Peter, and were so recognised; we were taken with Peter and the populace to Peter's mother's cottage, and there we ate bread and cheese, and drank milk and beer with everybody, and had a most sociable good time; and when we left we had a hand-shake all around, and were receiving and shouting back *Leb' wohl's* until a turn in the road separated us from our cordial and kindly new friends for ever.

We accomplished our undertaking. At half-past eight in the evening we stepped into Oppenau, just eleven hours and a half out from Allerheiligen—146 miles. This is the distance by pedometer; the guide-book and the Imperial Ordnance maps make it only ten and a quarter—a surprising blunder, for these two authorities are usually singularly accurate in the matter of distances.

CHAPTER 24

That was a thoroughly satisfactory walk, and the only one we were ever to have which was all the way down hill. We took the train next morning and returned to Baden-Baden through fearful fogs of dust. Every seat was crowded, too, for it was Sunday, and consequently everybody was taking a 'pleasure' excursion. Hot! the sky was an oven, and a sound one, too, with no cracks in it to let in any air. An odd time for a pleasure excursion, certainly.

Sunday is the great day on the Continent—the free day, the happy day. One can break the Sabbath in a hundred ways without committing any sin.

We do not work on Sunday, because the commandment forbids it; the Germans do not work on Sunday, because the commandment forbids it. We rest on Sunday, because the commandment requires it; the Germans rest on Sunday, because the commandment requires it. But in the definition of the word 'rest' lies all the difference. With us, its Sunday meaning is, stay in the house and keep still; with the Germans its Sunday and week-day meaning seems to be the same—rest the *tired part*, and never mind the other parts of the frame; rest the tired part, and use the means best calculated to rest that particular part. Thus, if one's duties have kept him in the house all the week, it will rest him to be out on Sunday; if his duties have required him to read weighty and serious matter all the week, it will rest him to read light matter on Sunday; if his occupation has busied him with death and funerals all the week, it will rest him to go to the theatre Sunday night and put in two or three hours laughing at a comedy; if he is tired with digging ditches or felling trees all the week, it will rest him to lie quiet in the house on Sunday; if the hand, the arm, the brain, the tongue, or any other member is fatigued with inanition, it is not to be rested by adding a day's inanition; but if a member is fatigued with exertion, inanition is the right rest for it. Such is the way in which the Germans seem to define the word 'rest,' that is to say, they rest a member by recreating, recuperating, restoring its forces. But our definition is less broad. We all rest alike on Sunday,—by secluding ourselves and keeping still, whether that is the surest way to rest the most of us or not. The Germans make the actors, the preachers, etc., work on Sunday. We encourage the preachers, the editors, the printers, etc., to work on Sunday, and imagine that none of the sin of it falls upon us; but I do not know how we are going to get around the fact that if it is wrong for the printer to work at his trade on Sunday, it must be equally wrong for the preacher to work at his, since the commandment has made no exception in his favour. We buy Monday morning's paper and read it, and thus encourage Sunday printing. But I shall never do it again.

The Germans remember the Sabbath day to keep it holy, by abstaining from work, as commanded; we keep it holy by abstaining from work as commanded, and by also abstaining from play, which is not commanded. Perhaps we constructively *break* the command to rest, because the resting we do is in most cases only a name, and not a fact.

These reasonings have sufficed, in a measure, to mend the rent in my conscience which I made by travelling to Baden-Baden that Sunday. We arrived in time to furbish up and get to the English church before services began. We arrived in considerable style, too, for the landlord had ordered the first carriage that could be found, since there was no time to lose, and our coachman was so splendidly liveried that we were probably mistaken for a brace of stray dukes; also why were we honoured with a pew all to ourselves, away up among the very elect at the left of the chancel? That was my first thought. In the pew directly in front of us sat an elderly lady, plainly and cheaply dressed; at her side sat a young lady with a very sweet face, and she also was quite simply dressed; but around us and about us were clothes and jewels which it would do anybody's heart good to worship in.

I thought it was pretty manifest that the elderly lady was embarrassed at finding herself in such a conspicuous place arrayed in such cheap apparel; I began to feel sorry for her and troubled about her. She tried to seem very busy with her prayer-book and her responses, and unconscious that she was out of place, but I said to myself, 'She is not succeeding,—there is a distressed tremulousness in her voice which betrays increasing embarrassment.' Presently the Saviour's name was mentioned, and in her flurry she lost her head completely, and rose and curtsied, instead of making a slight nod as everybody else did. The sympathetic blood surged to my temples and I turned and gave those fine birds what I intended to be a beseeching look which said, 'If any of you pets of fortune laugh at this poor soul, you will deserve to be flayed for it.' Things went from bad to worse, and I shortly found myself mentally taking the unfriended lady under my protection. My mind was wholly upon her, I forgot all about the sermon. Her embarrassment took stronger and stronger hold upon her; she got to snapping the lid of her smelling bottle,—it made a loud sharp sound, but in her trouble she snapped and snapped away, unconscious of what she was doing. The last extremity was reached when the collection-plate began its rounds; the moderate people threw in pennies, the nobles and the rich contributed silver, but she laid a twenty-mark gold piece upon the book-rest before her with a sounding slap! I said to myself, 'She has parted with all her little hoard to buy the consideration of these unpitying people,—it is a sorrowful spectacle.' I did not venture to look around this time; but as the service closed I said to myself, 'Let them laugh, it is their opportunity; but at the door of this church they shall see her step into our fine carriage with us, and our gaudy coachman shall drive her home.'

Then she rose,—and all the congregation stood while she walked down the aisle. She was the Empress of Germany!

No, she had not been so much embarrassed as I had supposed. My imagination had got started on the wrong scent, and that is always hopeless; one is sure, then, to go straight on misinterpreting everything, clear through to the end. The young lady with her Imperial Majesty was a maid of honour,—and I had been taking her for one of her boarders, all the time.

This is the only time I have ever had an Empress under my personal protection; and, considering my inexperience, I wonder I got through with it so well. I should have been a little embarrassed myself if I had known earlier what sort of a contract I had on my hands.

We found that the Empress had been in Baden-Baden several days. It is said that she never attends any but the English form of church service.

I lay a-bed and read and rested from my journey's fatigues the remainder of that Sunday, but I sent my agent to represent me at the afternoon service, for I never allow anything to interfere with my habit of attending church twice every Sunday.

There was a vast crowd in the public grounds that night to hear the band play the 'Fremersberg.' This piece tells one of the old legends of the region: how a great noble of the Middle Ages got lost in the mountains, and wandered about with his dogs in a violent storm, until at last the faint tones of a monastery bell, calling the monks to a midnight service, caught his ear, and he followed the direction the sounds came from and was saved. A beautiful air ran through the music, without ceasing; sometimes loud and strong, sometimes so soft that it could hardly be distinguished,—but it was always there; it swung grandly along through the shrill whistling of the storm-wind, the rattling patter of the rain, and the boom and crash of the thunder; it wound soft and low through the lesser sounds, the distant ones, such as the throbbing of the convent bell, the melodious winding of the hunter's horn, the distressed baying of his dogs, and the solemn chanting of the monks; it rose again, with a jubilant ring, and mingled itself with the country songs and dances of the peasants assembled in the convent hall to cheer up the rescued huntsman while he ate his supper. The instruments imitated all these sounds with a marvellous exactness. More than one man started to raise his umbrella when the storm burst forth and the sheets of mimic rain came driving by; it was hardly possible to keep from putting your hand to your hat when the fierce wind began to rage and shriek; and it was *not* possible to refrain from starting when those sudden and charmingly real thunder-crashes were let loose.

I suppose the Fremersberg is very low-grade music; I know, indeed, that it *must* be low-grade music, because it so delighted me, warmed me, moved me, stirred me, uplifted me, enraptured me, that I was full of cry all the time, and mad with enthusiasm. My soul had never had such a scouring out since I was born. The solemn and majestic chanting of the monks was not done by instruments, but by men's voices; and it rose and fell, and rose again in that rich confusion of warring sounds, and pulsing bells, and the stately swing of that ever-present enchanting air, and it seemed to me that nothing but the very lowest of low-grade music *could* be so divinely beautiful. The great crowd which the Fremersberg had called out was another evidence that it was low-grade music; for only the few are educated up to a point where high-grade music gives pleasure. I have never heard enough classic music to be able to enjoy it. I dislike the opera because I want to love it and can't.

I suppose there are two kinds of music,—one kind which one feels, just as an oyster might, and another sort which requires a higher faculty, a faculty which must be assisted and developed by teaching. Yet if base music gives certain of us wings, why should we want any other? But we do. We want it because the higher and better like it. But we want it without giving it the necessary time and trouble; so we climb into that upper tier, that dress circle, by a lie; we *pretend* we like it. I know several of that sort of people,—and I propose to be one of them myself when I get home with my fine European education.

And then there is painting. What a red rag is to a bull, Turner's 'Slave Ship' was to me before I studied Art. Mr. Ruskin is educated in art up to a point where that picture throws him into as mad an ecstasy of pleasure as it used to throw me into one of rage, last year, when I was ignorant. His cultivation enables him—and me, now—to see water in that glaring yellow mud, and natural effects in those lurid explosions of mixed smoke and flame, and crimson sunset glories; it reconciles him,—and me, now,—to the floating of iron cable-chains and other unfloatable things; it reconciles us to fishes swimming around on top of the mud,—I mean the water. The most of the picture is a manifest impossibility,—that is to say, a lie; and only rigid cultivation can enable a man to find truth in a lie. But it enabled Mr. Ruskin to do it, and it has enabled me to do it, and I am thankful for it. A Boston newspaper reporter went and took a look at the Slave Ship floundering about in that fierce conflagration of reds and yellows, and said it reminded him of a tortoise-shell cat having a fit in a platter of tomatoes. In my then uneducated state, that went home to my non-cultivation, and I thought here is a man with an unobstructed eye. Mr. Ruskin would have said: This person is an ass. That is what I would say, now.[1]

However, our business in Baden-Baden this time was to join our courier. I had thought it best to hire one, as we should be in Italy by-and-by, and we did not know that language. Neither did he. We found him at the hotel, ready to take charge of us. I asked him if he was 'all fixed.' He said he was. That was very true. He had a trunk, two small satchels, and an umbrella. I was to pay him 55 dollars a month and railway fares. On the Continent the railway fare on a trunk is about the same as it is on a man. Couriers do not have to pay any board and lodging. This seems a great saving to the tourist—at first. It does not occur to the tourist that *somebody* pays that man's board and lodging. It occurs to him by-and-by, however, in one of his lucid moments.

[1] Months after this was written, I happened into the National Gallery in London, and soon became so fascinated with the Turner pictures that I could hardly get away from the place. I went there often, afterwards, meaning to see the rest of the gallery, but the Turner spell was so strong; it could not be shaken off. However, the Turners which attracted me most did not remind me of the Slave Ship.

CHAPTER 25

Next morning we left in the train for Switzerland, and reached Lucerne about ten o'clock at night. The first discovery I made was that the beauty of the lake had not been exaggerated. Within a day or two I made another discovery. This was, that the lauded chamois is not a wild goat; that it is not a horned animal; that it is not shy; that it does not avoid human society; and that there is no peril in hunting it. The chamois is a black or brown creature no bigger than a mustard seed; you do not have to go after it, it comes after you; it arrives in vast herds and skips and scampers all over your body, inside your clothes; thus it is not shy, but extremely sociable; it is not afraid of man, on the contrary, it will attack him! its bite is not dangerous, but neither is it pleasant; its activity has not been overstated,—if you try to put your finger on it, it will skip a thousand times its own length at one jump, and no eye is sharp enough to see where it lights. A great deal of romantic nonsense has been written about the Swiss chamois and the perils of hunting it, whereas the truth is that even women and children hunt it, and fearlessly; indeed, everybody hunts it; the hunting is going on all the time, day and night, in bed and out of it. It is poetic foolishness to hunt it with a gun; very few people do that; there is not one man in a million who can hit it with a gun. It is much easier to catch it than it is to shoot it, and only the experienced chamois hunter can do either. Another common piece of exaggeration is that about the 'scarcity' of the chamois. It is the reverse of scarce. Droves of 100,000,000 chamois are not unusual in the Swiss hotels. Indeed, they are so numerous as to be a great pest. The romancers always dress up the chamois hunter in a fanciful and picturesque costume, whereas the best way to hunt this game is to do it without any costume at all. The article of commerce called chamois skin is another fraud; nobody could skin a chamois, it is too small. The creature is a humbug in every way, and everything which has been written about it is sentimental exaggeration. It was no pleasure to me to find the chamois out, for he had been one of my pet illusions; all my life it had been my dream to see him in his native wilds one day, and engage in the adventurous sport of chasing him from cliff to cliff. It is no pleasure to me to expose him now, and destroy the reader's delight in him and respect for him; but still it must be done, for when an honest writer discovers an imposition it is his simple duty to strip it bare and hurl it down from its place of honour, no matter who suffers by it: any other course would render him unworthy of the public confidence.

Lucerne is a charming place. It begins at the water's edge, with a fringe of hotels, and scrambles up and spreads itself over two or three sharp hills in a crowded, disorderly, but picturesque way, offering to the eye a heaped-up confusion of red roofs, quaint gables, dormer windows, toothpick steeples, with here and there a bit of ancient embattled wall bending itself over the ridges, worm-fashion, and here and there an old square tower of heavy masonry. And also here and there a town clock with only one hand—a hand which stretches straight across the dial and has no joint in it; such a clock helps out the picture, but you cannot tell the time of day by it. Between the curving line of hotels and the lake is a broad avenue with lamps and a double rank of low shade trees. The lake front is walled with masonry like a pier, and has a railing to keep people from walking overboard. All day long the vehicles dash along the avenue, and nurses, children, and tourists sit in the shade of the trees, or lean on the railing and watch the schools of fishes darting about in the clear water or gaze out over the lake at the stately border of snow-hooded mountain peaks. Little pleasure-steamers, black with people, are coming and going all the time; and everywhere one sees young girls and young men paddling about in fanciful row-boats, or skimming along by the help of sails when there is any wind. The front rooms of the hotels have little railed balconies, where one may take his private luncheon in calm cool comfort and look down upon this busy and pretty scene and enjoy it without having to do any of the work connected with it.

Most of the people, both male and female, are in walking costume, and carry alpenstocks. Evidently it is not considered safe to go about in Switzerland, even in town, without an alpenstock. If the tourist forgets, and comes down to breakfast without his alpenstock, he goes back and gets it, and stands it up in a corner. When his touring in Switzerland is finished, he does not throw that broomstick away, but lugs it home with him, to the far corners of the earth, although this costs him more trouble and bother than a baby or a courier could. You see, the alpenstock is his trophy; his name is burned upon it; and if he has climbed a hill, or jumped a brook, or traversed a brickyard with it, he has the names of those places burned upon it, too. Thus it is his regimental flag, so to speak, and bears the record of his achievements. It is worth three francs when he buys it, but a bonanza could not purchase it after his great deeds have been inscribed upon it. There are artisans all about Switzerland whose trade it is to burn these things upon the alpenstock of the tourist. And observe, a man is respected in Switzerland according to his alpenstock. I found I could get no attention there while I carried an unbranded one. However, branding is not expensive, so I soon remedied that. The effect upon the next detachment of tourists was very marked. I felt repaid for my trouble.

Half of the summer horde in Switzerland is made up of English people; the other half is made up of many nationalities, the Germans leading and the Americans coming next. The Americans were not as numerous as I had expected they would be.

The 7.30 *table d'hôte* at the great Schweitzerhof furnished a mighty array and variety of nationalities, but it offered a better opportunity to observe costumes than people, for the multitude sat at immensely long tables, and therefore the faces were mainly seen in perspective; but the breakfasts were served at small round tables, and then if one had the fortune to get a table in the midst of the assemblage he could have as many faces to study as he could desire. We used to try to guess out the nationalities, and generally succeeded tolerably well. Sometimes we tried to guess people's names, but that was a failure; that is a thing which probably requires a good deal of practice. We presently dropped it and gave our efforts to less difficult particulars. One morning I said—

'There is an American party.'

Harris said—

'Yes, but name the State.'

I named one State, Harris named another. We agreed upon one thing, however, that the young girl with the party was very beautiful, and very tastefully dressed. But we disagreed as to her age. I said she was eighteen, Harris said she was twenty. The dispute between us waxed warm and I finally said, with a pretence of being in earnest—

'Well, there is one way to settle the matter—I will go and ask her.'

Harris said, sarcastically, 'Certainly, that is the thing to do. All you need to do is to use the common formula over here: go and say, "I'm an American!" Of course she will be glad to see you.'

Then he hinted that perhaps there was no great danger of my venturing to speak to her.

I said, 'I was only talking—I didn't intend to approach her, but I see you do not know what an intrepid person I am. I am not afraid of any woman that walks. I will go and speak to this young girl.'

The thing I had in my mind was not difficult. I meant to address her in the most respectful way and ask her to pardon me if her strong resemblance to a former acquaintance of mine was deceiving me; and when she should reply that the name I mentioned was not the name she bore, I meant to beg pardon again, most respectfully, and retire. There would be no harm done. I walked to her table, bowed to the gentleman, then turned to her, and was about to begin my little speech when she exclaimed—

'I *knew* I wasn't mistaken—I told John it was you! John said it probably wasn't, but I knew I was right. I said you would recognize me presently and come over; and I'm glad you did, for I shouldn't have felt much flattered if you had gone out of this room without recognizing me. Sit down, sit down—how odd it is—you are the last person I was ever expecting to see again.'

This was a stupefying surprise. It took my wits clear away for an instant. However, we shook hands cordially all round, and I sat down. But truly this was the tightest place I ever was in. I seemed to vaguely remember the girl's face now, but I had no idea where I had seen it before, or what name belonged with it. I immediately tried to get up a diversion about Swiss scenery, to keep her from launching into topics that might betray that I did not know her, but it was of no use, she went right along upon matters which interested her more.

'O dear, what a night that was, when the sea washed the forward boats away,—do you remember it?'

'O, *don't* I!' said I,—but I didn't. I wished the sea had washed the rudder and the smoke-stack and the captain away,—then I could have located this questioner.

'And don't you remember how frightened poor Mary was, and how she cried?'

'Indeed I do!' said I. 'Dear me, how it all comes back!'

I fervently wished it *would* come back,—but my memory was a blank. The wise way would have been to frankly own up; but I could not bring myself to do that, after the young girl had praised me so for recognizing her; so I went on, deeper and deeper into the mire, hoping for a chance clue, but never getting one. The Unrecognizable continued, with vivacity,—

'Do you know, George married Mary, after all?'

'Why, no! Did he?'

'Indeed he did. He said he did not believe she was half as much to blame as her father was, and I thought he was right. Didn't you?'

'Of course he was. It was a perfectly plain case. I always said so.'

'Why, no you didn't!—at least that summer.'

'O, no, not that summer. No, you are perfectly right about that. It was the following winter that I said it.'

'Well, as it turned out, Mary was not in the least to blame,—it was all her father's fault,—at least his and old Darley's.'

It was necessary to say something,—so I said—

'I always regarded Darley as a troublesome old thing.'

'So he was, but then they always had a great affection for him, although he had so many eccentricities. You remember that when the weather was the least cold, he would try to come into the house.'

I was rather afraid to proceed. Evidently Darley was not a man,—he must be some other kind of animal,—possibly a dog, maybe an elephant. However, tails are common to all animals, so I ventured to say,—

'And what a tail he had!'

'*One*! He had a thousand!'

This was bewildering. I did not quite know what to say, so I only said,—

'Yes, he *was* rather well fixed in the matter of tails.'

'For a negro, and a crazy one at that, I should say he was,' said she.

It was getting pretty sultry for me. I said to myself, 'Is it possible she is going to stop there, and wait for me to speak? If she does, the conversation is blocked. A negro with a thousand tails is a topic which a person cannot talk about fluently and instructively without more or less preparation. As to diving rashly into such a vast subject—'

But here, to my gratitude, she interrupted my thought by saying—

'Yes, when it came to tales of his crazy woes, there was simply no end to them if anybody would listen. His own quarters were comfortable enough, but when the weather was cold, the family were sure to have his company,—nothing could keep him out of the house. But they always bore it kindly because he had saved Tom's life, years before. You remember Tom?'

'O, perfectly. Fine fellow he was, too.'

'Yes, he was. And what a pretty little thing his child was!'

'You may well say that. I never saw a prettier child.'

'I used to delight to pet it and dandle it and play with it.'

'So did I.'

'You named it. What *was* that name? I can't call it to mind.'

It appeared to me that the ice was getting pretty thin, here. I would have given something to know what the child's sex was. However, I had the good luck to think of a name that would fit either sex,—so I brought it out,—

'I named it Frances.'

'From a relative, I suppose? But you named the one that died, too,—one that I never saw. What did you call that one?'

I was out of neutral names, but as the child was dead and she had never seen it, I thought I might risk a name for it and trust to luck. Therefore I said—

'I called that one Thomas Henry.'

She said, musingly,—

'That is very singular ... very singular.'

I sat still and let the cold sweat run down. I was in a good deal of trouble, but I believed I could worry through if she wouldn't ask me to name any more children. I wondered where the lightning was going to strike next. She was still ruminating over that last child's title, but presently she said,—

'I have always been sorry you were away at the time,—I would have had you name my child.'

'*Your* child! Are you married?'

'I have been married thirteen years.'

'Christened, you mean.'

'No, married. The youth by your side is my son.'

'It seems incredible,—even impossible. I do not mean any harm by it, but would you mind telling me if you are any over eighteen?—that is to say, will you tell me how old you are?'

'I was just nineteen the day of the storm we were talking about. That was my birthday.'

That did not help matters much, as I did not know the date of the storm. I tried to think of some non-committal thing to say, to keep up my end of the talk and render my poverty in the matter of reminiscences as little noticeable as possible, but I seemed to be about out of non-committal things. I was about to say, 'You haven't changed a bit since then,'—but that was risky. I thought of saying 'You have improved ever so much since then,'—but that wouldn't answer, of course. I was about to try a shy at the weather, for a saving change, when the girl slipped in ahead of me and said,—

'How I have enjoyed this talk over those happy old times,—haven't you?'

'I never have spent such a half hour in all my life before!' said I, with emotion; and I could have added, with a near approach to truth, 'and I would rather be scalped than spend another one like it.' I was holily grateful to be through with the ordeal, and was about to make my good-byes and get out, when the girl said—

'But there is one thing that is ever so puzzling to me.'

'Why, what is that?'

'That dead child's name. What did you say it was?'

Here was another balmy place to be in: I had forgotten the child's name; I hadn't imagined it would be needed again. However, I had to pretend to know, anyway, so I said—

'Joseph William.'

The youth at my side corrected me, and said—

'No,—Thomas Henry.'

I thanked him,—in words,—and said, with trepidation,—

'O yes,—I was thinking of another child that I named,—I have named a great many, and I get them confused,—this one *was* named Henry Thompson—

'Thomas Henry,' calmly interposed the boy.

I thanked him again,—strictly in words,—and stammered out—

'Thomas Henry,—yes, Thomas Henry was the poor child's name. I named him for Thomas,—er, Thomas Carlyle, the great author, you know,—and Henry—er,—er, Henry VIII. The parents were very grateful to have a child named Thomas Henry.'

'That makes it more singular than ever,' murmured my beautiful friend.

'Does it? Why?

'Because when the parents speak of that child now, they

always call it Susan Amelia.'

That spiked my gun. I could not say anything. I was entirely out of verbal obliquities; to go further would be to lie, and that I would not do; so I simply sat still and suffered—sat mutely and resignedly there, and sizzled—for I was being slowly fried to death in my own blushes. Presently the enemy laughed a happy laugh and said,—

'I *have* enjoyed this talk over old times, but you have not. I saw very soon that you were only pretending to know me, and so as I had wasted a compliment on you in the beginning, I made up my mind to punish you. And I have succeeded pretty well. I was glad to see that you knew George and Tom and Darley, for I had never heard of them before, and therefore could not be sure that you had; and I was glad to learn the names of those imaginary children, too. One can get quite a fund of information out of you if one goes at it cleverly. Mary and the storm, and the sweeping away of the forward boats, were facts—all the rest was fiction. Mary was my sister, her full name was Mary——. *Now* do you remember me?'

'Yes,' I said, 'I do remember you now; and you are as hard-hearted as you were thirteen years ago in that ship, else you wouldn't have punished me so. You haven't changed your nature nor your person, in any way at all; you look just as young as you did then, you are just as beautiful as you were then, and you have transmitted a deal of your comeliness to this fine boy. There,—if that speech moves you any, let's fly the flag of truce, with the understanding that I am conquered and confess it.'

All of which was agreed to and accomplished, on the spot. When I went back to Harris, I said—

'Now you see what a person with talent and address can do.'

'Excuse me, I see what a person of colossal ignorance and simplicity can do. The idea of your going and intruding on a party of strangers, that way, and talking for half an hour; why, I never heard of a man in his right mind doing such a thing before. What did you say to them?'

'I never said any harm. I merely asked the girl what her name was.'

'I don't doubt it. Upon my word I don't. I think you were capable of it. It was stupid of me to let you go over there, and make such an exhibition of yourself. But you know I couldn't really believe you would do such an inexcusable thing. What will those people think of us! But how did you say it?—I mean the manner of it. I hope you were not abrupt.'

'No, I was careful about that. I said, "My friend and I would like to know what your name is, if you don't mind." '

'No, that was not abrupt. There is a polish about it that does you infinite credit. And I am glad you put me in; that was a delicate attention which I appreciate at its full value. What did she do?'

'She didn't do anything in particular. She told me her name.'

'Simply told you her name. Do you mean to say she did not show any surprise?'

'Well, now I come to think, she did show something; may be it was surprise; I hadn't thought of that,—I took it for gratification.'

'O, undoubtedly you were right; it must have been gratification; it could not be otherwise than gratifying to be assaulted by a stranger with such a question as that. Then what did you do?'

'I offered my hand, and the party gave me a shake.'

'I saw it! I did not believe my own eyes, at the time. Did the gentleman say anything about cutting your throat?'

'No, they all seemed glad to see me, as far as I could judge.'

'And do you know, I believe they were. I think they said to themselves, "Doubtless this curiosity has got away from his keeper—let us amuse ourselves with him." There is no other way of accounting for their facile docility. You sat down. Did they *ask* you to sit down?'

'No, they did not ask me, but I supposed they did not think of it.'

'You have an unerring instinct. What else did you do? What did you talk about?'

'Well, I asked the girl how old she was.'

'*Un*doubtedly. Your delicacy is beyond praise. Go on, go on,—don't mind my apparent misery,—I always look so when I

am steeped in a profound and reverent joy. Go on, she told you
her age?'

'Yes, she told me her age, and all about her mother, and her
grandmother, and her other relations, and all about herself.'

'Did she volunteer these statistics?'

'No, not exactly that. I asked the questions and she answered
them.'

'This is divine. Go on,—it is not possible that you forgot to
inquire into her politics?'

'No, I thought of that. She is a democrat, her husband is a
republican, and both of them are Baptists.'

'Her husband? Is that child married?'

'She is not a child. She is married, and that is her husband
who is there with her.'

'Has she any children?'

'Yes,—seven and a half.'

'That is impossible.'

'No, she has them. She told me herself.'

'Well, but seven and a *half*. How do you make out the half?
Where does the half come in?'

'That is a child which she had by another husband,—not this
one, but another one,—so it is a step-child, and they do not
count it full measure.'

'Another husband? Has she had another husband?'

'Yes, four. This one is number four.'

'I do not believe a word of it. It is impossible upon its face. Is
that boy there her brother?'

'No, that is her son. He is her youngest. He is not as old as he
looks; he is only eleven and a half.'

'These things are all manifestly impossible. This is a wretched
business. It is a plain case: they simply took your measure, and
concluded to fill you up. They seem to have succeeded. I am
glad I am not in the mess; they may at least be charitable
enough to think there ain't a pair of us. Are they going to stay
here long?'

'No, they leave before noon.'

'There is one man who is deeply grateful for that. How did
you find out? You asked, I suppose?'

'No, along at first I inquired into their plans in a general way and they said they were going to be here a week, and make trips round about; but toward the end of the interview, when I said you and I would tour around with them with pleasure, and offered to bring you over and introduce you, they hesitated a little, and asked if you were from the same establishment that I was. I said you were, and then they said they had changed their mind, and considered it necessary to start at once and visit a sick relative in Siberia.'

'Ah me, you struck the summit! You struck the loftiest altitude of stupidity that human effort has ever reached. You shall have a monument of jackass's skulls as high as the Strasburg spire if you die before I do. They wanted to know if I was from the same "establishment" that you hail from, did they? What did they mean by "establishment?" '

'I don't know; it never occurred to me to ask.'

"Well, *I* know. They meant an asylum—an *idiot* asylum, do you understand? So they *do* think there's a pair of us, after all. Now, what do you think of yourself?'

'Well I don't know. I didn't know I was doing any harm; I didn't *mean* to do any harm. They were very nice people, and they seemed to like me.'

Harris made some rude remarks and left for his bedroom,—to break some furniture, he said. He was a singularly irascible man; any little thing would disturb his temper.

I had been well scorched by the young woman, but no matter, I took it out of Harris. One should always 'get even' in some way, else the sore place will go on hurting.

CHAPTER 26

The Hofkirche is celebrated for its organ concerts. All summer long the tourists flock to that church about six o'clock in the evening, and pay their franc, and listen to the noise. They don't stay to hear all of it, but get up and tramp out over the sounding stone floor, meeting late comers who tramp in in a sounding and vigorous way. This tramping back and forth is kept up nearly all the time, and is accented by the continuous slamming of the door, and the coughing and barking and sneezing of the crowd. Meantime, the big organ is booming and crashing and thundering away, doing its best to prove that it is the biggest and loudest organ in Europe, and that a tight little box of a church is the most favourable place to average and appreciate its powers in. It is true there were some soft and merciful passages occasionally, but the tramp-tramp of the tourists only allowed one to get fitful glimpses of them, so to speak. Then right away the organist would let go another avalanche.

The commerce of Lucerne consists mainly in gimcrackery of the souvenir sort; the shops are packed with Alpine crystals, photographs of scenery, and wooden and ivory carvings. I will not conceal the fact that miniature figures of the Lion of Lucerne are to be had in them. Millions of them. But they are libels upon him, every one of them. There is a subtle something about the majestic pathos of the original which the copyist cannot get. Even the sun fails to get it; both the photographer and the carver give you a dying lion, and that is all. The shape is right, the attitude is right, the proportions are right, but that indescribable something which makes the Lion of Lucerne the most mournful and moving piece of stone in the world, is wanting.

The Lion lies in his lair in the perpendicular face of a low cliff—for he is carved from the living rock of the cliff. His size is colossal, his attitude is noble. His head is bowed, the broken spear is sticking in his shoulder, his protecting paw rests upon the lilies of France. Vines hang down the cliff and wave in the wind, and a clear stream trickles from above and empties into a pond at the base, and in the smooth surface of the pond the Lion is mirrored, among the water lilies.

Around about are green trees and grass. The place is a sheltered, reposeful, woodland nook, remote from noise and stir and confusion—and all this is fitting, for lions do die in such places, and not on granite pedestals in public squares fenced with fancy iron railings. The Lion of Lucerne would be impressive anywhere, but nowhere so impressive as where he is.

Martyrdom is the luckiest fate that can befall some people. Louis XVI. did not die in his bed, consequently history is very gentle with him; she is charitable toward his failings, and she finds in him high virtues which are not usually considered to be virtues when they are lodged in kings. She makes him out to be a person with a meek and modest spirit, the heart of a female saint, and a wrong head. None of these qualities are kingly, but the last. Taken together they make a character which would have fared harshly at the hands of history if its owner had had the ill luck to miss martyrdom. With the best intentions to do the right thing, he always managed to do the wrong one. Moreover, nothing could get the female saint out of him. He knew, well enough, that in national emergencies he must not consider how he ought to act as a man, but how he ought to act as a king: so he honestly tried to sink the man and be the king—but it was a failure, he only succeeded in being the female saint. He was not instant in season, but out of season. He could not be persuaded to do a thing while it could do any good—he was iron, he was adamant in his stubbornness then—but as soon as the thing had reached a point where it would be positively harmful to do it, do it he would, and nothing could stop him. He did not do it because it would be harmful, but because he hoped it was not yet too late to achieve by it the good which it would have done if applied earlier. His comprehension was always a train or two behindhand. If a national toe required amputating, he could not see that it needed anything more than poulticing; when others saw that the mortification had reached the knee, he first perceived that the toe needed cutting off—so he cut it off; and he severed the leg at the knee when others saw that the disease had reached the thigh. He was good, and honest, and well meaning, in the matter of chasing national diseases, but he never could overtake one. As a private man, he would have been lovable; but viewed as a king, he was strictly contemptible.

His was a most unroyal career, but the most pitiable spectacle in it was his sentimental treachery to his Swiss guard on that memorable 10th of August, when he allowed those heroes to be massacred in his cause, and forbade them to shed the 'sacred French blood' purporting to be flowing in the veins of the red-capped mob of miscreants that was raging around the palace. He meant to be kingly, but he was only the female saint once more. Some of his biographers think that upon this occasion the spirit of Saint Louis had descended upon him. It must have found pretty cramped quarters. If Napoleon I. had stood in the shoes of Louis XVI. that day, instead of being merely a casual and unknown looker-on, there would be no Lion of Lucerne now, but there would be a well-stocked Communist graveyard in Paris, which would answer just as well to remember August 10 by.

Martyrdom made a saint of Marie Queen of Scots three hundred years ago, and she has hardly lost all of her saintship yet. Martyrdom made a saint of the trivial and foolish Marie Antoinette, and her biographers still keep her fragrant with the odour of sanctity to this day, while unconsciously proving upon almost every page they write that the only calamitous instinct which her husband lacked, she supplied—the instinct to root out and get rid of an honest, able, and loyal official, wherever she found him. The hideous but beneficent French Revolution would have been deferred, or would have fallen short of completeness, or even might not have happened at all, if Marie Antoinette had made the unwise mistake of not being born. The world owes a great deal to the French Revolution, and consequently to its two chief promoters, Louis the Poor in Spirit and his queen.

We did not buy any wooden images of the Lion, nor any ivory, or ebony, or marble, or chalk, or sugar, or chocolate ones, or even any photographic slanders of him. The truth is, these copies were so common, so universal, in the shops and everywhere, that they presently became as intolerable to the wearied eye as the latest popular melody usually becomes to the harassed ear. In Lucerne, too, the wood carvings of other sorts, which had been so pleasant to look upon when one saw them occasionally at home, soon began to fatigue us. We grew very tired of seeing wooden quails and chickens picking and strutting around clock-faces, and still more tired of seeing wooden images of the alleged chamois skipping about wooden rocks, or lying upon them in family groups, or peering alertly up from behind them. The first day, I would have bought a hundred and fifty of these clocks if I had had the money—and I did buy three—but on the third day the disease had run its course, I had convalesced, and was in the market once more—trying to sell. However, I had no luck; which was just as well, for the things will be pretty enough, no doubt, when I get them home.

For years my pet aversion had been the cuckoo clock; now here I was, at last, right in the creature's home; so wherever I went, that distressing '*hoo*'hoo! *hoo*'hoo!' was always in my ears. For a nervous man, this was a fine state of things. Some sounds are hatefuller than others, but no sound is quite so inane, and silly, and aggravating as the '*hoo*'hoo' of a cuckoo clock, I think. I bought one, and am carrying it home to a certain person; for I have always said that if the opportunity ever happened, I would do that man an ill turn. What I meant, was, that I would break one of his legs, or something of that sort; but in Lucerne I instantly saw that I could impair his mind. That would be more lasting, and more satisfactory every way. So I bought the cuckoo clock; and if I ever get home with it, he is 'my meat,' as they say in the mines. I thought of another candidate—a book reviewer, whom I could name if I wanted to—but after thinking it over, I didn't buy him a clock. I couldn't injure his mind.

We visited the two long covered wooden bridges which span the green and brilliant Reuss just below where it goes plunging and hurrahing out of the lake. These rambling, swaybacked tunnels are very attractive things, with their alcoved outlooks upon the lovely and inspiriting water. They contain two or three hundred queer old pictures, by old Swiss masters—old boss sign painters, who flourished before the decadence of art.

The lake is alive with fishes, plainly visible to the eye, for the water is very clear. The parapets in front of the hotels were usually fringed with fishers of all ages. One day I thought I would stop and see a fish caught. The result brought to my mind, very forcibly, a circumstance which I had not thought of before for twelve years. This one:—

The Man Who Put Up At Gadsby's

When my odd friend Riley and I were newspaper correspondents in Washington, in the winter of '67, we were coming down Pennsylvania Avenue one night, near midnight, in a driving storm of snow, when the flash of a street lamp fell upon a man who was eagerly tearing along in the opposite direction. This man instantly stopped and exclaimed—

'This is lucky! You are Mr. Riley, ain't you?'

Riley was the most self-possessed and solemnly deliberate person in the republic. He stopped, looked his man over from head to foot, and finally said—

'I am Mr. Riley. Did you happen to be looking for me?'

'That's just what I was doing,' said the man joyously, 'and it's the biggest luck in the world that I've found you. My name is Lykins. I'm one of the teachers of the High School, San Francisco. As soon as I heard the San Francisco postmastership was vacant, I made up my mind to get it—and here I am.'

'Yes,' said Riley, slowly, 'as you have remarked ... Mr. Lykins ... here you are. And have you got it?'

'Well, not exactly *got* it, but the next thing to it. I've brought a petition, signed by the Superintendent of Public Instruction and all the teachers, and by more than two hundred other people. Now I want you, if you'll be so good, to go around with me to the Pacific delegation; for I want to rush this thing through and get along home.'

'If the matter is so pressing, you will prefer that we visit the delegation to-night,' said Riley, in a voice which had nothing mocking in it—to an unaccustomed ear.

'Oh, to-night, by all means! I haven't got any time to fool around. I want their promise before I go to bed—I ain't the talking kind, I'm the *doing* kind!'

'Yes ... you've come to the right place for that. When did you arrive?'

'Just an hour ago.'

'When are you intending to leave?'

'For New York to-morrow evening—for San Francisco next morning.'

'Just so ... What are you going to do to-morrow?'

'*Do*! Why, I've got to go to the President with the petition and the delegation, and get the appointment, haven't I?'

'Yes ... very true ... that is correct. And then what?'

'Executive Session of the Senate at 2 p.m.—got to get the appointment confirmed—I reckon you'll grant that?'

'Yes ... yes,' said Riley, meditatively, 'you are right again. Then you take the train for New York in the evening and the steamer for San Francisco next morning?'

'That's it—that's the way I map it out.'

Riley considered a while, and then said—

'You couldn't stay ... a day ... well, say two days longer?'

'Bless your soul, no! It's not my style. I ain't a man to go fooling around—I'm a man that *does* things, I tell you.'

The storm was raging, the thick snow blowing in gusts. Riley stood silent, apparently deep in a reverie, during a minute or more, then he looked up and said—

'Have you ever heard about that man who put up at Gadsby's once? ... But I see you haven't.'

He backed Mr. Lykins against an iron fence, button-holed him, fastened him with his eye, like the Ancient Mariner, and proceeded to unfold his narrative as placidly and peacefully as if we were all stretched comfortably in a blossomy summer meadow, instead of being persecuted by a wintry midnight tempest:—

'I will tell you about that man. It was in Jackson's time. Gadsby's was the principal hotel then. Well, this man arrived from Tennessee about nine o'clock one morning, with a black coachman and a splendid four-horse carriage and an elegant dog, which he was evidently fond and proud of; he drove up before Gadsby's, and the clerk and the landlord and everybody rushed out to take charge of him; but he said "Never mind," and jumped out and told the coachman to wait—said he hadn't time to take anything to eat, he only had a little claim against the Government to collect, would run across the way to the Treasury and fetch the money, and then get right along back to Tennessee, for he was in considerable of a hurry.

'Well, about eleven o'clock that night he came back and ordered a bed and told them to put the horses up—said he would collect the claim in the morning. This was in January, you understand—January 1834—the 3rd of January—Wednesday.

'Well, on the 5th of February he sold the fine carriage and bought a cheap secondhand one—said it would answer just as well to take the money home in, and he didn't care for style.

'On the 11th of August he sold a pair of the fine horses—said he'd often thought a pair was better than four, to go over the rough mountain roads with where a body had to be careful about his driving—and there wasn't so much of his claim but he could lug the money home with a pair easy enough.

'On the 13th of December he sold another horse—said two warn't necessary to drag that old light vehicle with—in fact, one could snatch it along faster than was absolutely necessary, now that it was good solid winter weather, and the roads in splendid condition.

'On the 17th of February, 1835, he sold the old carriage and bought a cheap secondhand buggy—said a buggy was just the trick to skim along mushy, slushy early spring roads with, and he had always wanted to try a buggy on those mountain roads, anyway.

'On the 1st of August he sold the buggy and bought the remains of an old sulky—said he just wanted to see those green Tennesseeans stare and gawk when they saw him come a-ripping along in a sulky—didn't believe they'd ever heard of a sulky in their lives.

'Well, on the 29th of August he sold his coloured coachman—said he didn't need a coachman for a sulky—wouldn't be room enough for two in it anyway—and besides it wasn't every day that Providence sent a man a fool who was willing to pay nine hundred dollars for such a third-rate negro as that—been wanting to get rid of the creature for years, but didn't like to *throw* him away.

'Eighteen months later—that is to say, on the 15th of February, 1837—he sold the sulky and bought a saddle—said horseback riding was what the doctor had always recommended *him* to take, and dog'd if he wanted to risk *his* neck going over those mountain roads on wheels in the dead of winter, not if he knew himself.

On the 9th of April he sold the saddle—said he wasn't going to risk his life with any perishable saddle-girth that ever was made, over a rainy, miry April road, while he could ride bareback and know and feel he was safe—always *had* despised to ride on a saddle, anyway.

'On the 24th of April he sold his horse—said, "I'm just fifty-seven to-day, hale and hearty—it would be a pretty howdy-do for me to be wasting such a trip as that and such weather as this on a horse, when there ain't anything in the world so splendid as a tramp on foot through the fresh spring woods and over the cheery mountains, to a man that *is* a man—and I can make my dog carry my claim in a little bundle anyway, when it's collected. So to-morrow I'll be up bright and early, make my little old collection, and mosey off to Tennessee, on my own hind legs, with a rousing Good-bye to Gadsby's."

'On the 22nd of June he sold his dog—said, "Dern a dog, anyway, where you're just starting off on a rattling bully pleasure-tramp through the summer woods and hills—perfect nuisance—chases the squirrels, barks at everything, goes a-capering and splattering around in the fords—man can't get any chance to reflect and enjoy nature—and I'd a blamed sight rather carry the claim myself, it's a mighty sight safer; a dog's mighty uncertain in a financial way—always noticed it—well, *good*-bye, boys—last call,—I'm off for Tennessee, with a good leg and a gay heart, early in the morning!" '

There was a pause and a silence—except the noise of the wind and the pelting snow. Mr. Lykins said, impatiently—

'Well?'

Riley said—

'Well—that was thirty years ago.'

'Very well, very well—what of it?'

'I'm great friends with that old patriarch. He comes every evening to tell me good-bye. I saw him an hour ago—he's off for Tennessee early to-morrow morning—as usual; said he calculated to get his claim through and be off before night-owls like me have turned out of bed. The tears were in his eyes, he was so glad he was going to see his old Tennessee and his friends once more.'

Another silent pause. The stranger broke it—

'Is that all?'

'That is all.'

'Well, for the *time* of night, and the *kind* of night, it seems to me the story was full long enough. But what's it all *for*?'

'Oh, nothing in particular.'

'Well, where's the point of it?'

'Oh, there isn't any particular point to it. Only, if you are not in *too* much of a hurry to rush off to San Francisco with that post-office appointment, Mr. Lykins, I'd advise you to "*put up at Gadsby's*" for a spell, and take it easy. Good-bye. *God* bless you!'

So saying, Riley blandly turned on his heel and left the astonished school teacher standing there, amusing and motionless snow image shining in the broad glow of the street lamp.

He never got that post-office.

To go back to Lucerne and its fishers, I concluded, after about nine hours' waiting, that the man who proposes to tarry till he sees somebody hook one of those well-fed and experienced fishes will find it wisdom to 'put up at Gadsby's' and take it easy. It is likely that a fish has not been caught on that lake pier for forty years; but no matter, the patient fisher watches his cork there all the day long just the same, and seems to enjoy it. One may see the fisher-loafers just as thick and contented and happy and patient all along the Seine at Paris, but tradition says that the only thing ever caught there in modern times is a thing they don't fish for at all—the recent dog and the translated cat.

CHAPTER 27.

Close by the Lion of Lucerne is what they call the 'Glacier Garden,' and it is the only one in the world. It is on high ground. Four or five years ago some workmen who were digging foundations for a house came upon this interesting relic of a long-departed age. Scientific men perceived in it a confirmation of their theories concerning the glacial period; so through their persuasions the little tract of ground was bought, and permanently protected against being built upon. The soil was removed, and there lay the rasped and guttered track which the ancient glacier had made as it moved along upon its slow and tedious journey. This track was perforated by huge pot-shaped holes in the bed-rock, formed by the furious washing around in them of boulders by the turbulent torrent which flows beneath all glaciers. These huge round boulders still remain in the holes; they and the walls of the holes are worn smooth by the long-continued chafing which they gave each other in those old days. It took a mighty force to churn these big lumps of stone around in that vigorous way. The neighbouring country had a very different shape at that time—the valleys have risen up and become hills since, and the hills have become valleys. The boulders discovered in the pots had travelled a great distance, for there is no rock like them nearer than the distant Rhone Glacier.

For some days we were content to enjoy looking at the blue Lake Lucerne, and at the piled-up masses of snow mountains that border it all round: an enticing spectacle this last, for there is a strange and fascinating beauty and charm about a majestic snow peak, with the sun blazing upon it or the moonlight softly enriching it; but finally, we concluded to try a bit of excursioning around on a steamboat, and a dash on foot at the Rigi. Very well, we had a delightful trip to Fluelen, on a breezy sunny day. Everybody sat on the upper deck, on benches, under an awning; everybody talked, laughed, and exclaimed at the wonderful scenery. In truth, a trip on that lake is almost the perfection of pleasuring. The mountains were a never-ceasing marvel. Sometimes they rose straight up out of the lake, and towered aloft and overshadowed our pigmy steamer with their prodigious bulk in the most impressive way. Not snow-clad mountains these, yet they climbed high enough towards the sky to meet the clouds and veil their foreheads in them. They were not barren and repulsive, but clothed in green, and restful and pleasant to the eye; and they were so almost straight-up-and-down sometimes that one could not imagine a man being able to keep his footing upon such a surface, yet there are paths, and the Swiss people go up and down them every day.

Sometimes one of these monster precipices had the slight inclination of the huge ship-houses in dock-yards; then high aloft towards the sky it took a little stronger inclination, like that of a mansard roof, and perched on this dizzy mansard one's eye detected little things like martin-boxes, and presently perceived that these were the dwellings of peasants—an airy place for a home, truly. And suppose a peasant should walk in his sleep, or his child should fall out of the front yard? The friends would have a tedious long journey down out of those cloud-heights, before they found the remains. And yet those faraway homes looked ever so seductive; they were so remote from the troubled world, they reposed in such an atmosphere of peace and of dreams—surely no one who had learned to live up there would ever want to live on a meaner level.

We swept through the prettiest little curving arms of the lake, among these colossal green walls, enjoying new delights always as the stately panorama unfolded itself before us and re-rolled and hid itself behind us; and now and then we had the thrilling surprise of bursting suddenly upon a tremendous white mass like the distant and dominating Jungfrau, or some kindred giant, looming head and shoulders above a tumbled waste of lesser Alps.

Once while I was hungrily taking in one of these surprises, and doing my best to get all I possibly could of it while it should last, I was interrupted by a young and care-free voice—

'You're an American, I think? So'm I.'

He was about eighteen, or possibly nineteen; slender, and of medium height; open, frank, happy face; a restless but independent eye; a snub nose, which had the air of drawing back with a decent reserve from the silky new-born moustache below it until it should be introduced; a loosely-hung jaw, calculated to work easily in the sockets. He wore a low-crowned, narrow-brimmed straw hat, with a broad blue ribbon around it, which had a white anchor embroidered on it in front; nobby short-tailed coat, pantaloons, vest—all trim and neat, and up with the fashion; red-striped stockings, very low—quarter patent leather shoes, tied with black ribbon; blue ribbon around his neck, wide-open collar; tiny diamond studs, wrinkleless kids, projecting cuffs, fastened with large oxydised silver sleeve-buttons bearing the device of a dog's face—English pug. He carried a slim cane, surmounted with an English pug's head with red glass eyes. Under his arm he carried a German Grammar, Otto's. His hair was short, straight, and smooth; and presently, when he turned his head a moment, I saw that it was nicely parted behind. He took a cigarette out of a dainty box, stuck it into a meerschaum holder which he carried in a morocco case, and reached for my cigar. While he was lighting, I said—

'Yes, I am an American.'

'I knew it. I can always tell them. What ship did you come over in?'

' "Holsatia." '

'We came in the "Batavia"—Cunard, you know. What kind of a passage did you have?'

'Tolerably rough.'

'So did we. Captain said he'd hardly ever seen it rougher. Where are you from?'

'New England.'

'So'm I. I'm from New Bloomfield. Anybody with you?'

'Yes, a friend.'

'Our whole family's along. It's awful slow going around alone, don't you think so.'

'Rather slow.'

'Ever been over here before?'

'Yes.'

'I haven't. My first trip. But we've been all around—Paris, and everywhere. I'm to enter Harvard next year. Studying German all the time now. Can't enter till I know German. I know considerable French. I get along pretty well in Paris, or anywhere where they speak French. What hotel are you stopping at?'

'Schweitzerhof.'

'No! Is that so? I never see you in the reception room. I go to the reception room a good deal of the time, because there's so many Americans there. I make lots of acquaintances. I know an American as soon as I see him, and so I speak to him and make his acquaintance. I like to be always making acquaintances, don't you?'

'Lord, yes!'

'You see it breaks up a trip like this, first rate. I never get bored on a trip like this, if I can make acquaintances and have somebody to talk to. But I think a trip like this would be an awful bore if a body couldn't find anybody to get acquainted with and talk to on a trip like this. I'm fond of talking, ain't you?'

'Passionately.'

'Have you felt bored on this trip?'

'Not all the time, part of it.'

'That's it—you see you ought to go around and get acquainted, and talk. That's my way. That's the way I always do—I just go 'round, 'round, 'round, and talk, talk, talk —never get bored. You been up the Rigi yet?'

'No.'

'Going?'

'I think so.'

'What hotel you going to stop at?'

'I don't know. Is there more than one?'

'Three. You stop at the Schreiber—you'll find it full of Americans. What ship did you say you came over in?'

' "City of Antwerp" '

'German, I guess. You going to Geneva?'

'Yes.'

'What hotel you going to stop at?'

'Hôtel de l'Ecu de Genève.'

'Don't you do it! No Americans there! You stop at one of those big hotels over the bridge—they're packed full of Americans.'

'But I want to practise my Arabic.'

'Good gracious, do you speak Arabic?'

'Yes—well enough to get along.'

'Why, hang it, you won't get along in Geneva—*they* don't speak Arabic, they speak French. What hotel are you stopping at here?'

'Hôtel Pension-Beaurivage.'

'Sho, you ought to stop at the Schweitzerhof. Didn't you know the Schweitzerhof was the best hotel in Switzerland? Look at your Baedeker.'

'Yes, I know—but I had an idea there warn't any Americans there.'

'No Americans! Why, bless your soul, it's just alive with them! I'm in the great reception room most all the time. I make lots of acquaintances there. Not as many as I did at first, because now only the new ones stop in there—the others go right along through. Where are you from?'

'Arkansaw.'

'Is that so? I'm from New England—New Bloomfield's my town when I'm at home. I'm having a mighty good time to-day, ain't you?'

'Divine.'

'That's what I call it. I like this knocking around, loose and easy, and making acquaintances and talking. I know an American soon as I see him; so I go and speak to him and make his acquaintance. I ain't ever bored on a trip like this if I can

make new acquaintances and talk. I'm awful fond of talking
when I can get hold of the right kind of a person, ain't you?'

'I prefer it to any other dissipation.'

'That's my notion, too. Now some people like to take a book
and sit down and read, and read, and read, or moon around
yawping at the lake or these mountains and things, but that ain't
my way; no, sir, if they like it, let 'em do it, I don't object; but as
for me, talking's what *I* like. You been up the Rigi?'

'Yes.'

'What hotel did you stop at?'

'Schreiber.'

'That's the place!—I stopped there too. *Full* of Americans,
wasn't it? It always is—always is. That's what they say.
Everybody says that. What ship did you come over in?'

' "Ville de Paris." '

'French, I reckon. What kind of a passage did ... Excuse me
a minute, there's some Americans I haven't seen before.'

And away he went. He went uninjured too. I had the
murderous impulse to harpoon him in the back with my
alpenstock, but as I raised the weapon the disposition left me; I
found I hadn't the heart to kill him, he was such a joyous,
innocent, good-natured numskull.

Half an hour later I was sitting on a bench inspecting, with
strong interest, a noble monolith which we were skimming
by—a monolith not shaped by man, but by Nature's free, great
hand—a massy pyramidal rock eighty feet high, devised by
Nature ten million years ago against the day when a man worthy
of it should need it for his monument. The time came at last, and
now this grand remembrancer bears Schiller's name in huge
letters upon its face. Curiously enough, this rock was not
degraded or defiled in any way. It is said that two years ago a
stranger let himself down from the top of it with ropes and
pulleys, and painted all over it, in blue letters bigger than those
in Schiller's name, these words:—

'Try Sozodont;'
'Buy Sun Stove Polish;'
'Helmbold's Buchu;'
'Try Benzaline For The Blood.'

He was captured, and it turned out that he was an American. Upon his trial the judge said to him:—

'You are from a land where any insolent that wants to is privileged to profane and insult Nature, and, through her, Nature's God, if by so doing he can put a sordid penny in his pocket. But here the case is different. Because you are a foreigner and ignorant, I will make your sentence light: if you were a native, I would deal strenuously with you. Hear and obey. You will immediately remove every trace of your offensive work from the Schiller monument; you will pay a fine of ten thousand francs; you will suffer two years' imprisonment at hard labour; you will then be horsewhipped, tarred and feathered, deprived of your ears, ridden on a rail to the confines of the canton, and banished for ever. The severer penalties are omitted in your case—not as a grace to you, but to that great republic which had the misfortune to give you birth.'

The steamer's benches were ranged back across the deck. My back hair was mingling innocently with the back hair of a couple of ladies. Presently they were addressed by someone and I overheard this conversation—

'You are Americans, I think? So'm I.'

'Yes—we are Americans.'

'I knew it—I can always tell them. What ship did you come over in?'

' "City of Chester." '

'Oh, yes—Inman line. We came in the "Batavia"—Cunard, you know. What kind of a passage did you have?'

'Pretty fair.'

'That was luck. We had it awful rough. Captain said he'd hardly ever seen it rougher. Where are you from?'

'New Jersey.'

'So'm I.'

'So'm I. No—I didn't mean that: I'm from New England. New Bloomfield's my place. These your children?—belong to both of you?'

'Only to one of us; they are mine; my friend is not married.'

'Single, I reckon? So'm I. Are you two ladies travelling alone?'

'No—my husband is with us.'

'Our whole family's along. It's awful slow, going around

alone—don't you think so?'

'I suppose it must be.'

'Hi, there's Mount Pilatus coming in sight again. Named after Pontius Pilate, you know, that shot the apple off of William Tell's head. Guidebook tells all about it, they say. I didn't read it—an American told me. I don't read when I'm knocking around like this, having a good time. Did you ever see the chapel where William Tell used to preach?'

'I did not know he ever preached there.'

'Oh, yes, he did. That American told me so. He don't ever shut up his guidebook. He knows more about this lake than the fishes in it. Besides, they *call* it "Tell's Chapel"—you know that yourself. You ever been over here before?'

'Yes.'

'I haven't. It's my first trip. But we've been all around—Paris, and everywhere. I'm to enter Harvard next year. Studying German all the time now. Can't enter till I know German. This book's Otto's Grammar. It's a mighty good book to get the *ich habe gehabt haben's* out of. But I don't really study when I'm knocking around this way. If the notion takes me, I just run over my little old *ich habe gehabt, du hast gehabt, er hat gehabt, wir haben gehabt, ihr habet gehabt, sie haben gehabt*—kind of "Now-I-lay-me-down-to-sleep" fashion, you know, and after that, maybe I don't buckle to it again for three days. It's awful undermining to the intellect, German is; you want to take it in small doses, or first you know your brains all run together, and you feel them sloshing around in your head same as so much drawn butter. But French is different; *French* ain't anything. I ain't any more afraid of French than a tramp's afraid of pie; I can rattle off my little *j'ai, tu as, il a,* and the rest of it, just as easy as a-b-c. I get along pretty well in Paris, or anywhere where they speak French. What hotel you stopping at?'

'The Schweitzerhof.'

'No! is that so? I never see you in the big reception room. I go in there a good deal of the time, because there's so many Americans there. I make lots of acquaintances. You been up the Rigi yet?'

'No.'

'Going?'

'We think of it.'

'What hotel you going to stop at?'

'I don't know.'

'Well, then, you stop at the Schreiber—it's full of Americans. What ship did you come over in?'

' "City of Chester." '

'Oh, yes, I remember I asked you that before. But I always ask everybody what ship they came over in, and so sometimes I forget and ask again. You going to Geneva?'

'Yes.'

'What hotel you going to stop at?'

'We expect to stop in a pension.'

'I don't hardly believe you'll like that; there's very few Americans in the pensions. What hotel are you stopping at here?'

'The Schweitzerhof.'

'Oh, yes, I asked you that before, too. But I always ask everybody what hotel they're stopping at, and so I've got my head all mixed up with hotels. But it makes talk, and I love to talk. It refreshes me up so—don't it you—on a trip like this?'

'Yes—sometimes.'

'Well, it does me, too. As long as I'm talking I never feel bored—ain't that the way with you?'

'Yes—generally. But there are exceptions to the rule.'

'Oh, of course. *I* don't care to talk to everybody *myself*. If a person starts in to jabber-jabber-jabber about scenery, and history, and pictures, and all sorts of tiresome things, I get the fan-tods mighty soon. I say, "Well, I must be going now—hope I'll see you again"—and then I take a walk. Where you from?'

'New Jersey.'

'Why, bother it all, I asked you *that* before, too. Have you seen the Lion of Lucerne?'

'Not yet.'

'Nor I, either. But the man who told me about Mount Pilatus says it's one of the things to see. It's twenty-eight feet long. It don't seem reasonable, but he said so, anyway. He saw it yesterday; said it was dying then, so I reckon it's dead by this time. But that ain't any matter, of course they'll stuff it. Did you say the children are yours—or *hers*?'

'Mine.'

'Oh, so you did. Are you going up the ... no, I asked you that. What ship ... no, I asked you that, too. What hotel are you ... no, you told me that. Let me see ... um ... oh, what kind of a voy ... no, we've been over that ground too. Um ... um ... well, I believe that is all. *Bonjour*—I am very glad to have made your acquaintance, ladies. *Guten Tag*.'

CHAPTER 28

The Rigi-Kulm is an imposing Alpine mass, 6,000 feet high, which stands by itself, and commands a mighty prospect of blue lakes, green valleys, and snowy mountains—a compact and magnificent picture three hundred miles in circumference. The ascent is made by rail, or horseback, or on foot, as one may prefer. I and my agent panoplied ourselves in walking costume, one bright morning, and started down the lake on the steamboat; we got ashore at the village of Wäggis, three-quarters of an hour distant from Lucerne. This village is at the foot of the mountain.

We were soon tramping leisurely up the leafy mule-path, and then the talk began to flow, as usual. It was twelve o'clock noon, and a breezy, cloudless day; the ascent was gradual, and the glimpses, from under the curtaining boughs, of blue water, and tiny sail-boats, and beetling cliffs, were as charming as glimpses of dreamland. All the circumstances were perfect—and the anticipations, too, for we should soon be enjoying, for the first time, that wonderful spectacle, an Alpine sunrise—the object of our journey. There was (apparently) no real need to hurry, for the guide-book made the walking distance from Wäggis to the summit only three hours and a quarter. I say 'apparently,' because the guide-book had already fooled us once—about the distance from Allerheiligen to Oppenau—and for aught I knew it might be getting ready to fool us again. We were only certain as to the altitudes—we calculated to find out for ourselves how many hours it is from the bottom to the top. The summit is 6,000 feet above the sea, but only 4,500 feet above the lake. When we had walked half an hour, we were fairly into the swing and humour of the undertaking, so we cleared for action; that is to say, we got a boy whom we met to carry our alpenstocks, and satchels, and overcoats and things for us; that left us free for business.

I suppose we must have stopped oftener to stretch out on the grass in the shade and take a bit of a smoke than this boy was used to, for presently he asked if it had been our idea to hire him by the job or by the year. We told him he could move along if he was in a hurry. He said he wasn't in such a very particular hurry, but he wanted to get to the top while he was young. We told him to clear out then, and leave the things at the uppermost hotel and say we should be along presently. He said he would secure us a hotel if he could, but if they were all full he would ask them to build another one and hurry up and get the paint and plaster dry against we arrived. Still gently chaffing us, he pushed ahead, up the trail, and soon disappeared. By six o'clock we were pretty high up in the air, and the view of lake and mountains had greatly grown in breadth and interest. We halted a while at a little public-house, where we had bread and cheese and a quart or two of fresh milk, out on the porch, with the big panorama all before us—and then moved on again.

Ten minutes afterwards we met a hot, red-faced man plunging down the mountain, with mighty strides, swinging his alpenstock ahead of him and taking a grip on the ground with its iron point to support these big strides. He stopped, fanned himself with his hat, swabbed the perspiration from his face and neck with a red handkerchief, panted a moment or two, and asked how far it was to Wäggis. I said three hours. He looked surprised and said—

'Why, it seems as if I could toss a biscuit into the lake from here, it's so close by. Is that an inn there?'

I said it was.

'Well,' said he, 'I can't stand another three hours, I've had enough for to-day: I'll take a bed there.'

I asked—

'Are we nearly to the top?'

'Nearly to the *top*! Why, bless your soul, you haven't really started yet.'

I said we would put up at the inn, too. So we turned back and ordered a hot supper, and had quite a jolly evening of it with this Englishman.

The German landlady gave us neat rooms and nice beds, and when I and my agent turned in, it was with the resolution to be up early and make the utmost of our first Alpine sunrise. But of course we were dead tired, and slept like policemen; so when we awoke in the morning and ran to the window it was already too late, because it was half-past eleven. It was a sharp disappointment. However, we ordered breakfast and told the landlady to call the Englishman, but she said he was already up and off at daybreak—and swearing mad about something or other. We could not find out what the matter was. He had asked the landlady the altitude of her place above the level of the lake, and she had told him fourteen hundred and ninety-five feet. That was all that was said; then he lost his temper. He said that between —— fools and guide-books, a man could acquire ignorance enough in twenty-four hours in a country like this to last him a year. Harris believed our boy had been loading him up with misinformation; and this was probably the case, for his epithet described that boy to a dot.

We got under way about the turn of noon, and pulled out for the summit again, with a fresh and vigorous step. When we had got about two hundred yards, and stopped to rest, I glanced to the left while I was lighting my pipe, and in the distance detected a long worm of black smoke crawling lazily up the steep mountain. Of course that was the locomotive. We propped ourselves on our elbows at once, to gaze, for we had never seen a mountain railway yet. Presently we could make out the train. It seemed incredible that the thing should creep straight up a sharp slant like the roof of a house—but there it was, and it was doing that very miracle.

In the course of a couple of hours we reached a fine breezy altitude where the little shepherd-huts had big stones all over their roofs to hold them down to the earth when the great storms rage. The country was wild and rocky about here, but there were plenty of trees, plenty of moss, and grass.

Away off on the opposite shore of the lake we could see some villages, and now for the first time we could observe the real difference between their proportions and those of the giant mountains at whose feet they slept. When one is in one of those villages it seems spacious, and its houses seem high and not out of proportion to the mountain that overhangs them—but from our altitude, what a change! The mountains were bigger and grander than ever, as they stood there thinking their solemn thoughts with their heads in the drifting clouds, but the villages at their feet—when the painstaking eye could trace them up and find them—were so reduced, so almost invisible, and lay so flat against the ground, that the exactest simile I can devise is to compare them to ant-deposits of granulated dirt overshadowed by the huge bulk of a cathedral. The steamboats skimming along under the stupendous precipices were diminished by distance to the daintiest little toys, the sail-boats and row-boats to shallops proper for fairies that keep house in the cups of lilies and ride to court on the backs of bumble-bees.

Presently we came upon half a dozen sheep nibbling grass in the spray of a stream of clear water that sprang from a rock wall a hundred feet high, and all at once our ears were startled with a melodious 'Lul...l...l...lul-lul-*la*hee-o-o-o!' pealing joyously from a near but invisible source, and recognised that we were hearing for the first time the famous Alpine *jodel* in its own native wilds. And we recognised, also, that it was that sort of quaint commingling of baritone and falsetto which at home we call 'Tyrolese warbling.'

The jodling (pronounced *yodling*—emphasis on the *o*) continued, and was very pleasant and inspiriting to hear. Now the jodler appeared—a shepherd boy of sixteen—and in our gladness and gratitude we gave him a franc to jodel some more. So he jodeled, and we listened. We moved on presently, and he generously jodeled us out of sight. After about fifteen minutes, we came across another shepherd boy who was jodeling, and gave him half a franc to keep it up. He also jodeled us out of

sight. After that, we found a jodler every ten minutes; we gave
the first one eight cents, the second one six cents, the third one
four cents, the fourth one a penny, contributed nothing to Nos.
5, 6, 7, and during the remainder of the day hired the rest of the
jodlers, at a franc apiece, not to jodel any more. There is
somewhat too much of this jodling in the Alps.

About the middle of the afternoon we passed through a
prodigious natural gateway called the Felsenthor, formed by two
enormous upright rocks, with a third lying across the top. There
was a very attractive little hotel close by, but our energies were
not conquered yet, so we went on.

Three hours afterward we came to the railway track. It was
planted straight up the mountain with the slant of a ladder that
leans against a house and it seemed to us that a man would need
good nerves who proposed to travel up it or down it either.

During the latter part of the afternoon we cooled our roasting
interiors with ice-cold water from clear streams, the only really
satisfying water we had tasted since we left home, for at the
hotels on the Continent they merely give you a tumbler of ice to
soak your water in, and that only modifies its hotness, doesn't
make it cold. Water can only be made cold enough for summer
comfort by being prepared in a refrigerator or a closed ice-
pitcher. Europeans say ice water impairs digestion. How do they
know?—they never drink any.

At ten minutes past six we reached the Kaltbad station, where
there is a spacious hotel with great verandahs which command a
majestic expanse of lake and mountain scenery. We were pretty
well fagged out now, but as we did not wish to miss the Alpine
sunrise, we got through with our dinner as quickly as possible
and hurried off to bed. It was unspeakably comfortable to
stretch our weary limbs between the cool damp sheets. And how
we did sleep!—for there is no opiate like Alpine pedestrianism.

In the morning we both awoke and leaped out of bed at the
same instant and ran and stripped aside the window curtains,
but we suffered a bitter disappointment again: it was already
half-past three in the afternoon.

We dressed sullenly and in ill spirits, each accusing the other
of over-sleeping. Harris said if we had brought the courier along,

as we ought to have done, we should not have missed these sunrises. I said he knew very well that one of us would have had to sit up and wake the courier; and I added that we were having trouble enough to take care of ourselves on this climb, without having to take care of a courier besides.

During breakfast our spirits came up a little, since we found by the guide-book that in the hotels on the summit the tourist is not left to trust to luck for his sunrise, but is roused betimes by a man who goes through the halls with a great Alpine horn, blowing blasts that would raise the dead. And there was another consoling thing: the guide-book said that up there on the summit the guests did not wait to dress much, but seized a red bed-blanket and sailed out arrayed like an Indian. This was good; this would be romantic; two hundred and fifty people grouped on the windy summit, with their hair flying and their red blankets flapping, in the solemn presence of the snowy ranges and the messenger splendours of the coming sun, would be a striking and memorable spectacle. So it was good luck, not ill luck, that we had missed those other sunrises.

We were informed by the guide-book that we were now 3,228 feet above the level of the lake—therefore full two-thirds of our journey had been accomplished. We got away at a quarter past four p.m.; a hundred yards above the hotel the railway divided; one track went straight up the steep hill, the other one turned square off to the right, with a very slight grade. We took the latter, and followed it more than a mile, turned a rocky corner and came in sight of a handsome new hotel. If we had gone on, we should have arrived at the summit, but Harris preferred to ask a lot of questions—as usual, of a man who didn't know anything—and he told us to go back and follow the other route. We did so. We could ill afford this loss of time.

We climbed and climbed; and we kept on climbing; we reached about forty summits; but there was always another one just ahead. It came on to rain, and it rained in dead earnest. We were soaked through, and it was bitter cold. Next a smoky fog of clouds covered the whole region densely, and we took to the railway ties to keep from getting lost. Sometimes we slopped along in a narrow path on the left-hand side of the track, but by-

and-by, when the fog blew aside a little and we saw that we were treading the rampart of a precipice, and that our left elbows were projecting over a perfectly boundless and bottomless vacancy, we gasped and jumped for the ties again.

The night shut down, dark, and drizzly, and cold. About eight in the evening the fog lifted and showed us a well-worn path which led up a very steep rise to the left. We took it, and as soon as we had got far enough from the railway to render the finding it again an impossibility, the fog shut down on us once more.

We were in a bleak unsheltered place now, and had to trudge right along in order to keep warm, though we rather expected to go over a precipice sooner or later. About nine o'clock we made an important discovery—that we were not in any path. We groped around a while on our hands and knees, but could not find it; so we sat down in the mud and the wet scant grass to wait. We were terrified into this by being suddenly confronted with a vast body which showed itself vaguely for an instant, and in the next instant was smothered in the fog again. It was really the hotel we were after, monstrously magnified by the fog, but we took it for the face of a precipice and decided not to try to claw up it.

We sat there an hour, with chattering teeth and quivering bodies, and quarrelled over all sorts of trifles, but gave most of our attention to abusing each other for the stupidity of deserting the railway track. We sat with our backs to the precipice, because what little wind there was came from that quarter. At some time or other the fog thinned a little; we did not know when, for we were facing the empty universe and the thinness could not show; but at last Harris happened to look around, and there stood a huge, dim, spectral hotel where the precipice had been. One could faintly discern the windows and chimneys, and a dull blur of lights. Our first emotion was deep, unutterable gratitude, our next was a foolish rage, born of the suspicion that possibly the hotel had been visible three-quarters of an hour while we sat there in those cold puddles quarrelling.

Yes, it was the Rigi-Kulm hotel—the one that occupies the extreme summit, and whose remote little sparkle of lights we had often seen glinting high aloft among the stars from our balcony away down yonder in Lucerne. The crusty portier and the crusty clerks gave us the surly reception which their kind deal in in prosperous times, but by mollifying them with an extra display of obsequiousness and servility we finally got them to show us to the room which our boy had engaged for us.

We got into some dry clothing, and while our supper was preparing we loafed forsakenly through a couple of vast cavernous drawing-rooms, one of which had a stove in it. This stove was in a corner, and densely walled around with people. We could not get near the fire, so we moved at large in the arctic spaces, among a multitude of people who sat silent, smileless, forlorn, and shivering—thinking what fools they were to come, perhaps. There were some Americans, and some Germans, but one could see that the great majority were English.

We lounged into an apartment where there was a great crowd, to see what was going on. It was a memento-magazine. The tourists were eagerly buying all sorts and styles of paper-cutters, marked 'Souvenir of the Rigi,' with handles made of the little curved horn of the ostensible chamois; there were all manner of wooden goblets and such things, similarly marked. I was going to buy a paper-cutter, but I believed I could remember the cold comfort of the Rigi-Kulm without it, so I smothered the impulse.

Supper warmed us, and we went immediately to bed; but first, as Mr. Baedeker requests all tourists to call his attention to any errors which they may find in his guide-books, I dropped him a line to inform him that when he said the foot journey from Wäggis to the summit was only three hours and a quarter, he missed it by just about three days. I had previously informed him of his mistake about the distance from Allerheiligen to Oppenau, and had also informed the Ordnance Department of the German Government of the same error in the Imperial maps. I will add, here, that I never got any answer to these letters, or any thanks from either of those sources; and what is still more discourteous, these corrections have not been made, either in the maps or the guide-books. But I will write again when I get time, for my letters may have miscarried.

We curled up in the clammy beds, and went to sleep without recking. We were so sodden with fatigue that we never stirred nor turned over till the blooming blasts of the Alpine horn aroused us. It may well be imagined that we did not lose any time. We snatched on a few odds and ends of clothing, cocooned ourselves in the proper red blankets and plunged along the halls and out into the whistling wind bare-headed. We saw a tall wooden scaffolding on the very peak of the summit, a hundred yards away, and made for it. We rushed up the stairs to the top of this scaffolding, and stood there, above the vast outlying world, with hair flying and ruddy blankets waving and cracking in the fierce breeze.

'Fifteen minutes too late, at least!' said Harris, in a vexed voice. 'The sun is clear above the horizon.'

'No matter,' I said, 'it is a most magnificent spectacle, and we will see it do the rest of its rising, anyway.'

In a moment we were deeply absorbed in the marvel before us, and dead to everything else. The great cloud-barred disk of the sun stood just above a limitless expanse of tossing white-caps—so to speak—a billowy chaos of massy mountain domes and peaks draped in imperishable snow, and flooded with an opaline glory of changing and dissolving splendours, whilst through rifts in a black cloud-bank above the sun, radiating lances of diamond dust shot to the zenith. The cloven valleys of the lower world swam in a tinted mist which veiled the ruggedness of their crags and ribs and ragged forests, and turned all the forbidding region into a soft and rich and sensuous paradise.

We could not speak. We could hardly breathe. We could only gaze in drunken ecstasy and drink it in. Presently Harris exclaimed—

'Why, ——nation, it's going *down!*'

Perfectly true. We had missed the *morning* horn-blow, and slept all day. This was stupefying. Harris said,—

'Look here, the sun isn't the spectacle—it's *us*—stacked up here on top of this gallows, in these idiotic blankets, and two hundred and fifty well-dressed men and women down here gawking up at us and not caring a straw whether the sun rises or sets, as long as they've got such a ridiculous spectacle as this to set down in their memorandum-books. They seem to be laughing their ribs loose, and there's one girl there that appears to be going all to pieces. I never saw such a man as you before. I think you are the very last possibility in the way of an ass.'

'What have *I* done?' I answered with heat.

'What have you done? You've got up at half-past seven o'clock in the evening to see the sun rise, that's what you've done.'

'And have you done any better, I'd like to know? I always used to get up with the lark, till I came under the petrifying influence of your turgid intellect.'

'*You* used to get up with the lark! Oh, no doubt; you'll get up with the hangman one of these days. But you ought to be ashamed to be jawing here like this in a red blanket, on a forty-foot scaffold on top of the Alps. And no end of people down here to boot; this isn't any place for an exhibition of temper.'

And so the customary quarrel went on. When the sun was fairly down, we slipped back to the hotel in the charitable gloaming, and went to bed again. We had encountered the horn-blower on the way, and he had tried to collect compensation, not only for announcing the sunset, which we did see, but for the sunrise, which we had totally missed, but we said no, we only took our solar rations on the 'European plain'—pay for what you get. He promised to make us hear his horn in the morning, if we were alive.

CHAPTER 29

He kept his word. We heard his horn and instantly got up. It was dark and cold and wretched. As I fumbled around for the matches, knocking things down with my quaking hands, I wished the sun would rise in the middle of the day, when it was warm and bright and cheerful, and one wasn't sleepy. We proceeded to dress by the gloom of a couple of sickly candles, but we could hardly button anything, our hands shook so. I thought of how many happy people there were in Europe, Asia, and America, and everywhere, who were sleeping peacefully in their beds and did not have to get up and see the Rigi sunrise—people who did not appreciate their advantage, as like as not, but would get up in the morning wanting more boons of Providence. While thinking these thoughts I yawned, in a rather ample way, and my upper teeth got hitched on a rail over the door, and whilst I was mounting a chair to free myself, Harris drew the window curtain and said—

'Oh, this is luck! We shan't have to go out at all; yonder are the mountains, in full view.'

That was glad news, indeed. It made us cheerful right away. One could see the grand Alpine masses dimly outlined against the black firmament, and one or two faint stars blinking through rifts in the night. Fully clothed, and wrapped in blankets, we huddled ourselves up, by the window, with lighted pipes, and fell into chat, while we waited in exceeding comfort to see how an

Alpine sunrise was going to look by candle-light. By-and-by a delicate, spiritual sort of effulgence spread itself by imperceptible degrees over the loftiest altitudes of the snowy wastes—but there the effort seemed to stop. I said, presently—

'There is a hitch about this sunrise somewhere. It doesn't seem to go. What do you reckon is the matter with it?'

'I don't know. It appears to hang fire somewhere. I never saw a sunrise act like that before. Can it be that the hotel is playing anything on us?'

'Of course not. The hotel merely has a property interest in the sun, it has nothing to do with the management of it. It is a precarious kind of property, too; a succession of total eclipses would probably ruin this tavern. Now what can be the matter with this sunrise?'

Harris jumped up and said—

'I've got it! I know what's the matter with it! We've been looking at the place where the sun *set* last night!'

'It is perfectly true! Why couldn't you have thought of that sooner? Now we've lost another one. And all through your blundering. It was exactly like you to light a pipe and sit down to wait for the sun to rise in the west.'

'It was exactly like to to find out the mistake, too. You never would have found it out. I find out all the mistakes.'

'You make them all, too, else your most valuable faculty would be wasted on you. But don't stop to quarrel now; maybe we are not too late yet.'

But we were. The sun was well up when we got to the exhibition ground.

On our way up we met the crowd returning—men and women dressed in all sorts of queer costumes, and exhibiting all degrees of cold and wretchedness in their gaits and countenances. A dozen still remained on the ground when we reached there, huddled together about the scaffold with their backs to the bitter wind. They had their red guide-books open at the diagram of the view, and were painfully picking out the several mountains, and trying to impress their names and positions on their memories. It was one of the saddest sights I ever saw.

Two sides of this place were guarded by railings, to keep people from being blown over the precipices. The view, looking sheer down into the broad valley, eastward, from this great elevation—almost a perpendicular mile—was very quaint and curious. Counties, towns, hilly ribs and ridges, wide stretches of green meadow, great forest tracks, winding streams, a dozen blue lakes, a flock of busy steamboats—we saw all this little world in unique circumstantiality of detail—saw it just as the birds see it—and all reduced to the smallest of scales and as sharply worked out and finished as a steel engraving. The numerous toy villages, with tiny spires projecting out of them, were just as the children might have left them when done with play the day before; the forest tracts were diminished to cushions of moss; one or two big lakes were dwarfed to ponds, the smaller ones to puddles—though they did not look like puddles but like blue ear-drops which had fallen and lodged in slight depressions, conformable to their shapes, among the moss-beds and the smooth levels of dainty green farm-land; the microscopic steamboats glided along as in a city reservoir, taking a mighty time to cover the distance between ports which seemed only a yard apart; and the isthmus which separated two lakes looked as if one might stretch out on it and lie with both elbows in the water, yet we knew invisible wagons were toiling across it and finding the distance a tedious one. This beautiful miniature world had exactly the appearance of those 'relief maps' which reproduce nature precisely, with the heights and depressions and other details graduated to a reduced scale, and with the rocks, trees, lakes, etc., coloured after nature.

I believed we could walk down to Wäggis or Vitznau in a day, but I knew we could go down by rail in about an hour, so I chose the latter method. I wanted to see what it was like, anyway. The train came along about the middle of the forenoon, and an odd thing it was. The locomotive boiler stood on end, and it and the whole locomotive were tilted sharply backward. There were two passenger cars, roofed, but wide open all around. These cars were not tilted back, but the seats were; this enabled the passenger to sit level while going down a steep incline.

There are three railway tracks; the central one is cogged; the 'lantern wheel' of the engine grips its way along these cogs, and pulls the train up the hill or retards its motion on the down trip. About the same speed—three miles an hour—is maintained both ways. Whether going up or down, the locomotive is always at the lower end of the train. It pushes, in the one case, braces back in the other. The passenger rides backwards going up, and faces forward going down.

We got front seats, and while the train moved along about fifty yards on level ground, I was not the least frightened; but now it started abruptly down stairs, and I caught my breath. And I, like my neighbours, unconsciously held back, all I could, and threw my weight to the rear, but of course that did no particular good. I had slidden down the balusters when I was a boy, and thought nothing of it, but to slide down the balusters in a railway train is a thing to make one's flesh creep. Sometimes we had as much as ten yards of almost level ground, and this gave us a few full breaths in comfort; but straightway·we would turn a corner and see a long steep line of rails stretching down below us, and the comfort was at an end. One expected to see the locomotive pause, or slack up a little, and approach this plunge cautiously, but it did nothing of the kind; it went calmly on, and when it reached the jumping-off place it made a sudden bow, and went gliding smoothly down stairs, untroubled by the circumstances.

It was wildly exhilarating to slide along the edge of the precipices after this grisly fashion, and look straight down upon that far-off valley which I was describing a while ago.

There was no level ground at the Kaltbad station; the rail-bed was as steep as a roof; I was curious to see how the stop was going to be managed. But it was very simple; the train came sliding down, and when it reached the right spot it just stopped—that was all there was 'to it'—stopped on the steep incline, and when the exchange of passengers and baggage had been made, it moved off and went sliding down again. The train can be stopped anywhere, at a moment's notice.

There was one curious effect, which I need not take the trouble to describe, because I can scissor a description of it out of the railway company's advertising pamphlet, and save my ink:—

'On the whole tour, particularly at the descent, we undergo an optical illusion which often seems to be incredible. All the shrubs, fir-trees, stables, houses, etc., seem to be bent in a slanting direction, as by an immense pressure of air. They are all standing awry, so much awry that the châlets and cottages of the peasants seem to be tumbling down. It is the consequence of the steep inclination of the line. Those who are seated in the carriage do not observe that they are going down a declivity of 20° to 25° (their seats being adapted to this course of proceeding and being bent down at their backs). They mistake their carriage and its horizontal lines for a proper measure of the normal plain, and therefore all the objects outside, which really are in a horizontal position, must show a disproportion of 20° to 25° declivity, in regard to the mountain.'

By the time one reaches Kaltbad, he has acquired confidence in the railway, and he now ceases to try to ease the locomotive by holding back. Thenceforward he smokes his pipe in serenity, and gazes out upon the magnificent picture below and about him with unfettered enjoyment. There is nothing to interrupt the view or the breeze; it is like inspecting the world on the wing. However, to be exact, there is one place where the serenity lapses for a while; this is while one is crossing the Schnurrtobel Bridge: a frail structure which swings its gossamer frame down through the dizzy air, over a gorge, like a vagrant spider strand.

One has no difficulty in remembering his sins while the train is creeping down this bridge; and he repents of them, too; though he sees, when he gets to Vitznau, that he need not have done it—the bridge was perfectly safe.

So ends the eventful trip which we made to the Rigi-Kulm to see an Alpine sunrise.

CHAPTER 30

An hour's sail brought us to Lucerne again. I judged it best to go to bed and rest several days, for I knew that the man who undertakes to make the tour of Europe on foot must take care of himself.

Thinking over my plans, as mapped out, I perceived that they did not take in the Furka Pass, the Rhone Glacier, the Finsteraarhorn, the Wetterhorn, etc. I immediately examined the guide-book to see if these were important, and found they were; in fact, a pedestrian tour of Europe could not be complete without them. Of course that decided me at once to see them, for I never allow myself to do things by halves, or in a slurring, slipshod way.

I called in my agent and instructed him to go without delay and make a careful examination of these noted places, on foot, and bring me back a written report of the result, for insertion in my book. I instructed him to go to Hospenthal as quickly as possible, and make his grand start from there; to extend his foot expedition as far as the Giesbach fall, and return to me from thence by diligence or mule. I told him to take the courier with him.

He objected to the courier, and with some show of reason, since he was about to venture upon new and untried ground; but I thought he might as well learn how to take care of the courier now as later, therefore I enforced my point. I said that the trouble, delay, and inconvenience of travelling with a courier were balanced by the deep respect which a courier's presence commands, and I must insist that as much style be thrown into my journeys as possible.

So the two assumed complete mountaineering costumes and departed. A week later they returned, pretty well used up, and my agent handed me the following

Official Report

Of a Visit to the Furka Region. By H. Harris, Agent.

About seven o'clock in the morning, with perfectly fine weather, we started from Hospenthal, and arrived at the *maison* on the Furka in a little under quatre hours. The want of variety in the scenery from Hospenthal made the *kakkahponeeka* wearisome; but let none be discouraged: no one can fail to be completely *recompensée* for his fatigue, when he sees, for the first time, the monarch of the Oberland, the tremendous Finsteraarhorn. A moment before all was dullness, but a *pas* further has placed us on the summit of the Furka; and exactly in front of us, at a *hopow* of only fifteen miles, this magnificent mountain lifts its snow-wreathed precipices into the deep blue sky. The inferior mountains on each side of the pass form a sort of frame for the picture of their dread lord, and close in the view so completely that no other prominent feature in the Oberland is visible from this *bong-a-bong*; nothing withdraws the attention from the solitary grandeur of the Finsteraarhorn and the dependent spurs which form the abutments of the central peak.

With the addition of some others, who were also bound for the Grimsel, we formed a large *xhvloj* as we descended the *steg* which winds round the shoulder of a mountain toward the Rhone glacier. We soon left the path and took to the ice; and after wandering amongst the crevasses *un peu*, to admire the wonders of these deep blue caverns, and hear the rushing of waters through their subglacial channels, we struck out a course towards *l'autre côtè* and crossed the glacier successfully, a little above the cave from which the infant Rhone takes its first bound from under the grand precipice of ice. Half a mile below this we began to climb the flowery side of the Meienwand. One of our party started before the rest, but the *Hitze* was so great that we found *ihm* quite exhausted, and lying at full length in the shade of a large *Gestein*. We sat down with him for a time, for all felt the heat exceedingly in the climb up this very steep *bolwoggoly*, and then we set out again together, and arrived at last near the Dead Man's Lake, at the foot of the Sidelhorn. This lonely spot, once used for an extempore burying-place, after a sanguinary *battue* between the French and Austrians, is the perfection of desolation: there is nothing in sight to mark the hand of man, except the line of weather-beaten whitened posts, set up to indicate the direction of the past in the *owdawakk* of winter. Near this point the footpath joins the wider track, which connects the Grimsel with the head of the Rhone *schnawp*: this has been carefully constructed, and leads with a tortuous course among and over *les pierres*, down to the bank of the gloomy little *swosh-swosh*, which almost washes against the walls of the Grimsel Hospice. We arrived a little before four o'clock at the end of our day's journey, hot enough to justify the step, taken by most of the *partie*, of plunging into the crystal water of the snow-fed lake.

The next afternoon we started for a walk up the Unteraar glacier, with the intention of, at all events, getting as far as the *Hütte* which is used as a sleeping-place by most of those who cross the Strahleck Pass to Grindelwald. We got over the tedious collection of stones and *débris* which covers the *pied* of the *Gletscher*, and had walked nearly three hours from the Grimsel, when, just as we were thinking of crossing over to the right, to climb the cliffs at the foot of the hut, the clouds, which had for some time assumed a threatening appearance, suddenly dropped, and a huge mass of them, driving towards us from the Finsteraarhorn, poured down a deluge of *haboolong* and hail. Fortunately, we were not far from a very large glacier table; it was a huge rock balanced on a pedestal of ice high enough to admit of our all creeping under it for *gowkarak*. A stream of *puckittypukk* had furrowed a course for itself in the ice at its base, and we were obliged to stand with one *Fuss* on each side of this, and endeavour to keep ourselves *chaud* by cutting steps in the steep bank of the pedestal, so as to get a higher place for standing on, as the *wasser* rose rapidly in its trench. A very cold *bzzzzzzzzeeeee* accompanied the storm, and made our position far from pleasant; and presently came a flash of *Blitzen*, apparently in the middle of our little party, with an instantaneous clap of *yokky*, sounding like a large gun fired close to our ears: the effect was startling; but in a few seconds our attention was fixed by the roaring echoes of the thunder against the tremendous mountains which completely surrounded us. This was followed by many more bursts, none of *welche*, however, was so dangerously near; and after waiting a long *demi*-hour in our icy prison, we sallied out to walk through a *haboolong* which, though not so heavy as before, was quite enough to give us a thorough soaking before our arrival at the Hospice.

The Grimsel is *certainement* a wonderful place; situated at the bottom of a sort of huge crater, the sides of which are utterly savage *Gebirge*, composed of barren rocks which cannot even support a single pine *arbre*, and afford only scanty food for a herd of *gmwkwllolp*, it looks as if it must be completely *begraben* in the winter snows. Enormous avalanches fall against it every spring, sometimes covering everything to the depth of thirty or forty feet; and, in spite of walls four feet thick, and furnished with outside iron shutters, the two men who stay here when the *voyageurs* are snugly quartered in their distant homes can tell you that the snow sometimes shakes the house to its foundations.

Next morning the *hogglebumgullup* still continued bad, but we made up our minds to go on, and make the best of it. Half an hour after we started the *Regen* thickened unpleasantly, and we attempted to get shelter under a projecting rock, but being far too *nass* already to make standing at all *agréable*, we pushed on for the Handeck, consoling ourselves with the reflection that from the furious rushing of the river Aar at our side, we should at all events see the celebrated *Wasserfall* in *grande perfection*. Nor were we *nappersocket* in our expectation; the water was roaring down its leap of 250 feet in a most magnificent frenzy, while the trees which cling to its rocky sides swayed to and fro in the violence of the hurricane which it brought down with it: even the stream, which falls into the main cascade at right angles, and *toutfois* forms a beautiful feature in the scene, was now swollen into a raging torrent; and the violence of this 'meeting of the waters,' about fifty feet below the frail bridge where we stood, was fearfully grand. While we were looking at it, *glücklicheweise* a gleam of sunshine came out, and instantly a beautiful rainbow was formed by the spray, and hung in mid air suspended over the awful gorge.

On going into the *châlet* above the fall, we were informed that a *Brücke* had broken down near Guttanen, and that it would be impossible to proceed for some time: accordingly we were kept in our drenched condition for *eine Stunde*, when some *voyageurs* arrived from Meiringen, and told us that there had been a trifling accident, *aben* that we could now cross. On arriving at the spot, I was much inclined to suspect that the whole story was a ruse to make us *slowwk*, and drink the more in the Handeck Inn; for only a few planks had been carried away, and though there might perhaps have been some difficulty with mules, the gap was certainly not larger than a *mmbglx* might cross with a very slight leap. Near Guttanen the *haboolong* happily ceased, and we had time to walk ourselves tolerably dry before arriving at Reichenbach, *wo* we enjoyed a good *diné* at the Hôtel des Alpes.

Next morning we walked to Rosenlaui, the *beau idéal* of Swiss scenery, where we spent the middle of the day in an excursion to the glacier. This was more beautiful than words can describe, for in the constant progress of the ice it has changed the form of its extremity, and formed a vast cavern, as blue as the sky above, and rippled like a frozen ocean. A few steps cut in the *whoopjamboreehoo* enabled us to walk completely under this, and feast our eyes upon one of the loveliest objects in creation. The glacier was all around divided by numberless fissures of the same exquisite colour, and the finest wood *Erdbeeren* were growing in abundance but a few yards from the ice. The inn stands in a *charmant* spot close to the *côté de la rivière* which, lower down, forms the Reichenbach fall, and embosomed in the richest of pinewoods, while the fine form of the Wellhorn looking down upon it completes the enchanting *bopple*. In the afternoon we walked over the Great Scheideck to Grindelwald, stopping to pay a visit to the Upper glacier by the way; but we were again overtaken by bad *hogglebumgullup*, and arrived at the hotel in *solche* a state that the landlord's wardrobe was in great request.

The clouds by this time seemed to have done their worst, for a lovely day succeeded, which we determined to devote to an ascent of the Faulhorn. We left Grindelwald just as a thunderstorm was dying away, and we hoped to find *guten Wetter* up above; but the rain, which had nearly ceased, began again, and we were struck by the rapidly increasing *froid* as we ascended. Two-thirds of the way up were completed when the rain was exchanged for *gnillic*, with which the *Boden* was thickly covered, and before we arrived at the top the *gnillic* and mist became so thick that we could not see one another at more than twenty *poopoo* distance, and it became difficult to pick our way over the rough and thickly covered ground. Shivering with cold we turned into bed with a double allowance of clothes, and slept comfortably while the wind howled *autour de la maison*: when I awoke, the wall and the window looked equally dark, but in another hour I found I could just see the form of the latter; so I jumped out of bed, and forced it open, though with difficulty, from the frost and the quantities of *gnillic* heaped up against it.

A row of huge icicles hung down from the edge of the roof, and anything more wintry than the whole *Anblick* could not well be imagined; but the sudden appearance of the great mountains in front was so startling that I felt no inclination to move towards bed again. The snow which had collected upon *la fenêtre* had increased the *Finsterniss oder der Dunkelheit*, so that when I looked out I was surprised to find that the daylight was considerable, and that the *balragooma* would evidently rise before long. Only the brightest of *les étoiles* were still shining; the sky was cloudless overhead, though small curling mists lay thousands of feet below us in the valleys, wreathed around the feet of the mountains, and adding to the splendour of their lofty summits. We were soon dressed and out of the house, watching the gradual approach of dawn, thoroughly absorbed in the first near view of the Oberland giants, which broke upon us unexpectedly after the intense obscurity of the evening before. '*Kabaugwakko songwashee Kum Wetterhorn snawpo!*' cried some one, as that grand summit gleamed with the first rose of dawn: and in a few moments the double crest of the Schreckhorn followed its example; peak after peak seemed warmed with life, the Jungfrau blushed even more beautifully than her neighbours, and soon, from the Wetterhorn in the East to the Wildstrubel in the West, a long row of fires glowed upon mighty altars, truly worthy of the gods. The *wlgw* was very severe; our sleeping place could hardly be *distinguee* from the snow around it, which had fallen to the depth of a *flirk* during the past evening, and we heartily enjoyed a rough scramble *en bas* to the Giesbach falls, where we soon found a warm climate. At noon the day before at Grindelwald the thermometer could not have stood at less than 100° Fahr. in the sun; and in the evening, judging from the icicles formed, and the state of the windows, there must have been at least twelve *dingblatter* of frost, thus giving a change of 80° during a few hours.

I said—

'You have done well, Harris; this report is concise, compact, well expressed; the language is crisp, the descriptions are vivid and not needlessly elaborated; your report goes straight to the point, attends strictly to business, and doesn't fool around. It is in many ways an excellent document. But it has a fault—it is too learned, it is much too learned. What is "*dingblatter*"?'

'Dingblatter is a Fiji word meaning "degrees." '

'You knew the English of it, then?'

'Oh yes.'

'What is "*gnillic*"?'

'That is the Esquimaux term for "snow." '

'So you knew the English for that too?'

'Why, certainly.'

'What does "*mmbglx*" stand for?'

'That is Zulu for "pedestrian." '

' "While the form of the Wellhorn looking down upon it completes the enchanting '*bopple*.' " What is "*bopple*"?'

' "Picture." It's Choctaw.'

'What is "*schnawp*"?'

' "Valley." That is Choctaw also.'

'What is "*bolwoggoly*"?'

'That is Chinese for "hill." '

'*Kahkaaponeeka*?'

' "Ascent." Choctaw.'

' "But we were again overtaken by bad "*hogglebumgullup*.' "
What does hogglebumgullup mean?'

'That is Chinese for "weather." '

'Is hogglebumgullup better than the English word? Is it any
more descriptive?'

'No, it means just the same.'

'And   dingblatter,   and   gnillic,—and   bopple,   and
schnawp,—are they better than the English words?'

'No, they mean just what the English ones do.'

'Then why do you use them? Why have you used all this
Chinese and Choctaw and Zulu rubbish?'

'Because I didn't know any French but two or three words,
and I didn't know any Latin or Greek at all.'

'That is nothing. Why should you want to use foreign words,
anyhow?'

'To adorn my page. They all do it.'

'Who is "all"?'

'Everybody. Everybody that writes elegantly. Anybody has a
right to that wants to.'

'I think you are mistaken.' I then proceeded in the following
scathing manner:— 'When really learned men write books for
other learned men to read, they are justified in using as many
learned words as they please—their audience will understand
them; but a man who writes a book for the general public to
read is not justified in disfiguring his pages with untranslated
foreign expressions. It is an insolence toward the majority of the
purchasers, for it is a very frank and impudent way of saying,
"Get the translations made yourself if you want them; this book
is not written for the ignorant classes." There are men who know
a foreign language so well, and have used it so long in their daily
life, that they seem to discharge whole volleys of it into their

English writings unconsciously, and so they omit to translate, as much as half the time. That is a great cruelty to nine out of ten of the man's readers. What is the excuse for this? The writer would say he only uses the foreign language where the delicacy of his point cannot be conveyed in English. Very well, then he writes his best things for the tenth man, and he ought to warn the other nine not to buy his book. However, the excuse he offers is at least an excuse; but there is another set of men who are like *you*: they know a *word* here and there, of a foreign language, or a few beggarly little three-word phrases. filched from the back of the Dictionary, and these they are continually peppering into their literature, with a pretence of knowing that language, or a few beggarly little three-word phrases, filched phrases which they use have their exact equivalent in a nobler language,—English; yet they think they "adorn their page" when they say *Strasse* for street, and *Bahnhof* for railway-station, and so on,—flaunting these fluttering rags of poverty in the reader's face, and imagining he will be ass enough to take them for the sign of untold riches held in reserve. I will let your "learning" remain in your report; you have as much right, I suppose, to "adorn your page" with Zulu and Chinese and Choctaw rubbish, as others of your sort have to adorn theirs with insolent odds and ends smouched from half-a-dozen learned tongues whose *a-b abs* they don't even know.'

When the musing spider steps upon the red-hot shovel, he first exhibits a wild surprise, then he shrivels up. Similar was the effect of these blistering words upon the tranquil and unsuspecting Agent. I can be dreadfully rough on a person when the mood takes me.

CHAPTER 31

We now prepared for a considerable walk—from Lucerne to Interlaken, over the Brünig Pass. But at the last moment the weather was so good that I changed my mind and hired a four-horse carriage. It was a huge vehicle, roomy, as easy in its motion as a palanquin, and exceedingly comfortable.

We got away pretty early in the morning, after a hot breakfast, and went bowling along over a hard, smooth road, through the summer loveliness of Switzerland, with near and distant lakes and mountains before and about us for the entertainment of the eye, and the music of multitudinous birds to charm the ear. Sometimes there was only the width of the road between the imposing precipices on the right and the clear cool water on the left with its shoals of uncatchable fishes skimming about through the bars of sun and shadow; and sometimes, in place of the precipices, the grassy land stretched away, in an apparently endless upward slant, and was dotted everywhere with snug little châlets, the peculiarly captivating cottage of Switzerland.

The ordinary châlet turns a broad, honest gable end to the road, and its ample roof hovers over the home in a protecting, caressing way, projecting its sheltering eaves far outward. The quaint windows are filled with little panes, and garnished with white muslin curtains, and brightened with boxes of blooming flowers. Across the front of the house, and up the spreading eaves, and along the fanciful railings of the shallow porch, are elaborate carvings—wreaths, fruits, arabesques, verses from Scripture, names, dates, etc. The building is wholly of wood, reddish brown in tint, a very pleasing colour. It generally has vines climbing over it. Set such a house against the fresh green of the hillside, and it looks ever so cosy and inviting and picturesque, and is a decidedly graceful addition to the landscape.

One does not find out what a hold the châlet has taken upon him until he presently comes upon a new house—a house which is aping the town fashions of Germany and France, a prim, hideous, straight-up-and-down thing, plastered all over on the outside to look like stone, and altogether so stiff, and formal, and ugly, and forbidding, and so out of tune with the gracious landscape, and so deaf and dumb and dead to the poetry of its surroundings, that it suggests an undertaker at a picnic, a corpse at a wedding, a puritan in Paradise.

In the course of the morning we passed the spot where Pontius Pilate is said to have thrown himself into the lake. The legend goes that after the Crucifixion his conscience troubled him and he fled from Jerusalem and wandered about the earth, weary of life and a prey to tortures of the mind. Eventually he hid himself away, on the heights of Mount Pilatus, and dwelt alone among the clouds and crags for years; but rest and peace were still denied him, so he finally put an end to his misery by drowning himself.

Presently we passed the place where a man of better odour was born. This was the children's friend Santa Claus, or St. Nicholas. There are some unaccountable reputations in the world. This saint's is an instance. He has ranked for ages as the peculiar friend of children, yet it appears he was not much of a friend to his own. He had ten of them, and when fifty years old he left them, and sought out as dismal a refuge from the world as possible and became a hermit in order that he might reflect upon pious themes without being disturbed by the joyous and other noises from the nursery, doubtless.

Judging by Pilate and St. Nicholas, there exists no rule for the construction of hermits: they seem made out of all kinds of material. But Pilate attended to the matter of expiating his sin while he was alive, whereas St. Nicholas will probably have to go on climbing down sooty chimneys, Christmas Eve, for ever, and conferring kindness on other people's children, to make up for deserting his own. His bones are kept in a church in a village (Sachseln), which we visited, and are naturally held in great reverence. His portrait is common in the farmhouses of the region, but is believed by many to be but an indifferent likeness. During his hermit life, according to the legend, he partook of the bread and wine of the communion once a month, but all the rest of the month he fasted.

A constant marvel with us, as we sped along the bases of the steep mountains, on this journey, was, not that avalanches occur, but that they are not occurring all the time. One does not understand why rocks and landslides do not plunge down these declivities daily. A land-slip occurred three quarters of a century ago, on the route from Arth to Brunnen, which was a formidable thing. A mass of conglomerate two miles long, a thousand feet broad, and a hundred feet thick, broke away from a cliff three thousand feet high and hurled itself into the valley below, burying four villages and five hundred people, as in a grave.

We had such a beautiful day, and such endless pictures of limpid lakes, and green hills and valleys, and majestic mountains, and milky cataracts dancing down the steeps and gleaming in the sun, that we could not help feeling sweet toward all the world; so we tried to drink all the milk, and eat all the grapes and apricots and berries, and buy all the bouquets of wild flowers which the little peasant boys and girls offered for sale; but we had to retire from this contract, for it was too heavy. At short distances—and they were entirely too short—all along the road, were groups of neat and comely children, with their wares nicely and temptingly set forth in the grass under the shade trees, and as soon as we approached they swarmed into the road, holding out their baskets and milk bottles, and ran beside the carriage, barefoot and bareheaded, and importuned us to buy. They seldom desisted early, but continued to run and insist—beside the waggon while they could, and behind it until they lost breath. Then they turned and chased a returning carriage back to their trading post again. After several hours of this, without any intermission, it becomes almost annoying. I do not know what we should have done without the returning carriages to draw off the pursuit. However, there were plenty of these, loaded with dusty tourists and piled high with luggage. Indeed, from Lucerne to Interlaken we had the spectacle, among other scenery, of an unbroken procession of fruit pedlars and tourist carriages.

Our talk was mostly anticipatory of what we should see on the down grade of the Brünig, by-and-by, after we should pass the summit. All our friends in Lucerne had said that to look down upon Meiringen, and the rushing blue-gray river Aar, and the broad level green valley; and across at the mighty Alpine precipices that rise straight up to the clouds out of that valley; and up at the microscopic châlets perched upon the dizzy eaves of those precipices and winking dimly and fitfully through the drifting veil of vapour; and still up and up, at the superb *Oltschibach* and the other beautiful cascades that leap from those rugged heights, robed in powdery spray, ruffled with foam, and girdled with rainbows—to look upon these things, they said, was to look upon the last possibility of the sublime and the enchanting. Therefore, as I say, we talked mainly of these coming wonders; if we were conscious of any impatience, it was to get there in favourable season; if we felt any anxiety, it was that the day might remain perfect, and enable us to see those marvels at their best.

As we approached the Kaiserstuhl, a part of the harness gave way. We were in distress for a moment, but only a moment. It was the fore-and-aft gear that was broken—the thing that leads aft from the forward part of the horse and is made fast to the thing that pulls the waggon. In America this would have been a heavy leathern strap; but all over the Continent it is nothing but a piece of rope the size of your little finger—clothes-line is what it is. Cabs use it, private carriages, freight carts and waggons, all sorts of vehicles have it. In Munich I afterwards saw it used on a long waggon laden with fifty-four half-barrels of beer; I had before noticed that the cabs in Heidelberg used it;—not new rope, but rope that had been in use since Abraham's time—and

I had felt nervous, sometimes, behind it, when the cab was tearing down a hill. But I had long been accustomed to it now, and had even become afraid of the leather strap which belonged in its place. Our driver got a fresh piece of clothes-line out of his locker and repaired the break in two minutes.

So much for one European fashion. Every country has its own ways. It may interest the reader to know how they 'put horses to' on the Continent. The man stands up the horses on each side of the thing that projects from the front end of the waggon, and then throws the tangled mass of gear on top of the horses, and passes the thing that goes forward through a ring, and hauls it aft, and passes the other thing through the other ring and hauls it aft on the other side of the other horse, opposite to the first one, after crossing them and bringing the loose end back, and then buckles the other thing underneath the horse, and takes another thing and wraps it around the thing I spoke of before, and puts another thing over each horse's head, with broad flappers to it to keep the dust out of his eyes, and puts the iron thing in his mouth for him to grit his teeth on, up hill, and brings the ends of these things aft over his back, after buckling another one around under his neck to hold his head up, and hitching another thing on a thing that goes over his shoulders to keep his head up when he is climbing a hill, and then takes the slack of the thing which I mentioned a while ago, and fetches it aft and makes it fast to the thing that pulls the waggon, and hands the other things up to the driver to steer with. I never have buckled up a horse myself, but I do not think we do it that way.

We had four very handsome horses, and the driver was very proud of his turn-out. He would bowl along on a reasonable trot, on the highway, but when he entered a village he did it on a furious run, and accompanied it with a frenzy of ceaseless whip crackings that sounded like volleys of musketry. He tore through the narrow streets and around the sharp curves like a moving earthquake, showering his volleys as he went, and before him swept a continuous tidal wave of scampering children, ducks, cats, and mothers clasping babies which they had snatched out of the way of the coming destruction; and as this living wave washed aside, along the walls, its elements, being safe, forgot their fears and turned their admiring gaze upon that gallant driver till he thundered around the next curve and was lost to sight.

He was a great man to those villagers, with his gaudy clothes and his terrific ways. Whenever he stopped to have his cattle watered and fed with loaves of bread, the villagers stood around admiring him while he swaggered about, the little boys gazed up at his face with humble homage, and the landlord brought out foaming mugs of beer and conversed proudly with him while he drank. Then he mounted his lofty box, swung his explosive whip, and away he went again, like a storm. I had not seen anything like this before since I was a boy, and the stage used to flourish through the village with the dust flying and the horn tooting.

When we reached the base of the Kaiserstuhl, we took two more horses; we had to toil along with difficulty for an hour and a half or two hours, for the ascent was not very gradual, but when we passed the backbone and approached the station, the driver surpassed all his previous efforts in the way of rush and clatter. He could not have six horses all the time, so he made the most of his chance while he had it.

Up to this point we had been in the heart of the William Tell region. The hero is not forgotten, by any means, or held in doubtful veneration. His wooden image, with his bow drawn, above the doors of taverns, was a frequent feature of the scenery.

About noon we arrived at the foot of the Brünig pass, and made a two-hour stop at the village hotel, another of those clean, pretty, and thoroughly well-kept inns which are such an astonishment to people who are accustomed to hotels of a dismally different pattern in remote country towns. There was a lake here, in the lap of the great mountains, the green slopes that rose toward the lower crags were graced with scattered Swiss cottages nestling among miniature farms and gardens, and from out a leafy ambuscade on the upper heights tumbled a brawling cataract.

Carriage after carriage, laden with tourists and trunks, arrived, and the quiet hotel was soon populous. We were early at the *table d'hôte*, and saw the people all come in. There were twenty-five, perhaps. They were of various nationalities, but we were the only Americans. Next to me sat an English bride, and next to her sat her new husband whom she called 'Neddy,' though he was big enough and stalwart enough to be entitled to his full name. They had a pretty little lovers' quarrel over what wine they should have. Neddy was for obeying the guide-book and taking the wine of the country; but the bride said—

'What, that nahsty stuff!'

'It isn't nahsty, Pet, it's quite good.'

'It *is* nahsty.'

'No, it *isn't* nahsty.'

'It's *o*ful nahsty, Neddy, and I shahn't drink it.'

Then the question was, what she must have. She said he knew very well that she never drank anything but champagne. She added—

'You know very well papa always has champagne on his table, and I've always been used to it.'

Neddy made a playful pretence of being distressed about the expense, and this amused her so much that she nearly exhausted herself with laughter, and this pleased *him* so much that he repeated his jest a couple of times, and added new and killing varieties to it. When the bride finally recovered, she gave Neddy a love-box on the arm with her fan, and said with arch severity—

'Well, you would *have* me—nothing else would do—so you'll have to make the best of a bad bargain. *Do* order the champagne, I'm *o*ful dry.'

So with a mock groan which made her laugh again, Neddy ordered the champagne.

The fact that this young woman had never moistened the selvedge edge of her soul with a less plebeian tipple than champagne had a marked and subduing effect upon Harris. He believed she belonged to the royal family. But I had my doubts.

We heard two or three different languages spoken by people at the table, and guessed out the nationalities of most of the guests to our satisfaction, but we failed with an elderly gentleman and his wife and a young girl who sat opposite us, and with a gentleman of about thirty-five who sat three seats beyond Harris. We did not hear any of these speak. But finally the last-named gentleman left while we were not noticing, but we looked up as he reached the far end of the table. He stopped there a moment, and made his toilet with a pocket comb. So he was a German; or else he had lived in German hotels long enough to catch the fashion. When the elderly couple and the young girl rose to leave they bowed respectfully to us. So they were Germans, too. This national custom is worth six of the other one, for export.

After dinner we talked with several Englishmen, and they inflamed our desire, to a hotter degree than ever, to see the sights of Meiringen from the heights of the Brünig pass. They said the view was marvellous, and that one who had seen it once could never forget it. They also spoke of the romantic nature of the road over the pass, and how in one place it had been cut through a flank of the solid rock, in such a way that the mountain overhung the tourist as he passed by; and they furthermore said that the sharp turns in the road and the abruptness of the descent would afford us a thrilling experience, for we should go down in a flying gallop and seem to be spinning around the rings of a whirlwind, like a drop of whisky descending the spirals of a corkscrew. I got all the information out of these gentlemen that we could need; and then, to make everything complete, I asked them if a body could get hold of a little fruit and milk here and there, in case of necessity. They threw up their hands in speechless intimation that the road was simply paved with refreshment pedlars. We were impatient to get away now, and the rest of our two-hour stop rather dragged. But finally the set time arrived and we began the ascent. Indeed, it was a wonderful road. It was smooth, and compact, and clean, and the side next the precipices was guarded all along by dressed stone posts about three feet high, placed at short distances apart. The road could not have been better built if Napoleon the First had built it. He seems to have been the introducer of the sort of roads which Europe now uses. All literature which describes life as it existed in England, France, and Germany up to the close of the last century is filled with pictures of coaches and carriages wallowing through these three countries in mud and slush half-wheel deep; but after Napoleon had floundered through a conquered kingdom he generally arranged things so that the rest of the world could follow dry shod.

We went on climbing, higher and higher, and curving hither and thither, in the shade of noble woods, and with a rich variety and profusion of wild flowers all about us; and glimpses of rounded grassy backbones below us occupied by trim châlets and nibbling sheep, and other glimpses of far lower altitudes, where distance diminished the châlets to toys and obliterated the sheep altogether; and every now and then some ermined monarch of the Alps swung magnificently into view for a moment, then drifted past an intervening spur and disappeared again.

It was an intoxicating trip, altogether; the exceeding sense of satisfaction that follows a good dinner added largely to the enjoyment; the having something especial to look forward to, and muse about, like the approaching grandeurs of Meiringen, sharpened the zest. Smoking was never so good before, solid comfort was never solider; we lay back against the thick cushions, silent, meditative, steeped in felicity.

* * *

I rubbed my eyes, opened them, and started. I had been dreaming I was at sea, and it was a thrilling surprise to wake up and find land all around me. It took me a couple of seconds to 'come to,' as you may say; then I took in the situation. The horses were drinking at a trough in the edge of a town, the driver was taking beer, Harris was snoring at my side; the courier, with folded arms and bowed head, was sleeping on the box; two dozen barefooted and bareheaded children were gathered about the carriage, with their hands crossed behind, gazing up with serious and innocent admiration at the dozing tourists baking there in the sun. Several small girls held night-capped babies nearly as big as themselves in their arms, and even these fat babies seemed to take a sort of sluggish interest in us.

We had slept an hour and a half and missed all the scenery! I did not need anybody to tell me that. If I had been a girl, I could have cursed for vexation. As it was, I woke up the agent and gave him a piece of my mind. Instead of being humiliated, he only upbraided me for being so wanting in vigilance. He said he had expected to improve his mind by coming to Europe, but a man might travel to the ends of the earth with me and never see anything, for I was manifestly endowed with the very genius of ill-luck. He even tried to get up some emotion about that poor courier, who never got a chance to see anything, on account of my heedlessness. But when I thought I had borne about enough of this kind of talk, I threatened to make Harris tramp back to the summit and make a report on that scenery, and this suggestion spiked his battery.

We drove sullenly through Brienz, dead to the seductions of its bewildering array of Swiss carvings and the clamorous *hoo*-hooing of its cuckoo clocks, and had not entirely recovered our spirits when we rattled across the bridge over the rushing blue river and entered the pretty town of Interlaken. It was just about sunset, and we had made the trip from Lucerne in ten hours.

CHAPTER 32

We located ourselves at the Jungfrau Hotel, one of those huge establishments which the needs of modern travel have created in every attractive spot on the Continent. There was a great gathering at dinner, and as usual one heard all sorts of languages.

The *table d'hôte* was served by waitresses dressed in the quaint and comely costume of the Swiss peasants. This consists of a simple *gros de laine*, trimmed with ashes of roses, with overskirt of *sacrebleu ventre saint gris*, cut bias on the off side, with facings of *petit polonaise* and narrow insertions of *pâté de foie gras* backstitched to the *mise-en-scène* in the form of a *je d'esprit*. It gives to the wearer a singularly piquant and alluring aspect.

One of these waitresses, a woman of forty, had side whiskers reaching half way down her jaw. They were two fingers broad, dark in colour, pretty thick, and the hairs were an inch long. One sees many women on the Continent with quite conspicuous moustaches, but this was the only woman I saw who had reached the dignity of whiskers.

After dinner the guests of both sexes distributed themselves about the front porches and the ornamental grounds belonging to the hotel, to enjoy the cool air; but as the twilight deepened towards darkness, they gathered themselves together in that saddest and solemnest and most constrained of all places, the great blank drawing-room which is a chief feature of all Continental summer hotels. There they grouped themselves about, in couples and threes, and mumbled in bated voices, and looked timid and homeless and forlorn.

There was a small piano in this room, a clattery, wheezy, asthmatic thing, certainly the very worst miscarriage in the way of a piano that the world has seen. In turn, five or six dejected and home-sick ladies approached it doubtingly, gave it a single inquiring thump, and retired with the lockjaw. But the boss of that instrument was to come, nevertheless; and from my own country—from Arkansaw. She was a brand-new bride, innocent, girlish, happy in herself and her grave and worshipping stripling of a husband; she was about eighteen, just out of school, free from affectations, unconscious of that passionless multitude around her; and the very first time she smote that old wreck one recognised that it had met its destiny. Her stripling brought an armful of aged sheet music from their room—for this bride went 'heeled,' as you might say—and bent himself lovingly over and got ready to turn the pages.

The bride fetched a swoop with her fingers from one end of the key-board to the other, just to get her bearings, as it were, and you could see the congregation set their teeth with the agony of it. Then, without any more preliminaries, she turned on all the horrors of the 'Battle of Prague,' that venerable shivaree, and waded chin-deep in the blood of the slain. She made a fair and honourable average of two false notes in every five, but her soul was in arms and she never stopped to correct. The audience stood it with pretty fair grit for a while, but when the cannonade waxed hotter and fiercer, and the discord-average rose to four in five, the procession began to move. A few stragglers held their ground ten minutes longer, but when the girl began to wring the true inwardness out of the 'cries of the wounded,' they struck their colours and retired in a kind of panic.

There never was a completer victory; I was the only non-combatant left on the field. I would not have deserted my countrywoman anyhow, but indeed I had no desires in that direction. None of us like mediocrity, but we all reverence perfection. This girl's music was perfection in its way; it was the worst music that had ever been achieved on our planet by a mere human being.

I moved up close, and never lost a strain. When she got through, I asked her to play it again. She did it with a pleased alacrity and a heightened enthusiasm. She made it *all* discords, this time. She got an amount of anguish into the cries of the wounded that shed a new light on human suffering. She was on the war-path all the evening. All the time, crowds of people gathered on the porches and pressed their noses against the windows to look and marvel, but the bravest never ventured in. The bride went off satisfied and happy with her young fellow, when her appetite was finally gorged, and the tourists swarmed in again.

What a change has come over Switzerland, and in fact all Europe, during this century! Seventy or eighty years ago Napoleon was the only man in Europe who could really be called a traveller; he was the only man who had devoted his attention to it and taken a powerful interest in it; he was the only man who had travelled extensively; but now everybody goes everywhere; and Switzerland, and many other regions which were unvisited and unknown remotenesses a hundred years ago, are in our days a buzzing hive of restless strangers every summer. But I digress.

In the morning when we looked out of our windows, we saw a wonderful sight. Across the valley, and apparently quite neighbourly and close at hand, the giant form of the Jungfrau rose cold and white into the clear sky, beyond a gateway in the nearer highlands. It reminded me, somehow, of our of those colossal billows which swell suddenly up beside one's ship, at sea, sometimes, with its crest and shoulders snowy white, and the rest of its noble proportions streaked downward with creamy foam.

It was hard to believe that the lofty wooded rampart on the left which so overtops the Jungfrau was not actually the higher of the two, but it was not, of course. It is only 2,000 or 3,000 feet high, and of course has no snow upon it in summer, whereas the Jungfrau is not much short of 14,000 feet high, and therefore that lowest verge of snow—on her side, which seems nearly down to the valley level—is really about 7,000 feet higher up in the air than the summit of that wooded rampart. It is the distance that makes the deception. The wooded height is but four or five miles removed from us, but the Jungfrau is four or five times that distance away.

Walking down the street of shops, in the forenoon, I was attracted by a large picture, carved, frame and all, from a single block of chocolate-coloured wood. There are people who know everything. Some of these had told us that continental shopkeepers always raise their prices on English and Americans. Many people had told us it was expensive to buy things through a courier, whereas I had supposed it was just the reverse. When I saw this picture I conjectured that it was worth more than the friend I proposed to buy it for would like to pay, but still it was worth while to inquire; so I told the courier to step in and ask the price, as if he wanted it for himself; I told him not to speak in English, and above all not to reveal the fact that he was a courier. Then I moved on a few yards, and waited.

The courier came presently and reported the price. I said to myself, 'It is a hundred francs too much,' and so dismissed the matter from my mind. But in the afternoon I was passing that place with Harris, and the picture attracted me again. We stepped in to see how much higher broken German would raise the price. The shop-woman named a figure just a hundred francs lower than the courier had named. This was a pleasant surprise. I said I would take it. After I had given directions as to where it was to be shipped, the shopwoman said, appealingly—

'If you please, do not let your courier know you bought it.'

This was an unexpected remark. I said—

'What makes you think I have a courier?'

'Ah, that is very simple; he told me himself.'

'He was very thoughtful. But tell me—why did you charge him more than you are charging me?'

'That is very simple, also: I do not have to pay you a percentage.'

'Oh, I begin to see. You would have had to pay the courier a percentage?'

'Undoubtedly. The courier always has his percentage. In this case it would have been a hundred francs.

'Then the tradesman does not pay a part of it—the purchaser pays all of it?'

'There are occasions when the tradesman and the courier agree upon a price which is twice or thrice the value of the article, then the two divide, and both get a percentage.'

'I see. But it seems to me that the purchaser does all the paying, even then.'

'Oh, to be sure! It goes without saying.'

'But I have bought this picture myself; therefore why shouldn't the courier know it?'

The woman exclaimed, in distress—

'Ah, indeed it would take all my little profit! He would come and demand his hundred francs, and I should have to pay.'

'He has not done the buying. You could refuse.'

'I could not dare to refuse. He would never bring travellers here again. More than that, he would denounce me to the other couriers, they would divert custom from me, and my business would be injured.'

I went away in a thoughtful frame of mind. I began to see why a courier could afford to work for fifty-five dollars a month and his fares. A month or two later I was able to understand why a courier did not have to pay any board and lodging, and why my hotel bills were always larger when I had him with me than when I left him behind, somewhere, for a few days.

Another thing was also explained, now, apparently. In one town I had taken the courier to the bank to do the translating when I drew some money. I had sat in the reading-room till the transaction was finished. Then a clerk had brought the money to me in person, and had been exceedingly polite, even going so far as to precede me to the door and hold it open for me and bow me out as if I had been a distinguished personage. It was a new experience. Exchange had been in my favour ever since I had been in Europe, but just that one time. I got simply the face of my draft, and no extra francs, whereas I had expected to get quite a number of them. This was the first time I had ever used the courier at a bank. I had suspected something then, and as long as he remained with me afterwards I managed bank matters by myself.

Still, if I felt that I could afford the tax, I would never travel without a courier, for a good courier is a convenience whose value cannot be estimated in dollars and cents. Without him, travel is a bitter harassment, a purgatory of little exasperating annoyances, a ceaseless and pitiless punishment—I mean to an irascible man who has no business capacity and is confused by details.

Without a courier, travel hasn't a ray of pleasure in it, anywhere; but with him it is a continuous and unruffled delight. He is always at hand, never has to be sent for; if your bell is not answered promptly—and it seldom is—you have only to open the door and speak, the courier will hear, and he will have the order attended to or raise an insurrection. You tell him what day you will start, and whither you are going—leave all the rest to him. You need not inquire about trains or fares, or car changes, or hotels, or anything else. At the proper time he will put you in a cab or an omnibus, and drive you to the train or the boat; he has packed your luggage and transferred it, he has paid all the bills. Other people have preceded you half an hour to scramble for impossible places and lose their tempers, but you can take your time, the courier has secured your seats for you, and you can occupy them at your leisure.

At the station, the crowd mash one another to pulp in the effort to get the weighers' attention to their trunks; they dispute hotly with these tyrants, who are cool and indifferent; they get their baggage billets, at last, and then have another squeeze and another rage over the disheartening business of trying to get them recorded and paid for, and still another over the equally disheartening business of trying to get near enough to the ticket office to buy a ticket; and now, with their tempers gone to the dogs, they must stand penned up and packed together, laden with wraps and satchels and shawl-straps, with the weary wife and babies, in the waiting-room, till the doors are thrown open—and then all hands make a grand final rush to the train, find it full, and have to stand on the platform and fret until some more cars are put on. They are in a condition to kill somebody by this time. Meantime you have been sitting in your car, smoking, and observing all this misery in the extremest comfort.

On the journey the guard is polite and watchful—won't allow anybody to get into your compartment—tells them you are just recovering from the small-pox and do not like to be disturbed. For the courier has made everything right with the guard. At way-stations the courier comes to your compartment to see if you want a glass of water, or a newspaper, or anything; at eating-stations he sends luncheon out to you, while the other people scramble and worry in the dining-rooms. If anything breaks, about the car you are in, and the station-master proposes to pack you and your agent into a compartment with strangers, the courier reveals to him confidently that you are a French duke, born deaf and dumb, and the official comes and makes affable signs that he has ordered a choice car to be added to the train for you.

At custom-houses the multitude file tediously through, hot and irritated, and look on while the officers burrow into the trunks and make a mess of everything; but you hand your keys to the courier and sit still. Perhaps you arrive at your destination in a rainstorm at ten at night—you generally do. The multitude spend half an hour verifying their baggage and getting it transferred to the omnibuses; but the courier puts you into a vehicle without a moment's loss of time, and when you reach your hotel you find your rooms have been secured two or three days in advance, everything is ready, you can go at once to bed. Some of those other people will have to drift around to two or three hotels, in the rain, before they find accommodations.

I have not set down half of the virtues that are vested in a good courier, but I think I have set down a sufficiency of them to show that an irritable man who can afford one and does not employ him is not a wise economist. My courier was the worst one in Europe, yet he was a good deal better than none at all. It could not pay him to be a better one than he was, because I could not afford to buy things through him. He was a good enough courier for the small amount he got out of his service. Yes, to travel with a courier is bliss, to travel without one is the reverse.

I have had dealings with some very bad couriers; but I have

also had dealings with one who might fairly be called perfection. He was a young Polander, named Joseph N. Verey. He spoke eight languages, and seemed to be equally at home in all of them; he was shrewd, prompt, posted, and punctual; he was fertile in resources, and singularly gifted in the matter of overcoming difficulties; he not only knew how to do everything in his line, but he knew the best ways and the quickest; he was handy with children and invalids; all his employer needed to do was to take life easy and leave everything to the courier. His address is, care of Mr. O.H. Caygill, 371 Strand, London. Excellent couriers are somewhat rare; if the reader is about to travel, he will find it to his advantage to make a note of this one.

CHAPTER 33

The beautiful Giesbach Fall is near Interlaken, on the other side of the lake of Brienz, and is illuminated every night with those gorgeous theatrical fires whose name I cannot call just at this moment. This is said to be a spectacle which the tourist ought by no means to miss. I was strongly tempted, but I could not go there with propriety, because one goes in a boat. The task which I had set myself was to walk over Europe on foot, not skim over it in a boat. I had made a tacit contract with myself; it was my duty to abide by it. I was willing to make boat-trips for pleasure, but I could not conscientiously make them in the way of business.

It cost me something of a pang to lose that fine sight, but I lived down the desire, and gained in my self-respect through the triumph. I had a finer and a grander sight, however, where I was. This was the mighty dome of the Jungfrau softly outlined against the sky and faintly silvered by the starlight. There was something subduing in the influence of that silent and solemn and awful presence; one seemed to meet the immutable, the indestructible, the eternal, face to face, and to feel the trivial and fleeting nature of his own existence the more sharply by the contrast. One had the sense of being under the brooding contemplation of a spirit, not an inert mass of rocks and ice—a spirit which had looked down, through the slow drift of the ages, upon a million vanished races of men, and judged them; and would judge a million more—and still be there, watching, unchanged and unchangeable, after all life should be gone and the earth have become a vacant desolation.

While I was feeling these things, I was groping, without knowing it, toward an understanding of what the spell is which people find in the Alps, and in no other mountains—that strange, deep, nameless influence which, once felt, cannot be forgotten—once felt, leaves always behind it a restless longing to feel it again—a longing which is like homesickness; a grieving, haunting yearning, which will plead, implore, and persecute till it has its will. I met dozens of people, imaginative and unimaginative, cultivated and uncultivated, who had come from far countries and roamed through the Swiss Alps year after year—they could not explain why. They had come first, they said, out of idle curiosity, because everybody talked about it; they had come since because they could not help it, and they should keep on coming, while they lived, for the same reason; they had tried to break their chains and stay away, but it was futile; now they had no desire to break them. Others came nearer formulating what they felt; they said they could find perfect rest and peace nowhere else when they were troubled; all frets and worries and chafings sank to sleep in the presence of the benignant serenity of the Alps; the Great Spirit of the Mountain breathed his own peace upon their hurt minds and sore hearts, and healed them; they could not think base thoughts or do mean and sordid things here, before the visible throne of God.

Down the road a piece was a Kursaal—whatever that may be—and we joined the human tide to see what sort of enjoyment it might afford. It was the usual open-air concert, in an ornamental garden, with wines, beer, milk, whey, grapes, etc.—the whey and the grapes being necessaries of life to certain invalids whom physicians cannot repair, and who only continue to exist by the grace of whey or grapes. One of these departed spirits told me, in a sad and lifeless way, that there was no way for him to live but by whey; never drank anything, now, but whey, and dearly, dearly loved whey, he didn't know whey he did, but he did. After making this pun he died—that is the whey it served him.

Some other remains, preserved from decomposition by the grape system, told me that the grapes were of a peculiar breed, highly medicinal in their nature, and that they were counted out and administered by the grape-doctors as methodically as if they were pills. The new patient, if very feeble, began with one grape before breakfast, took three during breakfast, a couple between meals, five at luncheon, three in the afternoon, seven at dinner, four for supper, and part of a grape just before going to bed by way of a general regulator. The quantity was gradually and regularly increased, according to the needs and capacities of the patient, until by-and-by you would find him disposing of his one grape per second all the day long, and his regular barrel per day.

He said that men cured in this way, and enabled to discard the grape system, never afterwards got over the habit of talking as if they were dictating to a slow amanuensis, because they always made a pause between each two words while they sucked the substance out of an imaginary grape. He said these were tedious people to talk with. He said that men who had been cured by the other process were easily distinguished from the rest of mankind because they always tilted their heads back between every two words, and swallowed a swig of imaginary whey. He said it was an impressive thing to observe two men who had been cured by the two processes engaged in conversation—said their pauses and accompanying movements were so continuous and regular that a stranger would think himself in the presence of a couple of automatic machines. One finds out a great many wonderful things by travelling if he stumbles upon the right person.

I did not remain long at the Kursaal; the music was good enough, but it seemed rather tame after the cyclone of that Arkansaw expert. Besides my adventurous spirit had conceived a formidable enterprise—nothing less than a trip from Interlaken, by the Gemmi and Visp, clear to Zermatt, on foot! So it was necessary to plan the details, and get ready for an early start. The courier (this was not the one I have just been speaking of) thought that the *portier* of the hotel would be able to tell us how to find our way. And so it turned out. He showed us the whole thing on a relief-map, and we could see our route, with all its elevations and depressions, its villages and its rivers, as clearly as if we were sailing over it in a balloon. A relief-map is a great thing. The *portier* also wrote down each day's journey and the nightly hotel on a piece of paper, and made our course so plain that we should never be able to get lost without high-priced outside help.

I put the courier in the care of a gentleman who was going to Lausanne, and then we went to bed, after laying out the walking costumes and putting them into condition for instant occupation in the morning.

However, when we came down to breakfast at 8 a.m., it looked so much like rain that I hired a two-horse top-buggy for the first third of the journey. For two or three hours we jogged along the level road which skirts the beautiful lake of Thun, with a dim and dreamlike picture of watery expanses and spectral Alpine forms always before us, veiled in a mellowing mist. Then a steady downpour set in, and hid everything but the nearest objects. We kept the rain out of our faces with umbrellas, and away from our bodies with the leather apron of the buggy; but the driver sat unsheltered, and placidly soaked the weather in and seemed to like it. We had the road all to ourselves, and I never had a pleasanter excursion.

The weather began to clear while we were driving up a valley called the Kienthal, and presently a vast black cloudbank in front of us dissolved away and uncurtained the grand proportions and the soaring loftinesses of the Blumis Alp. It was a sort of breath-taking surprise; for we had not supposed there was anything behind that low-hung blanket of sable cloud but level valley. What we had been mistaking for fleeting glimpses of sky away aloft there were really patches of the Blumis's snowy crest caught through shredded rents in the drifting pall of vapour.

We dined in the inn at Frutigen, and our driver ought to have dined there too, but he would not have had time to dine and get drunk both, so he gave his mind to making a masterpiece of the latter, and succeeded. A German gentleman and his two young lady daughters had been taking their nooning at the inn, and when they left, just ahead of us, it was plain that their driver was as drunk as ours, and as happy and good-natured too, which was saying a good deal. These rascals overflowed with attentions and information for their guests, and with brotherly love for each other. They tied their reins, and took off their coats and hats, so that they might be able to give unencumbered attention to conversation and to the gestures necessary for its illustration.

The road was smooth; it led up, and over and down a continual succession of hills; but it was narrow, the horses were used to it, and could not well get out of it anyhow; so why shouldn't the drivers entertain themselves and us? The noses of our horses projected sociably into the rear of the forward carriage, and as we toiled up the long hills our driver stood up and talked to his friend, and his friend stood up and talked back to him, with his rear to the scenery. When the top was reached, and we went flying down the other side, there was no change in the programme. I carry in my memory yet the picture of that forward driver, on his knees on his high seat, resting his elbows on its back, and beaming down on his passengers, with happy eye, and flying hair, and jolly red face, and offering his card to the old German gentleman, while he praised his hack and horses, and both teams were whizzing down a long hill with nobody in a position to tell whether we were bound to destruction or an undeserved safety.

Toward sunset we entered a beautiful green valley dotted with châlets, a cosy little domain, hidden away from the busy world in a cloistered nook, among giant precipices topped with snowy peaks that seemed to float like islands above the curling surf of the sea of vapour that severed them from the lower world. Down from vague and vaporous heights, little ruffled zigzag milky currents came crawling, and found their way to the verge of one of those tremendous overhanging walls, whence they plunged, a shaft of silver, shivered to atoms in mid-descent, and turned to an airy puff of luminous dust. Here and there, in grooved depressions among the snowy desolations of the upper altitudes, one glimpsed the extremity of a glacier, with its seagreen and honeycombed battlements of ice.

Up the valley, under a dizzy precipice, nestled the village of Kandersteg, our halting-place for the night. We were soon there, and housed in the hotel. But the waning day had such an inviting influence that we did not remain housed many moments, but struck out and followed a roaring torrent of ice-water up to its far source in a sort of little grass-carpeted parlour, walled in all around by vast precipices and overlooked by clustering summits of ice. This was the snuggest little croquet-ground imaginable; it was perfectly level, and not more than a mile long by half a mile wide. The walls around it were so gigantic, and everything about it was on so mighty a scale, that it was belittled, by contrast, to what I have likened it to—a cosy and carpeted parlour. It was so high above the Kandersteg valley that there was nothing between it and the snow-peaks. I had never been in such intimate relations with the high altitudes before; the snow-peaks had always been remote and unapproachable grandeurs hitherto, but now we were hob-a-nob—if one may use such a seemingly irreverent expression about creations so august as these.

We could see the streams which fed the torrent we had followed issuing from under the greenish ramparts of glaciers; but two or three of these, instead of flowing over the precipices, sank down into the rock and sprang in big jets out of holes in the mid-face of the walls.

The green nook which I have been describing is called the Gasternthal. The glacier streams gather and flow through it in a broad and rushing brook to a narrow cleft between lofty precipices; here the rushing brook becomes a mad torrent and goes booming and thundering down towards Kandersteg, lashing and thrashing its way over and among monster boulders, and hurling chance roots and logs about like straws. There was no lack of cascades along this route. The path by the side of the torrent was so narrow that one had to look sharp when he heard a cow-bell, and hunt for a place that was wide enough to accommodate a cow and a Christian side by side, and such places were not always to be had at an instant's notice. The cows wear church-bells, and that is a good idea in the cows, for where that torrent is you couldn't hear an ordinary cow-bell any further than you could hear the ticking of a watch.

I needed exercise, so I employed my agent in setting stranded logs and dead trees adrift, and I sat on a boulder and watched them go whirling and leaping head over heels down the boiling torrent. It was a wonderfully exhilarating spectacle. When I had had exercise enough, I made the agent take some, by running a race with one of those logs. I made a trifle by betting on the log.

After dinner we had a walk up and down the quiet Kandersteg valley, in the soft gloaming, with the spectacle of the dying lights of day playing about the crests and pinnacles of the still and solemn upper realms for contrast, and text for talk. There were no sounds but the dull complaining of the torrent and the occasional tinkling of a distant bell. The spirit of the place was a sense of deep, pervading peace; one might dream his life tranquilly away there, and not miss it or mind it when it was gone.

The summer departed with the sun, and winter came with the stars. It grew to be a bitter night in that little hotel, backed up against a precipice that had no visible top to it; but we kept warm, and woke in time in the morning to find that everybody else had left for the Gemmi three hours before—so our little plan of helping that German family (principally the old man) over the Pass was a blocked generosity.

CHAPTER 34

We hired the only guide left, to lead us on our way. He was over seventy, but he could have given me nine-tenths of his strength and still had all his age entitled him to. He shouldered our satchels, overcoats, and alpenstocks, and we set out up the path. It was hot work. The old man soon begged us to hand over our coats and waistcoats to him to carry, too, and we did it; one could not refuse so little a thing to a poor old man like that; he should have had them if he had been a hundred and fifty.

When we began that ascent, we could see a microscopic châlet perched away up against heaven on what seemed to be the highest mountain near us. It was on our right, across the narrow head of the valley. But when we got up abreast it, on its own level, mountains were towering high above on every hand, and we saw that its altitude was just about that of the little Gasternthal which we had visited the evening before. Still, it seemed a long way up in the air, in the waste and lonely wilderness of rocks. It had an unfenced grass-plot in front of it which seemed about as big as a billiard-table, and this grass-plot slanted so sharply downwards, and was so brief, and ended so exceedingly soon at the verge of the absolute precipice, that it was a shuddery thing to think of a person's venturing to trust his foot on an incline so situated at all. Suppose a man stepped on an orange-peel in that yard: there would be nothing for him to seize; nothing could keep him from rolling; five revolutions would bring him to the edge, and over he would go. What a frightful distance he would fall!—for there are very few birds that fly as high as his starting-point. He would strike and bounce, two or three times on his way down, but this would be no advantage to him. I would as soon take an airing on the slant of a rainbow as in such a front yard. I would rather, in fact, for the distance down would be about the same, and it is pleasanter to slide than to bounce. I could not see how the peasants got up to that châlet—the region seemed too steep for anything but a balloon.

As we strolled on, climbing up higher and higher, we were continually bringing neighbouring peaks into view, and lofty prominences which had been hidden behind lower peaks before; so, by-and-by, while standing before a group of these giants, we looked around for the châlet again: there it was, apparently on an inconspicuous ridge in the valley! It was as far below us, now, as it had been above us when we were beginning the ascent.

After a while the path led us along a railed precipice, and we looked over—far beneath us was the snug parlour again, the little Gasternthal, with its water-jets spouting from the face of its rock walls. We could have dropped a stone into it. We had been finding the top of the world all along—and always finding a still higher top stealing into view in a disappointing way just ahead; when we looked down into the Gasternthal we felt pretty sure that we had reached the genuine top at last, but it was not so; there were much higher altitudes to be scaled yet. We were still in the pleasant shade of forest trees, we were still in a region which was cushioned with beautiful mosses and aglow with the many-tinted lustre of innumerable wild-flowers.

We found, indeed, more interest in the wild-flowers than in anything else. We gathered a specimen or two of every kind which we were unacquainted with; so we had sumptuous bouquets. But one of the chief interests lay in chasing the seasons of the year up the mountain and determining them by the presence of flowers and berries which we were acquainted with. For instance, it was the end of August at the level of the sea; in the Kandersteg valley, at the base of the Pass, we found flowers which would not be due at the sea level for two or three weeks; higher up we entered October, and gathered fringed gentians. I made no notes, and have forgotten the details, but the construction of the floral calendar was very entertaining while it lasted.

In the high regions we found rich store of the splendid red flower called the Alpine rose, but we did not find any example of the ugly Swiss favourite called *Edelweiss*. Its name seems to indicate that it is a noble flower and that it is white. It may be noble enough, but it is not attractive, and it is not white. The fuzzy blossom is the colour of bad cigar ashes, and appears to be made of a cheap quality of grey plush. It has a noble and distant way of confining itself to the high altitudes, but that is probably on account of its looks; it apparently has no monopoly of those upper altitudes, however, for they are sometimes intruded upon by some of the loveliest of the valley families of wild-flowers. Everybody in the Alps wears a sprig of Edelweiss in his hat. It is the native's pet, and also the tourist's.

All the morning, as we loafed along, having a good time, other pedestrians went staving by us with vigorous strides, and with the intent and determined look of men who were walking for a wager. These wore loose knee-breeches, long yarn stockings, and hobnailed high-laced walking-shoes. They were gentlemen who would go home to England or Germany and tell how many miles they had beaten the guide-book every day. But I doubted if they ever had much real fun, outside of the mere magnificent exhilaration of the tramp through the green valleys and the breezy heights; for they were almost always alone, and even the finest scenery loses incalculably when there is no one to enjoy it with.

All the morning an endless double procession of mule-mounted tourists filed past us along the narrow path—the one procession going, the other coming. We had taken a good deal of trouble to teach ourselves the kindly German custom of saluting all strangers with doffed hat, and we resolutely clung to it that morning, although it kept us bare-headed most of the time and was not always responded to. Still we found an interest in the thing, because we naturally liked to know who were English and Americans among the passers-by. All Continental natives responded, of course; so did some of the English and Americans, but as a general thing these two races gave no sign. Whenever a man or a woman showed us cold neglect, we spoke up confidently in our own tongue and asked for such information as we happened to need, and we always got a reply in the same language. The English and American fold are not less kindly than other races, they are only more reserved, and that comes of habit and education. In one dreary, rocky waste, away above the line of vegetation, we met a procession of twenty-five mounted young men, all from America. We got answering bows enough from these, of course, for they were of an age to learn to do in Rome as Rome does, without much effort.

At one extremity of this patch of desolation, overhung by bare and forbidding crags which husbanded drifts of everlasting snow in their shaded cavities, was a small stretch of thin and discouraged grass, and a man and a family of pigs were actually here in some shanties. Consequently this place could be really reckoned as 'property'; it had a money value, and was doubtless taxed. I think it must have marked the limit of real estate in this world. It would be hard to set a money value upon any piece of earth that lies between that spot and the empty realm of space. That man may claim the distinction of owning the end of the world, for if there is any definite end to the world he has certainly found it.

From here forward we moved through a storm-swept and smileless desolation. All about us rose gigantic masses, crags, and ramparts of bare and dreary rock, with not a vestige or semblance of plant or tree or flower anywhere, or glimpse of any creature that had life. The frost and the tempests of unnumbered ages had battered and hacked at these cliffs, with a deathless energy, destroying them piecemeal; so all the region about their bases was a tumbled chaos of great fragments which had been split off and hurled to the ground. Soiled and aged banks of snow lay close about our path. The ghastly desolation of the place was as tremendously complete as if Doré had furnished the working plans for it. But every now and then, through the stern gateways around us, we caught a view of some neighbouring majestic dome, sheathed with glittering ice, and displaying its white purity at an elevation compared to which ours was grovelling and plebeian, and this spectacle always chained one's interest and admiration at once, and made him forget there was anything ugly in the world.

I have just said that there was nothing but death and desolation in these hideous places, but I forgot. In the most forlorn and arid and dismal one of all, where the racked and splintered *débris* was thickest, where the ancient patches of snow lay against the very path, where the winds blew bitterest and the general aspect was mournfullest and dreariest, and furthest from any suggestion of cheer or hope, I found a solitary wee forget-me-not flourishing away, not a droop about it anywhere, but holding its bright blue star up with the prettiest and gallantest air in the world, the only happy spirit, the only smiling thing, in all that grisly desert. She seemed to say, 'Cheer up!—as long as we are here, let us make the best of it.' I judged she had earned a right to a more hospitable place; so I plucked her up and sent her to America to a friend who would respect her for the fight she had made, all by her small self, to make a whole vast despondent Alpine desolation stop breaking its heart over the unalterable, and hold up its head and look at the bright side of things for once.

We stopped for a nooning at a strongly built little inn called the Schwarenbach. It sits in a lonely spot among the peaks, where it is swept by the trailing fringes of the cloud-rack, and is rained on, snowed on, and pelted and persecuted by the storms nearly every day of its life. It was the only habitation in the whole Gemmi Pass.

Close at hand, now, was a chance for a blood-curdling Alpine adventure. Close at hand was the snowy mass of the Great Altels cooling its top-knot in the sky and daring us to an ascent. I was fired with the idea, and immediately made up my mind to procure the necessary guides, ropes, etc., and undertake it. I instructed Harris to go to the landlord of the inn and set him about our preparations. Meantime I went diligently to work to read up and find out what this much-talked-of mountain-climbing was like, and how one should go about it—for in these matters I was ignorant. I opened Mr. Hinchcliff's 'Summer Months among the Alps' (published 1857), and selected his account of his ascent of Monte Rosa. It began—

'It is very difficult to free the mind from excitement on the evening before a grand expedition—'

I saw that I was too calm; so I walked the room a while and worked myself into a high excitement; but the book's next remark—that the adventurer must get up at two in the morning—came as near as anything to flatting it all out again. However, I reinforced it, and read on, about how Mr. Hinchliff dressed by candle-light and was 'soon down among the guides, who were bustling about in the passage, packing provisions, and making every preparation for the start'; and how he glanced out into the cold clear night and saw that—

'The whole sky was blazing with stars, larger and brighter than they appear through the dense atmosphere breathed by inhabitants of the lower parts of the earth. They seemed actually suspended from the dark vault of heaven, and their gentle light shed a fairy-like gleam over the snow-fields around the foot of the Matterhorn, which raised its stupendous pinnacle on high, penetrating to the heart of the Great Bear, and crowning itself with a diadem of his magnificent stars. Not a sound disturbed the deep tranquillity of the night, except the distant roar of streams which rush from the high plateau of the St. Theodule glacier, and fall headlong over precipitous rocks till they lose themselves in the mazes of the Gorner glacier.'

He took his hot toast and coffee, and then about half-past three his caravan of ten men filed away from the Riffel Hotel, and began the steep climb. At half-past five he happened to turn around, and 'beheld the glorious spectacle of the Matterhorn, just touched by the rosy-fingered morning, and looking like a huge pyramid of fire rising out of the barren ocean of ice and rock around it.' Then the Breithorn and the Dent Blanche caught the radiant glow; but 'the intervening mass of Monte Rosa made it necessary for us to climb many hours before we could hope to see the sun himself, yet the whole air soon grew warmer after the splendid birth of day.'

He gazed at the lofty crown of Monte Rosa and the wastes of

snow that guarded its steep approaches, and the chief guide delivered the opinion that no man could conquer their awful heights and put his foot upon that summit. But the adventurers moved steadily on, nevertheless.

They toiled up, and up, and still up; they passed the Grand Plateau; then toiled up a steep shoulder of the mountain, clinging like flies to its rugged face; and now they were confronted by a tremendous wall from which great blocks of ice and snow were evidently in the habit of falling. They turned aside to skirt this wall, and gradually ascended until their way was barred by a 'maze of gigantic snow crevasses'—so they turned aside again, and 'began a long climb of sufficient steepness to make a zigzag course necessary.'

Fatigue compelled them to halt frequently for a moment or two. At one of these halts somebody called out, 'Look at Mont Blanc!' and 'we were at once made aware of the very great height we had attained by actually seeing the monarch of the Alps and his attendant satellites right over the top of the Breithorn, itself at least 14,000 feet high!'

These people moved in single file, and were all tied to a strong rope, at regular distances apart, so that if one of them slipped on those giddy heights the others could brace themselves on their alpenstocks and save him from darting into the valley, thousands of feet below. By-and-by they came to an ice-coated ridge which was tilted up at a sharp angle and had a precipice on one side of it. They had to climb this, so the guide in the lead cut steps in the ice with his hatchet, and as fast as he took his toes out of one of these slight holes, the toes of the man behind him occupied it.

'Slowly and steadily we kept on our way over this dangerous part of the ascent, and I daresay it was fortunate for some of us that attention was distracted from the head by the paramount necessity of looking after the feet; *for, while on the left the incline of ice was so steep that it would be impossible for any man to save himself in case of a slip, unless the others could hold him up, on the right we might drop a pebble from the hand over precipices of unknown extent down upon the tremendous glacier below.*

'Great caution, therefore, was absolutely necessary, and in

this exposed situation we were attacked by all the fury of that grand enemy of aspirants to Monte Rosa—a severe and bitterly cold wind from the north. The fine powdery snow was driven past us in clouds, penetrating the interstices of our clothes, and the pieces of ice which flew from the blows of Peter's axe were whisked into the air, and then dashed over the precipice. We had quite enough to do to prevent ourselves from being served in the same ruthless fashion, and now and then, in the more violent gusts of wind, were glad to stick our alpenstocks into the ice and hold on hard.'

Having surmounted this perilous steep, they sat down and took a brief rest with their backs against a sheltering rock and their heels dangling over a bottomless abyss; then they climbed to the base of another ridge, a more difficult and dangerous one still:—

'The whole of the ridge was exceedingly narrow, and the fall on each side desperately steep, but the ice in some of these intervals between the masses of rock assumed the form of a mere sharp edge, almost like a knife; these places, though not more than three or four short paces in length, looked uncommonly awkward; but, like the sword leading true believers to the gates of Paradise, they must needs be passed before we could attain to the summit of our ambition. These were in one or two places so narrow, that in stepping over them with toes well turned out for greater security, *one end of the foot projected over the awful precipice on the right, while the other was on the beginning of the icy slope on the left, which was scarcely less steep than the rocks.*

On these occasions Peter would take my hand, and each of us stretching as far as we could, he was thus enabled to get a firm footing two paces or rather more from me, whence a spring would probably bring him to the rock on the other side; then, turning round, he called to me to come, and taking a couple of steps carefully, I was met at the third by his outstretched hand ready to clasp mine, and in a moment stood by his side. The others followed in much the same fashion. Once my right foot slipped on the side towards the precipice, but I threw out my left arm in a moment so that it caught the icy edge under my armpit as I fell, and supported me considerably; at the same instant I cast my eyes down the side on which I had slipped, and contrived to plant my right foot on a piece of rock as large as a cricket-ball, which chanced to protrude through the ice, on the very edge of the precipice. Being thus anchored fore and aft, as it were, I believe I could easily have recovered myself, even if I had been alone, though it must be confessed the situation would have been an awful one; as it was, however, a jerk from Peter settled the matter very soon, and I was on my legs all right in an instant. The rope is an immense help in places of this kind.'

Now they arrived at the base of a great knob or dome veneered with ice and powdered with snow—the utmost summit, the last bit of solidity between them and the hollow vault of heaven. They set to work with their hatchets, and were soon creeping, insect-like, up its surface, with their heels projecting over the thinnest kind of nothingness, thickened up a little with a few wandering shreds and films of cloud moving in lazy procession far below. Presently one man's toe-hold broke and he fell! There he dangled in mid-air at the end of the rope, like a spider, till his friends above hauled him into place again.

A little bit later the party stood upon the wee pedestal of the very summit, in a driving wind, and looked out upon the vast green expanses of Italy and a shoreless ocean of billowy Alps.

When I had read thus far, Harris burst into the room in a noble excitement and said the ropes and the guides were secured, and asked if I was ready. I said I believed I wouldn't ascend the Altels this time. I said Alp-climbing was a different thing from what I had supposed it was, and so I judged we had better study its points a little more before we went definitely into it. But I told him to retain the guides and order them to follow us to Zermatt, because I meant to use them there. I said I could feel the spirit of adventure beginning to stir in me, and was sure that the fell fascination of Alp-climbing would soon be upon me. I said he could make up his mind to it that we would do a deed before we were a week older which would make the hair of the timid curl with fright.

This made Harris happy, and filled him with ambitious anticipations. He went at once to tell the guides to follow us to Zermatt and bring all their paraphernalia with them.

CHAPTER 35

A great and priceless thing is a new interest! How it takes possession of a man! how it clings to him! how it rides him! I strode onward from the Schwarenbach hostelry a changed man, a reorganised personality. I walked in a new world, I saw with new eyes. I had been looking aloft at the giant snow-peaks only as things to be worshipped for their grandeur and magnitude, and their unspeakable grace of form; I looked up at them now, as also things to be conquered and climbed. My sense of their grandeur and their noble beauty was neither lost nor impaired; I had gained a new interest in the mountains without losing the old ones. I followed the steep lines up, inch by inch, with my eye, and noted the possibility or impossibility of following them with my feet. When I saw a shining helmet of ice projecting above the clouds, I tried to imagine I saw files of black specks toiling up it roped together with a gossamer thread.

We skirted the lonely little lake called the Daubensee, and presently passed close by a glacier on the right—a thing like a great river frozen solid in its flow and broken square off like a wall at its mouth. I had never been so near a glacier before.

Here we came upon a new board shanty, and found some men engaged in building a stone house; so the Schwarenbach was soon to have a rival. We bought a bottle or so of beer here; at any rate they called it beer, but I knew by the price that it was dissolved jewellery, and I perceived by the taste that dissolved jewellery is not good stuff to drink.

We were surrounded by a hideous desolation. We stepped

forward to a sort of jumping-off place, and were confronted by a
startling contrast; we seemed to look down into fairyland. Two
or three thousand feet below us was a bright green level, with a
pretty town in its midst, and a silvery stream winding among the
meadows; the charming spot was walled in on all sides by
gigantic precipices clothed with pines; and over the pines, out of
the softened distances, rose the snowy domes and peaks of the
Monte Rosa region. How exquisitely green and beautiful that
little valley down there was! The distance was not great enough
to obliterate details, it only made them little, and mellow, and
dainty, like landscapes and towns seen through the wrong end of
a spy-glass.

Right under us a narrow ledge rose up out of the valley, with
a green, slanting, bench-shaped top, and grouped about upon
this green-baize bench were a lot of black and white sheep which
looked merely like over-sized worms. The bench seemed lifted
well up into our neighbourhood, but that was a deception—it
was a long way down to it.

We began our descent, now, by the most remarkable road I
have ever seen. It wound in corkscrew curves down the face of
the colossal precipice—a narrow way, with always the solid
rock wall at one elbow, and perpendicular nothingness at the
other. We met an everlasting procession of guides, porters,
mules, litters, and tourists climbing up this steep and muddy
path, and there was no room to spare when you had to pass a
tolerably fat mule. I always took the inside, when I heard or saw
the mule coming, and flattened myself against the wall. I
preferred the inside, of course, but I should have had to take it
anyhow, because the mule prefers the outside. A mule's
preference—on a precipice—is a thing to be respected. Well, his
choice is always the outside. His life is mostly devoted to
carrying bulky panniers and packages which rest against his
body—therefore he is habituated to taking the outside edge of
mountain paths, to keep his bundles from rubbing against rocks
or banks on the other. When he goes into the passenger business
he absurdly clings to his old habit, and keeps one leg of his
passenger always dangling over the great deeps of the lower
world, while that passenger's heart is in the highlands, so to

speak. More than once I saw a mule's hind foot cave over the outer edge and send earth and rubbish into the bottomless abyss; and I noticed that upon these occasions the rider, whether male or female, looked tolerably unwell.

There was one place where an 18-inch breadth of light masonry had been added to the verge of the path, and as there was a very sharp turn here, a panel of fencing had been set up there at some ancient time, as a protection. This panel was old and grey and feeble, and the light masonry had been loosened by recent rains. A young American girl came along on a mule, and in making the turn the mule's hind foot caved all the loose masonry and one of the fence posts overboard; the mule gave a violent lurch inboard to save himself, and succeeded in the effort, but that girl turned as white as the snows of Mont Blanc for a moment.

The path here was simply a groove cut into the face of the precipice; there was a four-foot breadth of solid rock under the traveller, and a four-foot breadth of solid rock just above his head, like the roof of a narrow porch; he could look out from this gallery and see a sheer summitless and bottomless wall of rock before him, across a gorge or crack a biscuit's toss in width—but he could not see the bottom of his own precipice unless he lay down and projected his nose over the edge. I did not do this, because I did not wish to soil my clothes.

Every few hundred yards, at particularly bad places, one came across a panel or so of plank fencing; but they were always old and weak, and they generally leaned out over the chasm and did not make any rash promises to hold up people who might need support. There was one of these panels which had only its upper board left; a pedestrianising English youth came tearing down the path, was seized with an impulse to look over the precipice, and without an instant's thought he threw his weight upon that crazy board. It bent outward a foot! I never made a gasp before that came so near suffocating me. The English youth's face simply showed a lively surprise, but nothing more. He went swinging along valleywards again, as if he did not know he had just swindled a coroner by the closest kind of a shave.

The Alpine litter is sometimes like a cushioned box made fast between the middles of two long poles, and sometimes it is a chair with a back to it and a support for the feet. It is carried by relays of strong porters. The motion is easier than that of any other conveyance. We met a few men and a great many ladies in litters; it seemed to me that most of the ladies looked pale and nauseated; their general aspect gave me the idea that they were patiently enduring a horrible suffering. As a rule, they looked at their laps, and left the scenery to take care of itself.

But the most frightened creature I saw was a led horse that overtook us. Poor fellow! he had been born and reared in the grassy levels of the Kandersteg valley, and had never seen anything like this hideous place before. Every few steps he would stop short, glance wildly out from the dizzy height, and then spread his red nostrils wide and pant as violently as if he had been running a race; and all the while he quaked from head to heel as with a palsy. He was a handsome fellow, and he made a fine statuesque picture of terror, but it was pitiful to see him suffer so.

This dreadful path has had its tragedy. Baedeker, with his customary over-terseness, begins and ends the tale thus: 'The descent on horseback should be avoided. In 1861 a Comtesse d'Herlincourt fell from her saddle over the precipice and was killed on the spot.'

We looked over the precipice there, and saw the monument which commemorates the event. It stands in the bottom of the gorge, in a place which has been hollowed out of the rock to protect it from the torrent and the storms. Our old guide never spoke but when spoken to, and then limited himself to a syllable or two; but when we asked him about this tragedy he showed a strong interest in the matter. He said the Countess was very pretty, and very young—hardly out of her girlhood, in fact. She was newly married, and was on her bridal tour. The young husband was riding a little in advance, one guide was leading the husband's horse, another was leading the bride's. The old man continued—

'The guide that was leading the husband's horse happened to glance back, and there was that poor young thing sitting up

staring out over the precipice; and her face began to bend
downward a little, and she put up her two hands slowly and met
it—so—and put them flat against her eyes—so—and then she
sank out of the saddle, with a sharp shriek, and one caught only
the flash of a dress, and it was all over.'

Then after a pause—

'Ah, yes, that guide saw these things—yes, he saw them all.
He saw them all, just as I have told you.'

After another pause—

'Ah, yes, he saw them all. My God, that was *me*. I was that
guide!'

This had been the one event of the old man's life; so one may
be sure he had forgotten no detail connected with it. We listened
to all he had to say about what was done and what happened
and what was said after the sorrowful occurrence, and a painful
story it was.

When we had wound down toward the valley until we were
about on the last spiral of the corkscrew, Harris's hat blew over
the last remaining bit of precipice—a small cliff a hundred or a
hundred and fifty feet high—and sailed down towards a steep
slant composed of rough chips and fragments which the weather
had flaked away from the precipices. We went leisurely down
there, expecting to find it without any trouble, but we had made
a mistake as to that. We hunted during a couple of hours—not
because the old straw hat was valuable, but out of curiosity to
find out how such a thing could manage to conceal itself in open
ground where there was nothing for it to hide behind. When one
is reading in bed, and lays his paper-knife down, he cannot find
it again if it is smaller than a sabre; that hat was as stubborn as
any paper-knife could have been, and we finally had to give it
up; but we found a fragment that had once belonged to an
opera-glass, and by digging around and turning over the rocks
we gradually collected all the lenses and the cylinders and the
various odds and ends that go to make up a complete opera-
glass. We afterwards had the thing reconstructed, and the owner
can have his adventurous long-lost property by submitting
proofs and paying costs of rehabilitation. We had hopes of
finding the owner there, distributed around amongst the rocks,

for it would have made an elegant paragraph; but we were disappointed. Still, we were far from being disheartened, for there was a considerable area which we had not thoroughly searched; we were satisfied he was there, somewhere, so we resolved to wait over a day at Leuk and come back and get him. Then we sat down to polish off the perspiration and arrange about what we would do with him when we got him. Harris was for contributing him to the British Museum; but I was for mailing him to his widow. That is the difference between Harris and me: Harris is all for display, I am all for the simple right, even though I lose money by it. Harris argued in favour of his proposition and against mine; I argued in favour of mine and against his. The discussion warmed into a dispute; the dispute warmed into a quarrel. I finally said, very decidedly—

'My mind is made up. He goes to the widow.'

Harris answered sharply—

'And *my* mind is made up. He goes to the Museum.'

I said, calmly—

'The Museum may whistle when it gets him.'

Harris retorted—

'The widow may save herself the trouble of whistling, for I will see that she never gets him.'

After some angry bandying of epithets, I said—

'It seems to me that you are taking on a good many airs about these remains. I don't quite see what *you've* got to say about them?'

'*I*? I've got *all* to say about them. They'd never have been thought of if I hadn't found their opera-glass. The corpse belongs to me, and I'll do as I please with him.'

I was leader of the Expedition, and all discoveries achieved by it naturally belonged to me. I was entitled to these remains, and could have enforced my right; but rather than have bad blood about the matter, I said we would toss up for them. I threw heads and won, but it was a barren victory, for although we spent all the next day searching, we never found a bone. I cannot imagine what could ever have become of that fellow.

The town in the valley is called Leuk or Leukerbad. We pointed our course toward it, down a verdant slope which was adorned with fringed gentians and other flowers, and presently entered the narrow alleys of the outskirts and waded toward the middle of the town through liquid 'fertiliser.' They ought to either pave that village or organise a ferry.

Harris's body was simply a chamois-pasture; his person was populous with the little hungry pests; his skin, when he stripped, was splotched like a scarlet fever patient's; so, when we were about to enter one of the Leukerbad inns, and he noticed its sign, 'Chamois Hotel,' he refused to stop there. He said the chamois was plentiful enough, without hunting up hotels where they made a speciality of it. I was indifferent, for the chamois is a creature that will neither bite me nor abide with me: but to calm Harris, we went to the Hôtel des Alpes.

At the *table d'hôte* we had this for an incident. A very grave man—in fact his gravity amounted to solemnity, and almost to austerity—sat opposite us, and he was 'tight,' but doing his best to appear sober. He took up a *corked* bottle of wine, tilted it over his glass a while, then set it out of the way with a contented look, and went on with his dinner.

Presently he put his glass to his mouth, and of course found it empty. He looked puzzled and glanced furtively and suspiciously out of the corner of his eye at a benignant and unconscious old lady who sat at his right. Shook his head, as much as to say, 'No, she couldn't have done it.' He tilted the corked bottle over his glass again, meantime searching around with his watery eye to see if anybody was watching him. He ate a few mouthfuls, raised his glass to his lips, and of course it was still empty. He bent an injured and accusing side-gaze upon that unconscious old lady, which was a study to see. She went on eating and gave no sign. He took up his glass and his bottle, with a wise private nod of his head, and set them gravely on the left-hand side of his plate—poured himself another imaginary drink—went to work with his knife and fork once more—presently lifted his glass with good confidence, and found it empty, as usual.

This was almost a petrifying surprise. He straightened himself up in his chair and deliberately and sorrowfully inspected the busy old ladies at his elbows, first one and then the other. At last he softly pushed his plate away, set his glass directly in front of him, held on to it with his left hand, and proceeded to pour with his right. This time he observed that nothing came. He turned the bottle clear upside down; still nothing issued from it; a plaintive look came into his face, and he said, as if to himself. ' *'ic! They've got it all!*' Then he set the bottle down, resignedly, and took the rest of his dinner dry.

It was at that *table d'hôte*, too, that I had under inspection the largest lady I have ever seen in private life. She was over seven feet high, and magnificently proportioned. What had first called my attention to her was my stepping on an outlying flange of her foot, and hearing, from up toward the ceiling, a deep 'Pardon, m'sieu, but you encroach!'

That was when we were coming through the hall, and the place was dim, and I could see her only vaguely. The thing which called my attention to her the second time was, that at a table beyond ours were two very pretty girls, and this great lady came in and sat down between them and me and blotted out the view. She had a handsome face, and she was very finely formed—perfectly formed, I should say. But she made everybody around her look trivial and commonplace. Ladies near her looked like children, and the men about her looked mean. They looked like failures; and they looked as if they felt so, too. She sat with her back to us. I never saw such a back in my life. I would have so liked to see the moon rise over it. The whole congregation waited, under one pretext or another, till she finished her dinner and went out; they wanted to see her at her full altitude, and they found it worth tarrying for. She filled one's idea of what an empress ought to be, when she rose up in her unapproachable grandeur and moved superbly out of that place.

We were not at Leuk in time to see her at her heaviest weight. She had suffered from corpulence, and had come there to get rid of her extra flesh in the baths. Five weeks of soaking—five uninterrupted hours of it every day—had accomplished her purpose and reduced her to the right proportions.

Those baths remove fat, and also skin-diseases. The patients remain in the great tanks hours at a time. A dozen gentlemen and ladies occupy a tank together, and amuse themselves with rompings and various games. They have floating desks and tables, and they read or lunch or play chess in water that is breast-deep. The tourist can step in and view this novel spectacle if he chooses. There's a poor-box, and he will have to contribute. There are several of these big bathing-houses, and you can always tell when you are near one of them by the romping noises and shouts of laughter that proceed from it. The water is running water, and changes all the time, else a patient with a ringworm might take the bath with only a partial success, since while he was ridding himself of his ringworm he might catch the itch.

The next morning we wandered back up the green valley, leisurely, with the curving walls of those bare and stupendous precipices rising into the clouds before us. I had never seen a clean, bare precipice stretching up 5,000 feet above me before, and I never shall expect to see another one. They exist, perhaps, but not in places where one can easily get close to them. This pile of stone is peculiar. From its base to the soaring tops of its mighty towers, all its lines and all its details vaguely suggest human architecture. There are rudimentary bow windows, cornices, chimneys, demarcations of stories, &c. One could sit and stare up there and study the features and exquisite graces of this grand structure, bit by bit, and day after day, and never weary his interest. The termination, toward the town, observed in profile, is the perfection of shape. It comes down out of the clouds in a succession of rounded, colossal, terrace-like projections—a stairway for the gods; at its head spring several lofty storm-scarred towers, one above another, with faint films of vapour curling always about them like spectral banners. If there were a king whose realms included the whole world, here would be the palace meet and proper for such a monarch. He would only need to hollow it out and put in the electric light. He could give audience to a nation at a time under its roof.

Our search for those remains having failed, we inspected with a glass the dim and distant track of an old-time avalanche that once swept down from some pine-grown summits behind the town and swept away the houses and buried the people; then we struck down the road that leads toward the Rhone, to see the famous *Ladders*. These perilous things are built against the perpendicular face of a cliff two or three hundred feet high. The peasants, of both sexes, were climbing up and down them, with heavy loads on their backs. I ordered Harris to make the ascent, so I could put the thrill and horror of it in my book, and he accomplished the feat successfully, through a sub-agent, for three francs, which I paid. It makes me shudder yet when I think of what I felt when I was clinging there between heaven and earth in the person of that proxy. At times the world swam around me, and I could hardly keep from letting go, so dizzying was the appalling danger. Many a person would have given up and descended, but I stuck to my task, and would not yield until I had accomplished it. I felt a just pride in my exploit, but I would not have repeated it for the wealth of the world. I shall break my neck yet with some such foolhardy performance, for warnings never seem to have any lasting effect upon me. When the people of the hotel found that I had been climbing those crazy Ladders, it made me an object of considerable distinction.

Next morning, early, we drove to the Rhone valley and took the train for Visp. There we shouldered our knapsacks and things, and set out on foot, in a tremendous rain, up the winding gorge, towards Zermatt. Hour after hour we slopped along, by the roaring torrent, and under noble Lesser Alps which were clothed in rich velvety green all the way up, and had little atomy Swiss homes perched upon grassy benches along their mist-dimmed heights.

The rain continued to pour and torrent to boom, and we continued to enjoy both. At the one spot where this torrent tossed its white mane highest, and thundered loudest, and lashed the big boulders fiercest, the canton had done itself the honour to build the flimsiest wooden bridge that exists in the world. While we were walking over it, along with a party of horsemen, I noticed that even the larger rain-drops made it shake. I called Harris's attention to it, and he noticed it too. It seemed to me that if I owned an elephant that was a keep-sake, and I thought a good deal of him, I would think twice before I would ride him over that bridge.

We climbed up to the village of St. Nicholas, about half-past four in the afternoon, waded ankle-deep through the fertiliser-juice, and stopped at a new and nice hotel close by the little church. We stripped and went to bed, and sent our clothes down to be baked. All the horde of soaked tourists did the same. That chaos of clothing got mixed in the kitchen, and there were consequences. I did not get back the same drawers I sent down, when our things came up at 6.15; I got a pair on a new plan. They were merely a pair of white ruffle-cuffed absurdities, hitched together at the top with a narrow band, and they did not come quite down to my knees. They were pretty enough, but they made me feel like two people, and disconnected at that. The man must have been an idiot that got himself up like that, to rough it in the Swiss mountains. The shirt they brought me was shorter than the drawers, and hadn't any sleeves to it—at least it hadn't anything more than what Mr. Darwin would call 'rudimentary' sleeves; these had 'edging' around them, but the bosom was ridiculously plain. The knit silk under-shirt they brought me was on a new plan, and was really a sensible thing; it opened behind, and had pockets in it to put your shoulder-blades in; but they did not seem to fit mine, and so I found it a sort of uncomfortable garment. They gave my bobtail coat to somebody else, and sent me an ulster suitable for a giraffe. I had to tie my collar on, because there was no button behind on that foolish little shirt which I described a while ago.

When I was dressed for dinner at 6.30, I was too loose in some places and too tight in others, and altogether I felt slovenly and ill-conditioned. However, the people at the *table d'hôte* were no better off than I was; they had everybody's clothes but their own on. A long stranger recognised his ulster as soon as he saw the tail of it following me in, but nobody claimed my shirts or my drawers, though I described them as well as I was able. I gave them to the chambermaid that night when I went to bed, and she probably found the owner, for my own things were on a chair outside my door in the morning.

There was a loveable English clergyman who did not get to the *table d'hôte* at all. His breeches had turned up missing, and without any equivalent. He said he was not more particular than other people, but he had noticed that a clergyman at dinner without any breeches was almost sure to excite remark.

CHAPTER 36

We did not over-sleep at St. Nicholas. The church-bell began to ring at 4.30 in the morning, and from the length of time it continued to ring I judged that it takes the Swiss sinner a good while to get the invitation through his head. Most church-bells in the world are of poor quality, and have a harsh and rasping sound which upsets the temper and produces much sin, but the St. Nicholas bell is a good deal the worst one that has been contrived yet, and is peculiarly maddening in its operation. Still, it may have its right and its excuse to exist, for the community is poor and not every citizen can afford a clock, perhaps; but there cannot be any excuse for our church-bells at home, for there is no family in America without a clock, and consequently there is no fair pretext for the usual Sunday medley of dreadful sounds that issues from our steeples. There is much more profanity in America on Sunday than in all the other six days of the week put together, and it is of a more bitter and malignant character than the week-day profanity, too. It is produced by the cracked-pot clangour of the cheap church-bells.

We build our churches almost without regard to cost; we rear an edifice which is an adornment to the town, and we gild it, and fresco it, and mortgage it, and do everything we can think of to perfect it, and then spoil it all by putting a bell on it which afflicts everybody who hears it, giving some the headache, others St.

Vitus's dance, and the rest the blind-staggers.

An American village at ten o'clock on a summer Sunday is the quietest and peacefullest and holiest thing in nature; but it is a pretty different thing half an hour later. Mr. Poe's poem of the 'Bells' stands incomplete to this day; but it is well enough that it is so, for the public reciter or 'reader' who goes around trying to imitate the sounds of the various sorts of bells with his voice would find himself 'up a stump' when he got to the church-bell—as Joseph Addison would say. The church is always trying to get other people to reform; it might not be a bad idea to reform itself a little, by way of example. It is still clinging to one or two things which were useful once but which are not useful now, neither are they ornamental. One is the bell-ringing to remind a clock-caked town that it is church-time, and another is the reading from the pulpit of a tedious list of 'notices' which everybody who is interested has already read in the newspaper. The clergyman even reads the hymn through—a relic of an ancient time when hymn-books were scarce and costly; but everybody has a hymn-book now, and so the public reading is no longer necessary. It is not merely unnecessary, it is generally painful; for the average clergyman could not fire into his congregation with a shot-gun and hit a worse reader than himself, unless the weapon scattered shamefully. I am not meaning to be flippant and irreverent, I am only meaning to be truthful. The average clergyman, in all countries and of all denominations, is a very bad reader. One would think he would at least learn how to read the Lord's Prayer, by-and-by, but it is not so. He races through it as if he thought the quicker he got it in the sooner it would be answered. A person who does not appreciate the exceeding value of pauses, and does not know how to measure their duration judiciously, cannot render the grand simplicity and dignity of a composition like that effectively.

We took a tolerably early breakfast, and tramped off toward Zermatt through the reeking lanes of the village, glad to get away from that bell. By-and-by we had a fine spectacle on our right. It was the warlike butt-end of a huge glacier, which looked down on us from an Alpine height which was well up in the blue sky. It was an astonishing amount of ice to be compacted together in one mass. We ciphered upon it and decided that it was not less than several hundred feet from the base of the wall of solid ice on the top of it—Harris believed it was really twice that. We judged that if St. Paul's, St. Peter's, the Great Pyramid, the Strasburg Cathedral, and the Capitol at Washington were clustered against that wall, a man sitting on its upper edge could not hang his hat on the top of any one of them without reaching down three or four hundred feet—a thing which, of course, no man could do.

To me, that mighty glacier was very beautiful. I did not imagine that anybody could find fault with it; but I was mistaken. Harris had been snarling for several days. He was a rabid Protestant, and he was always saying—

'In the Protestant cantons you never see such poverty and dirt and squalor as you do in this Catholic one; you never see the lanes and alleys flowing with foulness; you never see such wretched little sties of houses; you never see an inverted tin turnip on top of a church for a dome; and as for a church-bell, why, you never hear a church-bell at all.'

All this morning he had been finding fault, straight along. First it was with the mud. He said, 'It ain't muddy in a Protestant canton when it rains.' Then it was with the dogs: 'They don't have those lop-eared dogs in a Protestant canton.' Then it was with the roads: 'They don't leave the roads to make themselves in a Protestant canton, the people make them—and they make a road that *is* a road, too.' Next it was the goats: 'You never see a goat shedding tears in a Protestant canton—a goat, there, is one of the cheerfullest objects in nature.' Next it was the chamois: 'You never see a Protestant chamois act like one of these—they take a bite or two and go; but these fellows camp with you and stay.' Then it was the guide-boards: 'In a Protestant canton you couldn't get lost if you wanted to, but you never see a guide-board in a Catholic canton.' Next, 'You never see any flower-boxes in the windows, here—never anything but now and then a cat—a torpid one; but you take a Protestant canton: windows perfectly lovely with flowers—and as for cats, there's just acres of them. These folks in this canton leave a road

to make itself, and then fine you three francs if you "trot" over
it—as if a horse could trot over such a sarcasm of a road.' Next
about the goître: '*They* talk about goître!—I haven't seen a
goître in this whole canton that I couldn't put in a hat.'

He had growled at everything, but I judged it would puzzle
him to find anything the matter with this majestic glacier. I
intimated as much; but he was ready, and said with surly
discontent—

'You ought to see them in the Protestant cantons.'

This irritated me. But I concealed the feeling, and asked—

'What is the matter with this one?'

'Matter? Why, it ain't in any kind of condition. They never
take any care of a glacier here. The moraine has been spilling
gravel around it, and got it all dirty.'

'Why, man, *they* can't help that.'

'*They*? You're right. That is, they *won't*. They could if they
wanted to. You never see a speck of dirt on a Protestant glacier.
Look at the Rhone glacier. It is fifteen miles long, and seven
hundred feet thick. If this was a Protestant glacier you wouldn't
see it looking like this, I can tell you.'

'That is nonsense. What would they do with it?'

'They would whitewash it. They always do.'

I did not believe a word of this, but rather than have trouble I
let it go; for it is a waste of breath to argue with a bigot. I even
doubted if the Rhone glacier *was* in a Protestant canton; but I
did not know, so I could not make anything by contradicting a
man who would probably put me down at once with
manufactured evidence.

About nine miles from St. Nicholas we crossed a bridge over
the raging torrent of the Visp, and came to a long strip of flimsy
fencing which was pretending to secure people from tumbling
over a perpendicular wall forty feet high and into the river.
Three children were approaching; one of them, a little girl about
eight years old, was running; when pretty close to us she
stumbled and fell, and her feet shot under the rail of the fence
and for a moment projected over the stream. It gave us a sharp
shock, for we thought she was gone, sure, for the ground slanted

steeply, and to save herself seemed a sheer impossibility; but she managed to scramble up, and ran by us laughing.

We went forward and examined the place and saw the long tracks which her feet had made in the dirt when they darted over the verge. If she had finished her trip she would have struck some big rocks on the edge of the water, and then the torrent would have snatched her down-stream among the half-covered boulders, and she would have been pounded to pulp in two minutes. We had come exceedingly near witnessing her death.

And now Harris's contrary nature and inborn selfishness were strikingly manifested. He has no spirit of self-denial. He began straight off, and continued for an hour, to express his gratitude that the child was not destroyed. I never saw such a man. That was the kind of person he was; just so *he* was gratified, he never cared anything about anybody else. I had noticed that trait in him, over and over again. Often, of course, it was mere heedlessness, mere want of reflection. Doubtless this may have been the case in most instances, but it was not the less hard to bear on that account—after all, its bottom, its groundwork, was selfishness. There is no avoiding that conclusion. In the instance under consideration, I did think the indecency of running on in that way might occur to him; but no, the child was saved and he was glad, that was sufficient—he cared not a straw for *my* feelings, or my loss of such a literary plum, snatched from my very mouth at the instant it was ready to drop into it. His selfishness was sufficient to place his own gratification in being spared suffering clear before all concern for me, his friend. Apparently he did not once reflect upon the valuable details which would have fallen like a windfall to me: fishing the child out—witnessing the surprise of the family and the stir the thing would have made among the peasants—then a Swiss funeral—then the roadside monument, to be paid for by us and have our names mentioned in it. And we should have gone into Baedeker and been immortal. I was silent. I was too much hurt to complain. If he could act so, and be so heedless and so frivolous at such a time, and actually seem to glory in it, after all I had done for him, I would have cut my hand off before I would let him see that I was wounded.

We were approaching Zermatt, consequently we were approaching the renowned Matterhorn. A month before this mountain had been only a name to us, but latterly we had been moving through a steadily thickening double row of pictures of it, done in oil, water, chromo, wood, steel, copper, crayon, and photography, and so it had at length become a shape to us—and a very distinct, decided, and familiar one, too. We were expecting to recognise that mountain whenever or wherever we should run across it. We were not deceived. The monarch was far away when we first saw him, but there was no such thing as mistaking him. He has the rare peculiarity of standing by himself. He is peculiarly steep, too, and is also most oddly shaped. He towers into the sky like a colossal wedge, with the upper third of its blade bent a little to the left. The broad base of this monster wedge is planted upon a grand glacier-paved Alpine platform whose elevation is ten thousand feet above sea level; as the wedge itself is some five thousand feet high, it follows that its apex is about fifteen thousand feet above sea level. So the whole bulk of this stately piece of rock, this sky-cleaving monolith, is above the line of eternal snow. Yet while all its giant neighbours have the look of being built of solid snow, from their waists up, the Matterhorn stands black and naked and forbidding the year round, or merely powdered or streaked with white in places, for its sides are so steep that the snow cannot stay there. Its strange form, its august isolation, and its majestic unkinship with its own kind, make it, so to speak, the Napoleon of the mountain world. 'Grand, gloomy, and peculiar,' is a phrase which fits it as aptly as it fitted the great captain.

Think of a monument a mile high, standing on a pedestal two miles high! This is what the Matterhorn is—a monument. Its office henceforth, for all time, will be to keep watch and ward over the secret resting-place of the young Lord Douglas, who in 1865 was precipitated from the summit over a precipice 4,000 feet high, and never seen again. No man ever had such a monument as this before. The most imposing of the world's other monuments are but atoms compared to it; and they will perish, and their places will pass from memory, but this will remain.[1]

A walk from St. Nicholas to Zermatt is a wonderful experience. Nature is built on a stupendous plan in that region. One marches continually between walls that are piled into the skies, with their upper heights broken into a confusion of sublime shapes that gleam white and cold against the background of blue; and here and there one sees a big glacier displaying its grandeurs on the top of a precipice, or a graceful cascade leaping and flashing down the green declivities. There is nothing tame, or cheap, or trivial—it is all magnificent. That short valley is a picture gallery of a notable kind, for it contains no mediocrities; from end to end the Creator has hung it with His masterpieces.

We made Zermatt at three in the afternoon, nine hours out from St. Nicholas. Distance, by guide-book, twelve miles; by pedometer, seventy-two. We were in the heart and home of the mountain-climbers now, as all visible things testified. The snow-peaks did not hold themselves aloof, in aristocratic reserve; they nestled close around, in a friendly sociable way; guides, with the ropes and axes, and other implements of their fearful calling slung about their persons, roosted in a long line upon a stone wall in front of the hotel, and waited for customers; sun-burned climbers in mountaineering costume, and followed by their guides and porters, arrived from time to time, from break-neck expeditions among the peaks and glaciers of the High Alps; male and female tourists, on mules, filed by in a continuous processsion, hotel-ward-bound, from wild adventures which would grow in grandeur every time they were described at the English or American fireside, and at last outgrow the possible itself.

---

[1] The accident which cost Lord Douglas his life (see Chapter 41) also cost the lives of three other men. These three fell four-fifths of a mile, and their bodies were afterwards found lying side by side upon a glacier, whence they were borne to Zermatt and buried in the churchyard. The remains of Lord Douglas have never been found. The secret of his sepulchre, like that of Moses, must remain a mystery always.

We were not dreaming; this was not a make-believe home of the Alp-climber, created by our heated imaginations; no, for here was Mr. Girdlestone himself, the famous Englishman who hunts his way to the most formidable Alpine summits without a guide. I was not equal to imagining a Girdlestone; it was all I could do to even realise him, while looking straight at him at short range. I would rather face whole Hyde Parks of artillery than the ghastly forms of death which he has faced among the peaks and precipices of the mountains. There is probably no pleasure equal to the pleasure of climbing a dangerous Alp; but it is a pleasure which is confined strictly to people who can find pleasure in it. I have not jumped to this conclusion; I have travelled to it per gravel train, so to speak. I have thought the thing all out, and am quite sure I am right. A born climber's appetite for climbing is hard to satisfy; when it comes upon him he is like a starving man with a feast before him; he may have other business on hand, but it must wait. Mr. Girdlestone had had his usual summer holiday in the Alps, and had spent it in his usual way, hunting for unique chances to break his neck; his vacation was over, and his luggage packed for England, but all of a sudden a hunger had come upon him to climb the tremendous Weisshorn once more, for he had heard of a new and utterly impossible route up it. His baggage was unpacked at once, and now he and a friend, laden with knapsacks, ice-axes, coils of rope, and canteens of milk, were just setting out. They would spend the night high up among the snows, somewhere, and get up at two in the morning and finish the enterprise. I had a strong desire to go with them, but forced it down—a feat which Mr. Girdlestone, with all his fortitude, could not do.

Even ladies catch the climbing mania, and are unable to throw it off. A famous climber of that sex had attempted the Weisshorn a few days before our arrival, and she and her guides had lost their way in a snowstorm high up among the peaks and glaciers, and been forced to wander around a good while before they could find a way down. When this lady reached the bottom she had been on her feet twenty-three hours!

Our guides, hired on the Gemmi, were already at Zermatt when we reached there. So there was nothing to interfere with our getting up an adventure whenever we should choose the time and the object. I resolved to devote my first evening in Zermatt to studying up the subject of Alpine climbing, by way of preparation.

I read several books, and here are some of the things I found out. One's shoes must be strong and heavy and have pointed hobnails in them. The alpenstock must be of the best wood, for if it should break loss of life might be the result. One should carry an axe to cut steps in the ice with, on the great heights. There must be a ladder, for there are steep bits of rock which can be surmounted with this instrument—or this utensil—but could not be surmounted without it; such an obstruction has compelled the tourist to waste hours hunting another route, when a ladder would have saved him all trouble. One must have from 150 to 500 feet of strong rope, to be used in lowering the party down steep declivities, which are too steep and smooth to be traversed in any other way. One must have a steel hook on another rope—a very useful thing; for when one is ascending, and comes to a low bluff which is yet too high for the ladder, he swings this rope aloft like a lasso, the hook catches at the top of the bluff, and then the tourist climbs the rope hand over hand—being always particular to try and forget that if the hook gives way he will never stop falling till he arrives in some part of Switzerland where they are not expecting him. Another important thing—there must be a rope to tie the whole party together with, so that if one falls from a mountain or down a bottomless chasm in a glacier, the others may brace back on the rope and save him. One must have a silk veil, to protect his face from snow, sleet, hail, and gale, and coloured goggles to protect his eyes from that dangerous enemy, snow-blindness. Finally, there must be some porters, to carry provisions, wine, and scientific instruments, and also blanket bags for the party to sleep in.

I closed my readings with a fearful adventure which Mr. Whymper once had on the Matterhorn when he was prowling around alone, 5,000 feet above the town of Breil. He was edging his way gingerly around the corner of a precipice where the upper edge of a sharp declivity of ice-glazed snow joined it. This declivity swept down a couple of hundred feet, into a gully which curved around and ended at a precipice 800 feet high, overlooking a glacier. His foot slipped, and he fell. He says:—

'My knapsack brought my head down first, and I pitched into some rocks about a dozen feet below; they caught something, and tumbled me off the edge, head over heels, into the gully; the baton was dashed from my hands, and I whirled downwards in a series of bounds, each longer than the last; now over ice, now into rocks, striking my head four or five times, each time with increased force. The last bound sent me spinning through the air in a leap of fifty or sixty feet, from one side of the gully to the other, and I struck the rocks, luckily, with the whole of my left side. They caught my clothes for a moment, and I fell back on to the snow with motion arrested. My head fortunately came the right side up, and a few frantic catches brought me to a halt in the neck of the gully and on the verge of the precipice. Baton, hat, and veil skimmed by and disappeared, and the crash of the rocks—which I had started—as they fell on to the glacier, told how narrow had been the escape from utter destruction. As it was, I fell nearly 200 feet in seven or eight bounds. Ten feet more would have taken me in one gigantic leap of 800 feet on to the glacier below.

'The situation was sufficiently serious. The rocks could not be let go for a moment, and the blood was spirting out of more than twenty cuts. The most serious ones were in the head, and I vainly tried to close them with one hand, whilst holding on with the other. It was useless; the blood gushed out in blinding jets at each pulsation. At last, in a moment of inspiration, I kicked out a big lump of snow and stuck it as plaister on my head. The idea was a happy one, and the flow of blood diminished. Then, scrambling up, I got, not a moment too soon, to a place of safety, and fainted away. The sun was setting when consciousness returned, and it was pitch-dark before the Great Staircase was descended; but by a combination of luck and care, the whole 4,700 feet of descent to Breil was accomplished without a slip, or once missing the way.'

His wounds kept him a-bed some days. Then he got up and climbed that mountain again. This is the way with a true Alp-climber; the more fun he has, the more he wants.

CHAPTER 37

After I had finished my readings I was no longer myself; I was tranced, uplifted, intoxicated, by the almost incredible perils and adventures I had been following my authors through, and the triumphs I had been sharing with them. I sat silent some time, then turned to Harris, and said—

'My mind is made up.'

Something in my tone struck him; and when he glanced at my eye and read what was written there, his face paled perceptibly. He hesitated a moment, then said—

'Speak.'

I answered with perfect calmness—

'I WILL ASCEND THE RIFFELBERG.'

If I had shot my poor friend he could not have fallen from his chair more suddenly. If I had been his father he could not have pleaded harder to get me to give up my purpose. But I turned a deaf ear to all he said. When he perceived at last that nothing could alter my determination he ceased to urge, and for a while the deep silence was broken only by his sobs. I sat in marble resolution, with my eyes fixed upon vacancy, for in spirit I was already wrestling with the perils of the mountains, and my friend sat gazing at me in adoring admiration through his tears. At last he threw himself upon me in a loving embrace, and exclaimed in broken tones—

'Your Harris will never desert you. We will die together!'

I cheered the noble fellow with praises, and soon his fears were forgotten, and he was eager for the adventure. He wanted to summon the guides at once and leave at two in the morning, as he supposed the custom was; but I explained that nobody was looking at that hour, and that the start in the dark was not usually made from the village, but from the first night's resting-place on the mountain side. I said we would leave the village at three or four p.m. on the morrow; meantime he could notify the guides, and also let the public know of the attempt which we proposed to make.

I went to bed, but not to sleep. No man can sleep when he is about to undertake one of these Alpine exploits. I tossed feverishly all night long, and was glad enough when I heard the clock strike half-past eleven, and knew it was time to get up for dinner. I rose jaded and rusty, and went to the noon meal, where I found myself the centre of interest and curiosity, for the news was already abroad. It is not easy to eat calmly when you are a lion, but it is very pleasant, nevertheless.

As usual, at Zermatt, when a great ascent is about to be undertaken, everybody, native and foreign, laid aside his own projects and took up a good position to observe the start. The expedition consisted of 198 persons, including the mules, or 205, including the cows. As follows:—

CHIEFS OF SERVICE	SUBORDINATES
Myself.	1 Veterinary Surgeon.
Mr. Harris.	1 Butler.
17 Guides.	12 Waiters.
4 Surgeons.	1 Footman.
1 Geologist.	1 Barber.
1 Botanist.	1 Head Cook.
3 Chaplains.	9 Assistants.
2 Draftsmen.	4 Pastry Cooks.
15 Barkeepers.	1 Confectionery Artist.
1 Latinist.	

TRANSPORTATION, etc.

27	Porters.	1	Fine ditto.
44	Mules.	7	Cows.
44	Muleteers.	2	Milkers.
3	Coarse Washers and Ironers.		

Total, 154 men, 51 animals. Grand Total, 205.

RATIONS, etc.		APPARATUM	
16	Cases Hams.	25	Spring Mattresses.
2	Barrels Flour.	2	Hair ditto.
22	Barrels Whisky.		Bedding for same.
1	Barrel Sugar.	2	Mosquito Nets.
1	Keg Lemons.	29	Tents.
2,000	Cigars.		Scientific Instruments.
1	Barrel Pies.	97	Ice-axes.
1	Ton of Pemmican.	5	Cases Dynamite.
143	Pair Crutches.	7	Cans Nitro-glycerine.
2	Barrels Arnica.	22	40-foot Ladders.
1	Bale of Lint.	2	Miles of Rope.
27	Kegs Paregoric.	154	Umbrellas.

It was full four o'clock in the afternoon before my cavalcade was entirely ready. At that hour it began to move. In point of numbers and spectacular effect it was the most imposing expedition that had ever marched from Zermatt.

I commanded the chief guide to arrange the men and animals in single file, twelve feet apart, and lash them all together on a strong rope. He objected that the first two miles was a dead level, with plenty of room, and that the rope was never used except in very dangerous places. But I would not listen to that. My reading had taught me that many serious accidents had happened in the Alps simply from not having the people tied up soon enough; I was not going to add one to the list. The guide then obeyed my order.

When the procession stood at ease, roped together, and ready to move, I never saw a finer sight. It was 3,122 feet long—over half a mile; every man but Harris and me was on foot, and had on his green veil and his blue goggles, and his white rag around his hat, and his coil of rope over one shoulder and under the other, and his ice-axe in his belt, and carried his alpenstock in his left hand, his umbrella (closed) in his right, and his crutches slung at his back. The burdens of the pack mules and the horns of the cows were decked with the Edelweiss and the Alpine rose.

I and my agent were the only persons mounted. We were in the post of danger in the extreme rear, and tied securely to five guides apiece. Our armour-bearers carried our ice-axes, alpenstocks, and other implements for us. We were mounted upon very small donkeys, as a measure of safety; in time of peril we could straighten our legs and stand up, and let the donkey walk from under. Still, I cannot recommend this sort of animal—at least for excursions of mere pleasure—because his ears interrupt the view. I and my agent possessed the regulation mountaineering costumes, but concluded to leave them behind. Out of respect for the great numbers of tourists of both sexes who would be assembled in front of the hotels to see us pass, and also out of respect for the many tourists whom we expected to encounter on our expedition, we decided to make the ascent in evening dress.

At fifteen minutes past four I gave the command to move, and my subordinates passed it along the line. The great crowd in front of the Monte Rosa hotel parted in twain, with a cheer, as the procession approached, and as the head of it was filing by I gave the order, 'Unlimber—make ready—HOIST!' and with one impulse up went my half mile of umbrellas. It was a beautiful sight, and a total surprise to the spectators. Nothing like that had ever been seen in the Alps before. The applause it brought forth was deeply gratifying to me, and I rode by with my plug hat in my hand to testify my appreciation of it. It was the only testimony I could offer, for I was too full to speak.

We watered the caravan at the cold stream which rushes down a trough near the end of the village, and soon afterward left the haunts of civilisation behind us. About half-past five o'clock we arrived at a bridge which spans the Visp, and after throwing over a detachment to see if it was safe, the caravan crossed without accident. The way now led, by a gentle ascent, carpeted with fresh green grass, to the church of Winkelmatten. Without stopping to examine this edifice, I executed a flank movement to the right and crossed the bridge over the Findelenbach, after first testing its strength. Here I deployed to the right again, and presently entered an inviting stretch of meadow land which was unoccupied save by a couple of deserted huts toward its furthest extremity. These meadows offered an excellent camping-place. We pitched our tents, supped, established a proper guard, recorded the events of the day, and then went to bed.

We rose at two in the morning and dressed by candle-light. It was a dismal and chilly business. A few stars were shining, but the general heavens were overcast, and the great shaft of the Matterhorn was draped in a sable pall of clouds. The chief guide advised a delay; he said he feared it was going to rain. We waited until nine o'clock, and then got away in tolerably clear weather.

Our course led up some terrific steeps, densely wooded with larches and cedars, and traversed by paths which the rains had guttered and which were obstructed by loose stones. To add to the danger and inconvenience, we were constantly meeting returning tourists on foot or horseback, and as constantly being crowded and battered by ascending tourists who were in a hurry and wanted to get by.

Our troubles thickened. About the middle of the afternoon the seventeen guides called a halt and held a consultation. After consulting an hour they said their first suspicion remained intact—that is to say, they believed they were lost. I asked if they did not *know* it? No, they said, they *couldn't* absolutely know whether they were lost or not, because none of them had ever been in that part of the country before. They had a strong instinct that they were lost, but they had no proofs, except that they did not know where they were. They had met no tourists for some time, and they considered that a suspicious sign.

Plainly we were in an ugly fix. The guides were naturally unwilling to go alone and seek a way out of the difficulty; so we all went together. For better security we moved slowly and cautiously, for the forest was very dense. We did not move up the mountain, but around it, hoping to strike across the old trail. Toward nightfall, when we were about tired out, we came up against a rock as big as a cottage. This barrier took all the remaining spirit out of the men, and a panic of fear and despair ensued. They moaned and wept, and said they should never see their homes and their dear ones again. Then they began to upbraid me for bringing them upon this fatal expedition. Some even muttered threats against me.

Clearly it was no time to show weakness. So I made a speech in which I said that other Alp-climbers had been in as perilous a position as this, and yet by courage and perseverance had escaped. I promised to stand by them; I promised to rescue them. I closed by saying we had plenty of provisions to maintain us for quite a siege; and did they suppose Zermatt would allow half a mile of men and mules to mysteriously disappear during any considerable time, right above their noses, and make no inquiries? No, Zermatt would send out searching expeditions, and we should be saved.

This speech had a great effect. The men pitched the tents with some little show of cheerfulness, and we were snugly under cover when the night shut down. I now reaped the reward of my wisdom in providing one article which is not mentioned in any book of Alpine adventure but this. I refer to the paregoric. But for that beneficent drug, not one of those men would have slept a moment during that fearful night. But for the gentle persuader they must have tossed, unsoothed, the night through; for the whisky was for me. Yes, they would have risen in the morning unfitted for their heavy task. As it was, everybody slept but my agent and me—only we two and the barkeepers. I would not permit myself to sleep at such a time. I considered myself responsible for all those lives. I meant to be on hand and ready, in case of avalanches. I am aware now that there were no avalanches up there, but I did not know it then.

We watched the weather all through that awful night, and kept an eye on the barometer, to be prepared for the least change. There was not the slightest change recorded by the instrument, during the whole time. Words cannot describe the comfort that that friendly, hopeful, steadfast thing was to me in that season of trouble. It was a defective barometer, and had no hand but the stationary brass pointer, but I did not know that until afterwards. If I should be in such a situation again, I should not wish for any barometer but that one.

All hands rose at two in the morning and took breakfast, and as soon as it was light we roped outselves together and went at that rock. For some time we tried the hook-rope and other means of scaling it, but without success—that is, without perfect success. The hook caught once, and Harris started up it, hand over hand, but the hold broke, and if there had not happened to be a chaplain sitting underneath at the time, Harris would certainly have been crippled. As it was, it was the chaplain. He took to his crutches, and I ordered the hook-rope to be laid aside. It was too dangerous an implement where so many were standing around.

We were puzzled for a while; then somebody thought of the ladders. One of these was leaned against the rock, and the men went up it tied together in couples. Another ladder was sent up for use in descending. At the end of half an hour everybody was over, and that rock was conquered. We gave our first grand shout of triumph. But the joy was short-lived, for somebody asked how we were going to get the animals over.

This was a serious difficulty; in fact, it was an impossibility. The courage of the men began to waver immediately; once more we were threatened with a panic. But when the danger was most imminent, we were saved in a mysterious way. A mule which had attracted attention from the beginning by its disposition to experiment, tried to eat a five-pound can of nitro-glycerine. This happened right alongside the rock. The explosion threw us all to the ground, and covered us with dirt and *débris*; it frightened us extremely, too, for the crash it made was deafening, and the violence of the shock made the ground tremble. However, we were grateful, for the rock was gone. Its place was occupied by a new cellar, about thirty feet across, by fifteen feet deep. The explosion was heard as far as Zermatt; and an hour and a half afterwards many citizens of that town were knocked down and quite seriously injured by descending portions of mule meat, frozen solid. This shows, better than any estimate in figures, how high the experimenter went.

We had nothing to do now but bridge the cellar and proceed on our way. With a cheer the men went at their work. I attended to the engineering myself. I appointed a strong detail to cut down trees with ice-axes and trim them for piers to support the bridge. This was a slow business, for ice-axes are not good to cut wood with. I caused my piers to be firmly set up in ranks in the cellar, and upon them I laid six of my forty-foot ladders, side by side, and laid six more on top of them. Upon this bridge I caused a bed of boughs to be spread, and on top of the boughs a bed of earth six inches deep. I stretched ropes upon either side to serve as railings, and then my bridge was complete. A train of elephants could have crossed it in safety and comfort. By nightfall the caravan was on the other side, and the ladders taken up.

Next morning we went on in good spirits for a while, though our way was slow and difficult, by reason of the steep and rocky nature of the ground and the thickness of the forest; but at last a dull despondency crept into the men's faces, and it was apparent that not only they, but even the guides, were now convinced that we were lost. The fact that we still met no tourists was a circumstance that was but too significant. Another thing seemed to suggest that we were not only lost, but very badly lost; for there must surely be searching parties on the road before this time, yet we had seen no sign of them.

Demoralisation was spreading; something must be done, and done quickly too. Fortunately, I am not unfertile in expedients. I contrived one now which commended itself to all, for it promised well. I took three-quarters of a mile of rope and fastened one end of it around the waist of a guide, and told him to go and find the road, whilst the caravan waited. I instructed him to guide himself back by the rope, in case of failure; in case of success, he was to give the rope a series of violent jerks, whereupon the Expedition would go to him at once. He departed, and in two minutes had disappeared among the trees. I paid out the rope myself, while everybody watched the crawling thing with eager eyes. The rope crept away quite slowly, at times, at other times with some briskness. Twice or thrice we seemed to get the signal, and a shout was just ready to break from the men's lips when they perceived it was a false alarm. But at last, when over half a mile of rope had slidden away, it stopped gliding and stood absolutely still—one minute—two minutes—three—while we held our breath and watched.

Was the guide resting? Was he scanning the country from some high point? Was he inquiring of a chance mountaineer? Stop—had he fainted from excess of fatigue and anxiety?

This thought gave us a shock. I was in the very act of detailing an expedition to succour him, when the cord was assailed with a series of such frantic jerks that I could hardly keep hold of it. The huzza that went up, then, was good to hear. 'Saved! saved!' was the word that rang out, all down the long rank of the caravan.

We rose up and started at once. We found the route to be good enough for a while, but it began to grow difficult, by-and-by, and this feature steadily increased. When we judged we had gone half a mile, we momently expected to see the guide; but no, he was not visible anywhere; neither was he waiting, for the rope was still moving, consequently he was doing the same. This argued that he had not found the road yet, but was marching to it with some peasant. There was nothing for us to do but plod along, and this we did. At the end of three hours we were still plodding. This was not only mysterious, but exasperating. And very fatiguing, too; for we had tried hard, along at first, to catch up with the guide, but had only fagged ourselves in vain; for although he was travelling slowly he was yet able to go faster than the hampered caravan over such ground.

At three in the afternoon we were nearly dead with exhaustion—and still the rope was slowly gliding out. The murmurs against the guide had been growing steadily, and at last they were become loud and savage. A mutiny ensued. The men refused to proceed. They declared that we had been travelling over and over the same ground all day, in a kind of circle. They demanded that our end of the rope be made fast to a tree, so as to halt the guide until we could overtake him and kill him. This was not an unreasonable requirement, so I gave the order.

As soon as the rope was tied, the Expedition moved forward with that alacrity which the thirst for vengeance usually inspires. But after a tiresome march of almost half a mile, we came to a hill covered thick with a crumbly rubbish of stones, and so steep that no man of us all was now in a condition to climb it. Every attempt failed, and ended in crippling somebody. Within twenty minutes I had five men on crutches. Whenever a climber tried to assist himself by the rope, it yielded and let him tumble backwards. The frequency of this result suggested an idea to me. I ordered the caravan to 'bout face and form in marching order; I then made the tow-rope fast to the rear mule, and gave the command—

'Mark time—by the right flank—forward—march!'

The procession began to move, to the impressive strains of a battle chant, and I said to myself, 'Now, if the rope don't break, I judge *this* will fetch that guide into the camp.' I watched the rope gliding down the hill, and presently when I was all fixed for triumph I was confronted by a disappointment: there was no guide tied to the rope, it was only a very indignant old black ram. The fury of the baffled Expedition exceeded all bounds. They even wanted to wreak their unreasoning vengeance on this innocent dumb brute. But I stood between them and their prey, menaced by a bristling wall of ice-axes and alpenstocks, and proclaimed that there was but one road to this murder, and it was directly over my corpse. Even as I spoke I saw that my doom was sealed, except a miracle supervened to divert these madmen from their fell purpose. I see that sickening wall of weapons now; I see that advancing host as I saw it then, I see the hate in those cruel eyes; I remember how I dropped my head upon my breast; I feel again the sudden earthquake shock in my rear, administered by the very ram I was sacrificing myself to save; I hear once more the typhoon of laughter that burst from the assaulting column as I clove it from van to rear like a Sepoy shot from a Rodman gun.

I was saved. Yes, I was saved, and by the merciful instinct of ingratitude which nature had planted in the breast of that treacherous beast. The grace which eloquence had failed to work in those men's hearts had been wrought by a laugh. The ram was set free and my life was spared.

We lived to find out that that guide had deserted us as soon as he had placed a half-mile between himself and us. To avert suspicion, he had judged it best that the line should continue to move; so he caught that ram, and at the time that he was sitting on it making the rope fast to it, we were imagining he was lying in a swoon, overcome by fatigue and distress. When he allowed the ram to get up, it fell to plunging around trying to rid itself of the rope, and this was the signal which we had risen up with glad shouts to obey. We had followed this ram round and round in a circle all day—a thing which was proved by the discovery that we had watered the Expedition seven times at one and the same spring in seven hours. As expert a woodman as I am, I had somehow failed to notice this until my attention was called to it by a hog. This hog was always wallowing there, and as he was the only hog we saw, his frequent repetition, together with his unvarying similarity to himself, finally caused me to reflect that he must be the same hog, and this led me to the deduction that this must the same spring also—which indeed it was.

I made a note of this curious thing, as showing in a striking manner the relative difference between glacial action and the action of the hog. It is now a well-established fact that glaciers move; I consider that my observations go to show, with equal conclusiveness, that a hog in a spring does not move. I shall be glad to receive the opinions of other observers upon this point.

To return, for an explanatory moment, to that guide, and then I shall be done with him. After leaving the ram tied to the rope, he had wandered at large a while, and then happened to run across a cow. Judging that a cow would naturally know more than a guide, he took her by the tail, and the result justified his judgment. She nibbled her leisurely way down-hill till it was near milking time; then she struck for home and towed him into Zermatt.

CHAPTER 38

We went into camp on that wild spot to which that ram had brought us. The men were greatly fatigued. Their conviction that we were lost was forgotten in the cheer of a good supper, and before the reaction had a chance to set in, I loaded them up with paregoric and put them to bed.

Next morning I was considering in my mind our desperate situation and trying to think of a remedy, when Harris came to me with a Baedeker map which showed conclusively that the mountain we were on was still in Switzerland—yes, every part of it was in Switzerland. So we were not lost, after all. This was an immense relief; it lifted the weight of two such mountains from my breast. I immediately had the news disseminated and the map exhibited. The effect was wonderful. As soon as the men saw with their own eyes that they knew where they were, and that it was only the summit that was lost and not themselves, they cheered up instantly and said with one accord, let the summit take care of itself, they were not interested in its troubles.

Our distresses being at an end, I now determined to rest the men in camp and give the scientific department of the Expedition a chance. First I made a barometric observation, to get our altitude, but I could not perceive that there was any result. I knew, by my scientific reading, that either thermometers or barometers ought to be boiled, to make them accurate; I did not know which it was, so I boiled both. There was still no result; so I examined these instruments and discovered that they possessed radical blemishes: the barometer had no hand but the brass pointer, and the ball of the thermometer was stuffed with tin foil. I might have boiled those things to rags, and never found out anything.

I hunted up another barometer; it was new and perfect. I boiled it half an hour in a pot of bean soup which the cooks were making. The result was unexpected: the instrument was not affected at all, but there was such a strong barometer taste to the soup that the head cook, who was a most conscientious person, changed its name in the bill of fare. The dish was so greatly liked by all, that I ordered the cook to have barometer soup every day. It was believed that the barometer might eventually be injured, but I did not care for that. I had demonstrated to my satisfaction that it could not tell how high a mountain was, therefore I had no real use for it. Changes of the weather I could take care of without it; I did not wish to know when the weather was going to be good; what I wanted to know was when it was going to be bad, and this I could find out from Harris's corns. Harris had had his corns tested and regulated at the government observatory in Heidelberg, and one could depend upon them with confidence. So I transferred the new barometer to the cooking department, to be used for the official mess. It was found that even a pretty fair article of soup could be made with the defective barometer; so I allowed that one to be transferred to the subordinate messes.

I next boiled the thermometer, and got a most excellent result; the mercury went up to about 200° Fahrenheit. In the opinion of the other scientists of the Expedition, this seemed to indicate that we had attained the extraordinary altitude of 200,000 feet above sea level. Science places the line of eternal snow at about 10,000 feet above sea level. There was no snow where we were, consequently it was proven that the eternal snow line ceases somewhere above the 10,000 foot level and does not begin any more. This was an interesting fact, and one which had not been observed by any observer before. It was as valuable as interesting, too, since it would open up the deserted summits of the highest Alps to population and agriculture. It was a proud thing to be where we were, yet it caused us a pang to reflect that but for that ram we might just as well have been 200,000 feet higher.

The success of my last experiment induced me to try an experiment with my photographic apparatus. I got it out, and boiled one of my cameras, but the thing was a failure: it made the wood swell up and burst, and I could not see that the lenses were any better than they were before.

I now concluded to boil a guide. It might improve him, it could not impair his usefuless. But I was not allowed to proceed. Guides have no feeling for science, and this one would not consent to be made uncomfortable in its interest.

In the midst of my scientific work, one of those needless accidents happened which are always occurring among the ignorant and thoughless. A porter shot at a chamois and missed it and crippled the Latinist. This was not a serious matter to me, for a Latinist's duties are as well performed on crutches as otherwise—but the fact remained that if the Latinist had not happened to be in the way a mule would have got that load. That would have been quite another matter, for when it comes down to a question of value there is a palpable difference between a Latinist and a mule. I could not depend on having a Latinist in the right place every time; so, to make things safe, I ordered that in future the chamois must not be hunted within the limits of the camp with any other weapon than the forefinger.

My nerves had hardly grown quiet after this affair when they got another shake-up—one which utterly unmanned me for a moment: a rumour swept suddenly through the camp that one of the barkeepers had fallen over a precipice.

However, it turned out that it was only a chaplain. I had laid in an extra force of chaplains, purposely to be prepared for emergencies like this, but by some unaccountable oversight had come away rather short-handed in the matter of barkeepers.

On the following morning we moved on, well refreshed and in good spirits. I remember this day with peculiar pleasure, because it saw our road restored to us. Yes, we found our road again, and in quite an extraordinary way. We had plodded along some two hours and a half, when we came up against a solid mass of rock about twenty feet high. I did not need to be instructed by a mule this time.—I was already beginning to know more than any mule in the Expedition.—I at once put in a blast of dynamite, and lifted that rock out of the way. But to my surprise and mortification, I found that there had been a châlet on top of it.

I picked up such members of the family as fell in my vicinity, and subordinates of my corps collected the rest. None of these poor people were injured, happily, but they were much annoyed. I explained to the head chaleteer just how the thing happened, and that I was only searching for the road, and would certainly have given him timely notice if I had known he was up there. I said I had meant no harm, and hoped I had not lowered myself in his estimation by raising him a few rods in the air. I said many other judicious things, and finally when I offered to rebuild his châlet, and pay for breakages, and throw in the cellar, he was mollified and satisfied. He hadn't any cellar at all, before; he would not have as good a view, now, as formerly, but what he had lost in view he had gained in cellar, by exact measurement. He said there wasn't another hole like that in the mountains—and he would have been right if the late mule had not tried to eat up the nitro-glycerine.

I put a hundred and sixteen men at work, and they rebuilt the châlet from its own *débris* in fifteen minutes. It was a good deal more picturesque than it was before, too. The man said we were now on the Feli-Stutz, above the Schwegmatt—information which I was glad to get, since it gave us our position to a degree of particularity which we had not been accustomed to for a day or so. We also learned that we were standing at the foot of the Riffelberg proper, and that the initial chapter of our work was completed.

We had a fine view, from here, of the energetic Visp, as it makes its first plunge into the world from under a huge arch of solid ice, worn through the foot-wall of the great Gorner Glacier; and we could also see the Furggenbach, which is the outlet of the Furggen Glacier.

The mule-road to the summit of the Riffelberg passed right in front of the châlet, a circumstance which we almost immediately noticed, because a procession of tourists was filing along it pretty much all the time.[1] The chaleteer's business consisted in furnishing refreshments to tourists. My blast had interrupted this trade for a few minutes, by breaking all the bottles on the place; but I gave the man a lot of whisky to sell for Alpine champagne, and a lot of vinegar which would answer for Rhine wine, consequently trade was soon as brisk as ever.

Leaving the Expedition outside to rest, I quartered myself in the châlet, with Harris, purposing to correct my journals and scientific observations before continuing the ascent. I had hardly begun my work when a tall, slender, vigorous American youth of about twenty-three, who was on his way down the mountain, entered and came toward me with that breezy self-complacency which is the adolescent's idea of the well-bred ease of the man of the world. His hair was short and parted accurately in the middle, and he had all the look of an American person who would be likely to begin his signature with an initial, and spell his middle name out. He introduced himself, smiling a smirky smile borrowed from the courtiers of the stage, extended a fair-skinned talon, and whilst he gripped my hand in it he bent his body forward three times at the hips, as the stage-courtier does, and said in the airiest and most condescending and patronising way—I quote his exact language—

'Very glad to make your acquaintance, 'm sure; very glad indeed, assure you. I've read all your little efforts and greatly admired them, and when I heard you were here, I ...'

I indicated a chair, and he sat down. This grandee was the' grandson of an American of considerable note in his day, and not wholly forgotten yet—a man who came so near being a great man that he was quite generally accounted one while he lived.

I slowly paced the floor, pondering scientific problems, and heard this conversation:—

Grandson. First visit to Europe?

[1] 'Pretty much' may not be elegant English, but it is high time it was. There is no elegant word or phrase which means just what it means.—M.T.

Harris. Mine? Yes.

G.S. (With a soft reminiscent sigh suggestive of bygone joys that may be tasted in their freshness but once.) Ah, I know what it is to you. A first visit!—ah, the romance of it! I wish I could feel it again.

H. Yes, I find it exceeds all my dreams. It is enchantment. I go ...

G.S. (With a dainty gesture of the hand signifying, 'Spare me your callow enthusiasms, good friend.'... Yes, *I* know, I know; you go to cathedrals, and exlaim; and you drag through league-long picture-galleries and exclaim; and you stand here, and there, and yonder, upon historic ground, and continue to exclaim; and you are permeated with your first crude conceptions of Art, and are proud and happy. Ah, yes, proud and happy—that expresses it. Yes, yes, enjoy it—it is right—it is an innocent revel.

H. And you? Don't you do these things now?

G.S. I? Oh, that is *very* good! My dear sir, when you are as old a traveller as I am, you will not ask such a question as that. *I* visit the regulation cathedral, do the worn round of the regulation sights, *yet*?—Excuse me!

H. Well, what *do* you do, then?

G.S. Do? I flit—and flit—for I am ever on the wing—but I avoid the herd. To-day I am in Paris, to-morrow in Berlin, anon in Rome; but you would look for me in vain in the galleries of the Louvre or the common resorts of the gazers in those other capitals. If you would find me, you must look in the unvisited nooks and corners where others never think of going. One day you will find me making myself at home in some obscure peasant's cabin, another day you will find me in some forgotten castle, worshipping some little gem of art which the careless eye has overlooked and which the inexperienced would despise; again you will find me a guest in the inner sanctuaries of palaces while the herd is content to get a hurried glimpse of the unused chambers by feeing a servant.

H. You are a *guest* in such places?

G.S. And a welcome one.

H. It is surprising. How does it come?

G.S. My grandfather's name is a passport to all the courts in Europe. I have only to utter that name and every door is open to me. I flit from court to court at my own free will and pleasure, and am always welcome. I am as much at home in the palaces of Europe as you are among your relatives. I know every titled person in Europe, I think. I have my pockets full of invitations all the time. I am under promise now to go to Italy, where I am to be the guest of a succession of the noblest houses in the land. In Berlin my life is a continued round of gaiety in the Imperial palace. It is the same wherever I go.

H. It must be very pleasant. But it must make Boston seem a little slow when you are at home.

G.S. Yes, of course it does. But I don't go home much. There's no life there—little to feed a man's higher nature. Boston's very narrow, you know. She doesn't know it, and you couldn't convince her of it; so I say nothing when I'm there: where's the use? Yes, Boston is very narrow, but she has such a good opinion of herself that she can't see it. A man who has travelled as much as I have, and seen as much of the world, sees it plain enough, but he can't cure it, you know, so the best way is to leave it and seek a sphere which is more in harmony with his tastes and culture. I run across there once a year perhaps, when I have nothing important on hand, but I'm very soon back again. I spend my time in Europe.

H. I see. You map out your plans and——

G.S. No, excuse me. I don't map out any plans. I simply follow the inclination of the day. I am limited by no ties, no requirements; I am not bound in any way. I am too old a traveller to hamper myself with deliberate purposes. I am simply a traveller—an inveterate traveller—a man of the world, in a word—I can call myself by no other name. I do not say, 'I am going here, or I am going there;' I say nothing at all, I only act. For instance, next week you may find me the guest of a grandee of Spain, or you may find me off for Venice, or flitting toward Dresden. I shall probably go to Egypt presently; friends will say to friends, 'He is at the Nile cataracts;' and at that very moment they will be surprised to learn that I'm away off yonder to India somewhere. I am a constant surprise to people. They are always saying, 'Yes, he was in Jerusalem when we heard of him last, but goodness knows where he is now.'

Presently the Grandson rose to leave—discovered he had an appointment with some Emperor, perhaps. He did his graces over again: gripped me with one talon, at arm's length, pressed his hat against his stomach with the other, bent his body in the middle three times, murmuring—

'Please,'m sure; great pleasure, 'm sure. Wish you much success.'

Then he removed his gracious presence. It is a great and solemn thing to have a grandfather.

I have not purposed to misrepresent this boy in any way, for what little indignation he excited in me soon passed and left nothing behind it but compassion. One cannot keep up a grudge against a vacuum. I have tried to repeat the lad's very words; if I have failed anywhere, I have at least not failed to reproduce the marrow and meaning of what he said. He and the innocent chatterbox whom I met on the Swiss lake are the most unique and interesting specimens of Young America I came across during my foreign tramping. I have made honest portraits of them, not caricatures. The grandson of twenty-three referred to himself five or six times as an 'old traveller,' and as many as three times (with a serene complacency which was maddening) as a 'man of the world.' There was something very delicious about his leaving Boston to her 'narrowness,' unreproved and uninstructed.

I formed the caravan in marching order presently, and after riding down the line to see that it was properly roped together, gave the command to proceed. In a little while the road carried us to open, grassy land. We were above the troublesome forest now, and had an uninterrupted view, straight before us, of our summit—the summit of the Riffelberg.

We followed the mule road, a zigzag course, now to the right, now to the left, but always up, and always crowded and incommoded by going and coming files of reckless tourists who were never, in a single instance, tied together. I was obliged to exert the utmost care and caution, for in many places the road was not two yards wide, and often the lower side of it sloped away in slanting precipices eight and even nine feet deep. I had to encourage the men constantly, to keep them from giving way to their unmanly fears.

We might have made the summit before night but for a delay caused by the loss of an umbrella. I was for allowing the umbrella to remain lost, but the men murmured, and with reason, for in this exposed region we stood in peculiar need of protection against avalanches; so I went into camp and detached a strong party to go after the missing article.

The difficulties of the next morning were severe, but our courage was high, for our goal was near. At noon we conquered the last impediment—we stood at last upon the summit—and without the loss of a single man, except the mule that ate the gylcerine. Our great achievement was achieved—the possibility of the impossible was demonstrated, and Harris and I walked proudly into the great dining-room of the Riffelberg Hotel and stood our alpenstocks up in the corner.

Yes, I had made the grand ascent; but it was a mistake to do it in evening dress. The plug hats were battered, the swallow-tails were fluttering rags, mud added no grace, the general effect was unpleasant and even disreputable.

There are about seventy-five tourists at the hotel—mainly ladies and little children—and they gave us an admiring welcome which paid us for all our privations and sufferings. The ascent had been made, and the names and dates now stand recorded on a stone monument there to prove it to all future tourists.

I boiled a thermometer and took an altitude, with a most curious result: *the summit was not as high as the point on the mountain side where I had taken the first altitude.* Suspecting that I had made an important discovery, I prepared to verify it. There happened to be a still higher summit (called the Gorner Grat) above the hotel, and notwithstanding the fact that it overlooks a glacier from a dizzy height, and that the ascent is difficult and dangerous, I resolved to venture up there and boil a thermomenter. So I sent a strong party with some borrowed hoes, in charge of two chiefs of service, to dig a stairway in the soil all the way, and this I ascended, roped to the guides.

This breezy height was the summit proper—so I accomplished even more than I had originally purposed to do. This foolhardy exploit is recorded on another stone monument.

I boiled my thermometer, and sure enough this spot, which purported to be 2,000 feet higher than the locality of the hotel, turned out to be 9,000 feet *lower*. Thus the fact was clearly demonstrated that, *above a certain point, the higher a point seems to be, the lower it actually is.* Our ascent itself was a great achievement, but this contribution to science was an inconceivably greater matter.

Cavillers object that water boils at a lower and lower temperature the higher and higher you go, and hence the apparent anomaly. I answer that I do not base my theory upon what the boiling water does, but upon what a boiled thermometer says. You can't go behind the thermometer.

I had a magnificent view of Monte Rosa, and apparently all the rest of the Alpine world, from that high place. All the circling horizon was piled high with a mighty tumult of snowy crests. One might have imagined he saw before him the tented camps of a beleaguering host of Brobdingnagians.

But lonely, conspicuous, and superb rose that wonderful upright wedge, the Matterhorn. Its precipitous sides were powdered over with snow, and the upper half hidden in thick clouds which now and then dissolved to cobweb films and gave brief glimpses of the imposing tower as through a veil. A little later the Matterhorn[1] took to himself the semblance of a volcano; he was stripped naked to his apex—around this circled vast wreaths of white cloud which strung slowly out and streamed away slantwise toward the sun, a twenty-mile stretch of rolling and tumbling vapour, and looking just as if it were pouring out of a crater. Later again, one of the mountain's sides

---

[1] NOTE.—I had the very unusual luck to catch one little momentary glimpse of the Matterhorn wholly unencumbered by clouds. I levelled my photographic apparatus at it without the loss of an instant, and should have got an elegant picture if my donkey had not interfered. It was my purpose to draw this photograph all by myself for my book, but I was obliged to put the mountain part of it into the hands of the professional artist because I found I could not do landscape well.

was clean and clear, and another side densely clothed from base to summit in thick smoke-like cloud which feathered off and blew around the shaft's sharp edge like the smoke around the corners of a burning building. The Matterhorn is always experimenting, and always gets up fine effects too. In the sunset, when all the lower world is palled in gloom, it points toward heaven out of the pervading blackness like a finger of fire. In the sunrise—well, they say it is very fine in the sunrise.

Authorities agree that there is no such tremendous 'lay out' of snowy Alpine magnitude, grandeur, and sublimity to be seen from any other accessible point as the tourist may see from the summit of the Riffelberg. Therefore let the tourist rope himself up and go there, for I have shown that with nerve, caution, and judgment the thing can be done.

I wish to add one remark here—in parentheses, so to speak—suggested by the word 'snowy,' which I have just used. We have all seen hills and mountains and levels with snow on them, and so we think we know all the aspects and effects produced by snow. But indeed we do not, until we have seen the Alps. Possibly mass and distance add something—at any rate something *is* added. Among other noticeable things, there is a dazzling, intense whiteness about the distant Alpine snow when the sun is on it, which one recognises as peculiar, and not familiar to the eye. The snow which one is accustomed to has a tint to it—painters usually give it a bluish cast—but there is no perceptible tint to the distant Alpine snow when it is trying to look its whitest. As to the unimaginable splendour of it when the sun is blazing down on it—well, it simply *is* unimaginable.

CHAPTER 39

A Guide-Book is a queer thing. The reader has just seen what a man who undertakes the great ascent from Zermatt to the Riffelberg Hotel must experience. Yet Baedeker makes these strange statements concerning this matter:—

1, Distance—three hours.

2. The road cannot be mistaken.

3. Guide unnecessary.

4. Distance from Riffelberg Hotel to the Gorner Grat, one hour and a half.

5. Ascent simple and easy. Guide unnecessary.

6. Elevation of Riffelberg Hotel above sea level, 5,315 feet.

7. Elevation of the Gorner Grat above sea level, 10,289 feet.

I have pretty effectually throttled these errors by sending him the following demonstrated facts:—

1. Distance from Zermatt to Riffelberg Hotel, seven days.

2. The road *can* be mistaken. If I am the first that did it, I want the credit of it too.

3. Guides *are* necessary, for none but a native can read those finger-boards.

4. The estimate of the elevation of the several localities above sea level is pretty correct—for Baedeker. He only misses it about a hundred and eighty or ninety thousand feet.

I found my arnica invaluable. My men were suffering excruciatingly from the friction of sitting down so much. During

two or three days not one of them was able to do more than lie
down or walk about; yet so effective was the arnica, that on the
fourth all were able to sit up. I consider that, more than to
anything else, I owe the success of our great undertaking to
arnica and paregoric.

My men being restored to health and strength, my main
perplexity now was how to get them down the mountain again. I
was not willing to expose the brave fellows to the perils, fatigues,
and hardships of that fearful route again if it could be helped.
First I thought of balloons; but of course I had to give that idea
up, for balloons were not procurable. I thought of several other
expedients, but upon consideration discarded them for cause. But
at last I hit it. I was aware that the movement of glaciers is an
established fact, for I had read it in Baedeker; so I resolved to
take passage for Zermatt on the great Gorner Glacier.

Very good. The next thing was, how to get down to the glacier
comfortably—for the mule-road to it was long, and winding,
and wearisome. I set my mind at work, and soon thought out a
plan. One looks straight down upon the vast frozen river called
the Gorner Glacier from the Gorner Grat—a sheer precipice
1,200 feet high. We had 154 umbrellas—and what is an
umbrella but a parachute?

I mentioned this noble idea to Harris with enthusiasm, and
was about to order the expedition to form on the Gorner Grat,
with their umbrellas, and prepare for flight by platoons, each
platoon in command of a guide, when Harris stopped me and
urged me not to be too hasty. He asked me if this method of
descending the Alps had ever been tried before. I said, 'No, I had
not heard of an instance.' Then, in his opinion, it was a matter of
considerable gravity; in his opinion it would not be well to send
the whole command over the cliff at once; a better way would be
to send down a single individual first, and see how he fared.

I saw the wisdom of this idea instantly. I said as much, and
thanked my agent cordially, and told him to take his umbrella
and try the thing right away, and wave his hat when he got
down, if he struck in a soft place, and then I would ship the rest
right along.

Harris was greatly touched with this mark of confidence, and said so in a voice that had a perceptible tremble in it; but at the same time he said he did not feel himself worthy of so conspicuous a favour; that it might cause jealousy in the command, for there were plenty who would not hesitate to say he had used underhand means to get the appointment, whereas his conscience would bear him witness that he had not sought it at all, not even, in his secret heart, desired it.

I said these words did him extreme credit, but that he must not throw away the imperishable distinction of being the first man to descend an Alp per parachute, simply to save the feelings of some envious underlings. No, I said, he *must* accept the appointment—it was no longer an invitation, it was a command.

He thanked me with effusion, and said that putting the thing in this form removed every objection. He retired, and soon returned with his umbrella, his eyes flaming with gratitude and his cheeks pallid with joy. Just then the head guide passed along. Harris's expression changed to one of infinite tenderness, and he said—

'That man did me a cruel injury four days ago, and I said in my heart he should live to perceive and confess that the only noble revenge a man can take upon his enemy is to return good for evil. I resign in his favour. Appoint him.'

I threw my arms around the generous fellow and said—

'Harris, you are the noblest soul that lives. You shall not regret this sublime act, neither shall the world fail to know of it. You shall have opportunities far transcending this one, too, if I live—remember that.'

I called the head guide to me and appointed him on the spot. But the thing aroused no enthusiasm in him. He did not take to the idea at all. He said—

'Tie myself to an umbrella and jump over the Gorner Grat; excuse me, there are a great many pleasanter roads to the devil than that.'

Upon a discussion of the subject with him, it appeared that he considered the project distinctly and decidedly dangerous. I was not convinced, yet I was not willing to try the experiment in any risky way—that is, in a way that might cripple the strength and efficiency of the Expedition. I was about at my wits' end when it occurred to me to try it on the Latinist.

He was called in. But he declined, on the plea of inexperience, diffidence in public, lack of curiosity, and I don't know what all. Another man declined on account of a cold in the head; thought he ought to avoid exposure. Another could not jump well—never *could* jump well—did not believe he could jump so far without long and patient practice. Another was afraid it was going to rain, and his umbrella had a hole in it. Everybody had an excuse. The result was what the reader has by this time guessed: the most magnificent idea that was ever conceived had to be abandoned from sheer lack of a person with enterprise enough to carry it out. Yes, I actually had to give that thing up—whilst doubtless, I should live to see somebody use it, and take all the credit from me.

Well, I had to go overland—there was no other way. I marched the Expedition down the steep and tedious mule-path, and took up as good a position as I could upon the middle of the glacier, because Baedeker said the middle part travels the fastest. As a measure of economy, however, I put some of the heavier baggage on the shoreward parts, to go as slow freight.

I waited and waited, but the glacier did not move. Night was coming on, the darkness began to gather—still we did not budge. It occurred to me then that there might be a time-table in Baedeker, it would be well to find out the hours of starting. I called for the book—it could not be found. Bradshaw would certainly contain a time-table, but no Bradshaw could be found.

Very well, I must make the best of the situation. So I pitched the tents, picketed the animals, milked the cows, had supper, paregoricked the men, established the watch, and went to bed—with orders to call me as soon as we came in sight of Zermatt.

I awoke about half-past-ten next morning and looked around. We hadn't budged a peg! At first I could not understand it: then it occurred to me that the old thing must be aground. So I cut down some trees and rigged a spar on the starboard and another on the port side, and fooled away upwards of three hours trying to spar her off. But it was no use, she was a half a mile wide and fifteen or twenty miles long, and there was no telling just whereabouts she *was* aground. The men began to show uneasiness too, and presently they came flying to me with ashy faces, saying she had sprung a leak.

Nothing but my cool behaviour at this critical time saved us from another panic. I ordered them to show me the place. They led me to a spot where a huge boulder lay in a deep pool of clear and brilliant water. It did look like a pretty bad leak, but I kept that to myself. I made a pump and set the men to work to pump out the glacier. We made a success of it. I perceived then that it was not a leak at all. This boulder had descended from a precipice and stopped on the ice in the middle of the glacier, and the sun had warmed it up every day, and consequently it had melted its way deeper and deeper into the ice, until at last it reposed, as we had found it, in a deep pool of the clearest and coldest water.

Presently Baedeker was found again, and I hunted eagerly for the time-table. There was none. The book simply said the glacier was moving all the time. This was satisfactory, so I shut up the book and chose a good position to view the scenery as we passed along. I stood there some time enjoying the trip, but at last it occurred to me that we did not seem to be gaining any on the scenery. I said to myself, 'This confounded old thing's aground again, sure'—and opened Baedeker to see if I could run across any remedy for these annoying interruptions. I soon found a sentence which threw a dazzling light upon the matter. It said, 'The Gorner Glacier travels at an average rate of a little less than an inch a day.' I have seldom felt so outraged. I have seldom had my confidence so wantonly betrayed. I made a small calculation: 1 inch a day, say 30 feet a year; estimated distance to Zermatt, 3 1-18 miles. Time required to go by glacier, *a little over five hundred years!* I said to myself, 'I can *walk* it quicker, and before I will patronise such a fraud as this, I will do it.'

When I revealed to Harris the fact that the passenger-part of this glacier—the central part—the lightning-express part, so to speak—was not due in Zermatt till the summer of 2,378, and that the baggage, coming along the slow edge, would not arrive until some generations later, he burst out with—

'That is European management all over! An inch a day—think of that! Five hundred years to go a trifle over three miles! But I am not a bit surprised. It's a Catholic glacier. You can tell by the look of it. And the management!'

I said no, I believed nothing but the extreme end of it was in a Catholic canton.

'Well, then, it's a Government glacier,' said Harris. 'It's all the same. Over here the Government runs everything—so everything's slow; slow and ill-managed. But with us, everything's done by private enterprise, and then there ain't much lolling around, you can depend on it. I wish Tom Scott could get his hands on this torpid old slab once—you'd see it take a different gait from this.'

I said I was sure he would increase the speed, if there was trade enough to justify it.

'He'd *make* trade,' said Harris. 'That's the difference between Governments and individuals. Governments don't care, individuals do. Tom Scott would take all the trade; in two years Gornèr stock would go to 200, and inside of two more you would see all the other glaciers under the hammer for taxes'. After a reflective pause, Harris added, 'A little less than an inch a day; a little less than an *inch*, mind you. Well, I am losing my reverence for glaciers.'

I was feeling much the same way myself. I have travelled by canal boat, ox-waggon, raft, and by the Ephesus and Smyrna railway, but when it comes down to good solid honest slow motion, I bet my money on the glacier. As a means of passenger transportation I consider the glacier a failure; but as a vehicle for slow freight, I think she fills the bill. In the matter of putting the fine shades on that line of business, I judge she could teach the Germans something.

I ordered the men to break camp and prepare for the land journey to Zermatt. At this moment a most interesting find was made; a dark object, bedded in the glacial ice, was cut out with the ice-axes, and it proved to be a piece of the undressed skin of some animal—a hair trunk, perhaps; but a close inspection disabled the hair trunk theory, and further discussion and examination exploded it entirely—that is, in the opinion of all the scientists except the one who had advanced it. This one clung to his theory with the affectionate fidelity characteristic of originators of scientific theories, and afterwards won many of the first scientists of the age to his view, by a very able pamphlet which he wrote, entitled, 'Evidences going to show that the hair trunk, in a wild state, belonged to the early glacial period, and roamed the wastes of chaos in company with the cave bear, primeval man, and the other Oolitics of the Old Silurian family.'

Each of our scientists had a theory of his own, and put forward an animal of his own as a candidate for the skin. I sided with the geologist of the Expedition in the belief that this patch of skin had once helped to cover a Siberian elephant in some old forgotten age—but we divided there, the geologist believing that this discovery proved that Siberia had formerly been located where Switzerland is now, whereas I held the opinion that it merely proved that the primeval Swiss was not the dull savage he is represented to have been, but was a being of high intellectual development, who liked to go the menagerie.

We arrived that evening, after many hardships and adventures, in some fields close to the great ice-arch where the mad Visp boils and surges out from under the foot of the great Gorner Glacier, and here we camped, our perils over, and our magnificent undertaking successfully completed. We marched into Zermatt the next day, and were received with the most lavish honours and applause. A document, signed and sealed by all the authorities, was given to me which established and endorsed the fact that I had made the ascent of the Riffelberg. This I wear around my neck, and it will be buried with me when I am no more.

CHAPTER 40

I am not so ignorant about glacial movement now as I was when I took passage on the Gorner Glacier. I have 'read up' since. I am aware that these vast bodies of ice do not travel at the same rate of speed; whilst the Gorner Glacier makes less than an inch a day, the Unter-Aar Glacier makes as much as eight; and still other glaciers are said to go 12, 16, and even 20 inches a day. One writer says that the slowest glacier travels 25 feet a year, and the fastest 400.

What is a glacier? It is easy to say it looks like a frozen river which occupies the bed of a winding gorge or gully between mountains. But that gives no notion of its vastness, for it is sometimes 600 feet thick, and we are not accustomed to rivers 600 feet deep; no, our rivers are 6 feet, 20 feet, and sometimes 50 feet deep; we are not quite able to grasp so large a fact as an ice-river 600 feet deep.

The glacier's surface is not smooth and level, but has deep swales and swelling elevations, and sometimes has the look of a tossing sea whose turbulent billows were frozen hard in the instant of their most violent motion; the glacier's surface is not a flawless mass, but is a river with cracks or crevasses, some narrow, some gaping wide. Many a man, the victim of a slip or a mis-step, has plunged down one of these and met his death. Men have been fished out of them alive, but it was when they did not go to a great depth; the cold of the great depths would quickly stupefy a man, whether he was hurt or unhurt. These cracks do not go straight down; one can seldom see more than 20 to 40 feet down them; consequently men who have disappeared in them have been sought for, in the hope that they had stopped within helping distance, whereas their case, in most instances, had really been hopeless from the beginning.

In 1864 a party of tourists was descending Mont Blanc, and while picking their way over one of the mighty glaciers of that lofty region, roped together, as was proper, a young porter disengaged himself from the line, and started across an ice-bridge which spanned a crevasse. It broke under him with a crash and he disappeared. The others could not see how deep he had gone, so it might be worth while to try and rescue him. A brave young guide named Michel Payot volunteered.

Two ropes were made fast to his leather belt, and he bore the end of the third one in his hand to tie to the victim in case he found him. He was lowered into the crevasse, he descended deeper and deeper between the clear blue walls of solid ice, he approached a bend in the crack and disappeared under. Down, and still down, he went into this profound grave; when he had reached a depth of 80 feet he passed under another bend in the crack, and thence descended 80 feet lower, as between perpendicular precipices. Arrived at this stage of 160 feet below the surface of the glacier, he peered through the twilight dimness and perceived that the chasm took another turn and stretched away at a steep slant to unknown deeps, for its course was lost in darkness. What a place that was to be in—especially if that leather belt should break! The compression of the belt threatened to suffocate the intrepid fellow; he called to his friends to draw him up, but could not make them hear. They still lowered him deeper and deeper. Then he jerked his third cord as vigorously as he could; his friends understood, and dragged him out of those icy jaws of death.

Then they attached a bottle to a cord and sent it down 200 feet, but it found no bottom. It came up covered with congelations—evidence enough that even if the poor porter reached the bottom with unbroken bones, a swift death from cold was sure anyway.

A glacier is a stupendous, ever progressing, resistless plough. It pushes ahead of it masses of boulders which are packed together, and they stretch across the gorge, right in front of it, like a long grave or a long, sharp roof. This is called a moraine. It also shoves out a moraine along each side of its course.

Imposing as the modern glaciers are, they are not so huge as were some that once existed. For instance, Mr. Whymper says:—

'At some very remote period the valley of Aosta was occupied by a vast glacier, which flowed down its entire length from Mont Blanc to the plain of Piedmont, remained stationary, or nearly so, at its mouth for many centuries, and deposited there enormous masses of *débris*. The length of this glacier exceeded *eighty miles*, and it drained a basin twenty-five to thirty-five miles across, bounded by the highest mountains in the Alps. The great peaks rose several thousand feet above the glaciers, and then, as now, shattered by sun and frost, poured down their showers of rocks and stones, in witness of which there are the immense piles of angular fragments that constitute the moraines of Ivria.

'The moraines around Ivria are of extraordinary dimensions. That which was on the left bank of the glacier is about *thirteen miles* long, and in some places rises to a height of *two thousand one hundred and thirty feet* above the floor of the valley! The terminal moraines (those which are pushed in front of the glaciers) cover something like twenty square miles of country. At the mouth of the valley of the Aosta the thickness of the glacier must have been at least *two thousand feet*, and its width at that part *five miles and a quarter*.'

It is not easy to get at a comprehension of a mass of ice like that. If one could cleave off the butt end of such a glacier—an oblong block two or three miles wide by five and a quarter long and 2,000 feet thick—he could completely hide the city of New York under it, and Trinity steeple would only stick up into it relatively as far as a shingle nail would stick up into the bottom of a Saratoga trunk.

'The boulders from Mont Blanc, upon the plain below Ivria, assure us that the glacier which transported them existed for a prodigious length of time. Their present distance from the cliffs from which they were derived is about 420,000 feet, and if we assume that they travelled at the rate of 400 feet per annum, their journey must have occupied them no less than 1,055 years! In all probability they did not travel so fast.'

Glaciers are sometimes hurried out of their characteristic snail-pace. A marvellous spectacle is presented then. Mr. Whymper refers to a case which occurred in Iceland in 1721:—

'It seems that in the neighbourhood of the mountain Kotlugja, large bodies of water formed underneath, or within the glaciers (either on account of the interior heat of the earth or from other causes), and at length acquired irresistible power, tore the glaciers from their mooring on the land, and swept them over every obstacle into the sea. Prodigious masses of ice were thus borne for a distance of about ten miles over land in the space of a few hours; and their bulk was so enormous, that they covered the sea for seven miles from the shore, and remained aground in 600 feet of water! The denudation of the land was upon a grand scale. All superficial accumulations were swept away, and the bed-rock was exposed. It was described, in graphic language, how all irregularities and depressions were obliterated, and a smooth surface of several miles area laid bare, and that this area had the appearance of having been *planed by a plane.*'

The account translated from the Icelandic says that the mountain-like ruins of this majestic glacier so covered the sea that as far as the eye could reach no open water was discoverable, even from the highest peaks. A monster wall or barrier of ice was built across a considerable stretch of land, too, by this strange irruption:—

'One can form some idea of the altitude of this barrier of ice when it is mentioned that from Hofdabrekka farm, which lies high up on a fjeld, one could not see Hjorleifshofdi opposite, which is a fell 640 feet in height; but in order to do so had to clamber up a mountain slope east of Hofdabrekka, 1,200 feet high.'

These things will help the reader to understand why it is that a man who keeps company with glaciers comes to feel tolerably insignificant by and by. The Alps and the glaciers together are able to take every bit of conceit out of a man and reduce his self-importance to zero if he will only remain within the influence of their sublime presence long enough to give it a fair and reasonable chance to do its work.

The Alpine glaciers move—that is granted now by everybody. But there was a time when people scoffed at the idea; they said you might as well expect leagues of solid rock to crawl along the ground as expect solid leagues of ice to do it. But proof after proof was furnished, and finally the world had to believe.

The wise men not only said the glacier moved, but they timed its movement. They ciphered out a glacier's gait, and then said confidently that it would travel just so far in so many years. There is record of a striking and curious example of the accuracy which may be attained in these reckonings.

In 1820 the ascent of Mont Blanc was attempted by a Russian and two Englishmen, with seven guides. They had reached a prodigious altitude, and were approaching the summit, when an avalanche swept several of the party down a sharp slope of two hundred feet and hurled five of them (all guides) into one of the crevasses of a glacier. The life of one of the five was saved by a long barometer which was strapped to his back—it bridged the crevasse and suspended him until help came. The alpenstock or baton of another saved its owner in a similar way. Three men were lost—Pierre Balmat, Pierre Carrier, and Auguste Tairraz. They had been hurled down into the fathomless great deeps of the crevasse.

Dr. Forbes, the English geologist, had made frequent visits to the Mont Blanc region, and had given much attention to the disputed question of the movement of glaciers. During one of these visits he completed his estimates of the rate of movement of the glacier which had swallowed up the three guides, and uttered the prediction that the glacier would deliver up its dead at the foot of the mountain thirty-five years from the time of the accident, or possibly forty.

A dull, slow journey—a movement imperceptible to any eye—but it was proceeding, nevertheless, and without cessation. It was a journey which a rolling stone would make in a few seconds—the lofty point of departure was visible from the village below in the valley.

The prediction cut curiously close to the truth; forty-one years after the catastrophe the remains were cast forth at the foot of the glacier.

I find an interesting account of the matter in the 'Histoire du Mont Blanc,' by Stephen d'Arve. I will condense this account as follows:—

'On the 12th of August, 1861, at the hour of the close of mass, a guide arrived out of breath at the mairie of Chamonix, and bearing on his shoulders a very lugubrious burden. It was a sack filled with human remains which he had gathered from the orifice of a crevasse in the Glacier des Bossons. He conjectured that these were remains of the victims of the catastrophe of 1820, and a minute inquest, immediately instituted by the local authorities, soon demonstrated the correctness of his supposition. The contents of the sack were spread upon a long table, and officially inventoried as follows:—

'Portions of three human skulls. Several tufts of black and blonde hair. A human jaw, furnished with fine white teeth. A fore-arm and hand, all the fingers of the latter intact. The flesh was white and fresh, and both the arm and hand preserved a degree of flexibility in the articulations.

'The ring finger had suffered a slight abrasion, and the stain of the blood was still visible and unchanged after forty-one years. A left foot, the flesh white and fresh.

'Along with these fragments were portions of waistcoats, hats, hob-nailed shoes, and other clothing; a wing of a pigeon, with black feathers; a fragment of an alpenstock; a tin lantern; and lastly, a boiled leg of mutton, the only flesh among all the remains that exhaled an unpleasant odour. The guide said that the mutton had no odour when he took it from the glacier; an hour's exposure to the sun had already begun the work of decomposition upon it.

'Persons were called for to identify these poor pathetic relics, and a touching scene ensued. Two men were still living who had witnessed the grim catastrophe of nearly half a century before—Marie Couttet (saved by his baton) and Julien Davouassoux (saved by the barometer). These aged men entered and approached the table. Davouassoux, more than 80 years old, contemplated the mournful remains mutely and with a vacant eye, for his intelligence and his memory were torpid with age; but Couttet's faculties were still perfect at seventy-two, and he exhibited strong emotion. He said—

' "Pierre Balmat was fair; he wore a straw hat. This bit of skull, with the tuft of blonde hair, was his; this is his hat. Pierre Carrier was very dark; this skull was his, and this felt hat. This is Balmat's hand, I remember it so well!" and the old man bent down and kissed it reverently, then closed his fingers upon it in an affectionate grasp, crying out, "I could never have dared to believe that before quitting this world it would be granted me to press once more the hand of one of those brave comrades, the hand of my good friend Balmat."

'There is something weirdly pathetic about the picture of that white-haired veteran greeting with his loving hand-shake this friend who had been dead forty years. When these hands had met last, they were alike in the softness and freshness of youth; now, one was brown, and wrinkled and horny with age, while the other was still as young, and fair, and blemishless as if those forty years had come and gone in a single moment, leaving no mark of their passage. Time had gone on in the one case; it had stood still in the other. A man who has not seen a friend for a generation keeps him in mind always as he saw him last, and is somehow surprised, and is also shocked, to see the ageing change the years have wrought when he sees him again. Marie Couttet's experience, in finding his friend's hand unaltered from the image of it which he had carried in his memory for forty years, is an experience which stands alone in the history of man, perhaps.

'Couttet identified other relics—

' "This hat belonged to Auguste Tairraz. He carried the cage of pigeons which we proposed to set free upon the summit. Here is the wing of one of those pigeons. And here is the fragment of my broken baton; it was by grace of the baton that my life was saved. Who could have told me that I should one day have the satisfaction to look again upon this bit of wood that supported me above the grave that swallowed up my unfortunate companions!" '

No portions of the body of Tairraz had been found. A diligent search was made, but without result. However, another search was instituted a year later, and this had better success. Many fragments of clothing which had belonged to the lost guides were discovered; also part of a lantern, and a green veil, with blood stains on it. But the interesting feature was this—

One of the searchers came suddenly upon a sleeved arm projecting from a crevice in the ice-wall, with the hand outstretched as if offering greeting! 'The nails of this white hand were still rosy, and the pose of the extended fingers seem to express an eloquent welcome to the long lost light of day.'

The hand and arm were alone; there was no trunk. After being removed from the ice the flesh tints quickly faded out and the rosy nails took on the alabaster hue of death. This was the third *right* hand found; therefore all three of the lost men were accounted for beyond cavil or question.

Dr. Hamel was the Russian gentleman of the party which made the ascent at the time of the famous disaster. He left Chamonix as soon as he conveniently could after the descent; and as he had shown a chilly indifference about the calamity, and offered neither sympathy nor assistance to the widows and orphans, he carried with him the cordial execrations of the whole community. Four months before the first remains were found, a Chamonix guide named Balmat—a relative of one of the lost men—was in London, and one day encountered a hale old gentleman in the British Museum, who said,—

'I overheard your name. Are you from Chamonix, Monsieur Balmat?'

'Yes, sir.'

'Haven't they found the bodies of my three guides yet? I am Dr. Hamel.'

'Alas, no, monsieur.'

'Well, you'll find them sooner or later.'

'Yes, it is the opinion of Dr. Forbes and Mr. Tyndall that the glacier will sooner or later restore to us the remains of the unfortunate victims.'

'Without a doubt, without a doubt. And it will be a great thing for Chamonix, in the matter of attracting tourists. You can get up a museum with those remains that will draw!'

This savage idea had not improved the odour of Dr. Hamel's name in Chamonix by any means. But, after all, the man was sound on human nature. His idea was conveyed to the public officials of Chamonix, and they gravely discussed it around the official council table. They were only prevented from carrying it into execution by the determined opposition of the friends and descendants of the lost guides, who insisted on giving the remains Christian burial, and succeeded in their purpose.

A close watch had to be kept upon all the poor remnants and fragments, to prevent embezzlement. A few accessory odds and ends were sold. Rags and scraps of the coarse clothing were parted with at a rate equal to about twenty dollars a yard; a piece of a lantern and one or two other trifles brought nearly their weight in gold; and an Englishman offered a pound sterling for a single breeches-button.

CHAPTER 41

One of the most memorable of all the Alpine catastrophes was that of July 1865, on the Matterhorn—already slightly referred to a few pages back. The details of it are scarcely known in America. To the vast majority of readers they are not known at all. Mr. Whymper's account is the only authentic one. I will import the chief portion of it into this book, partly because of its intrinsic interest, and partly because it gives such a vivid idea of what the perilous pastime of Alp-climbing is. This was Mr. Whymper's *ninth* attempt during a series of years to vanquish that steep and stubborn pillar of rock; it succeeded, the other eight were failures. No man had ever accomplished the ascent before, though the attempts had been numerous.

Mr. Whymper's Narrative

We started from Zermatt on July 13, at half-past five, on a brilliant and perfectly cloudless morning. We were eight in number—Crox (guide), old Peter Taugwalder (guide), and his two sons; Lord F. Douglas, Mr. Hadow, Rev. Mr. Hudson, and I. To ensure steady motion, one tourist and one native walked together. The youngest Taugwalder fell to my share. The wine-bags also fell to my lot to carry, and throughout the day after each drink I replenished them secretly with water, so that at the next halt they were found fuller than before! This was considered a good omen, and little short of miraculous.

On the first day we did not intend to ascend to any great height, and we mounted accordingly very leisurely. Before twelve o'clock we had found a good position for the tent at a height of 11,000 feet. We passed the remaining hours of daylight—some basking in the sunshine, some sketching, some collecting; Hudson made tea, I coffee, and at length we retired, each one to his blanket-bag.

We assembled together before dawn on the 14th and started directly it was light enough to move. One of the young Taugwalders returned to Zermatt. In a few minutes we turned the rib which had intercepted the view of the eastern face from our tent platform. The whole of this great slope was now revealed, rising for 3,000 feet like a huge natural staircase. Some parts were more, and others were less easy, but we were not once brought to a halt by any serious impediment, for when an obstruction was met in front it could always be turned to the right or to the left. For the greater part of the way there was no occasion, indeed, for the rope, and sometimes Hudson led, sometimes myself. At 6.20 we had attained a height of 12,800 feet, and halted for half an hour; we then continued the ascent without a break until 9.55, when we stopped for fifty minutes, at a height of 14,000 feet.

We had now arrived at the foot of that part which, seen from the Riffelberg, seems perpendicular or overhanging. We could no longer continue on the eastern side. For a little distance we ascended by snow upon the arête—that is, the ridge—then turned over to the right, or northern side. The work became difficult, and required caution. In some places there was little to hold; the general slope of the mountain was *less* than 40°, and snow had accumulated in, and had filled up, the interstices of the rock-face, leaving only occasional fragments projecting here and there. These were at times covered with a thin film of ice. It was a place which any fair mountaineer might pass in safety. We bore away nearly horizontally for about 400 feet, then ascended directly towards the summit for about 60 feet, then doubled back to the ridge which descends towards Zermatt. A long stride round a rather awkward corner brought us to snow once more.

The last doubt vanished! The Matterhorn was ours! Nothing but 200 feet of easy snow remained to be surmounted.

The higher we rose, the more intense became the excitement. The slope eased off, at length we could be detached, and Croz and I, dashing away, ran a neck-and-neck race, which ended in a dead heat. At 1.40 p.m. the world was at out feet, and the Matterhorn was conquered.

The others arrived. Croz now took the tent-pole and planted it in the highest snow. 'Yes,' we said, 'there is the flag-staff, but where is the flag?' 'Here it is,' he answered, pulling off his blouse and fixing it to the stick. It made a poor flag, and there was no wind to float it out, yet it was seen all around. They saw it at Zermatt—at the Riffel—in the Val Tournanche.

*　*　*

We remained on the summit for one hour—

One crowded hour of glorious life.

It passed away too quickly, and we began to prepare for the descent.

Hudson and I consulted as to the best and safest arrangement of the party. We agreed that it was best for Croz to go first, and Hadow second; Hudson, who was almost equal to a guide in sureness of foot, wished to be third; Lord Douglas was placed next, and old Peter, the strongest of the remainder, after him. I suggested to Hudson that we should attach a rope to the rocks on our arrival at the difficult bit, and hold it as we descended, as an additional protection. He approved the idea, but it was not definitely decided that it should be done. The party was being arranged in the above order whilst I was sketching the summit, and they had finished and were waiting for me to be tied in line, when some one remembered that our names had not been left in a bottle. They requested me to write them down, and moved off while it was being done.

A few minutes afterwards I tied myself to young Peter, ran down after the others, and caught them just as they were commencing the descent of the difficult part. Great care was being taken. Only one man was moving at a time; when he was firmly planted the next advanced, and so on. They had not, however, attached the additional rope to rocks, and nothing was said about it. The suggestion was not made for my own sake, and I am not sure that it even occurred to me again. For some little distance we two followed the others, detached from them, and should have continued so had not Lord Douglas asked me, about 3 p.m., to tie on to old Peter, as he feared, he said, that Taugwalder would not be able to hold his ground if a slip occurred.

A few minutes later a sharp-eyed lad ran into the Monte Rosa Hotel at Zermatt, saying that he had seen an avalanche fall from the summit of the Matterhorn on to the Matterhorn glacier. The boy was reproved for telling idle stories; he was right, nevertheless, and this was what he saw.

Michel Croz had laid aside his axe, and in order to give Mr. Hadow greater security was absolutely taking hold of his legs, and putting his feet, one by one, into their proper positions. As far as I know, no one was actually descending. I cannot speak with certainty, because the two leading men were partially hidden from my sight by an intervening mass of rock, but it is my belief, from the movements of their shoulders, that Croz, having done as I have said, was in the act of turning round to go down a step or two himself; at this moment Mr. Hadow slipped, fell against him, and knocked him over. I heard one startled exclamation from Croz, then saw him and Mr. Hadow flying downwards; in another moment Hudson was dragged from his steps, and Lord Douglas immediately after him. All this was the work of a moment. Immediately we heard Croz's exclamation, old Peter and I planted ourselves as firmly as the rocks would permit; the rope was taut between us, and the jerk came on us both as on one man. We held; but the rope broke midway between Taugwalder and Lord Francis Douglas. For a few seconds we saw our unfortunate companions sliding downwards on their backs, and spreading out their hands, endeavouring to save themselves. They passed from our sight uninjured, disappeared one by one, and fell from precipice to precipice on to the Matterhorn glacier below, a distance of nearly 4,000 feet in height. From the moment the rope broke it was impossible to help them. So perished our comrades!

* * *

For more than two hours afterwards I thought almost every moment that the next would be my last, for the Taugwalders, utterly unnerved, were not only incapable of giving assistance, but were in such a state that a slip might have been expected from them at any moment. After a time we were able to do that which should have been done at first, and fixed rope to firm rocks, in addition to being tied together. These ropes were cut from time to time, and were left behind. Even with their assurance the men were afraid to proceed, and several times old Peter turned, with ashy face and faltering limbs, and said, with terrible emphasis, '*I cannot!*'

About 6 p.m. we arrived at the snow upon the ridge descending towards Zermatt, and all peril was over. We frequently looked, but in vain, for traces of our unfortunate companions; we bent over the ridge and cried to them, but no sound returned. Convinced at last that they were neither within sight nor hearing, we ceased from our useless efforts; and, too cast down for speech, silently gathered up our things, and the little effects of those who were lost, and then completed the descent.

Such is Mr. Whymper's graphic and thrilling narrative. Zermatt gossip darkly hints that the elder Taugwalder cut the rope when the accident occurred in order to preserve himself from being dragged into the abyss; but Mr. Whymper says that the ends of the rope showed no evidence of cutting but only of breaking. He adds that if Taugwalder had had the disposition to cut the rope, he would not have had time to do it, the accident was so sudden and unexpected.

Lord Douglas's body has never been found. It probably lodged upon some inaccessible shelf in the face of the mighty precipice. Lord Douglas was a youth of nineteen. The three other victims fell nearly 4,000 feet, and their bodies lay together upon the glacier when found by Mr. Whymper and the other searchers the next morning. Their graves are beside the little church in Zermatt.

CHAPTER 42

Switzerland is simply a large, humpy, solid rock, with a thin skin of grass stretched over it. Consequently they do not dig graves, they blast them out with powder and fuse. They cannot afford to have large graveyards, the grass skin is too circumscribed and too valuable. It is all required for the support of the living.

The graveyard in Zermatt occupies only about one-eighth of an acre. The graves are sunk in the living rock, and are very permanent; but occupation of them is only temporary; the occupant can only stay till his grave is needed by a later subject, he is removed then, for they do not bury one body on top of another. As I understand it, a family owns a grave just as it owns a house. A man dies and leaves his house to his son, and at the same time this dead father succeeds to his own father's grave. He moves out of the house and into the grave, and his predecessor moves out of the grave and into the cellar of the chapel. I saw a black box lying in the churchyard, with skull and cross-bones painted on it, and was told that this was used in transferring remains to the cellar.

In that cellar the bones and skulls of several hundreds of former citizens were compactly corded up. They made a pile 18 feet long, 7 feet high, and 8 feet wide. I was told that in some of the receptacles of this kind in the Swiss villages the skulls were all marked, and if a man wished to find the skulls of his ancestors for several generations back he could do it by these marks, preserved in the family records.

An English gentleman who had lived some years in this region said it was the cradle of compulsory education. But he said that the English idea that compulsory education would reduce bastardy and intemperance was an error—it has not that effect. He said there was more seduction in the Protestant than in the Catholic cantons, because the confessional protected the girls. I wonder why it doesn't protect married women in France and Spain?

This gentleman said that among the poorer peasants in the Valais it was common for the brothers in a family to cast lots to determine which of them should have the coveted privilege of marrying. Then the lucky one got married, and his brethren—doomed bachelors—heroically banded themselves together to help support the new family.

We left Zermatt in a waggon—and in a rain storm, too—for St. Nicholas about ten o'clock one morning. Again we passed between those grass-clad prodigious cliffs, specked with wee dwellings peeping over at us from velvety green walls ten and twelve hundred feet high. It did not seem possible that the imaginary chamois even could climb those precipices. Lovers on the opposite cliffs probably kiss through a spy-glass and correspond with a rifle.

In Switzerland the farmer's plough is a wide shovel, which scrapes up and turns over the thin earthy skin of his native rock—and there the man of the plough is a hero. Now here, by our St. Nicholas road, was a grave, and it had a tragic story. A ploughman was skinning his farm one morning—not the steepest part of it, but still a steep part—that is, he was not skinning the front of his farm, but the roof of it, near the eaves—when he absent-mindedly let go of the plough-handles to moisten his hands in the usual way: he lost his balance and fell out of his farm backwards. Poor fellow, he never touched anything till he struck the bottom 1,500 feet below.[1] We throw a halo of heroism around the life of the soldier and the sailor, because of the deadly dangers they are facing all the time. But

---

[1] This was on a Sunday,—M.T.

we are not used to looking upon farming as an heroic occupation. This is because we have not lived in Switzerland.

From St. Nicholas we struck out for Visp—or Vispach—on foot. The rain storms had been at work during several days, and had done a deal of damage in Switzerland and Savoy. We came to one place where a stream had changed its course and plunged down the mountain in a new place, sweeping everything before it. Two poor but precious farms by the roadside were ruined. One was washed clear away, and the bed-rock exposed; the other was buried out of sight under a tumbled chaos of rocks, gravel, mud, and rubbish. The resistless might of water was well exemplified. Some saplings which had stood in the way were bent to the ground, stripped clean of their bark, and buried under rocky *débris*. The road had been swept away too.

In another place, where the road was high up on the mountain's face, and its outside edge protected by flimsy masonry, we frequently came across spots where this masonry had caved off and left dangerous gaps for mules to get over; and with still more frequency we found the masonry slightly crumbled, and marked by mule hoofs, thus showing that there had been danger of an accident to somebody. When at last we came to a badly ruptured bit of masonry, with hoof-prints evidencing a desperate struggle to regain the lost foothold, I looked quite hopefully over the dizzy precipice. But there was nobody down there.

They take exceedingly good care of their rivers in Switzerland and other portions of Europe. They wall up both banks with slanting solid stone masonry—so that from end to end of these rivers the banks look like the wharves at St. Louis and other towns on the Mississippi River.

It was during this walk from St. Nicholas, in the shadow of the majestic Alps, that we came across some little children amusing themselves in what seemed, at first, a most odd and original way—but it wasn't, it was in simply a natural and characteristic way. They were roped together with a string, they had mimic alpenstocks and ice-axes, and were climbing a meek and lowly manure pile with a most blood-curdling amount of care and caution. The 'guide' at the head of the line cut imaginary steps in a laborious and painstaking way, and not a monkey budged till the step above him was vacated. If we had waited we should have witnessed an imaginary accident, no doubt; and we should have heard the intrepid band hurrah when they made the summit and looked around upon the 'magnificent view,' and seen them throw themselves down in exhausted attitudes for a rest in that commanding situation.

In Nevada I used to see the children play at silver mining. Of course, the great thing was an accident in a mine, and there were two 'star' parts: that of the man who fell down the mimic shaft, and that of the daring hero who was lowered into the depths to bring him up. I knew one small chap who always insisted on playing *both* of these parts—and he carried his point. He would tumble into the shaft and die, and then come to the surface and go back after his own remains.

It is the smartest boy that gets the hero-part everywhere: he is head guide in Switzerland, head miner in Nevada, head bull-fighter in Spain, &c., but I knew a preacher's son, seven years old, who once selected a part for himself compared to which those just mentioned are tame and unimpressive. Jimmy's father stopped him from driving imaginary horse-cars on Sunday—stopped him from playing captain of an imaginary steamboat next Sunday—stopped him from leading an imaginary army to battle the following Sunday—and so on. Finally the little fellow said—

'I've tried everything, and they won't any of them do. What *can* I play?'

'I hardly know, Jimmy; but you *must* play only things that are suitable to the Sabbath day.'

Next Sunday the preacher stepped softly to a back room door to see if the children were rightly employed. He peeped in. A chair occupied the middle of the room, and on the back of it hung Jimmy's cap; one of the little sisters took the cap down, nibbled at it, then passed it to another small sister and said, 'Eat of this fruit, for it is good.' The Reverend took in the situation—alas, they were playing the Expulsion from Eden! Yet he found one little crumb of comfort. He said to himself, 'For once Jimmy has yielded the chief *rôle*—I have been wronging him, I did not believe there was so much modesty in him; I should have expected him to be either Adam or Eve.' This crumb of comfort lasted but a very little while; he glanced around and discovered Jimmy standing in an imposing attitude in a corner, with a dark and deadly frown on his face. What that meant was very plain—*he was personating the Deity!* Think of the guileless sublimity of that idea.

We reached Vispach at 8 p.m., only about seven hours out from St. Nicholas. So we must have made fully a mile and a half an hour, and it was all down hill too, and very muddy at that. We stayed all night at the Hôtel du Soleil; I remember it because the landlady, the portier, the waitress, and the chambermaid were not separate persons, but were all contained in one neat and chipper suit of spotless muslin, and she was the prettiest young creature I saw in all that region. She was the landlord's daughter. And I remember that the only native match to her I saw in all Europe was the young daughter of the landlord of a village inn in the Black Forest. Why don't more people in Europe marry and keep hotel?

Next morning we left with a family of English friends and went by train to Brevet, and thence by boat across the lake to Ouchy (Lausanne).

Ouchy is memorable to me, not on account of its beautiful situation and lovely surroundings—although these would make it stick long in one's memory—but as the place where I caught the London 'Times' dropping into humour. It was not aware of it, though. It did not do it on purpose. An English friend called my attention to this lapse, and cut out the reprehensible paragraph for me. Think of encountering a grin like this on the face of that grim journal:—

ERRATUM.—We are requested by Reuter's Telegram Company to correct an erroneous announcement made in their Brisbane telegram of the 2nd inst., published in our impression of the 5th inst., stating that 'Lady Kennedy had given birth to twins, the eldest being a son.' The Company explain that the message they received contained the words 'Governor of Queensland, *twins first son*.' Being, however, subsequently informed that Sir Arthur Kennedy was unmarried, and that there must be some mistake, a telegraphic repetition was at once demanded. It has been received to-day (11th inst.), and shows that the words really telegraphed by Reuter's agent were, 'Governor Queensland *turns first sod*,' alluding to the Maryborough-Gympie Railway in course of construction. The words in italics were mutilated by the telegraph in transmission from Australia, and reaching the company in the form mentioned above gave rise to the mistake.

I had always had a deep and reverent compassion for the sufferings of the 'prisoner of Chillon,' whose story Byron has told in such moving verse; so I took the steamer and made pilgrimage to the dungeons of the Castle of Chillon, to see the place where poor Bonivard endured his dreary captivity 300 years ago. I am glad I did that, for it took away some of the pain I was feeling on the prisoner's account. His dungeon was a nice, cool, roomy place, and I cannot see why he should have been so dissatisfied with it. If he had been imprisoned in a St. Nicholas private dwelling, where the fertilizer prevails, and the goat sleeps with the guest, and the chickens roost on him, and the cow comes in and bothers him when he wants to muse, it would have been another matter altogether; but he surely could not have had a very cheerless time of it in that pretty dungeon. It has romantic window-slits that let in generous bars of light, and it has tall, noble columns, carved apparently from the living rock; and, what is more, they are written all over with thousands of names, some of them—like Byron's and Victor Hugo's—of the first celebrity. Why didn't he amuse himself reading these names? Then there are the couriers and tourists—swarms of them every day—what was to hinder him from having a good time with them? I think Bonivard's sufferings have been overrated.

Next, we took train and went to Martigny, on the way to Mont Blanc. Next morning we started, about eight o'clock, on foot. We had plenty of company in the way of waggon-loads and mule-loads of tourists—and dust. This scattering procession of travellers was perhaps a mile long. The road was up-hill—interminably up-hill—and tolerably steep. The weather was blistering hot, and the man or woman who had to sit on a creeping mule or in a crawling waggon, and broil in the beating sun, was an object to be pitied. We could dodge among the bushes, and have the relief of the shade, but those people could not. They paid for a conveyance, and to get their money's worth they rode.

We went by the way of the Tête Noire, and after we reached high ground there was no lack of fine scenery. In one place the road was tunnelled through a shoulder of the mountain; from there one looked down into a gorge with a rushing torrent in it, and on every hand was a charming view of rocky buttresses and wooded heights. There was a liberal allowance of pretty waterfalls, too, on the Tête Noire route.

About half an hour before we reached the village of Argentière a vast dome of snow, with the sun blazing on it, drifted into view and framed itself in a strong V-shaped gateway of the mountains, and we recognised Mont Blanc, the 'monarch of the Alps.' With every step after that this stately dome rose higher and higher into the blue sky, and at last seemed to occupy the zenith.

Some of Mont Blanc's neighbours—bare, light-brown, steeple-like rocks—were very peculiarly shaped. Some were whittled to a sharp point, and slightly bent at the upper end, like a lady's finger; one monster sugar-loaf resembled a bishop's hat: it was too steep to hold snow on its sides, but had some in the division.

While we were still on very high ground, and before the descent toward Argentière began, we looked up toward a neighbouring mountain-top, and saw exquisite prismatic colours playing about some white clouds which were so delicate as to almost resemble gossamer webs. The faint pinks and greens were peculiarly beautiful; none of the colours were deep, they were the lightest shades. They were bewitchingly commingled. We sat down to study and enjoy this singular spectacle. The tints remained during several minutes—flitting, changing, melting into each other; paling almost away for a moment, then reflushing—a shifting, restless, unstable succession of soft opaline gleams, shimmering over that airy film of white cloud, and turning it into a fabric dainty enough to clothe an angel with.

By and by we perceived what those super-delicate colours,

and their continuous play and movement, reminded us of: it is what one sees in a soap-bubble that is drifting along, catching changes of tint from the objects it passes. A soap-bubble is the most beautiful thing, and the most exquisite, in nature: that lovely phantom fabric in the sky was suggestive of a soap-bubble split open and spread out in the sun. I wonder how much it would take to buy a soap-bubble if there was only one in the world? One could buy a hatful of Koh-i-Noors with the same money, no doubt.

We made the tramp from Martigny to Argentière in eight hours. We beat all the mules and waggons; we didn't usually do that. We hired a sort of open baggage-waggon for the trip down the valley to Chamonix, and then devoted an hour to dining. This gave the driver time to get drunk. He had a friend with him, and this friend also had had time to get drunk.

When we drove off, the driver said all the tourists had arrived and gone by while we were at dinner; 'but,' said he, impressively, 'be not disturbed by that—remain tranquil—give yourselves no uneasiness—their dust rises far before us, you shall see it fade and disappear far behind us. Rest you tranquil, leave all to me—I am the king of drivers. Behold!'

Down came his whip, and away we clattered. I never had such a shaking up in my life. The recent flooding rains had washed the road clear away in places, but we never stopped, we never slowed down, for anything. We tore right along, over rocks, rubbish, gullies, open fields—sometimes with one or two wheels on the ground, but generally with none. Every now and then that calm, good-natured madman would bend a majestic look over his shoulder at us and say, 'Ah, you perceive? It is as I have said—I am the king of drivers.' Every time we just missed going to destruction he would say, with tranquil happiness, 'Enjoy it, gentlemen, it is very rare, it is very unusual—it is given to few to ride with the king of drivers—and observe it as as I have said, *I* am he.'

He spoke in French, and punctuated with hiccups. His friend was French too, but spoke in German—using the same system of punctuation, however. The friend called himself the 'Captain of Mont Blanc,' and wanted us to make the ascent with him. He said he had made more ascents that any other man—forty-seven—and his brother had made thirty-seven. His brother was the best guide in the world, except himself—but he, yes, observe him well—he was the 'Captain of Mont Blanc'—that title belonged to none other.

The 'king' was as good as his word—he overtook that long procession of tourists and went by it like a hurricane. The result was that we got choicer rooms at the hotel in Chamonix than we should have done if his majesty had been a slower artist—or, rather, if he hadn't most providentially got drunk before he left Argentière.

CHAPTER 43

Everybody was out of doors; everybody was in the principal street of the village—not on the side-walks, but all over the street; everybody was lounging, loafing, chatting, waiting, alert, expectant, interested—for it was train-time. That is to say, it was diligence-time—the half-dozen big diligences would soon be arriving from Geneva, and the village was interested, in many ways, in knowing how many people were coming, and what sort of folk they might be. It was altogether the livest-looking street we had seen in any village on the Continent.

The hotel was by the side of a booming torrent, whose music was loud and strong; we could not see this torrent, for it was dark now, but one could locate it without a light. There was a large enclosed yard in front of the hotel, and this was filled with groups of villagers waiting to see the diligences arrive, or to hire themselves to excursionists for the morrow. A telescope stood in the yard, with its huge barrel canted up towards the lustrous evening star. The long porch of the hotel was populous with tourists, who sat in shawls and wraps under the vast overshadowing bulk of Mont Blanc, and gossiped or meditated.

Never did a mountain seem so close; its big sides seemed at one's very elbow, and its majestic dome, and the lofty cluster of slender minarets that were its neighbours, seemed to be almost over one's head. It was night in the streets, and the lamps were sparkling everywhere; the broad bases and shoulders of the mountains were in deep gloom, but their summits swam in a strange, rich glow which was really daylight, and yet had a mellow something about it which was very different from the hard white glare of the kind of daylight I was used to. Its radiance was strong and clear, but at the same time it was singularly soft, and spiritual, and benignant. No, it was not our harsh, aggressive, realistic daylight—it seemed properer to an enchanted land—or to heaven.

I had seen moonlight and daylight together before, but I had not seen daylight and black night elbow to elbow before. At least I had not seen the daylight resting upon an object sufficiently close at hand before to make the contrast startling and at war with nature.

The daylight passed away. Presently the moon rose up behind some of those sky-piercing fingers or pinnacles of bare rock of which I have spoken—they were a little to the left of the crest of Mont Blanc, and right over our heads—but she couldn't manage to climb high enough toward heaven to get entirely above them. She would show the glittering arch of her upper third occasionally, and scrape it along behind the comb-like row; sometimes a pinnacle stood straight up, like a statuette of ebony, against that glittering white shield, then seemed to glide out of it by its own volition and power, and become a dim spectre, whilst the next pinnacle glided into its place and blotted the spotless disk with the black exclamation point of its presence. The top of one pinnacle took the shapely, clean-cut form of a rabbit's head, in the inkiest silhouette, while it rested against the moon. The unillumined peaks and minarets, hovering vague and phantom-like above us while the others were painfully white and strong with snow and moonlight, made a peculiar effect.

But when the moon, having passed the line of pinnacles, was hidden behind the stupendous white swell of Mont Blanc, the masterpiece of the evening was flung on the canvas. A rich greenish radiance sprang into the sky from behind the mountain, and in this some airy shreds and ribbons of vapour floated about, and being flushed with that strange tint, went waving to and fro like pale green flames. After a while, radiating bars—vast broadening fan-shaped shadows—grew up and stretched away to the zenith from behind the mountain. It was a spectacle to take one's breath, for the wonder of it and the sublimity.

Indeed, those mighty bars of alternate light and shadow streaming up from behind that dark and prodigious form, and occupying the half of the dull and opaque heavens, were the most imposing and impressive marvel I had ever looked upon. There is no simile for it, for nothing is like it. If a child had asked me what it was, I should have said, 'Humble yourself in this presence, it is the glory flowing from the hidden head of the Creator.' One falls shorter of the truth than that, sometimes, in trying to explain mysteries to the little people. I could have found out the cause of this awe-compelling miracle by inquiring, for it is not infrequent at Mont Blanc—but I did not wish to know. We have not the reverent feeling for the rainbow that a savage has, because we know how it is made. We have lost as much as we gained by prying into that matter.

We took a walk down street, a block or two, and at a place where four streets met and the principal shops were clustered, found the groups of men in the roadway thicker than ever—for this was the Exchange of Chamonix. These men were in the costumes of guides and porters, and were there to be hired.

The office of that great personage, the Guide-in-Chief of the Chamonix Guild of Guides, was near by. This guild is a close corporation, and is governed by strict laws. There are many excursion routes, some dangerous and some not, some that can be made safely without a guide, and some that cannot. The bureau determines these things. Where it decides that a guide is necessary, you are forbidden to go without one. Neither are you allowed to be a victim of extortion; the law states what you are to pay. The guides serve in rotation; you cannot select the man who is to take your life into his hands, you must take the worst in the lot if it is his turn.

A guide's fee ranges all the way up from a half dollar (for some trifling excursion of a few rods) to twenty dollars, according to the distance traversed and the nature of the ground. A guide's fee for taking a person to the summit of Mont Blanc and back is twenty dollars—and he earns it. The time employed is usually three days, and there is enough early rising in it to make a man far more 'healthy and wealthy and wise' than any one man has any right to be. The porter's fee for the same trip is ten dollars. Several fools—no, I mean several tourists—usually go together, and divide up the expense, and thus make it light; for if only one f—tourist, I mean—went, he would have to have several guides and porters, and that would make the matter costly.

We went into the Chief's office. There were maps of mountains on the walls, also one or two lithographs of celebrated guides and a portrait of the scientist De Saussure.

In glass cases were some labelled fragments of boots and batons, and other suggestive relics and remembrances of casualties on Mont Blanc. In a book was a record of all the ascents which have ever been made, beginning with Nos. 1 and 2—being those of Jacques Balmat and De Saussure, in 1787, and ending with No. 685, which wasn't cold yet. In fact No. 685 was standing by the official table waiting to receive the precious official diploma which should prove to his German household and to his descendants that he had once been indiscreet enough to climb to the top of Mont Blanc. He looked very happy when he got his document; in fact, he spoke up and said he *was* happy.

I tried to buy a diploma for an invalid friend at home who had never travelled, and whose desire all his life has been to ascend Mont Blanc, but the Guide-in-Chief rather insolently refused to sell me one. I was very much offended. I said I did not propose to be discriminated against on account of my nationality; that he had just sold a diploma to this German gentleman, and my money was as good as his; I would see to it that he couldn't keep shop for Germans and deny his produce to Americans; I would have his licence taken away from him at the dropping of a handkerchief; if France refused to break him, I would make an international matter of it and bring on a war; the soil should be drenched with blood; and not only that, but I would set up an opposition shop and sell diplomas at half price.

For two cents I would have done these things, too; but nobody offered me the two cents. I tried to move that German's feelings, but it could not be done; he would not give me his diploma, neither would he sell it to me. I *told* him my friend was sick and could not come himself, but he said he did not care a *verdammtes pfennig*, he wanted his diploma for himself—did I suppose he was going to risk his neck for that thing and then give it to a sick stranger? Indeed he wouldn't, so he wouldn't. I resolved, then, that I would do all I could to injure Mont Blanc.

In the record book was a list of all the fatal accidents which had happened on the mountain. It began with the one in 1820, when the Russian Dr. Hamel's three guides were lost in a crevasse of the glacier, and it recorded the delivery of the remains in the valley by the slow-moving glacier forty-one years later. The latest catastrophe bore date 1877.

We stepped out and roved about the village a while. In front of the little church was a monument to the memory of the bold guide Jacques Balmat, the first man who ever stood upon the summit of Mont Blanc. He made that wild trip solitary and alone. He accomplished the ascent a number of times afterwards. A stretch of nearly half a century lay between his first ascent and his last one. At the ripe old age of seventy-two he was climbing around a corner of a lofty precipice of the Pic du Midi—nobody with him—when he slipped and fell. So he died in harness.

He had grown very avaricious in his old age, and used to go off stealthily to hunt for non-existent and impossible gold among those perilous peaks and precipices. He was on a quest of that kind when he lost his life. There was a statue to him, and another to De Saussure, in the hall of our hotel, and a metal plate on the door of a room upstairs bore an inscription to the effect that that room had been occupied by Albert Smith. Balmat and De Saussure discovered Mont Blanc—so to speak—but it was Smith who made it a paying property. His articles in *Blackwood* and his lectures on Mont Blanc in London advertised it and made people as anxious to see it as if it owed them money.

As we strolled along the road we looked up and saw a red signal light glowing in the darkness of the mountain side. It seemed but a trifling way up—perhaps a hundred yards, a climb of ten minutes. It was a lucky piece of sagacity in us that we concluded to stop a man whom we met and get a light for our pipes from him instead of continuing the climb to that lantern to get a light, as had been our purpose. The man said that that lantern was on the Grands Mulets, some 6,500 feet above the valley! I knew by our Riffelberg experience that it would have taken us a good part of a week to go up there. I would sooner not smoke at all than take all that trouble for a light.

Even in the daytime the foreshortening effect of the mountain's close proximity creates curious deceptions. For instance, one sees with the naked eye a cabin up there beside the glacier, and a little above and beyond he sees the spot where that red light was located; he thinks he could throw a stone from the one place to the other. But he couldn't, for the difference between the two altitudes is more than 3,000 feet. It looks impossible, from below, that this can be true, but it is true, nevertheless.

While strolling about, we kept the run of the moon all the time, and we still kept an eye on her after we got back to the hotel portico. I had a theory that the gravitation of refraction being subsidiary to atmospheric compensation, the refrangibility of the earth's surface would emphasize this effect in regions where great mountain ranges occur, and possibly so even-handedly impact the odic and idyllic forces together, the one upon the other, as to prevent the moon from rising higher than 12,200 feet above sea level. This daring theory had been received with frantic scorn by some of my fellow-scientists, and with an eager silence by others. Among the former I may mention Prof. H——y, and among the latter Prof. T——l. Such is professional jealousy; a scientist will never show any kindness for a theory which he did not start himself. There is no feeling of brotherhood among these people. Indeed, they always resent it when I call them brother. To show how far their ungenerosity can carry them, I will state that I offered to let Prof H——y publish my great theory as his own discovery; I even begged him to do it; I even proposed to print it myself as his theory. Instead of thanking me, he said that if I tried to fasten that theory on him he would sue me for slander. I was going to offer it to Mr. Darwin, whom I understood to be a man without prejudices, but

it occurred to me that perhaps he would not be interested in it
since it did not concern heraldry.

But I am glad now that I was forced to father my intrepid
theory myself, for on the night of which I am writing it was
triumphantly justified and established. Mont Blanc is nearly
16,000 feet high; he hid the moon utterly; near him is a peak
which is 12,216 feet high; the moon slid along behind the
pinnacles, and when she approached that one I watched her with
intense interest, for my reputation as a scientist must stand or
fall by its decision. I cannot describe the emotions which surged
like tidal waves through my breast when I saw the moon glide
behind that lofty needle and pass it by without exposing more
than two feet four inches of her upper rim above it! I was secure,
then. I knew she could rise no higher, and I was right. She sailed
behind all the peaks and never succeeded in hoisting her disk
above a single one of them.

While the moon was behind one of those sharp fingers, its
shadow was flung athwart the vacant heavens—a long, slanting,
clean-cut, dark ray, with a streaming and energetic suggestion of
force about it, such as the ascending jet of water from a
powerful fire engine affords. It was curious to see a good strong
shadow of an earthly object cast upon so intangible a field as the
atmosphere.

We went to bed at last, and went quickly to sleep, but I woke
up, after about three hours, with throbbing temples, and a head
which was physically sore, outside and in. I was dazed, dreamy,
wretched, seedy, unrefreshed. I recognised the occasion of all
this; it was that torrent. In the mountain villages of Switzerland,
and along the roads, one has always the roar of the torrent in his
ears. He imagines it is music, and he thinks poetic things about
it; he lies in his comfortable bed and is lulled to sleep by it. But
by-and-by he begins to notice that his head is very sore...he
cannot account for it; in solitudes where the profoundest silence
reigns, he notices a sullen, distant, continuous roar in his ears,
which is like what he would experience if he had sea-shells
pressed against them—he cannot account for it; he is drowsy
and absent-minded; there is no tenacity to his mind, he cannot
keep hold of a thought and follow it out; if he sits down to write,

his vocabulary is empty, no suitable words will come, he forgets what he started to do, and remains there, pen in hand, head tilted up, eyes closed, listening painfully to the muffled roar of a distant train in his ears. In his soundest sleep the strain continues, he goes on listening, always listening, intently, anxiously, and wakes at last, harassed, irritable, unrefreshed. He cannot manage to account for these things. Day after day he feels as if he had spent his nights in a sleeping car. It actually takes him weeks to find out that it is those persecuting torrents that have been making all the mischief. It is time for him to get out of Switzerland then, for as soon as he has discovered the cause, the misery is magnified several fold. The roar of the torrent is maddening then, for his imagination is assisting; the physical pain it inflicts is exquisite. When he finds he is approaching one of those streams, his dread is so lively that he is disposed to fly the track and avoid the implacable foe.

Eight or nine months after the distress of the torrents had departed from me, the roar and thunder of the streets of Paris brought it all back again. I moved to the sixth storey of the hotel to hunt for peace. About midnight the noises dulled away, and I was sinking to sleep, when I heard a new and curious sound. I listened: evidently some joyous lunatic was softly dancing a 'double shuffle' in the room over my head. I had to wait for him to get through, of course. Five long, long minutes he smoothly shuffled away—a pause followed, then something fell with a heavy thump on the floor. I said to myself, 'There—he is pulling off his boots—thank heavens he is done.' Another slight pause—he went to shuffling again! I said to myself, 'Is he trying to see what he can do with only one boot on?' Presently came another pause and another thump on the floor. I said, 'Good, he has pulled off his other boot—*now* he is done.' But he wasn't. The next moment he was shuffling again. I said 'Confound him, he is at it in his slippers!' After a little came that same old pause, and right after it that thump on the floor once more. I said, 'Hang him, he had on *two* pair of boots!' For an hour that magician went on shuffling and pulling off boots till he had shed as many as twenty-five pair, and I was hovering on the verge of lunacy. I got my gun and stole up there. The fellow was in the midst of an acre of sprawling boots, and he had a boot in his hand, shuffling it—no, I mean *polishing* it. The mystery was explained. He hadn't been dancing. He was the 'Boots' of the hotel, and was attending to business.

CHAPTER 44

After breakfast, that next morning in Chamonix, we went out in the yard and watched the gangs of excursionising tourists arriving and departing with their mules and guides and porters; then we took a look through the telescope at the snowy hump of Mont Blanc. It was brilliant with sunshine, and the vast smooth bulge seemed hardly five hundred yards away. With the naked eye we could dimly make out the house at the Pierre Pointue, which is located by the side of the great glacier, and is more than 3,000 feet above the level of the valley, but with the telescope we could see all its details. While I looked, a woman rode by the house on a mule, and I saw her with sharp distinctness; I could have described her dress. I saw her nod to the people of the house, and rein up her mule, and put her hand up to shield her eyes from the sun. I was not used to telescopes; in fact, I never had looked through a good one before; it seemed incredible to me that this woman could be so far away. I was satisfied that I could see all these details with my naked eye; but when I tried it, the mule and those vivid people had wholly vanished, and the house itself had become small and vague. I tried the telescope again, and again everything was vivid. The strong black shadows of the mule and the woman were flung against the side of the house, and I saw the mule's silhouette wave its ears.

The telescopulist—or the telescopulariat—I do not know which is right—said a party were making the grand ascent, and would come in sight on the remote upper heights, presently; so we waited to observe this performance.

Presently I had a superb idea. I wanted to stand with a party on the summit of Mont Blanc, merely to be able to say I had done it, and I believed the telescope could set me within seven feet of the uppermost man. The telescoper assured me that it could. I then asked him how much I owed him for as far as I had got? He said, one franc. I asked him how much it would cost me to make the entire ascent? Three francs. I at once determined to make the entire ascent. But first I inquired if there was any danger? He said no—not by telescope; and he had taken a great many parties to the summit, and never lost a man. I asked what he would charge to let my agent go with me, together with such guides and porters as might be necessary? He said he would let Harris go for two francs; and that unless we were unusually timid, he should consider guides and porters unnecessary; it was not customary to take them when going by telescope, for they were rather an incumbrance than a help. He said that the party now on the mountain were approaching the most difficult part, and if we hurried we should overtake them within ten minutes, and could then join them and have the benefit of their guides and porters without their knowledge, and without expense to us.

I then said we would start immediately. I believe I said it calmly, though I was conscious of a shudder and of a paling cheek, in view of the nature of the exploit I was so unreflectingly engaging in. But the old dare-devil spirit was upon me, and I said that as I had committed myself, I would not back down; I would ascend Mont Blanc if it cost me my life. I told the man to slant his machine in the proper direction, and let us be off.

Harris was afraid and did not want to go, but I heartened him up and said I would hold his hand all the way; so he gave his consent, though he trembled a little at first. I took a last pathetic look upon the pleasant summer scene about me, then boldly put my eye to the glass and prepared to mount among the grim glaciers and the everlasting snows.

We took our way carefully and cautiously across the great Glacier des Bossons, over yawning and terrific crevasses and amongst imposing crags and buttresses of ice, which were fringed with icicles of gigantic proportions. The desert of ice that stretched far and wide about us was wild and desolate beyond description, and the perils which beset us were so great that at times I was minded to turn back. But I pulled my pluck together and pushed on.

We passed the glacier safely and began to mount the steeps beyond, with great celerity. When we were seven minutes out from the starting point, we reached an altitude where the scene took a new aspect; an apparently limitless continent of gleaming snow was tilted heavenward before our faces. As my eye followed that awful acclivity far away up into the remote skies, it seemed to me that all I had ever seen before of sublimity and magnitude was small and insignificant compared with this.

We rested a moment, and then began to mount with speed. Within three minutes we caught sight of the party ahead of us, and stopped to observe them. They were toiling up a long, slanting ridge of snow—twelve persons, roped together some fifteen feet apart, marching in single file, and strongly marked against the clear blue sky. One was a woman. We could see them lift their feet and put them down; we saw them swing their alpenstocks forward in unison, like so many pendulums, and then bear their weight upon them; we saw the lady wave her handkerchief. They dragged themselves upwards in a worn and weary way, for they had been climbing steadily from the Grands Mulets, on the Glacier des Bossons, since three in the morning, and it was eleven now. We saw them sink down in the snow and rest, and drink something from a bottle. After a while they moved on, and as they approached the final short dash of the home-stretch we closed up on them and joined them.

Presently we all stood together on the summit! What a view was spread out below! Away off under the north-western horizon rolled the sillent billows of the Farnese Oberland, their snowy crests glinting softly in the subdued lights of distance; in the north rose the giant form of the Wobblehorn, draped from peak to shoulder in sable thunder-clouds; beyond him, to the right, stretched the grand processional summits of the Cisalpine Cordillera, drowned in a sensuous haze; to the east loomed the colossal masses of the Yodelhorn, the Fuddlehorn, and the

Dinnerhorn, their cloudless summits flashing white and cold in the sun; beyond them shimmered the faint far line of the Ghauts of Jubbulpore and the Aiguilles des Alleghenies; in the south towered the smoking peak of Popocatapetl and the unapproachable altitudes of the peerless Scrabblehorn; in the west-south-west the stately range of the Himalayas lay dreaming in a purple gloom; and thence all around the curving horizon the eye roved over a troubled sea of sunkissed Alps, and noted here and there the noble proportions and soaring domes of the Bottlehorn, and the Saddlehorn, and the Shovelhorn, and the Powderhorn, all bathed in the glory of noon, and mottled with softly-gliding blots, the shadows flung from drifting clouds.

Overcome by the scene, we all raised a triumphant, tremendous shout, in unison. A startled man at my elbow said—

'Confound you, what do you yell like that for, right here in the street?'

That brought me down to Chamonix like a flirt. I gave that man some spiritual advice and disposed of him, and then paid the telescope man his full fee, and said that we were charmed with the trip, and would remain down, and not re-ascend and require him to fetch us down by telescope. This pleased him very much, for of course we could have stepped back to the summit and put him to the trouble of bringing us home if we had wanted to.

I judged we could get diplomas, now anyhow; so we went after them, but the Chief Guide put us off, with one pretext or another, during all the time we stayed in Chamonix, and we ended by never getting them at all. So much for his prejudice against people's nationality. However, we worried him enough to make him remember us and our ascent for some time. He even said, once, that he wished there was a lunatic asylum in Chamonix. This shows that he really had fears that we were going to drive him mad. It was what we intended to do, but lack of time defeated it.

I cannot venture to advise the reader one way or the other, as to ascending Mont Blanc. I say only this: if he is at all timid, the enjoyments of the trip will hardly make up for the hardships and sufferings he will have to endure. But if he has good nerve, youth, health, and a bold, firm will, and could leave his family comfortably provided for in case the worst happened, he would find the ascent a wonderful experience, and the view from the top a vision to dream about, and tell about, and recall with exultation all the days of his life.

While I do not advise such a person to attempt the ascent, I do not advise him against it. But if he elects to attempt it, let him be warily careful of two things: choose a calm clear day; and do not pay the telescope man in advance. There are dark stories of his getting advance-payers on the summit, and then leaving them there to rot.

A frightful tragedy was once witnessed through the Chamonix telescopes. Think of questions and answers like these, on an inquest:—

Coroner. You saw deceased lose his life?

Witness. I did.

C. Where was he at the time?

W. Close to the summit of Mont Blanc.

C. Where were you?

W. In the main street of Chamonix.

C. What was the distance between you?

W. A little over five miles, as the bird flies.

This accident occurred in 1866 a year and a month after the disaster on the Matterhorn. Three adventurous English gentlemen[1] of great experience in mountain climbing, made up their minds to ascend Mont Blanc without guides or porters. All endeavours to dissuade them from their project failed. Powerful telescopes are numerous in Chamonix. These huge brass tubes, mounted on their scaffoldings and pointing skyward from every choice vantage-ground, have the formidable look of artillery, and give the town the general aspect of getting ready to repel a charge of angels. The reader may easily believe that the telescopes had plenty of custom on that August morning in 1866, for everybody knew of the dangerous undertaking which was on foot, and all had fears that misfortune would result. All the morning the tubes remained directed towards the mountain

---

[1] Sir George Young and his brothers James and Albert.

heights, each with its anxious group around it; but the white deserts were vacant.

At last, towards eleven o'clock, the people who were looking through the telescopes cried out, 'There they are!'—and sure enough, far up on the loftiest terraces of the Grand Plateau, the three pygmies appeared, climbing with remarkable vigour and spirit. They disappeared in the 'Corridor,' and were lost to sight during an hour. Then they reappeared, and were presently seen standing together upon the extreme summit of Mont Blanc. So far, all was well. They remained a few minutes on that highest point of land in Europe, a target for all the telescopes, and were then seen to begin the descent. Suddenly all three vanished. An instant after, they appeared again, *two thousand feet below!*

Evidently they had tripped and been shot down an almost perpendicular slope of ice to a point where it joined the border of the upper glacier. Naturally the distant witnesses supposed they were now looking upon three corpses; so they could hardly believe their eyes when they presently saw two of the men rise to their feet and bend over the third. During two hours and a half they watched the two busying themselves over the extended form of their brother, who seemed entirely inert. Chamonix's affairs stood still; everybody was in the street, all interest was centred upon what was going on upon that lofty and isolated stage five miles away. Finally the two—one of them walking with great difficulty—were seen to begin the descent abandoning the third, who was no doubt lifeless. Their movements were followed, step by step, until they reached the 'Corridor' and disappeared behind its ridge. Before they had had time to traverse the 'Corridor' and reappear, twilight was come, and the power of the telescopes was at an end.

The survivors had a most perilous journey before them in the gathering darkness, for they must get down to the Grands Mulets before they would find a safe stopping-place—a long and tedious descent, and perilous enough even in good daylight. The oldest guides expressed the opinion that they could not succeed; that all the chances were that they would lose their lives.

Yet those brave men did succeed. They reached the Grands Mulets in safety. Even the fearful shock which their nerves had sustained was not sufficient to overcome their coolness and courage. It would appear from the official account that they were threading their way down through those dangers from the closing in of twilight until two o'clock in the morning, or later; because the rescuing party from Chamonix reached the Grands Mulets about three in the morning, and moved thence towards the scene of the disaster under the leadership of Sir George Young, 'who had only just arrived.'

After having been on his feet twenty-four hours in the exhausting work of mountain-climbing, Sir George began the re-ascent at the head of the relief party of six guides, to recover the corpse of his brother. This was considered a new imprudence, as the number was too few for the service required. Another relief party presently arrived at the cabin on the Grands Mulets, and quartered themselves there to await events. Ten hours after Sir George's departure towards the summit, this new relief were still scanning the snowy altitudes above them from their own high perch among the ice-deserts 10,000 feet above the level of the sea; but the whole forenoon had passed without a glimpse of any living thing appearing up there.

This was alarming. Half a dozen of their number set out, then, early in the afternoon, to seek and succour Sir George and his guides. The persons remaining at the cabin saw these disappear, and then ensued another distressing wait. Four hours passed without tidings. Then at five o'clock another relief, consisting of three guides, set forward from the cabin. They carried food and cordials for the refreshments of their predecessors; they took lanterns with them too. Night was coming on; and, to make matters worse, a fine, cold rain had begun to fall.

At the same hour that these three began their dangerous ascent the official Guide-in-Chief of the Mont Blanc region undertook the dangerous descent to Chamonix, all alone, to get reinforcements. However, a couple of hours later, at 7 p.m., the anxious solicitude came to an end, and happily. A bugle note was heard, and a cluster of black specks was distinguishable against the snows of the upper heights. The watchers counted these specks eagerly—fourteen. Nobody was missing. An hour and a half later they were all safe under the roof of the cabin. They had brought the corpse with them. Sir George Young tarried there but a few minutes, and then began the long and troublesome descent from the cabin to Chamonix. He probably reached there about two or three o'clock in the morning, after having been afoot among the rocks and glaciers during two days and two nights. His endurance was equal to his daring.

The cause of the unaccountable delay of Sir George and the relief parties among the heights where the disaster had happened was a thick fog; or partly that, and partly the slow and difficult work of conveying the dead body down the perilous steeps.

The corpse, upon being viewed at the inquest, showed no bruises, and it was some time before the surgeons discovered that the neck was broken. One of the surviving brothers had sustained some unimportant injuries, but the other had suffered no hurt at all. How these men could fall 2,000 feet almost perpendicularly, and live afterwards, is a most strange and unaccountable thing.

A great many women have made the ascent of Mont Blanc. An English girl, Miss Stratton, conceived the daring idea, two or three years ago, of attempting the ascent in the middle of winter. She tried it, and she succeeded. Moreover, she froze two of her fingers on the way up; she fell in love with her guide on the summit, and she married him when she got to the bottom again. There is nothing in romance, in the way of a striking 'situation,' which can beat this love scene in mid-heaven on an isolated ice-crest with the thermometer at zero and an Arctic gale blowing.

The first woman who ascended Mont Blanc was a girl aged twenty-two, Mdlle. Maria Paradis—1809. Nobody was with her but her sweetheart, and he was not a guide. The sex then took a rest for about thirty years, when a Mdlle. d'Angeville made the ascent—1838. In Chamonix I picked up a rude old lithograph of that day which pictured her 'in the act.' However, I value it less as a work of art than as a fashion-plate. Miss D'Angeville put on a pair of men's pantaloons to climb in, which was wise; but she cramped their utility by adding her petticoat, which was idiotic.

One of the mournfullest calamities which men's disposition to climb dangerous mountains has resulted in happened on Mont Blanc in September 1870. Mr. D'Arve tells the story briefly in his 'Histoire du Mont Blanc.' In the next chapter I will copy its chief features.

CHAPTER 45

A Catastrophe Which Cost Eleven Lives

On September 5, 1870, a caravan of eleven persons departed from Chamonix to make the ascent of Mont Blanc. Three of the party were tourists: Messrs. Randall and Bean, Americans, and Mr. George Corkindale, a Scotch gentleman; there were three guides and five porters. The cabin on the Grands Mulets was reached that day; the ascent was resumed early the next morning, September 6. The day was fine and clear, and the movements of the party were observed through the telescopes of Chamonix; at two o'clock in the afternoon they were seen to reach the summit. A few minutes later they were seen making the first steps of the descent; then a cloud closed around them and hid them from view.

Eight hours passed, the cloud still remained, night came, no one had returned to the Grands Mulets. Sylvain Couttet, keeper of the cabin there, suspected a misfortune, and sent down to the valley for help. A detachment of guides went up, and by the time they had made the tedious trip and reached the cabin, a raging storm had set in. They had to wait; nothing could be attempted in such a tempest.

The wild storm lasted *more than a week,* without ceasing; but on the 17th, Couttet, with several guides, left the cabin and succeeded in making the ascent. In the snowy wastes near the summit they came upon five bodies, lying upon their sides in a reposeful attitude, which suggested that possibly they had fallen asleep, there, while exhausted with fatigue and hunger, and benumbed with cold, and never knew when death stole upon them. Couttet moved a few steps farther and discovered five more bodies. The eleventh corpse—that of a porter—was not found, although diligent search was made for it.

In the pocket of Mr. Bean, one of the Americans, was found a note-book in which had been pencilled some sentences which admit us in flesh and spirit, as it were, to the presence of these men during their last hours of life, and to the grisly horrors which their fading vision looked upon and their failing consciousness took cognizance of:—

Tuesday, Sept. 6.—I have made the ascent of Mont Blanc, with ten persons—eight guides, and Mr. Corkindale and Mr. Randall. We reached the summit at half-past two. Immediately after quitting it, we were enveloped in clouds of snow. We passed the night in a grotto hollowed in the snow, which afforded but poor shelter, and I was ill all night.

Sept. 7, Morning.—The cold is excessive. The snow falls heavily and without interruption. The guides take no rest.

Evening.—My Dear Hessie, we have been two days on Mont Blanc, in the midst of a terrible hurricane of snow, we have lost our way, and are in a hole scooped in the snow, at an altitude of 15,000 feet. I have no longer any hope of descending.

They had wandered around, and around, in that blinding snow storm, hopelessly lost, in a space only a hundred yards square; and when cold and fatigue vanquished them at last, they scooped their cave and lay down there to die by inches, *unaware that five steps more would have brought them into the true path.* They were so near to life and safety as that, and did not suspect it! The thought of this gives the sharpest pang that the tragic story conveys.

The author of the 'Histoire du Mont Blanc' introduces the closing sentences of Mr. Bean's pathetic record thus:—

'Here the characters are large and unsteady; the hand which traces them is become chilled and torpid; but the spirit survives, and the faith and resignation of the dying man are expressed with a sublime simplicity.'

Perhaps this note-book will be found and sent to you. We have nothing to eat, my feet are already frozen, and I am exhausted; I have strength to write only a few words more. I have left means for C.'s education; I know you will employ them wisely. I die with faith in God, and with loving thoughts of you. Farewell to all. We shall meet again, in Heaven ... I think of you always.

It is the way of the Alps to deliver death to their victims with a merciful swiftness, but here the rule failed. These men suffered the bitterest death that has been recorded in the history of these mountains, freighted as that history is with grisly tragedies.

CHAPTER 46

Mr. Harris and I took some guides and porters, and ascended to the Hôtel des Pyramides, which is perched on the high moraine which borders the Glacier des Bossons. The road led sharply up hill, all the way, through grass and flowers and woods, and was a pleasant walk, barring the fatigue of the climb.

From the hotel we could view the huge glacier at very close range. After a rest we followed down a path which had been made in the steep inner frontage of the moraine, and stepped upon the glacier itself. One of the shows of the place was a tunnel-like cavern, which had been hewn in the glacier. The proprietor of this tunnel took candles, and conducted us into it. It was three or four feet wide and about six feet high. Its walls of pure and solid ice emitted a soft and rich blue light that produced a lovely effect, and suggested enchanted caves, and that sort of thing. When we had proceeded some yards and were entering darkness, we turned about and had a dainty sun-lit picture of distant woods and heights framed in the strong arch of the tunnel and seen through the tender blue radiance of the tunnel's atmosphere.

The cavern was nearly a hundred yards long, and when we reached its inner limit the proprietor stepped into a branch tunnel with his candles, and left us buried in the bowels of the glacier, and in pitch darkness. We judged his purpose was murder and robbery; so we got out our matches and prepared to sell our lives as dearly as possible by setting the glacier on fire if the worse came to the worst—but we soon perceived that this man had changed his mind; he began to sing, in a deep melodious voice, and woke some curious and pleasing echoes. By-and-by he came back and I pretended that that was what he had gone behind there for. We believed as much of that as we wanted to.

Thus our lives had been once more in imminent peril, but by the exercise of the swift sagacity and cool courage which had saved us so often, we had added another escape to the long list. The tourist should visit that ice-cavern, by all means, for it is well worth the trouble; but I would advise him to go only with a strong and well armed force. I do not consider artillery necessary, yet it would not be unadvisable to take it along if convenient. The journey, going and coming, is about three miles and a half, three of which are on level ground. We made it in less than a day, but I would counsel the unpractised, if not pressed for time, to allow themselves two. Nothing is gained in the Alps by over-exertion; nothing is gained by crowding two days' work into one for the poor sake of being able to boast of the exploit afterwards. It will be found much better, in the long run, to do the thing in two days, and then subtract one of them from the narrative. This saves fatigue, and does not injure the narrative. All the more thoughtful among the Alpine tourists do this.

We now called upon the Guide-in-Chief, and asked for a squadron of guides and porters for the ascent of the Montanvert. This idiot glared at us, and said—

'You don't need guides and porters to go to the Montanvert.'

'What do we need, then?'

'Such as *you*?—an ambulance!'

I was so stung by this brutal remark that I took my custom elsewhere.

Betimes, next morning, we had reached an altitude of 5,000 feet above the level of the sea. Here we camped and breakfasted. There was a cabin there—the spot is called the *Caillet*—and a spring of ice-cold water. On the door of the cabin was a sign, in French, to the effect that 'One may here see a living chamois for 50 centimes.' We did not invest; what we wanted was to see a dead one.

A little after noon we ended the ascent, and arrived at the new hotel on the Montanvert, and had a view of six miles, right up the great glacier, the famous Mer de Glace. At this point it is like a sea whose deep swales and long rolling swells have been caught in mid-movement and frozen solid; but farther up it is broken up into wildly-tossing billows of ice.

We descended a ticklish path in the steep side of the moraine, and invaded the glacier. There were tourists of both sexes scattered far and wide over it everywhere, and it had the festive look of a skating rink.

The Empress Josephine came this far once. She ascended the Montanvert in 1810—but not alone; a small army of men preceded her to clear the path—and carpet it, perhaps,—and she followed, under the protection of *sixty-eight* guides.

Her successor visited Chamonix later, but in far different style. It was seven weeks after the first fall of the Empire, and poor Marie Louise, ex-Empress, was a fugitive. She came at night, and in a storm, with only two attendants, and stood before a peasant's hut, tired, bedraggled, soaked with rain, 'the red print of her lost crown still girdling her brow,' and implored admittance—and was refused! A few days before, the adulations and applause of a nation were sounding in her ears, and now she was come to this!

We crossed the Mer de Glace in safety, but we had misgivings. The crevasses in the ice yawned deep and blue and mysterious, and it made one nervous to traverse them. The huge round waves of ice were slippery and difficult to climb, and the chances of tripping and sliding down them and darting into a crevasse, were too many to be comfortable.

In the bottom of a deep swale between two of the biggest of the ice-waves, we found a fraud who pretended to be cutting steps to ensure the safety of tourists. He was 'soldiering' when we came upon him, but he hopped up and chipped out a couple of steps about big enough for a cat, and charged us a franc or two for it. Then he sat down again, to doze till the next party should come along. He had collected black mail from two or three hundred people already, that day, but had not chipped out ice enough to impair the glacier perceptibly. I have heard of a good many soft sinecures, but it seems to me that keeping tollbridge on a glacier is the softest one I have encountered yet.

That was a blazing hot day, and it brought a persistent and persecuting thirst with it. What an unspeakable luxury it was to slake that thirst with the pure and limpid ice-water of the glacier! Down the sides of every great rib of ice poured limpid rills in gutters carved by their own attrition; better still, wherever a rock had laid, there was now a bowl-shaped hole, with smooth white sides and bottom of ice, and this bowl was brimming with water of such absolute clearness that the careless observer would not see it at all, but would think the bowl was empty. These fountains had such an alluring look that I often stretched myself out when I was not thirsty and dipped my face in and drank till my teeth ached. Everywhere among the Swiss mountains we had at hand the blessing—not to be found in Europe, *except* in the mountains,—of water capable of quenching thirst. Everywhere in the Swiss highlands brilliant little rills of exquisitely cold water went dancing along by the roadsides, and my comrade and I were always drinking and always delivering our deep gratitude.

But in Europe everywhere, except in the mountains, the water is flat and insipid beyond the power of words to describe. It is served lukewarm; but no matter, ice could not help it; it is incurably flat, incurably insipid. It is only good to wash with; I wonder it doesn't occur to the average inhabitant to try it for that. In Europe the people say contemptuously, 'Nobody drinks water here.' Indeed they have a sound and sufficient reason. In many places they even have what may be called prohibitory reasons. In Paris and Munich, for instance, they say, 'Don't drink the water, it is simply poison.'

Either America is healthier than Europe, notwithstanding her 'deadly' indulgence in ice-water, or she does not keep the run of her death-rate as sharply as Europe does. I think we do keep up the death statistics accurately; and if we do, our cities are healthier than the cities of Europe. Every month the German government tabulates the death-rate of the world and publishes it. I scrap-booked these reports during several months, and it was curious to see how regular and persistently each city repeated its same death-rate month after month. The tables might as well have been stereotyped, they varied so little. These tables were based upon weekly reports showing the average of deaths in each 1,000 of population for a year. Munich was always present with her 33 deaths in each 1,000 of her population (yearly average), Chicago was as constant with her 15 or 17, Dublin with her 48—and so on.

Only a few American cities appear in these tables, but they are scattered so widely over the country, that they furnish a good general average of *city* health in the United States; and I think it will be granted that our towns and villages are healthier than our cities.

Here is the average of the only American cities reported in the German tables:—

Chicago, deaths in 1,000 of population annually, 16; Philadelphia, 18, St. Louis, 18; San Francisco, 19; New York (the Dublin of America), 23.

See how the figures jump up, as soon as one arrives at the Transatlantic list:—

Paris, 27; Glasgow, 27; London, 28; Vienna, 28; Augsburg, 28; Braunschweig, 28; Königsberg, 29; Cologne, 29; Dresden, 29; Hamburg, 29; Berlin, 30; Bombay, 30; Warsaw, 31; Breslau, 31; Odessa, 32; Munich, 33; Strasburg, 33; Pest, 35; Cassel, 35; Lisbon, 36; Liverpool, 36; Prague, 37; Madras, 37; Bucharest, 39; St. Petersburg, 40; Trieste, 40; Alexandria (Egypt), 43; Dublin, 48, Calcutta, 55.

Edinburgh is as healthy as New York—23; but there is no *city* in the entire list which is healthier, except Frankfort-on-the-Main—20. But Frankfort is not as healthy as Chicago, San Francisco, St. Louis, or Philadelphia.

Perhaps a strict average of the world might develop the fact that where 1 in 1,000 of America's population dies, 2 in 1,000 of the other populations of the earth succumb.

I do not like to make insinuations, but I do think the above statistics darkly suggest that these people over here drink this detestable water 'on the sly.'

We climbed the moraine on the opposite side of the glacier, and then crept along its sharp ridge a hundred yards or so, in pretty constant danger of a tumble to the glacier below. The fall would only have been 100 feet, but it would have closed me out as effectually as 1,000 feet, therefore I respected the distance accordingly, and was glad when the trip was done. A moraine is an ugly thing to assault head-first. At a distance it looks like an endless grave of fine sand, accurately shaped and nicely smoothed; but close by, it is found to be made mainly of rough boulders of all sizes, from that of a man's head to that of a cottage. By-and-by we came to the *Mauvais Pas*, or, the Villainous Road, to translate it feelingly. It was a break-neck path around the face of a precipice forty or fifty feet high, and nothing to hang on to but some iron railings. I got along, slowly, safely, and uncomfortably, and finally reached the middle. My hopes began to rise a little, but they were quickly blighted; for there I met a hog—a long-nosed bristly fellow, that held up his snout and worked his nostrils at me inquiringly. A hog on a pleasure excursion in Switzerland—think of it. It is striking and unusual; a body might write a poem about it. He could not retreat, if he had been disposed to do it. It would have been foolish to stand upon our dignity in a place where there was hardly room to stand upon our feet, so we did nothing of the sort. There were twenty or thirty ladies and gentlemen behind us; we all turned about and went back, and the hog followed behind. The creature did not seem set up by what he had done; he had probably done it before.

We reached the restaurant on the height called the Château at four in the afternoon. It was a memento factory, and the stock was large, cheap and varied. I bought the usual papercutter to remember the place by, and had Mont Blanc, the Mauvais Pas, and the rest of the region branded on my alpenstock; then we descended to the valley, and walked home without being tied together. This was not dangerous, for the valley was five miles wide, and quite level.

We reached the hotel before nine o'clock. Next morning we left for Geneva on top of the diligence, under shelter of a gay awning. If I remember rightly, there were more than twenty people up there. It was so high that the ascent was made by ladder. The huge vehicle was full everywhere, inside and out. Five other diligences left at the same time, all full. We had engaged our seats two days beforehand, to make sure, and paid the regulation price, five dollars each; but the rest of the company were wiser; they had trusted Baedeker, and waited; consequently, some of them got their seats for one or two dollars. Baedeker knows all about hotels, railway and diligence companies, and speaks his mind freely. He is a trustworthy friend of the traveller.

We never saw Mont Blanc at his best until we were many miles away; then he lifted his majestic proportions high into the heavens, all white and cold and solemn, and made the rest of the world seem little and plebeian, and cheap and trivial.

As he passed out of sight at last, an old Englishman settled himself in his seat and said—

'Well, I am satisfied. I have seen the principal features of Swiss scenery—Mont Blanc and the goître—now for home!'

CHAPTER 47

We spent a few pleasant restful days at Geneva, that delightful city where accurate time-pieces are made for all the rest of the world, but whose own clocks never give the correct time of day by any accident.

Geneva is filled with pretty little shops, and the shops are filled with the most enticing gimcrackery; but if one enters one of these places he is at once pounced upon, and followed up, and so persecuted to buy this, that, and the other thing, that he is very grateful to get out again, and is not at all apt to repeat his experiment. The shopkeepers of the smaller sort, in Geneva, are as troublesome and persistent as are the salesmen of that monster hive in Paris, the Grand Magasin du Louvre—an establishment where ill-mannered pestering, pursuing and insistence have been reduced to a science.

In Geneva, prices in the smaller shops are very elastic—that is another bad feature. I was looking in at a window at a very pretty string of beads, suitable for a child. I was only admiring them; I had no use for them; I hardly ever wear beads. The shopwoman came out and offered them to me for thirty-five francs. I said it was cheap, but I did not need them.

'Ah, but, monsieur, they are so beautiful!'

I confessed it, but said they were not suitable for one of my age and simplicity of character. She darted in and brought them out, and tried to force them into my hands, saying—

'Ah, but only see how lovely they are! Surely monsieur will take them; monsieur shall have them for thirty francs. There, I have said it—it is a loss, but one must live!'

I dropped my hands and tried to move her to respect my unprotected situation. But no, she dangled the beads in the sun before my face, exclaiming, 'Ah, monsieur *cannot* resist them!' She hung them on my coat button, folded her hands resignedly, and said, 'Gone—and for thirty francs, the lovely things, it is incredible! but the good God will sanctify the sacrifice to me.'

I removed them gently, returned them, and walked away, shaking my head and smiling a smile of silly embarrassment, while the passers-by halted to observe. The woman leaned out of her door, shook the beads, and screamed after me—

'Monsieur shall have them for twenty-eight!'

I shook my head.

'Twenty-seven! It is a cruel loss, it is ruin—but take them, only take them.'

I still retreated, still wagging my head.

'*Mon Dieu*, they shall even go for twenty-six! There, I have said it. Come!'

I wagged another negative. A nurse and a little English girl had been near me, and were following me, now. The shopwoman ran to the nurse, thrust the beads into her hands and said—

'Monsieur shall have them for twenty-five! Take them to the hotel—he shall send me the money to-morrow—next day—when he likes.' Then to the child: 'When thy father sends me the money, come thou also, my angel, and thou shalt have something, oh so pretty.'

I was thus providentially saved. The nurse refused the beads squarely and firmly, and that ended the matter.

The 'sights' of Geneva are not numerous. I made one attempt to hunt up the houses once inhabited by those two disagreeable people, Rousseau and Calvin, but had no success. Then I concluded to go home. I found it was easier to propose to do that than to do it; for that town is a bewildering place. I got lost in a tangle of narrow and crooked streets, and stayed lost for an hour or two. Finally I found a street which looked familiar, and said to myself, 'Now I am at home, I judge.' But I was wrong;

this was '*Hell* Street.' Presently I found another place which had a familiar look, and said to myself, 'Now I am at home, sure.' It was another error. This was '*Purgatory* Street.' After a little I said, '*Now* I've got to the right place, anyway ... no, this is "*Paradise* Street"'; I'm farther from home than I was at the beginning.' Those were queer named—Calvin was the author of them, likely. 'Hell' and 'Purgatory' fitted those two streets like a glove, but the 'Paradise' appeared to be sarcastic.

I came out on the lake front, at last, and then I knew where I was. I was walking along before the glittering jewellery shops when I saw a curious performance. A lady passed by, and a trim dandy lounged across the walk in such an apparently carefully-timed way as to bring himself exactly in front of her when she got to him; he made no offer to step out of the way; he did not apologize; he did not even notice her. She had to stop still and let him lounge by. I wondered if he had done that piece of brutality purposely. He strolled to a chair and seated himself at a small table; two or three other males were sitting at similar tables sipping sweetened water. I waited; presently a youth came by, and this fellow got up and served him the same trick. Still, it did not seem possible that anyone could do such a thing deliberately. To satisfy my curiosity I went around the block, and, sure enough, as I approached, at a good round speed, he got up and lounged lazily across my path, fouling my course exactly at the right moment to receive all my weight. This proved that his previous performance had not been accidental, but intentional.

I saw that dandy's curious game played afterwards in Paris, but not for amusement; not with a motive of any sort, indeed, but simply from a selfish indifference to other people's comforts and rights. One does not see it as frequently in Paris as he might expect to, for there the law says, in effect, 'It is the business of the weak to get out of the way of the strong.' We fine a cabman if he runs over a citizen; Paris fines the citizen for being run over. At least so everybody says—but I saw something which caused me to doubt; I saw a horseman run over an old woman one day—the police arrested him and took him away. That looked as if they meant to punish him.

It will not do for me to find merit in American manners—for are they not the standing butt for the jests of critical and polished Europe? Still I must venture to claim one little matter of superiority in our manners—a lady may traverse our streets all day going and coming as she chooses, and she will never be molested by any man; but if a lady unattended walks abroad in the streets of London, even at noonday, she will be pretty likely to be accosted and insulted; and not by drunken sailors, but by men who carry the look and wear the dress of gentlemen. It is maintained that these people are not gentlemen, but are a lower sort disguised as gentlemen. The case of Colonel Valentine Baker obstructs that argument, for a man cannot become an officer in the British army except he hold the rank of gentleman. This person, finding himself alone in a railway compartment with an unprotected girl—but it is an atrocious story, and doubtless the reader remembers it well enough. London must have been more or less accustomed to Bakers, and the ways of Bakers, else London would have been offended and excited. Baker was 'imprisoned'—in a parlour; and he could not have been more visited, or more overwhelmed with attentions, if he had committed six murders, and then—while the gallows was preparing—'got religion'—after the manner of the holy Charles Peace, of saintly memory. Arkansaw—it seems a little indelicate to be trumpeting forth our own superiorities, and comparisons are always odious, but still—Arkansaw would certainly have hanged Baker. I do not say she would have tried him first, but she would have hanged him, anyway.

Even the most degraded woman can walk our streets unmolested, her sex and her weakness being her sufficient protection. She will encounter less polish than she would in the old world, but she will run across enough humanity to make up for it.

The music of a donkey awoke us early in the morning, and we rose up and made ready for a pretty formidable walk—to Italy; but the road was so level that we took the train. We lost a good deal of time by this, but it was no matter, we were not in a hurry. We were four hours going to Chambery. The Swiss trains go upwards of three miles an hour, in places, but they are quite safe.

That aged French town of Chambery was as quaint and crooked as Heilbronn. A drowsy reposeful quiet reigned in the back streets which made strolling through them very pleasant, barring the almost unbearable heat of the sun. In one of these streets, which was eight feet wide, gracefully curved, and built up with small antiquated houses, I saw three fat hogs lying asleep, and a boy (also asleep), taking care of them. From queer old-fashioned windows along the curve, projected boxes of bright flowers, and over the edge of one of these boxes hung the head and shoulders of a cat—asleep. The five sleeping creatures were the only living things visible in that street. There was not a sound; absolute stillness prevailed. It was Sunday; one is not used to such dreamy Sundays on the Continent. In our part of the town it was different that night. A regiment of brown and battered soldiers had arrived home from Algiers, and I judged they got thirsty on the way. They sang and drank till dawn, in the pleasant open air.

We left for Turin at ten the next morning by a railway, which was profusely decorated with tunnels. We forgot to take a lantern along, consequently we missed all the scenery. Our compartment was full. A ponderous tow-headed Swiss woman, who put on many fine-lady airs, but was evidently more used to washing linen than wearing it, sat in a corner seat and put her legs across into the opposite one, propping them intermediately with her up-ended valise. In the seat thus pirated sat two Americans, greatly incommoded by that woman's majestic coffin-clad feet. One of them begged her, politely, to remove them. She opened her eyes and gave him a stare, but answered nothing. By-and-by he preferred his request again, with great respectfulness. She said, in good English, and in deeply offended tone, that she had paid her passage and was not going to be bullied out of her 'rights' by ill-bred foreigners, even if she *was* alone and unprotected.

'But I have rights also, madam. My ticket entitles me to a seat, but you are occupying half of it.'

'I will not talk with you, sir. What right have you to speak to me? I do not know you. One would know you came from a land where there are no gentlemen. No *gentleman* would treat a lady as you have treated me.'

'I come from a region where a lady would hardly give me the same provocation.'

'You have insulted me, sir! You have intimated that I am not a lady—and I hope I am *not* one, after the pattern of your country.'

'I beg that you will give yourself no alarm on that head, madam; but at the same time I must insist—always respectfully—that you let me have my seat.'

Here the fragile laundress burst into tears and sobs

'I never was so insulted before! Never, never! It is shameful, it is brutal, it is base, to bully and abuse an unprotected lad who has lost the use of her limbs and cannot put her feet to the floor without agony!'

'Good heavens, madam, why didn't you say that at first! I offer a thousand pardons. And I offer them most sincerely. I did not know—I *could* not know—that anything was the matter. You are most welcome to the seat, and would have been from the first if I had only known. I am truly sorry it all happened, I do assure you.'

But he couldn't get a word of forgiveness out of her. She simply sobbed and snuffled in a subdued but wholly unappeasable way for two long hours, meantime crowding the man more than ever with her undertaker-furniture, and paying no sort of attention to his frequent and humble little efforts to do something for her comfort. Then the train halted at the Italian line, and she hopped up and marched out of the car with as firm a leg as any washerwoman of all her tribe! And how sick I was to see how she had fooled me!

Turin is a very fine city. In the matter of roominess it transcends anything that was ever dreamed of before, I fancy. It sits in the midst of a vast dead-level, and one is obliged to imagine that land may be had for the asking, and no taxes to pay, so lavishly do they use it. The streets are extravagantly wide, the paved squares are prodigious, the houses are huge and handsome, and compacted into uniform blocks that stretch away as straight as an arrow, into the distance. The side walks are about as wide as ordinary European *streets*, and are covered over with a double arcade, supported on great stone piers or columns. One walks from one end to the other of these spacious streets, under shelter all the time, and all his course is lined with the prettiest of shops and the most inviting dining-houses.

There is a wide and lengthy court, glittering with the most wickedly enticing shops, which is roofed with glass, high aloft over head, and paved with soft-toned marbles laid in graceful figures; and at night, when this place is brilliant with gas and populous with a sauntering and chatting and laughing multitude of pleasure-seekers, it is a spectacle worth seeing.

Everything is on a large scale; the public buildings, for instance—and they are architecturally imposing too, as well as large. The big squares have big bronze monuments in them. At the hotel they gave us rooms that were alarming for size, and a parlour to match. It was well the weather required no fire in the parlour, for I think one might as well have tried to warm a park. The place would have a warm look though in any weather, for the window curtains were of red silk damask, and the walls were covered with the same fire-hued goods—so, also, were the four sofas and the brigade of chairs. The furniture, the ornaments, the chandeliers, the carpets were all new and bright and costly. We did not need a parlour at all, but they said it belonged to the two bedrooms and we might use it if we chose. Since it was to cost nothing, we were not averse from using it, of course.

Turin must surely read a good deal, for it has more book stores to the square rod than any other town I know of. And it has its own share of military folk. The Italian officers' uniforms are very much the most beautiful I have ever seen; and as a general thing the men in them were as handsome as the clothes. They were not large men, but they had fine forms, fine features, rich olive complexions, and lustrous black eyes.

For several weeks I had been culling all the information I could about Italy, from tourists. The tourists were all agreed upon one thing—one must expect to be cheated at every turn by the Italians. I took an evening walk in Turin, and presently came across a little Punch and Judy show in one of the great squares. Twelve or fifteen people constituted the audience. This miniature theatre was not much bigger than a man's coffin stood on end; the upper part was open and displayed a tinselled parlour—a good-sized handkerchief would have answered for a drop-curtain; the footlights consisted of a couple of candle-ends an inch long; various manikins the size of dolls appeared on the stage and made long speeches at each other, gesticulating a good deal, and they generally had a fight before they got through. They were worked by strings from above, and the illusion was not perfect, for one saw, not only the strings, but the brawny hand that manipulated them—and the actors and actresses all talked in the same voice too. The audience stood in front of the theatre, and seemed to enjoy the performance heartily.

When the play was done, a youth in his shirt-sleeves started around with a small copper saucer to make a collection. I did not know how much to put in, but thought I would be guided by my predecessors. Unluckily I only had two of these, and they did not help me much because they did not put in anything. I had no Italian money, so I put in a small Swiss coin worth about ten cents. The youth finished his collection trip and emptied the result on the stage; he had some very animated talk with the concealed manager, then he came working his way through the little crowd—seeking me, I thought. I had a mind to slip away, but concluded I wouldn't; I would stand my ground, and confront the villainy, whatever it was. The youth stood before me and held up that Swiss coin, sure enough, and said something. I did not understand him, but I judged he was requiring Italian money of me. The crowd gathered close to listen. I was irritated, and said—in English of course—

'I know it's Swiss, but you'll take that or none. I haven't any other.'

He tried to put the coin in my hand, and spoke again. I drew my hand away, and said—

'*No*, sir. I know all about you people. You can't play any of your fraudful tricks on me. If there is a discount on that coin, I am sorry, but I am not going to make it good. I noticed that some of the audience didn't pay you anything at all. You let them go without a word, but you come after me because you think I'm a stranger and will put up with an extortion rather than have a scene. But you are mistaken this time—you'll take that Swiss money or none.'

The youth stood there with the coin in his fingers nonplussed and bewildered; of course he had not understood a word. An English-speaking Italian spoke up now, and said—

'You are misunderstanding the boy. He does not mean any harm. He did not suppose you gave him so much money purposely, so he hurried back to return you the coin lest you might get away before you discovered your mistake. Take it, and give him a penny—that will make everything smooth again.'

I probably blushed then, for there was occasion. Through the interpreter I begged the boy's pardon, but I nobly refused to take back the ten cents. I said I was accustomed to squandering large sums in that way—it was the kind of person I was. Then I retired to make a note to the effect that in Italy persons connected with the drama do not cheat.

The episode with the showman reminds me of a dark chapter in my history. I once robbed an aged and blind beggar-woman of four dollars—in a church. It happened in this way. When I was out with the Innocents Abroad, the ship stopped in the Russian port of Odessa, and I went ashore with others to view the town. I got separated from the rest, and wandered about, alone, until late in the afternoon, when I entered a Greek church to see what it was like. When I was ready to leave, I observed two wrinkled old women standing stiffly upright, against the inner wall, near the door, with their brown palms open to receive alms. I contributed to the nearer one, and passed out. I had gone fifty yards, perhaps, when it occurred to me that I must remain ashore all night, as I had heard that the ship's business would carry her away at four o'clock and keep her away until morning. It was a little after four now. I had come ashore with only two pieces of money, both about the same size, but differing largely in value—one was a French gold piece worth four dollars, the other a Turkish coin worth two cents and a half. With a sudden and horrified misgiving, I put my hand in my pocket, now, and sure enough I fetched out that Turkish penny!

Here was a situation. A hotel would require pay in advance—I must walk the streets all night, and perhaps be arrested as a suspicious character. There was but one way out of the difficulty—I flew back to the church, and softly entered.

There stood the old women yet, and in the palm of the nearest one still lay my gold piece. I was grateful. I crept close, feeling unspeakably mean; I got my Turkish penny ready, and was extending a trembling hand to make the nefarious exchange, when I heard a cough behind me. I jumped back as if I had been accused, and stood quaking while a worshipper entered and passed up the aisle.

I was there a year trying to steal that money; that is, it seemed a year, though of course it must have been much less. The worshippers went and came; there were hardly ever three in the church at once, but there was always one or more. Every time I tried to commit my crime somebody came in or somebody started out, and I was prevented; but at last my opportunity came, for one moment there was nobody in the church but the two beggar-women and me. I whipped the gold piece out of the poor old pauper's palm and dropped my Turkish penny in its place. Poor old thing, she murmured her thanks—they smote me to the heart. Then I sped away in a guilty hurry, and even when I was a mile from the church I was still glancing back, every moment, to see if I was being pursued.

That experience has been of priceless value and benefit to me; for I resolved then, that as long as I lived I would never again rob a blind beggar-woman in a church; and I have always kept my word. The most permanent lessons in morals are those which come not of booky teaching, but of experience.

CHAPTER 48

In Milan we spent most of our time in the vast and beautiful Arcade or Gallery, or whatever it is called. Blocks of tall new buildings of the most sumptuous sort, rich with decoration and graced with statues, the streets between these blocks roofed over with glass at a great height, the pavements all of smooth and variegated marble, arranged in tasteful patterns—little tables all over these marble streets, people sitting at them, eating, drinking, or smoking—crowds of other people strolling by—such is the Arcade. I should like to live in it all the time. The windows of the sumptuous restaurants stand open, and one breakfasts there and enjoys the passing show.

We wandered all over the town, enjoying whatever was going on in the streets. We took one omnibus ride, and as I did not speak Italian and could not ask the price, I held out some copper coins to the conductor, and he took two. Then he went and got his tariff-card and showed me that he had taken only the right sum. So I made a note—Italian omnibus conductors do not cheat.

Near the cathedral I saw another instance of probity. An old man was peddling dolls and toy fans. Two small American children bought fans, and one gave the old man a franc and three copper coins, and both started away; but they were called back, and the franc and one of the coppers were restored to them. Hence it is plain that in Italy parties connected with the drama, and with the omnibus and toy interests do not cheat.

The stocks of goods in the shops were not extensive, generally. In the vestibule of what seemed to be a clothing store, we saw eight or ten wooden dummies grouped together, clothed in woollen business-suits, and each suit marked with its price. One suit was marked forty-five francs—nine dollars. Harris stepped in, and said he wanted a suit like that. Nothing easier; the old merchant dragged in the dummy, brushed him off with a broom, stripped him and shipped the clothes to the hotel. He said he did not keep two suits of the same kind in stock, but manufactured a second when it was needed to re-clothe the dummy.

In another quarter we found six Italians engaged in a violent quarrel. They danced fiercely about, gesticulating with their heads, their arms, their legs, their whole bodies; they would rush forward occasionally in a sudden access of passion and shake their fists in each other's very faces. We lost half an hour there, waiting to help cord up the dead, but they finally embraced each other affectionately, and the trouble was all over. The episode was interesting, but we could not have afforded all that time to it if we had known nothing was going to come of it but a reconciliation. Note made—in Italy, people who quarrel cheat the spectator.

We had another disappointment afterwards. We approached a deeply interested crowd, and in the midst of it found a fellow wildly chattering and gesticulating over a box on the ground, which was covered with a piece of old blanket. Every little while he would bend down and take hold of the edge of the blanket with the extreme tips of his fingers, as if to show there was no deception—chattering away all the while—but always, just as I was expecting to see a wonderful feat of legerdemain, he would let go the blanket and rise to explain further. However, at last he uncovered the box and got out a spoon with a liquid in it, and held it fair and frankly around, for people to see that it was all right and he was taking no advantage—his chatter became more excited than ever. I supposed he was going to set fire to the liquid and swallow it, so I was greatly wrought up and interested. I got a cent ready in one hand and a florin in the other, intending to give him the former if he survived and the latter if he killed himself—for his loss would be my gain in a literary way, and I was willing to pay a fair price for the item—but this imposter ended his intensely moving performance by simply adding some powder to the liquid and polishing the spoon! Then he held it aloft, and he could not have shown a wilder exultation if he had achieved an immortal miracle. The crowd applauded in a gratified way, and it seemed to me that history speaks the truth when it says these children of the South are easily entertained.

We spent an impressive hour in the noble cathedral, where long shafts of tinted light were cleaving through the solemn dimness from the lofty windows, and falling on a pillar here, a picture there, and a kneeling worshipper yonder. The organ was muttering, censers were swinging, candles were glinting on the distant altar, and the robed priests were filing silently past them. The scene was one to sweep all frivolous thoughts away, and steep the soul in a holy calm. A trim young American lady paused a yard or two from me, fixed her eyes on the mellow sparks flecking the far-off altar, bent her head reverently a moment, then straightened up, kicked her train into the air with her heel, caught it deftly in her hand, and marched briskly out.

We visited the picture galleries and the other regulation 'sights' of Milan—not because I wanted to write about them again, but to see if I had learned anything in twelve years. I afterwards visited the great galleries of Rome and Florence for the same purpose. I found I had learned one thing. When I wrote about the Old Masters before, I said the copies were better than the originals. That was a mistake of large dimensions. The Old Masters were still unpleasing to me, but they were truly divine contrasted with the copies. The copy is to the original as the pallid, smart, inane new waxwork group is to the vigorous, earnest, dignified group of living men and women whom it professes to duplicate. There is a mellow richness, a subdued colour, in the old pictures, which is to the eye what muffled and mellowed sound is to the ear. That is the merit which is most loudly praised in the old picture, and is the one which the copy most conspicuously lacks, and which the copyist must not hope to compass. It was generally conceded by the artists with whom I talked, that that subdued splendour, that mellow richness, is imparted to the picture by *age*. Then why should we worship the Old Master for it, who didn't impart it, instead of worshipping Old Time, who did? Perhaps the picture was a clanging bell until Time muffled it and sweetened it.

In conversation with an artist in Venice, I asked—

'What is it that people see in the Old Masters? I have been in the Doge's palace, and I saw several acres of very bad drawing, very bad perspective, and very incorrect proportions. Paul Veronese's dogs do not resemble dogs; all the horses look like bladders on legs; one man had a *right* leg on the left side of his body; in the large picture, where the Emperor (Barbarossa?) is prostrate before the Pope, there are three men in the foreground who are over thirty feet high, if one may judge by the size of a kneeling little boy in the centre of the foreground; and according to the same scale, the Pope is seven feet high, and the Doge is a shrivelled dwarf of four feet.'

The artist said—

'Yes, the Old Masters often drew badly; they did not care much for truth and exactness in minor details. But, after all, in spite of bad drawing, bad perspective, bad proportions, and a choice of subjects which no longer appeal to people as strongly as they did three hundred years ago, there is a *something* about their pictures which is divine—something which is above and beyond the art of any epoch since—a something which would be the despair of artists, but that they never hope or expect to attain it, and therefore do not worry about it.'

That is what he said—and he said what he believed; and not only believed, but felt.

Reasoning—especially reasoning without technical knowledge—must be put aside in cases of this kind. It cannot assist the inquirer. It will lead him, in the most logical progression, to what, in the eyes of artists, would be a most illogical conclusion. Thus, bad drawing, bad proportion, bad perspective, indifference to truthful detail, colour which gets its merit from time, and not from the artist—these things constitute the Old Master; conclusion, the Old Master was a bad painter, the Old Master was not an Old Master at all, but an Old Apprentice. Your friend the artist will grant your premises, but deny your conclusion; he will maintain that notwithstanding this formidable list of confessed defects, there is still a something that is divine and unapproachable about the Old Master, and that there is no arguing the fact away by any system of reasoning whatever.

I can believe that. There are women who have an indefinable charm in their faces which makes them beautiful to their intimates; but a cold stranger who tried to reason the matter out and find this beauty would fail. He would say of one of these women: 'This chin is too short, this nose is too long, this forehead is too high, this hair is too red, this complexion is too pallid, the perspective of the entire composition is incorrect; conclusion, the woman is not beautiful.' But her nearest friend might say, and say truly, 'Your premises are right, your logic is faultless, but your conclusion is wrong, nevertheless; she is an Old Master—she is beautiful, but only to such as know her; it is a beauty which cannot be formulated, but it is there just the same.'

I found more pleasure in contemplating the Old Masters this time than I did when I was in Europe in former years, but still it was a calm pleasure; there was nothing overheated about it. When I was in Venice before, I think I found no picture which stirred me much; but this time there were two which enticed me to the Doge's palace day after day, and kept me there hours at a time. One of these was Tintoretto's three-acre picture in the Great Council Chamber. When I saw it twelve years ago I was not strongly attracted to it—the guide told me it was an insurrection in heaven—but this was an error.

The movement of this great work is very fine. There are ten thousand figures, and they are all doing something. There is a wonderful 'go' to the whole composition. Some of the figures are diving headlong downward, with clasped hands, others are swimming through the cloud-shoals—some on their faces, some on their backs—great processions of bishops, martyrs, and angels are pouring swiftly centrewards from various outlying directions—everywhere is enthusiastic joy, there is rushing movement everywhere. There are fifteen or twenty figures scattered here and there with books, but they cannot keep their attention on their reading—they offer the books to others, but no one wishes to read now. The Lion of St. Mark is there, with his book; St. Mark is there, with his pen uplifted; he and the Lion are looking at each other earnestly in the face, disputing about the way to spell a word—the Lion looks up in rapt admiration while St. Mark spells. This is wonderfully interpreted by the artist. It is the master-stroke of this incomparable painting.

I visited the place daily and never grew tired of looking at that grand picture. As I have intimated, the movement is almost unimaginably vigorous; the figures are singing, hosannahing, and many are blowing trumpets. So vividly is noise suggested, that spectators who become absorbed in the picture almost always fall to shouting comments in each other's ears, making ear-trumpets of their curved hands, fearing they may not otherwise be heard. One often sees a tourist, with the eloquent tears pouring down his cheeks, funnel his hands at his wife's ear, and hears him roar through them.

'O to be there and at rest!'

None but the supremely great in art can produce effects like these with the silent brush.

Twelve years ago I could not have appreciated this picture. One year ago I could not have appreciated it. My study of art in Heidelberg has been a noble education to me. All that I am to-day in art I owe to that.

The other great work which fascinated me was Bassano's immortal Hair Trunk. This is in the Chamber of the Council of Ten. It is in one of the three forty-foot pictures which decorate the walls of the room. The composition of this picture is beyond praise. The Hair Trunk is not hurled at the stranger's head—so to speak—as the chief feature of an immortal work so often is. No; it is carefully guarded from prominence, it is subordinated, it is restrained, it is most deftly and cleverly held in reserve, it is most cautiously and ingeniously led up to, by the master, and consequently when the spectator reaches it at last, he is taken unawares, he is unprepared, and it bursts upon him with a stupefying surprise.

One is lost in wonder at all the thought and care which this elaborate planning must have cost. A general glance at the picture could never suggest that there was a hair trunk in it; the Hair Trunk is not mentioned in the title even, which is, 'Pope Alexander III. and the Doge Ziani, the Conqueror of the Emperor Frederick Barbarossa.' You see the title is actually utilised to help divert attention from the trunk; thus, as I say, nothing suggests the presence of the trunk by any hint, yet everything studiedly leads up to it, step by step. Let us examine into this, and observe the exquisite artful artlessness of the plan.

At the extreme left end of the picture are a couple of women, one of them with a child looking over her shoulder at a wounded man sitting with bandaged head on the ground. These people seem needless; but no, they are there for a purpose. One cannot look at them without seeing the gorgeous procession of grandees, bishops, halberdiers, and banner-bearers which is passing along behind them. One cannot see the procession without feeling a curiosity to follow it and learn whither it is going. It leads him to the Pope in the centre of the picture, who is talking with the bonnetless Doge—talking tranquilly, too, although within twelve feet of them a man is beating a drum, and not far from the drummer two persons are blowing horns, and many horsemen are plunging and rioting about—indeed, twenty-two feet of this great work is all a deep and happy holiday serenity and Sunday-school procession, and then we come suddenly upon eleven and a half feet of turmoil, and racket, and insubordination. This latter state of things is not an accident, it has its purpose. But for it, one would linger upon the Pope and the Doge, thinking them to be the motive and supreme feature of the picture; whereas one is drawn along, almost unconsciously, to see what the trouble is about. Now at the very *end* of this riot, within four feet of the end of the picture, and full thirty-six feet from the beginning of it, the Hair Trunk bursts with an electrifying suddenness upon the spectator, in all its matchless perfection, and the great master's triumph is sweeping and complete. From that moment no other thing in those forty feet of canvas has any charm. One sees the Hair Trunk and the

Hair Trunk only—and to see it is to worship it. Bassano even
placed objects in the immediate vicinity of the supreme feature
whose pretended purpose was to divert attention from it yet a
little longer, and thus delay and augment the surprise; for
instance, to the right of it he has placed a stooping man, with a
cap so red that it is sure to hold the eye for a moment— to the
left of it, some six feet away, he has placed a red-coated man on
an inflated horse, and that coat plucks your eye to that locality
the next moment. Then, between the trunk and the red
horseman, he has intruded a man, naked to his waist, who is
carrying a fancy flour-sack on the middle of his back, instead of
on his shoulder—this admirable feat interests you, of
course—keeps you at bay a little longer, like a sock or a jacket
thrown to the pursuing wolf—but at last, in spite of all
distractions and detentions, the eye of even the most dull and
heedless spectator is sure to fall upon the world's masterpiece,
and in that moment he totters to his chair or leans upon his
guide for support.

Descriptions of such a work as this must necessarily be
imperfect, yet they are of value. The top of the Trunk is arched;
the arch is a perfect half-circle, in the Roman style of
architecture, for in the then rapid decadence of Greek art the
rising influence of Rome was already beginning to be felt in the
art of the Republic. The Trunk is bound or bordered with leather
all around where the lid joins the main body. Many critics
consider this leather too cold in tone; but I consider this its
highest merit, since it was evidently made so to emphasise by
contrast the impassioned fervour of the hasp. The high lights in
this part of the work are cleverly managed, the *motif* is
admirably subordinated to the ground tints, and the *technique* is
very fine. The brass nail-heads are in the purest style of the early
Renaissance. The strokes here are very firm and bold—every
nail-head is a portrait. The handle on the end of the trunk has
evidently been retouched—I think, with a piece of chalk—but
one can still see the inspiration of the Old Master in the tranquil,
almost too tranquil, hang of it. The hair of this trunk is *real*
hair—so to speak—white in patches, brown in patches. The
details are finely worked out; the repose proper to hair in a

recumbent and inactive attitude is charmingly expressed. There is a feeling about this part of the work which lifts it to the highest altitude of art; the sense of sordid realism vanished away—one recognises that there is *soul* here. View this Trunk as you will, it is a gem, it is a marvel, it is a miracle. Some of the effects are very daring, approaching even to the boldest flights of the rococo, the sirocco, and the Byzantine schools—yet the master's hand never falters—it moves on, calm, majestic, confident—and with that art which conceals art, it finally casts over the *tout ensemble*, by mysterious methods of its own, a subtle something which refines, subdues, etherealises the arid components, and endues them with the deep charm and gracious witchery of poesy.

Among the art-treasures of Europe there are pictures which approach the Hair Trunk—there are two which may be said to equal it, possibly—but there is none that surpasses it. So perfect is the Hair Trunk that it moves even persons who ordinarily have no feeling for art. When an Erie baggage-master saw it two years ago, he could hardly keep from checking it; and once when a customs inspector was brought into its presence, he gazed upon it in silent rapture for some moments, then slowly and unconsciously placed one hand behind him with the palm uppermost, and got out his chalk with the other. These facts speak for themselves.

CHAPTER 49

One lingers about the Cathedral a good deal, in Venice. There is a strong fascination about it—partly because it is so old, and partly because it is so ugly. Too many of the world's famous buildings fail of one chief virtue—harmony; they are made up of a methodless mixture of the ugly and the beautiful; this is bad; it is confusing, it is unrestful. One has a sense of uneasiness, of distress, without knowing why. But one is calm before St. Mark, one is calm within it, one would be calm on top of it, calm in the cellar; for its details are masterfully ugly, no misplaced and impertinent beauties are intruded anywhere; and the consequent result is a grand harmonious whole, of soothing, entrancing, tranquillising, soul-satisfying ugliness. One's admiration of a perfect thing always grows, never declines; and this is the surest evidence to him that it *is* perfect. St. Mark is perfect. To me it soon grew to be so nobly, so augustly ugly, that it was difficult to stay away from it, even for a little while. Every time its squat domes disappeared from my view, I had a despondent feeling; whenever they reappeared, I felt an honest rapture—I have not known any happier hours than those I daily spent in front of Florian's, looking across the Great Square at it. Propped on its long row of low thick-legged columns, its back knobbed with domes, it seemed like a vast warty bug taking a meditative walk.

St. Mark is not the oldest building in the world, of course; but it seems the oldest, and looks the oldest—especially inside.

When the ancient mosaics in its walls become damaged they are repaired, but not altered; the grotesque old pattern is preserved. Antiquity has a charm of its own, and to smarten it up would only damage it. One day I was sitting on a red marble bench in the vestibule, looking up at an ancient piece of apprentice-work in mosaic, illustrative of the command to 'multiply and replenish the earth.' The cathedral itself had seemed very old: but this picture was illustrating a period in history which made the building seem young by comparison. But I presently found an antique which was older than either the battered cathedral or the date assigned to that piece of history: it was a spiral-shaped fossil as large as the crown of a hat. It was embedded in the marble bench, and had been sat upon by tourists until it was worn smooth. Contrasted with the inconceivable antiquity of this modest fossil, those other things were flippantly modern, jejune, mere matters of day-before-yesterday. The sense of the oldness of the cathedral vanished away under the influence of this truly venerable presence.

St. Mark's is monumental. It is an imperishable remembrancer of the profound and simple piety of the Middle Ages. Whoever could ravish a column from a Pagan temple did it, and contributed his swag to this Christian one. So this fane is upheld by several hundred acquisitions procured in that peculiar way. In our day it would be immoral to go on the highway to get bricks for a church, but it was no sin in the old times. St. Mark's was itself the victim of a curious robbery once. The thing is set down in the History of Venice; but it might be smuggled into the 'Arabian Nights,' and not seem out of place there.

Nearly four hundred and fifty years ago, a Canadian named Stammato, in the suite of a Prince of the House of Este, was allowed to view the riches of St. Mark. His sinful eye was dazzled, and he hid himself behind an altar with an evil purpose in his heart; but a priest discovered him, and turned him out. Afterwards he got in again, by false keys this time. He went there night after night, and worked hard and patiently all alone, overcoming difficulty after difficulty with his toil, and at last succeeded in removing a great block of the marble panelling which walled the lower part of the treasury. This block he fixed so that he could take it out and put it in at will. After that, for weeks he spent all his midnights in his magnificent mine, inspecting it in security, gloating over its marvels at his leisure, and always slipping back to his obscure lodgings before dawn with a duke's ransom under his cloak. He did not need to grab haphazard, and run; there was no hurry. He could make deliberate and well-considered selections. He could consult his aesthetic tastes. One comprehends how undisturbed he was, and how safe from any danger of interruption, when it is stated that he even carried off a unicorn's horn—a mere curiosity—which would not pass through the egress entire, but had to be sawn in two—a bit of work which cost him hours of tedious labour. He continued to store up his treasures at home until his occupation lost the charm of novelty, and became monotonous; then he ceased from it, contented. Well he might be; for his collection, raised to modern values, represented nearly 50,000,000 dols.!

He could have gone home much the richest citizen of his country, and it might have been years before the plunder was missed, but he was human: he could not enjoy his delight alone, he must have somebody to talk about it with. So he exacted a solemn oath from a Canadian noble named Crioni, then led him to his lodgings, and nearly took his breath away with a sight of his glittering hoard. He detected a look in his friend's face which excited his suspicion, and was about to slip a stiletto into him, when Crioni saved himself by explaining that that look was only an expression of supreme and happy astonishment. Stammato made Crioni a present of one of the State's principal jewels—a huge carbuncle, which afterwards figured in the ducal cap of state; and the pair parted. Crioni went at once to the palace, denounced the criminal, and handed over the carbuncle as evidence. Stammato was arrested, tried, and condemned, with the old-time Venetian promptness. He was hanged between the two great columns in the Piazza—with a gilded rope, out of compliments to his love of gold, perhaps. He got no good of his booty at all; it was *all* recovered.

In Venice we had a luxury which very seldom fell to our lot on the Continent—a home dinner with a private family. If one could always stop with private families when travelling, Europe would have a charm which it now lacks. As it is, one must live in the hotels, of course, and that is a sorrowful business. A man accustomed to American food and American domestic cookery would not starve to death suddenly in Europe, but I think he would gradually waste away and eventually die. He would have to do without his accustomed morning meal. That is too formidable a change altogether, he would necessarily suffer from it. He could get the shadow, the sham, the base counterfeit of that meal; but that would do him no good, and money could not buy the reality.

To particularise: the average American's simplest and commonest form of breakfast consists of coffee and beefsteak; well, in Europe, coffee is an unknown beverage. You can get what the European hotel keeper thinks is coffee, but it resembles the real thing as hypocrisy resembles holiness. It is a feeble, characterless, uninspiring sort of stuff, and almost as undrinkable as if it had been made in an American hotel. The milk used for it is what the French call 'Christian' milk—milk which has been baptised.

After a few months' acquaintance with European 'coffee,' one's mind weakens, and his faith with it, and he begins to wonder if the rich beverage of home, with its clotted layer of yellow cream on top of it, is not a mere dream after all, and a thing which never existed.

Next comes the European bread—fair enough, good enough, after a fashion, but cold; cold and tough, and unsympathetic; and never any change, never any variety—always the same tiresome thing.

Next, the butter—the sham and tasteless butter; no salt in it, and made of goodness knows what.

Then, there is the beefsteak. They have it in Europe, but they don't know how to cook it. Neither will they cut it right. It comes on the table in a small round pewter platter. It lies in the centre of this platter, in a bordering bed of grease-soaked potatoes; it is the size, shape, and thickness of a man's hand with the thumb and fingers cut off. It is a little overdone, is rather dry, it tastes pretty insipidly, it rouses no enthusiasm.

Imagine a poor exile contemplating that inert thing; and

imagine an angel suddenly sweeping down out of a better land
and setting before him a mighty porter-house steak an inch and
a half thick, hot and spluttering from the griddle; dusted with
fragrant pepper; enriched with little melting bits of butter of the
most unimpeachable freshness and genuineness; the precious
juices of the meat trickling out and joining the gravy,
archipelagoed with mushrooms; a township or two of tender
yellowish fat gracing an outlying district of this ample county of
beefsteak; the long white bone which divides the sirloin from the
tender loin still in its place; and imagine that the angel also adds
a great cup of American home-made coffee, with the cream a-
froth on top, some real butter, firm and yellow and fresh, some
smoking hot biscuits, a plate of hot buckwheat cakes, with
transparent syrup—could words describe the gratitude of this
exile?

The European dinner is better than the European breakfast,
but it has its faults and inferiorities, it does not satisfy. He comes
to the table eager and hungry—he swallows his soup—there is
an undefinable lack about it somewhere; thinks the fish is going
to be the thing he wants—eats it and isn't sure; thinks the next
dish is perhaps the one that will hit the hungry place—tries it,
and is conscious that there was a something wanting about it
also. And thus he goes on, from dish to dish, like a boy after a
butterfly which just misses getting caught every time it alights,
but somehow doesn't get caught after all; and at the end the exile
and the boy have fared about alike: the one is full, but grievously
unsatisfied, the other has had plenty of exercise, plenty of
interest, and a fine lot of hopes, but he hasn't got any butterfly.
There is here and there an American who will say he can
remember rising from an European *table d'hôte* perfectly
satisfied; but we must not overlook the fact, that there is also
here and there an American who will lie.

The number of dishes is sufficient; but then it is such a
monotonous variety of *unstriking* dishes. It is an inane dead
level of 'fair-to-middling.' There is nothing to *accent* it. Perhaps
if the roast of mutton or of beef—a big generous one—were
brought on the table and carved in full view of the client, that
might give the right sense of earnestness and reality to the thing;

but they don't do that, they pass the sliced meat around on a dish, and so you are perfectly calm, it does not stir you in the least. Now a vast roast turkey, stretched on the broad of his back, with his heels in the air, and the rich juices oozing from his fat sides ... but I may as well as stop there, for they would not know how to cook him. They can't even cook a chicken respectably; and as for carving it, they do that with a hatchet. This is about the customary *table d'hôte* bill in summer:—

Soup (characterless).

Fish—sole, salmon, or whiting—usually tolerably good.

Roast—mutton or beef—tasteless—and some last year's potatoes.

A pâté, or some other made-dish—usually good, 'considering.'

One vegetable—brought on in state, and all alone—usually insipid lentils, or string beans, or indifferent asparagus.

Roast chicken, as tasteless as paper.

Lettuce-salad—tolerably good.

Decayed strawberries or cherries.

Sometimes the apricots and figs are fresh, but this is no advantage, as these fruits are of no account anyway.

The grapes are generally good, and sometimes there is a tolerably good peach, by mistake.

The variations of the above bill are trifling. After a fortnight one discovers that the variations are only apparent, not real; in the third week you get what you had the first, and in the fourth week you get what you had the second. Three or four months of this weary sameness will kill the robustest appetite.

It has now been many months, at the present writing, since I have had a nourishing meal, but I shall soon have one—a modest, private affair, all to myself. I have selected a few dishes, and made out a little bill of fare, which will go home in the steamer that precedes me, and be hot when I arrive—as follows:—

Radishes. Baked apples, with cream

Fried oysters; stewed oysters. Frogs.

American coffee, with real cream.

American butter.

Fried chicken, Southern style.

Porter-house steak.
Saratoga potatoes.
Broiled chicken, American style.
Hot biscuits, Southern style.
Hot wheat-bread. Southern style.
Hot buckwheat cakes.
American toast. Clear maple syrup.
Virginia bacon, broiled
Blue points, on the half shell.
Cherry-stone clams.
San Francisco mussels, steamed.
Oyster soup. Clam soup.
Philadelphia terrapin soup.
Oysters roasted in shell— Northern style.
Soft-shelled crabs. Connecticut shad.
Baltimore perch.
Brook trout, from Sierra Nevadas.
Lake trout, from Tahoe.
Sheep-head and croakers, from New Orleans.
Black bass, from the Mississippi.
Hot-egg bread, Southern style.
Hot light-bread, Southern style.
Buttermilk. Iced sweet milk.
Apple dumplings, with real cream.
Apple pie. Apple fritters.
American roast beef.
Roast turkey, Thanksgiving style.

Cranberry sauce. Celery.
Roast wild turkey. Woodcock.
Canvas-back-duck, from Baltimore.
Prairie hens, from Illinois.
Missouri partridges, broiled.
Possum. Coon.
Boston bacon and beans.
Bacon and greens, Southern style.
Hominy. Boiled onions, Turnips.
Pumpkin. Squash. Asparagus.
Butter beans. Sweet potatoes.
Lettuce. Succotash. String beans.
Mashed potatoes. Catsup.
Boiled potatoes, in the skins.
New potatoes, minus their skins.
Early rose potatoes roasted in the ashes, Southern style, served hot.
Sliced tomatoes, with sugar or vinegar. Stewed tomatoes.
Green corn, cut from the ear, and served with butter and pepper.
Green corn, on the ear.
Hot corn-pone, with chitlings, Southern style.
Hot hoe-cake, Southern style.
Apple puffs, Southern style.
Peach cobbler, Southern style.
Peach pie. American mince pie.
Pumpkin pie. Squash pie.
All sorts of American pastry.

Fresh American fruits of all sorts, including strawberries, which are not to be doled out as if they were jewellery, but in a more liberal way.

Ice-water—not prepared in the ineffectual goblet, but in the sincere and capable refrigerator.

Americans intending to spend a year or so in European hotels will do well to copy this bill and carry it along. They will find it an excellent thing to get up an appetite with, in the dispiriting presence of the squalid *table d'hôte*.

Foreigners cannot enjoy our food, I suppose, any more than we can enjoy theirs. It is not strange; for tastes are made, not born. I might glorify my bill of fare until I was tired; but after all, the Scotchman would shake his head and say, 'Where's your haggis?' and the Fijian would sigh and say, 'Where's your missionary?'

I have a neat talent in matters pertaining to nourishment. This has met with professional recognition. I have often furnished recipes for cook-books. Here are some designs for pies and things which I recently prepared for a friend's projected cook-book, but as I forgot to furnish diagrams and perspectives, they had to be left out, of course:—

Recipe for an Ash-cake

Take a lot of water and add to it a lot of coarse Indian meal and about a quarter of a lot of salt. Mix well together, knead into the form of a 'pone,' and let the pone stand awhile—not on its edge, but the other way. Rake away a place among the embers, lay it there, and cover it an inch deep with hot ashes. When it is done, remove it; blow off all the ashes but one layer; butter that one and eat.

N.B. No household should ever be without this talisman. It has been noticed that tramps never return for another ash-cake.

Recipe for New England Pie.

To make this excellent breakfast dish, proceed as follows:— Take a sufficiency of water and a sufficiency of flour and construct a bullet-proof dough. Work this into the form of a disk, with the edges turned up some three-fourths of an inch. Toughen and kiln-dry it a couple of days in a mild but unvarying temperature. Construct a cover for this redoubt in the same way and of the same material. Fill with stewed dried apples; aggravate with cloves, lemon peel, and slabs of citron; add two portions of New Orleans sugar, then solder on the lid and set in a safe place till it petrifies. Serve cold at breakfast and invite your enemy.

Recipe for German Coffee.

Take a barrel of water and bring it to a boil; rub a chicory berry against a coffee berry, then convey the former into the water. Continue the boiling and evaporation until the intensity of the flavour and aroma of the coffee and chicory has been diminished to a proper degree; then set aside to cool. Now unharness the remains of a once cow from the plough, insert them in a hydraulic press, and when you shall have acquired a teaspoonful of that pale blue juice which a German superstition regards as milk, modify the malignity of its strength in a bucket of tepid water and ring up the breakfast. Mix the beverage in a cold cup, partake with moderation, and keep a wet rag around your head to guard against over-excitement.

To Carve Fowls in the German Fashion.

Use a club, and avoid the joints.

CHAPTER 50

I wonder why some things are? For instance, Art is allowed as much indecent licence to-day as in earlier times; but the privileges of Literature in this respect have been sharply curtailed within the past eighty or ninety years. Fielding and Smollett could portray the beastliness of their day in the beastliest language; we have plenty of foul subjects to deal with in our day, but we are not allowed to approach them very near, even with nice and guarded forms of speech. But not so with Art. The brush may still deal freely with any subject, however revolting or indelicate. It makes a body ooze sarcasm at every pore, to go about Rome and Florence and see what this last generation has been doing with the statues. These works, which had stood in innocent nakedness for ages, are all fig-leaved now. Yes, every one of them. Nobody noticed their nakedness before, perhaps; nobody can help noticing it now, the fig-leaf makes it so conspicuous. But the comical thing about it all is, that the fig-leaf is confined to cold and pallid marble, which would be still cold and unsuggestive without this sham and ostentatious symbol of modesty, whereas warm-blooded paintings which do really need it have in no case been furnished with it.

At the door of the Ufizzi, in Florence, one is confronted by statues of a man and a woman, noseless, battered, black with accumulated grime—they hardly suggest human beings—yet these ridiculous creatures have been thoughtfully and conscientiously fig-leaved by this fastidious generation. You enter, and proceed to that most-visited little gallery that exists in the world—the Tribune—and there, against the wall, without obstructing rag or leaf, you may look your fill upon the foulest, the vilest, the obscenest picture the world possesses—Titian's Venus. It isn't that she is naked and stretched out on a bed; no, it is the attitude of one of her arms and hand. If I ventured to describe that attitude, there would be a fine howl; but there the Venus lies, for anybody to gloat over that wants to; and there she has a right to lie, for she is a work of art, and Art has its privileges. I saw young girls stealing furtive glances at her; I saw young men gaze long and absorbedly at her; I saw aged, infirm men hang upon her charms with a pathetic interest. How I should like to describe her—just to see what a holy indignation I could stir up in the world—just to hear the unreflecting average man deliver himself about my grossness and coarseness, and all that. The world says that no worded description of a moving spectacle is a hundredth part as moving as the same spectacle seen with one's own eyes; yet the world is willing to let its son and its daughter and itself look at Titian's beast, but won't stand a description of it in words. Which shows that the world is not as consistent as it might be.

There are pictures of nude women which suggest no impure thought; I am well aware of that. I am not railing at such. What I am trying to emphasise is the fact that Titian's Venus is very far from being one of that sort. Without any question it was painted for a bagnio, and it was probably refused because it was a trifle too strong. In truth it is too strong for any place but a public Art Gallery. Titian has two Venuses in the Tribune; persons who have seen them will easily remember which one I am referring to.

In every gallery in Europe there are hideous pictures of blood, carnage, oozing brains, putrefaction—pictures portraying intolerable suffering—pictures alive with every conceivable horror, wrought out in dreadful detail—and similar pictures are being put on the canvas every day and publicly exhibited—without a growl from anybody, for they are innocent, they are inoffensive, being works of art. But suppose a literary artist ventured to go into a painstaking and elaborate description of one of these grisly things, the critics would skin him alive. Well, let it go, it cannot be helped; Art retains her privileges, Literature has lost hers. Somebody else may cipher out they whys and the wherefors and the consistencies of it—I haven't got time.

Titian's Venus defiles and disgraces the Tribune, there is no softening that fact; but his 'Moses' glorifies it. The simple truthfulness of this noble work wins the heart and the applause of every visitor, be he learned or ignorant. After wearying oneself with the acres of stuffy, sappy, expressionless babies that populate the canvases of the Old Masters in Italy, it is refreshing to stand before this peerless child and feel that thrill which tells you you are at last in the presence of the real thing. This is a human child, this is genuine. You have seen him a thousand times—you have seen him just as he is here—and you confess, without reserve, that Titian *was* a Master. The doll-faces of other painted babes may mean one thing, they may mean another, but with the 'Moses' the case is different. The most famous of all the art critics has said, 'There is no room for doubt here—plainly this child is in trouble.'

I consider that the 'Moses' has no equal among the works of the Old Masters, except it be the divine Hair Trunk of Bassano. I feel sure that if all the other Old Masters were lost, and only these two preserved, the world would be the gainer by it.

My sole purpose is going to Florence was to see this immortal 'Moses,' and by good fortune I was just in time, for they were already preparing to remove it to a more private and better-protected place, because a fashion of robbing the great galleries was prevailing in Europe at the time.

I got a capable artist to copy the picture; Pannemaker, the engraver of Doré's books, engraved it for me, and I have the pleasure of laying it before the reader as the frontispiece to this volume.

We took a turn to Rome and some other Italian cities; then to Munich, and thence to Paris, partly for exercise, but mainly because these things were in our projected programme, and it was only right that we should be faithful to it.

From Paris I branched out and walked through Holland and Belgium, procuring an occasional lift by rail or canal when tired, and I had a tolerably good time of it 'by and large.' I worked Spain and other regions through agents, to save time and shoe leather.

We crossed to England, and then made the homeward passage in the Cunarder 'Gallia,' a very fine ship. I was glad to get home—immeasurably glad; so glad, in fact, that it did not seem possible that anything could ever get me out of the country again. I had not enjoyed a pleasure abroad which seemed to me to compare with the pleasure I felt in seeing New York harbour again. Europe has many advantages which we have not, but they do not compensate for a good many still more valuable ones which exist nowhere but in our own country. Then we are such a homeless lot when we are over there! So are Europeans themselves, for that matter. They live in dark and chilly vast tombs, costly enough, maybe, but without conveniences. To be condemned to live as the average European family lives would make life a pretty heavy burden to the average American family.

On the whole, I think that short visits to Europe are better for us than long ones. The former preserve us from becoming Europeanised; they keep our pride of country intact, and at the same time they intensify our affection for our country and our people; whereas long visits have the effect of dulling those feelings, at least in the majority of cases. I think that one who mixes much with Americans long resident abroad must arrive at this conclusion.

APPENDIX

Nothing gives such weight and
dignity to a book as an Appendix.

Herodotus.

APPENDIX A

The Portier

Omar Khayam, the poet-prophet of Persia, writing more than eight hundred years ago, has said:—

> In the four parts of the earth are many that are able to write learned books, many that are able to lead armies, and many also that are able to govern kingdoms and empires; but few there be that can keep hotel.

A word about the European hotel *portier*. He is a most admirable invention, a most valuable convenience. He always wears a conspicuous uniform; he can always be found when he is wanted, for he sticks closely to his post at the front door; he is as polite as a duke; he speaks from four to ten languages; he is your surest help and refuge in time of trouble or perplexity. He is not the clerk, he is not the landlord; he ranks above the clerk, and represents the landlord, who is seldom seen. Instead of going to the clerk for information, as we do at home, you go to the portier. It is the pride of the portier to know everything. You ask the portier at what hours the trains leave—he tells you instantly; or you ask him who is the best physician in town; or what is the hack tariff; or how many children the mayor has; or what days the galleries are open, and whether a permit is required, and where you are to get it, and what you must pay for it; or when the theatres open and close, what the plays are to be, and the price of seats; or what is the newest thing in hats; or how the bills of mortality average; or 'who struck Billy Patterson.' It does not matter what you ask him: in nine cases out of ten he knows, and in the tenth case he will find out for you before you can turn around three times. There is nothing he will not put his hand to. Suppose you tell him you wish to go from Hamburg to Pekin by the way of Jericho, and are ignorant of routes and prices—the next morning he will hand you a piece of paper with the whole thing worked out on it to the last detail. Before you have been long on European soil, you find yourself still *saying* you are relying on Providence, but when you come to look closer you will see that in reality you are relying on the portier. He discovers what is puzzling you, or what is troubling you, or what your need is, before you can get the half of it out, and he promptly says, 'Leave that to me.' Consequently you easily drift into the habit of leaving everything to him. There is a certain embarrassment about applying to the average American hotel clerk, a certain hesitancy, a sense of insecurity against rebuff; but you feel no embarrassment in your intercourse with the portier; he receives your propositions with an enthusiasm which cheers, and plunges into their accomplishment with an alacrity which almost inebriates. The more requirements you can pile upon him, the better he likes it. Of course the result is that you cease from doing anything for yourself. He calls a hack when you want one; puts you into it; tells the driver whither to take you; receives you like a long-lost child when you return; sends you about your business, does all the quarrelling with the hackman himself, and pays him his money out of his own pocket. He sends for your theatre tickets, and pays for them; he sends for any possible article you can require, be it a doctor, an elephant, or a postage-stamp; and when you leave, at last, you will find a subordinate seated with the cab-driver, who will put you in your railway compartment, buy your tickets, have your baggage weighed, bring you the printed tags, and tell you everything is in your bill and paid for. At home you get such elaborate, excellent, and willing service as this only in the best hotels of our large cities; but in Europe you get in the mere back country towns just as well.

What is the secret of the portier's devotion? It is very simple: he gets *fees, and no salary.* His fee is pretty closely regulated, too. If you stay a week in the house, you give him five marks—a dollar and a quarter, or about eighteen cents a day. If you stay a month, you reduce this average somewhat. If you stay two or three months or longer, you cut it down half, or even more than half. If you stay only one day, you give the portier a mark.

The head waiter's fee is a shade less than the portier's; the Boots, who not only blacks your boots and brushes your clothes, but is usually the porter and handles your baggage, gets a somewhat smaller fee than the head waiter; the chambermaid's fee ranks below that of the Boots. You fee only these four, and no one else. A German gentleman told me that when he remained a week in an hotel, he gave the portier five marks, the head waiter four, the Boots three, and the chambermaid two; and if he stayed three months he divided ninety marks among them, in about the above proportions. Ninety marks make $22.50.

None of these fees are ever paid until you leave the hotel, though it be a year—except one of these four servants should go away in the meantime; in that case he will be sure to come and bid you good-bye and give you the opportunity to pay him what is fairly coming to him. It is considered very bad policy to fee a servant while you are still to remain longer in the hotel, because if you gave him too little he might neglect you afterwards, and if you gave him too much he might neglect somebody else to attend to you. It is considered best to keep his expectations 'on a string' until your stay is concluded.

I do not know whether hotel servants in New York get any wages or not, but I do know that in some of the hotels there the feeing system in vogue is a heavy burden. The waiter expects a quarter a breakfast—and gets it. You have a different waiter at luncheon, and so he gets a quarter. Your waiter at dinner is another stranger—consequently he gets a quarter. The boy who carries your satchel to your room and lights your gas, fumbles around and hangs around significantly, and you fee him to get rid of him. Now you may ring for ice-water; and ten minutes later a lemonade; and ten minutes afterwards, for a cigar; and by-and-by for a newspaper—and what is the result? Why, a new boy has appeared every time, and fooled and fumbled around until you have paid him something. Suppose you boldly put your foot down, and say it is the hotel's business to pay its servants?—and suppose you stand your ground and stop feeing? You will have to ring your bell ten or fifteen times before you get a servant there; and when he goes to fill your order you will grow old and infirm before you see him again. You may struggled nobly for twenty-four hours, may be, if you are an adamantine sort of person, but in the meantime you will have been so wretchedly served, and so insolently, that you will haul down your colours, and go to impoverishing yourself with fees.

It seems to me that it would be a happy idea to import the European feeing system into America. I believe it would result in getting even the bells of the Philadelphia hotels answered, and cheerful service rendered.

The greatest American hotels keep a number of clerks and a cashier, and pay them salaries which mount up to a considerable total in the course of a year. The great Continental hotels keep a cashier on a trifling salary, and a portier *who pays the hotel a salary*. By the latter system both the hotel and the public save money and are better served than by our system. One of our consuls told me that the portier of a great Berlin hotel paid $5,000 a year for his position, and yet cleared $6,000 for himself. The position of portier in the chief hotels of Saratoga, Long Branch, New York, and similar centres of resort would be one which the holder could afford to pay even more than $5,000 for, perhaps.

When we borrowed the feeing fashion from Europe a dozen years ago, the salary system ought to have been discontinued, of course. We might make this correction now, I should think. And we might add the portier too. Since I first began to study the portier, I have had opportunities to observe him in the chief cities of Germany, Switzerland, and Italy; and the more I have seen of him, the more I have wished that he might be adopted in America, and become there, as he is in Europe, the stranger's guardian angel.

Yes, what was true eight hundred years ago is just as true to-day: 'Few there be that can keep hotel.' Perhaps it is because the landlords and their subordinates have in too many cases taken up their trade without first learning it. In Europe the trade of hotel-keeper is taught. The apprentice begins at the bottom of the ladder and masters the several grades one after the other. Just as in our country printing-offices the apprentice first learns how to sweep out and bring water; then learns to 'roll;' then to sort 'pi;' then to set type; and finally rounds and completes his education with job-work and press-work: so the landlord-apprentice serves as call-boy; then as under-waiter; then as a parlour-waiter; then as head-waiter, in which position he often has to make out all the bills; then as clerk or cashier; then as portier. His trade is learned now, and by-and-by he will assume the style and dignity of landlord, and be found conducting an hotel of his own.

Now in Europe, the same as in America, when a man has kept an hotel so thoroughly well during a number of years as to give it a great reputation, he has his reward. He can live prosperously on that reputation. He can let his hotel run down to the last degree of shabbiness and yet have it full of people all the time. For instance, there is the Hôtel de Ville in Milan. It swarms with mice and fleas, and if the rest of the world were destroyed it could furnish dirt enough to start another with. The food would create an insurrection in a poorhouse; and yet if you go outside to get your meals that hotel makes up its loss by overcharging you on all sorts of trifles—and without making any denials or excuses about it either. But the Hôtel de Ville's old excellent reputation still keeps its dreary rooms crowded with travellers who would be elsewhere if they had only had some wise friend to warn them.

APPENDIX B

Heidelberg Castle

Heidelberg Castle must have been very beautiful before the French battered and bruised and scorched it two hundred years ago. The stone is brown, with a pinkish tint, and does not seem to stain easily. The dainty and elaborate ornamentation upon its two chief fronts is as delicately carved as if it had been intended for the interior of a drawing-room rather than for the outside of a house. Many fruit and flower-clusters, human heads, and grim projecting lion's heads are still as perfect in every detail as if they were new. But the statues which are ranked between the windows have suffered. These are life-size statues of old-time emperors, electors, and similar grandees, clad in mail and bearing ponderous swords. Some have lost an arm, some a head, and one poor fellow is chopped off at the middle. There is a saying that if a stranger will pass over the drawbridge and walk across the court to the Castle front without saying anything, he can make a wish and it will be fulfilled. But they say that the truth of this thing has never had a chance to be proved, for the reason that before any stranger can walk from the drawbridge to the appointed place, the beauty of the palace front will extort an exclamation of delight from him.

A ruin must be rightly situated, to be effective. This one could not have been better placed. It stands upon a commanding elevation, it is buried in green woods, there is no level ground about it, but on the contrary there are wooded terraces upon terraces, and one looks down through shining leaves into profound chasms and abysses where twilight reigns and the sun cannot intrude. Nature knows how to garnish a ruin to get the best effect. One of these old towers is split down the middle, and one half has tumbled aside. It tumbled in such a way as to establish itself in a picturesque attitude. Then all it lacked was a fitting drapery, and Nature has furnished that; she has robed the rugged mass in flowers and verdure, and made it a charm to the eye. The standing half exposes its arched and cavernous rooms to you, like open, toothless mouths; there, too, the vines and flowers have done their work of grace. The rear portion of the tower has not been neglected, either, but is clothed with a clinging garment of polished ivy which hides the wounds and stains of time. Even the top is not left bare, but is crowned with a flourishing group of trees and shrubs. Misfortune has done for this old tower what it has done for the human character sometimes—improved it.

A gentleman remarked, one day, that it might have been fine to live in the Castle in the day of its prime, but that we had one advantage which its vanished inhabitants lacked—the advantage of having a charming ruin to visit and muse over. But that was a hasty idea. Those people had the advantage of *us*. They had the fine Castle to live in, and they could cross the Rhine valley and muse over the stately ruin of Trifels besides. The Trifels people, in their day, five hundred years ago, could go and muse over majestic ruins which have vanished, now, to the last stone. There have always been ruins, no doubt; and there have always been pensive people to sigh over them, and asses to scratch upon them their names and the important date of their visit. Within a hundred years after Adam left Eden, the guide probably gave the usual general flourish with his hand and said: 'Place where the animals were named, ladies and gentlemen; place where the tree of the forbidden fruit stood; exact spot where Adam and Eve first met; and here, ladies and gentlemen, adorned and hallowed by the names and addresses of three generations of tourists, we have the crumbling remains of Cain's altar—fine old ruin!' Then, no doubt, he taxed them a shekel apiece and let them go.

An illumination of Heidelberg Castle is one of the sights of Europe. The Castle's picturesque shape; its commanding situation, midway up the steep and wooded mountain side; its vast size—these features combine to make an illumination a most effective spectacle. It is necessarily an expensive show, and consequently rather infrequent. Therefore, whenever one of these exhibitions is to take place, the news goes about in the papers, and Heidelberg is sure to be full of people on that night. I and my agent had one of these opportunities, and improved it.

About half-past seven on the appointed evening we crossed the lower bridge, with some American students, in a pouring rain, and started up the road which borders the Neunheim side of the river. This roadway was densely packed with carriages and foot passengers; the former of all ages, and the latter of all ages and both sexes. This black and solid mass was struggling painfully onward, through the slop, the darkness, and the deluge. We waded along for three-quarters of a mile, and finally took up a position in an unsheltered beer-garden directly opposite the Castle. We could not *see* the Castle—or anything else, for that matter—but we could dimly discern the outlines of the mountain over the way, through the pervading blackness, and knew whereabouts the Castle was located. We stood on one of the hundred benches in the garden, under our umbrellas; the other ninety-nine were occupied by standing men and women, and they also had umbrellas. All the region round about, and up and down the river-road, was a dense wilderness of humanity hidden under an unbroken pavement of carriage tops and umbrellas. Thus we stood during two drenching hours. No rain fell on my head, but the converging whalebone points of a dozen neighbouring umbrellas poured little cooling streams of water down my neck, and sometimes into my ears, and thus kept me from getting hot and impatient. I had the rheumatism, too, and had heard that this was good for it. Afterwards, however, I was led to believe that the water treatment is *not* good for rheumatism. There were even little girls in that dreadful place. A man held one in his arms, just in front of me, for as much as an hour, with umbrella-drippings soaking into her clothing all the time.

In the circumstances, two hours was a good while for us to have to wait, but when the illumination did at last come, we felt repaid. It came unexpectedly, of course—things always do that have been long looked and longed for. With a perfectly breath-taking suddenness several vast sheaves of vari-coloured rockets were vomited skyward out of the black throats of the Castle towers, accompanied by a thundering crash of sound, and instantly every detail of the prodigious ruin stood revealed against the mountain side and glowing an an almost intolerable splendour of fire and colour. For some little time the whole building was a blinding crimson mass, the towers continued to spout thick columns of rockets aloft, and overhead the sky was radiant with arrowy bolts which clove their way to the zenith, paused, curved gracefully downward, then burst into brilliant fountain sprays of richly coloured sparks. The red fires died slowly down within the Castle, and presently the shell grew nearly black outside; the angry glare that shone out through the broken arches and innumerable sashless windows now reproduced the aspect which the Castle must have borne in the old time when the French spoilers saw the monster bonfire which they had made there fading and smouldering towards extinction.

While we still gazed and enjoyed, the ruin was suddenly enveloped in rolling and tumbling volumes of vaporous green fire; then in dazzling purple ones; then a mixture of many colours followed, and drowned the great fabric in its blended splendours. Meantime the nearest bridge had been illuminated, and from several rafts anchored in the river meteor showers of rockets, Roman candles, bombs, serpents, and Catharine wheels were being discharged in wasteful profusion into the sky—a marvellous sight indeed to a person as little used to such spectacles as I was. For a while the whole region about us seemed as bright as day, and yet the rain was falling in torrents all the time. The evening's entertainment presently closed, and we joined the innumerable caravan of half-drowned spectators, and waded home again.

The Castle grounds are very ample and very beautiful; and as they joined the hotel grounds, with no fences to climb, but only some nobly shaded stone stairways to descend, we spent a part of nearly every day in idling through their smooth walks and leafy groves. There was an attractive spot among the trees where were a great many wooden tables and benches; and there one could sit in the shade and pretend to sip at his foamy beaker of beer while he inspected the crowd. I say pretend, because I only pretended to sip, without really sipping. That is the polite way; but when you are ready to go, you empty the beaker at a draught. There was a brass band, and it furnished excellent music every afternoon. Sometimes so many people came that every seat was occupied, every table filled. And never a rough in the assemblage—all nicely dressed fathers and mothers, young gentlemen and ladies and children; and plenty of university students and glittering officers; with here and there a grey professor, or a peaceful old lady with her knitting; and always a sprinkling of gawky foreigners. Everybody had his glass of beer before him, or his cup of coffee, or his bottle of wine, or his hot cutlet and potatoes; young ladies chatted, or fanned themselves, or wrought at their crocheting or embroidering; the students fed sugar to their dogs, or discussed duels, or illustrated new fencing-tricks with their little canes; and everywhere was comfort and enjoyment, and everywhere peace and goodwill to men. The trees were jubilant with birds, and the paths with rollicking children. One could have a seat in that place and plenty of music, any afternoon, for about eight cents or a family ticket for the season for two dollars.

For a change, when you wanted one, you could stroll to the Castle, and burrow among its dungeons, or climb about its ruined towers, or visit its interior shows—the great Heidelberg Tun, for instance. Everybody has heard of the great Heidelberg Tun, and most people have seen it, no doubt. It is a wine-cask as big as a cottage, and some traditions say it holds eighteen hundred thousand bottles, and other traditions say it holds eighteen hundred million barrels. I think it likely that one of these statements is a mistake, and the other one a lie. However, the mere matter of capacity is a thing of no sort of consequence, since the cask is empty, and indeed has always been empty, history says. An empty cask the size of a cathedral could excite but little emotion in me. I do not see any wisdom in building a monster cask to hoard up emptiness in, when you can get a better quality, outside, any day, free of expense. What could this cask have been built for? The more one studies over that, the more uncertain and unhappy he becomes. Some historians say that thirty couples, some say thirty thousand couples, can dance on the head of this cask at the same time. Even this does not seem to me to account for the building of it. It does not even throw light on it. A profound and scholarly Englishman—a specialist—who had made the great Heidelberg Tun his sole study for fifteen years, told me he had at last satisfied himself that the ancients built it to make German cream in. He said that the average German cow yielded from one to two and a half teaspoonfuls of milk, when she was not worked in the plough or the hay waggon more than eighteen or nineteen hours a day. This milk was very sweet and good, and of a beautiful transparent bluish tint; but in order to get cream from it in the most economical way, a peculiar process was necessary. Now he believed that the habit of the ancients was to collect several milkings in a teacup, pour it into the Great Tun, fill up with water, and then skim off the cream from time to time as the needs of the German Empire demanded.

This began to look reasonable. It certainly began to account for the German cream which I had encountered and marvelled over in so many hotels and restaurants. But a thoughts struck me—

'Why did not each dairyman take his own teacup of milk and his own cask of water, and mix them, without making a government matter of it?'

'Where could he get a cask large enough to contain the right proportion of water?'

'Very true.' It was plain that the Englishman had studied the matter from all sides. Still I thought I might catch him on one point; so I asked him why the modern empire did not make the nation's cream in the Heidelberg Tun, instead of leaving it to rot away unused. But he answered as one prepared—

'A patient and diligent examination of the modern German cream has satisfied me that they do not use the Great Tun now, because they have got a *bigger* one hidden away somewhere. Either that is the case, or they empty the spring milkings into the mountain torrents, and then skim the Rhine all summer.'

There is a museum of antiquities in the Castle, and among its most treasured relics are ancient manuscripts connected with German history. There are hundreds of these, and their dates stretch back through many centuries. One of them is a decree signed and sealed by the hand of a successor of Charlemagne in the year 896. A signature made by a hand which vanished out of this life near a thousand years ago is a more impressive thing than even a ruined castle. Luther's wedding-ring was shown me; also a fork belonging to a time anterior to our era, and an early bootjack. And there was a plaster cast of the head of a man who was assassinated about sixty years ago. The stab-wounds in the face were duplicated with unpleasant fidelity. One or two real hairs still remained sticking in the eyebrows of the cast. That trifle seemed to almost change the counterfeit into a corpse.

There are many aged portraits—some valuable, some worthless; some of great interest, some of none at all. I bought a couple—one a gorgeous duke of the olden time, and the other a comely blue-eyed damsel, a princess, may be. I bought them to start a portrait gallery of my ancestors with. I paid a dollar and a half for the duke, and two and a half for the princess. One can lay in ancestors at even cheaper rates than these, in Europe if he will mouse among old picture shops, and look out for chances.

APPENDIX C

The College Prison

It seems that the student may break a good many of the public laws without having to answer to the public authorities. His case must come before the University for trial and punishment. If a policeman catches him in an unlawful act and proceeds to arrest him, the offender proclaims that he is a student, and perhaps shows his matriculation card, whereupon the officer asks for his address, then goes his way, and reports the matter at headquarters. If the offence is one over which the city has no jurisdiction, the authorities report the case officially to the University, and give themselves no further concern about it. The University court send for the student, listen to the evidence, and pronounce judgment. The punishment usually inflicted is imprisonment in the University prison. As I understand it, a student's case is often tried without his being present at all. Then something like this happens: A constable in the service of the University visits the lodgings of the said student, knocks, is invited to come in, does so, and says politely—

'If you please, I am here to conduct you to prison.'

'Ah,' says the student, 'I was not expecting it. What have I been doing?'

'Two weeks ago the public peace had the honour to be disturbed by you.'

'It is true; I had forgotten it. Very well; I have been complained of, tried, and found guilty—is that it?'

'Exactly. You are sentenced to two days' solitary confinement in the college prison, and I am sent to fetch you.

Student. 'Oh, I can't go to-day!'

Officer. 'If you please—why?'

Student. 'Because I've got an engagement.'
Officer. 'To-morrow, then, perhaps?'
Student. 'No, I am going to the opera to-morrow.'
Officer. 'Could you come Friday?'
Student. (Reflectively.) 'Let me see—Friday—Friday. I don't seem to have anything on hand Friday.'
Officer. 'Then, if you please, I will expect you on Friday.'
Student. 'All right, I'll come around Friday.'
Officer. 'Thank you. Good day, sir.'
Student. 'Good day.'

So on Friday the student goes to the prison of his own accord, and is admitted.

It is questionable if the world's criminal history can show a custom more odd than this. Nobody knows, now, how it originated. There have always been many noblemen among the students, and it is presumed that all students are gentlemen; in the old times it was usual to mar the convenience of such folk as little as possible; perhaps this indulgent custom owes its origin to this.

One day I was listening to some conversation upon this subject, when an American student said that for some time he had been under sentence for a slight breach of the peace and had promised the constable that he would presently find an unoccupied day and betake himself to prison. I asked the young gentleman to do me the kindness to go to jail as soon as he conveniently could, so that I might try to get in there and visit him, and see what college-captivity was like. He said he would appoint the very first day he could spare.

His confinement was to endure twenty-four hours. He shortly chose his day, and sent me word. I started immediately. When I reached the University Place, I saw two gentlemen talking together, and as they had portfolios under their arms I judged they were tutors or elderly students; so I asked them in English to show me the college jail. I had learned to take it for granted that anybody in Germany who knows anything knows English, so I had stopped afflicting people with my German. These gentlemen seemed a trifle amused—and a trifle confused, too—but one of them said he would walk around the corner with me and show me the place. He asked me why I wanted to get in there, and I said, to see a friend—and for curiosity. He doubted if I would be admitted, but volunteered to put in a word or two for me with the custodian.

He rang the bell, a door opened, and we stepped into a paved way and then into a small living-room, where we were received by a hearty and good-natured German woman of fifty. She threw up her hands with a surprised 'Ach Gott, Herr Professor!' and exhibited a mighty deference for my new acquaintance. By the sparkle in her eye I judged she was a good deal amused, too. The 'Herr Professor' talked to her in German, and I understood enough of it to know that he was bringing very plausible reasons to bear for admitting me. They were successful. So the Herr Professor received my earnest thanks and departed. The old dame got her keys, took me up two or three flights of stairs, unlocked a door, and we stood in the presence of the criminal. Then she went into a jolly and eager description of all that had occurred downstairs, and what the Herr Professor had said, and so forth and so on. Plainly she regarded it as quite a superior joke that I had waylaid a Professor and employed him in so odd a service. But I wouldn't have done it if I had known he was a Professor; therefore my conscience was not disturbed.

Now the dame left us to ourselves. The cell was not a roomy one; still it was a little larger than an ordinary prison cell. It had a window of good size, iron-grated; a small stove; two wooden chairs; two oaken tables, very old and most elaborately carved with names, mottoes, faces, armorial bearings, etc.—the work of several generations of imprisoned students; and a narrow wooden bedstead with a villainous old straw mattress, but no sheets, pillows, blankets or coverlets—for these the student must furnish at his own cost if he wants . them. There was no carpet, of course. The ceiling was completely covered with names, dates, and monograms, done with candle-smoke. The walls were thickly covered with pictures and portraits (in profile), some done with ink, some with soot, some with a pencil, and some with red, blue, and green chalks; and wherever an inch or two of space had remained between the pictures, the captives had written plaintive verses, or names and dates. I do not think I was ever in a more elaborately frescoed apartment.

Against the wall hung a placard containing the prison laws. I made a note of one or two of these. For instance: The prisoner must pay, for the 'privilege' of entering, a sum equivalent to 20 cents of our money; for the privilege of leaving, when his term has expired, 20 cents; for every day spent in the prison, 12 cents; for fire and light, 12 cents a day. The jailor furnishes coffee, mornings, for a small sum; dinners and suppers may be ordered from outside if the prisoner chooses—and he is allowed to pay for them, too.

Here and there, on the walls, appeared the names of American students, and in one place the American arms and motto were displayed in coloured chalks.

With the help of my friend I translated many of the inscriptions.

Some of them were cheerful, others the reverse. I will give the reader a
few specimens:—

'In my tenth semestre (my best one), I am cast here through the
complaints of others. Let those who follow me take warning.'

'III Tage ohne Grund angeblich aus Neugierde.' Which is to say, he
had a curiosity to know what prison-life was like; so he made a breach
in some law and got three days for it. It is more than likely that he
never had the same curiosity again.

(*Translation.*) 'E. Glinicke, four days for being too eager a
spectator of a row.'

'F. Graf Bismarck—27–29, II, '74.' Which means that Count
Bismarck, son of the great statesman, was a prisoner two days in
1874.

(*Translation.*) 'R. Diergandt—for Love—four days.' Many people
in this world have caught it heavier than that for the same indiscretion.

This one is terse. I translate—

'Four weeks for *misinterpreted gallantry*.'

I wish the sufferer had explained a little more fully. A four weeks'
term is a rather serious matter.

There were many uncomplimentary references, on the walls, to a
certain unpopular college dignitary. One sufferer had got three days
for not saluting him. Another had 'here two days slept and three nights
lain awake,' on account of this same 'Dr. K.' In one place was a
picture of Dr. K. hanging on a gallows.

Here and there, lonesome prisoners had eased the heavy time by
altering the records left by predecessors. Leaving the name standing,
and the date and length of the captivity, they had erased the
description of the misdemeanour, and written in its place, in staring
capitals, 'FOR THEFT!' or 'FOR MURDER!' or some other gaudy
crime. In one place, all by itself, stood this blood-curdling word—
'RACHE!'[1]
There was no name signed, and no date. It was an inscription well
calculated to pique curiosity. One would greatly like to know the
nature of the wrong that had been done, and what sort of vengeance
was wanted, and whether the prisoner ever achieved it or not. But
there was no way of finding out these things.

Occasionally a name was followed simply by the remark, "II days,
for disturbing the peace,' and without comment upon the justice or
injustice of the sentence.

[1] 'Revenge.'

In one place was a hilarious picture of a student of the green-cap corps with a bottle of champagne in each hand; and below was the legend: 'These make an evil fate endurable.'

There were two prison cells, and neither had space left on walls or ceiling for another name or portrait or picture. The inside surfaces of the two doors were completely covered with cartes de visite of former prisoners, ingeniously let into the wood and protected from dirt and injury by glass.

I very much wanted one of the sorry old tables which the prisoners had spent so many years in ornamenting with their pocket knives, but red tape was in the way. The custodian could not sell one without an order from a superior; and that superior would have to get it from *his* superior; and this one would have to get it from a higher one—and so on up and up until the faculty should sit on the matter and deliver final judgment. The system was right, and nobody could find fault with it; but it did not seem justifiable to bother so many people, so I proceeded no further. It might have cost me more than I could afford, anyway; for one of those prison tables, which was at that time in a private museum in Heidelberg, was afterwards sold at auction for two hundred and fifty dollars. It was not worth more than a dollar, or possibly a dollar and a half, before the captive students began their work on it. Persons who saw it at the auction said it was so curiously and wonderfully carved that it was worth the money that was paid for it.

Among the many who have tasted the college prison's dreary hospitality was a lively young fellow from one of the Southern States of America, whose first year's experience of German university life was rather peculiar. The day he arrived in Heidelberg he enrolled his name on the college books, and was so elated with the fact that his dearest hope had found fruition and he was actually a student of the old and renowned university, that he set to work that very night to celebrate the event by a grand lark in company with some other students. In the course of his lark he managed to make a wide breach in one of the university's most stringent laws. Sequel: before noon, next day, he was in the college prison—booked for three months. The twelve long weeks dragged slowly by, and the day of deliverance came at last. A great crowd of sympathising fellow-students received him with a rousing demonstration as he came forth, and of course there was another grand lark—in the course of which he managed to make a wide breach in one of the *city's* most stringent laws. Sequel: before noon, next day, he was safe in the city lock-up—booked for three months. This second tedious captivity drew to an end in the course of time, and again a great crowd of sympathising fellow-students gave him a rousing reception as he came forth; but his delight in his freedom was so boundless that he could not proceed soberly and calmly, but must go hopping and skipping and jumping down the sleety street from sheer excess of joy. Sequel: he slipped and broke his leg, and actually lay in the hospital during the next three months!

When he at last became a free man again, he said he believed he would hunt up a brisker seat of learning; the Heidelberg lectures might be good, but the opportunities of attending them were too rare, the educational process too slow; he said he had come to Europe with the idea that the acquirement of an education was only a matter of time, but if he had averaged the Heidelberg system correctly, it was rather a matter of eternity.

APPENDIX D

The Awful German Language

A little learning makes the whole world kin.—*Proverbs* xxxii 7.

I went often to look at the collection of curiosities in Heidelberg Castle, and one day I surprised the keeper of it with my German. I spoke entirely in that language. He was greatly interested; and after I had talked awhile he said my German was very rare, possibly a 'unique;' and wanted to add it to his museum.

If he had known what it had cost me to acquire my art, he would also have known that it would break any collector to buy it. Harris and I had been hard at work on our German during several weeks at that time, and although we had made good progress, it had been accomplished under great difficulty and annoyance, for three of our teachers had died in the meantime. A person who has not studied German can form no idea what a perplexing language it is.

Surely there is not another language that is so slipshod and systemless, and so slippery and elusive to the grasp. One is washed about in it, hither and hither, in the most helpless way; and when at last he thinks he has captured a rule which offers firm ground to take a rest on amid the general rage and turmoil of the ten parts of speech, he turns over the page and reads, 'Let the pupil make careful note of the following *exceptions*.' He runs his eye down and finds that there are more exceptions to the rule than instances of it. So overboard he goes again, to hunt for another Ararat and find another quicksand. Such has been, and continues to be, my experience. Every time I think I have got one of these four confusing 'cases' where I am master of it, a seemingly insignificant preposition intrudes itself into my sentence, clothed with an awful and unsuspected power, and crumbles the ground from under me. For instance, my book inquires after a certain bird—(it is always inquiring after things which are of no sort of consequence to anybody): 'Where is the bird?' Now the answer to this question—according to the book—is that the bird is waiting in the blacksmith shop on account of the rain. Of course no bird would do that, but then you must stick to the book. Very well, I begin to cipher out the German for that answer. I begin at the wrong end, necessarily, for that is the German idea. I say to myself, '*Regen* (rain) is masculine—or maybe it is feminine—or possibly neuter—it is too much trouble to look, now. Therefore, it is either *der* (the) Regen, or *die* (the) Regen, or *das* (the) Regen, according to which gender it may turn out to be when I look. In the interest of science, I will cipher it out on the hypothesis that it is masculine. Very well—then *the* rain is *der* Regen, if it is simply in the quiescent state of being *mentioned*, without enlargement or discussion—Nominative case; but if this rain is lying around, in a kind of a general way on the ground, it is then definitely located, it is *doing something*—that is, *resting* (which is one of the German grammar's ideas of doing something), and this throws the rain into the Dative case, and makes it *dem* Regen. However, this rain is not resting, but is doing something *actively*—it is falling—to interfere with the bird, likely—and this indicates *movement*—which has the effect of sliding it into the Accusative case and changing *dem* Regen into *den* Regen.' Having completed the grammatical horoscope of this matter, I answer up confidently and state in German that the bird is staying in the blacksmith shop 'wegen (on account of) *den* Regen.' Then the teacher lets me softly down with the remark that whenever the word 'wegen' drops into a sentence, it *always* throws that subject into the *Genitive* case, regardless of consequences—and that therefore this bird stayed in the blacksmith shop 'wegen *des* Regens.'

N.B.—I was informed later, by a higher authority, that there was an 'exception' which permits one to say 'wegen *den* Regen' in certain peculiar and complex circumstances, but that this exception is not extended to anything but rain.

There are ten parts of speech, and they are all troublesome. An average sentence in a German newspaper is a sublime and impressive curiosity; it occupies a quarter of a column; it contains all the ten parts of speech—not in regular order, but mixed; it is built mainly of compound words constructed by the writer on the spot, and not to be found in any dictionary—six or seven words compacted into one, without joint or seam—that is, without hyphens; it treats of fourteen or fifteen different subjects, each enclosed in a parenthesis of its own, with here and there extra parentheses which re-enclose three or four of the minor parentheses, making pens within pens; finally, all the parentheses and re-parentheses are massed together between a couple of king-parentheses, one of which is placed in the first line of the majestic sentence and the other in the middle of the last line of it—*after which comes the* VERB, and you find out for the first time what the man has been talking about; and after the verb—merely by way of ornament, as far as I can make out—the writer shovels in '*haben sind gewesen gehabt haben geworden sein*,' or words to that effect, and the monument is finished. I suppose that this closing hurrah is in the nature of the flourish to a man's signature—not necessary, but pretty. German books are easy enough to read when you hold them before the looking-glass or stand on your head—so as to reverse the construction—but I think that to learn to read and understand a German newspaper is a thing which must always remain an impossibility to a foreigner.

Yet even the German books are not entirely free from attacks of the Parenthesis distemper—though they are usually so mild as to cover only a few lines, and therefore when you at last get down to the verb it carries some meaning to your mind because you are able to remember a good deal of what has gone before.

Now here is a sentence from a popular and excellent German novel—with a slight parenthesis in it. I will make a perfectly literal translation, and throw in the parenthesis-marks and some hyphens for the assistance of the reader—though in the original there are no parenthesis-marks or hyphens, and the reader is left to flounder through to the remote verb the best way he can:—

'But when he, upon the street, the (in-satin-and-silk-covered-now-very-unconstrainedly-after-the-newest-fashion-dressed) government counsellor's wife *met*,' etc., etc.[1]

That is from 'The Old Mamselle's Secret,' by Mrs. Marlitt. And that sentence is constructed upon the most approved German model. You observe how far that verb is from the reader's base of operations; well, in a German newspaper they put their verb away over the next page; and I have heard that sometimes after stringing along on exciting preliminaries and parentheses for a column or two, they get in a hurry and have to go to press without getting to the verb at all. Of course, then, the reader is left in a very exhausted and ignorant state.

We have the Parenthesis disease in our literature, too; and one may see cases of it every day in our books and newspapers; but with us it is

---

[1] Wenn er aber auf der Strasse der in Sammt und Seide gehüllten jetz sehr ungenirt nach der neusten mode gekleideten Regierungsrathin begegnet.'

the mark and sign of an unpractised writer or a cloudy intellect, whereas with the Germans it is doubtless the mark and sign of a practised pen and of the presence of that sort of luminous intellectual fog which stands for clearness among these people. For surely it is *not* clearness—it necessarily can't be clearness. Even a jury would have penetration enough to discover that. A writer's ideas must be a good deal confused, a good deal out of line and sequence, when he starts out to say that a man met a counsellor's wife in the street, and then right in the midst of this so simple undertaking halts these approaching people and makes them stand still until he jots down an inventory of the woman's dress. That is manifestly absurd. It reminds a person of those dentists who secure your instant and breathless interest in a tooth by taking a grip on it with the forceps, and then stand there and drawl through a tedious anecdote before they give the dreaded jerk. Parentheses in literature and dentistry are in bad taste.

The Germans have another kind of parenthesis, which they make by splitting a verb in two and putting half of it at the beginning of an exciting chapter and the *other half* at the end of it. Can anyone conceive of anything more confusing than that? These things are called 'separable verbs.' The German grammar is blistered all over with separable verbs; and the wider the two portions of one of them are spread apart, the better the author of the crime is pleased with his performance. A favourite one is *reiste ab* which means *departed*. Here is an example which I culled from a novel and reduced to English:—

'The trunks being now ready, he DE- after kissing his mother and sisters, and once more pressing to his bosom his adored Gretchen, who, dressed in simple white muslin, with a single tuberose in the ample folds of her rich brown hair, had tottered feebly down the stairs, still pale from the terror and excitement of the past evening, but longing to lay her poor aching head yet once again upon the breast of him whom she loved more dearly than life itself, PARTED.'

However, it is not well to dwell too much on the separable verbs. One is sure to lose his temper early; and if he sticks to the subject, and will not be warned, it will at last either soften his brain or petrify it. Personal pronouns and adjectives are a fruitful nuisance in this language, and should have been left out. For instance, the same sound, *sie*, means *you*, and it means *she*, and it means *her*, and it means *it*, and it means *they*, and it means *them*. Think of the ragged poverty of a language which has to make one word do the work of six—and a poor little weak thing of only three letters at that. But mainly, think of the exasperation of never knowing which of these meanings the speaker is trying to convey. This explains why, whenever a person says *sie* to me, I generally try to kill him, if a stranger.

Now observe the adjective. Here was a case where simplicity would have been an advantage; therefore, for no other reason, the inventor of this language complicated it all he could. When we wish to speak of our 'good friend or friends,' in our enlightened tongue, we stick to the one form and have no trouble or hard feeling about it; but with the German tongue it is different. When a German gets his hands on an adjective, he declines it, and keeps on declining it until the common sense is all declined out of it. It is as bad as Latin. He says, for instance:—

SINGULAR

Nominative—Mein gut*er* Freund, my good friend.
Genitive—Mein*es* gut*en* Freund*es*, of my good friend.
Dative—Mein*em* gut*en* Freund, to my good friend.
Accusative—Mein*en* gut*en* Freund, my good friend.

PLURAL

N.—Mein*e* gut*en* Freund*e*, my good friends.
G.—Mein*er* gut*en* Freund*e*, of my good friends.
D.—Nein*en* gut*en* Freund*en*, to my good friends.
A.—Mein*e* gut*en* Freund*e*, my good friends.

Now let the candidate for the asylum try to memorise those variations, and see how soon he will be elected. One might better go without friends in Germany than take all this trouble about them. I have shown what a bother it is to decline a good (male) friend; well, this is only a third of the work, for there is a variety of new distortions of the adjective to be learned when the object is feminine, and still another when the object is neuter. Now there are more adjectives in this language than there are black cats in Switzerland, and they must all be as elaborately declined as the examples above suggested. Difficult?—troublesome?—these words cannot describe it. I heard a Californian student in Heidelberg say, in one of his calmest moods, that he would rather decline two drinks than one German adjective.

The inventor of the language seems to have taken pleasure in complicating it in every way he could think of. For instance, if one is casually referring to a house, *Haus*, or a horse, *Pferd*, or a dog, *Hund*, he spells these words as I have indicated; but if he is referring to them in the Dative case, he sticks on a foolish and unnecessary *e* and spells them Hause, Pferde, Hunde. So, as an added *e* often signifies the plural, as the *s* does with us, the new student is likely to go on for a month making twins out of a Dative dog before he discovers his mistake; and on the other hand, many a new student who could ill afford loss, has bought and paid for two dogs and only got one of them, because he ignorantly bought that dog in the Dative singular when he really supposed he was talking plural—which left the law on the seller's side, of course, by the strict rules of grammar, and therefore a suit for recovery could not lie.

In German, all the Nouns begin with a capital letter. Now that is a good idea; and a good idea in this language is necessarily conspicuous from its lonesomeness. I consider this capitalising of nouns a good idea, because by reason of it you are almost always able to tell a noun the minute you see it. You fall into error occasionally, because you mistake the name of a person for the name of a thing, and waste a good deal of time trying to dig a meaning out of it. German names almost always do mean something, and this helps to deceive the student. I translated a passage one day, which said that 'the infuriated tigress broke loose and utterly ate up the unfortunate fir-forest' (*Tannenwald*). When I was girding up my loins to doubt this, I found out that Tannenwald, in this instance, was a man's name.

Every noun has a gender, and there is no sense or system in the distribution; so the gender of each must be learned separately and by heart. There is no other way. To do this one has to have a memory like a memorandum book. In German a young lady has no sex, while a turnip has. Think what overwrought reverence that shows for the turnip, and what callous disrespect for the girl. See how it looks in print. I translate this from a conversation in one of the best of the German Sunday-school books:—

Gretchen. 'Wilhelm, where is the turnip?'

Wilhem.. 'She has gone to the kitchen.'

Gretchen. 'Where is the accomplished and beautiful English maiden?'

Wilhelm. 'It has gone to the opera.'

To continue with the German genders: a tree is male, its buds are female, its leaves are neuter; horses are sexless, dogs are male, cats are female—Tom-cats included, of course; a person's mouth, neck, bosom, elbows, fingers, nails, feet, and body are of the male sex, and his head is male or neuter according to the word selected to signify it, and *not* according to the sex of the individual who wears it—for in Germany all the women wear either male heads or sexless ones; a person's nose, lips, shoulders, breast, hands, hips, and toes are of the female sex; and his hair, ears, eye, chin, legs, knees, heart, and conscience haven't any sex at all. The inventor of the language probably got what he knew about a conscience from hearsay.

Now, by the above dissection, the reader will see that in Germany a man may *think* he is a man, but when he comes to look into the matter closely he is bound to have his doubts; he finds that in sober truth he is a most ridiculous mixture; and if he ends by trying to comfort himself with the thought that he can at least depend on a third of this mess as being manly and masculine, the humiliating second thought will quickly remind him that in this respect he is no better off than any woman or cow in the land.

In *the* German it is true that, by some oversight of the inventor of the language, a Woman is a female, but a Wife (*Weib*) is not—which is unfortunate. A wife here has no sex; she is neuter; so, according to the grammar, a fish is *he*, his scales are *she*, but a fish-wife is neither. To describe a wife as sexless may be called under-description; that is bad enough, but over-description is surely worse. A German speaks of an Englishman as the *Engländer*; to change the sex he adds *in*, and that stands for Englishwoman—*Engländerin*. That seems descriptive enough, but still it is not exact enough for a German; so he precedes the word with that article which indicates that the creature to follow is feminine, and writes it down thus: '*Die* Engländer*in*'—which means 'the *she-Englishwoman*.' I consider that that person is over-described.

Well, after the student has learned the sex of a great number of nouns he is still in difficulty, because he finds it impossible to persuade his tongue to refer to things as '*he*' and '*she*,' and '*him*' and '*her*.' which it has been always accustomed to refer to as '*it*.' When he even frames a German sentence in his mind, with the hims and hers in the right places, and then works up his courage to the utterance point, it is no use—the moment he begins to speak his tongue flies the track, and all those laboured males and females come out as '*its*.' And even when he is reading German to himself he always calls those things '*it*,' whereas he ought to read in this way:—

Tale of the Fishwife and Its Sad Fate[1]

It is a bleak Day. Hear the Rain, how he pours, and the Hail, how he rattles; and see the Snow, how he drifts along, and oh, the Mud, how deep he is! Ah, the poor Fishwife, it is stuck fast in the Mire; it has dropped its Basket of Fishes; and its Hands have been cut by the Scales as it seized some of the falling Creatures; and one Scale has even got into its Eye, and it cannot get her out. It opens its Mouth to

---

[1] I capitalise the nouns, in the German (and ancient English) fashion.

cry for Help, but if any Sound comes out of him, alas! he is drowned by the raging of the Storm. And now a Tomcat has got one of the Fishes, and she will surely escape with him. No; she bites off a Fin, she holds her in her Mouth—will she swallow her? No the Fishwife's brave Mother-Dog deserts his Puppies and rescues the Fin; which he eats himself as his Reward. O horror; the Lightning has struck the Fishbasket! he sets him on Fire! See the Flame, how she licks the doomed Utensil with her red and angry Tongue! Now she attacks the helpless Fishwife's Foot—she burns him up all but the big Toe, and even *she* is partly consumed; and still she spreads, still she waves her fiery tongues! She attacks the Fishwife's Leg and destroys *it*; she attacks its Hand and destroys *her*; she attacks its poor worn Garment and destroys *her* also; she attacks its Body and consumes *him*; she wreathes herself about its Heart and *it* is consumed; next about its Breast and in a Moment *she* is a Cinder; now she reaches its Neck—*he* goes; now its Chin—*it* goes; now its Nose—*she* goes. In another moment, except Help come, the Fishwife will be no more! Time presses—is there none to succour and save? Yes! Joy, you! with flying Feet the she-Englishwoman comes! But alas! the generous she-Female is too late! Where how is the fated Fishwife? It has ceased from its Sufferings; it has gone to a better Land; all that is left of it for its loved Ones to lament over is this poor smouldering Ash-heap. Ah, woful, woful Ash-heap! Let us take him up tenderly, reverently, upon the lowly Shovel, and bear him to his long Rest, with the Prayer that when he rises again it will be in a Realm where he will have one good square responsible Sex, and have it all to himself, instead of having a mangy lot of assorted Sexes scattered all over him in Spots.

There, now, the reader can see for himself that this pronoun-business is a very awkward thing for the unaccustomed tongue.

I suppose that in all languages the similarities of look and sound between words which have no similarity in meaning are a fruitful source of perplexity to the foreigner. It is so in our tongue, and it is notably the case in the German. Now there is that troublesome word *vermählt*: to me it has so close a resemblance—either real or fancied—to three or four other words, that I never know whether it means despised, painted, suspected, or married, until I look in the dictionary, and then I find it means the latter. There are lots of such words, and they are a great torment. To increase the difficulty there are words which *seem* to resemble each other, and yet do not; but they make just as much trouble as if they did. For instance, there is the word *vermiethen* (to let, to lease, to hire), and the word *verheirathen* (another way of saying to *marry*). I heard of an

Englishman who knocked at a man's door in Heidelberg and proposed, in the best German he could command, to 'verheirathen' that house. Then there are some words which mean one thing when you emphasise the first syllable, but mean something very different if you throw the emphasis on the last syllable. For instance, there is a word which means a runaway, or the act of glancing through a book, according to the placing of the emphasis; and another word which signifies to *associate* with a man, or to *avoid* him, according to where you put the emphasis—and you can generally depend on putting it in the wrong place and getting into trouble.

There are some exceedingly useful words in this language: *Schlag*, for example, and *Zug*. There are three-quarters of a column of Schlags in the dictionary, and a column and a half of Zugs. The word Schlag means Blow, Stroke, Dash, Hit, Shock, Clap, Slap, Time, Bar, Coin, Stamp, Kind, Sort, Manner, Way, Apoplexy, Wood-cutting, Enclosure, Field, Forest-clearing. This is its simple and *exact* meaning—that is to say, its restricted, its fettered meaning; but there are ways by which you can set it free, so that it can soar away, as on the wings of the morning, and never be at rest. You can hang any word you please to its tail, and make it mean anything you want to. You can begin with *Schlag-ader*, which means artery, and you can hang on the whole dictionary, word by word, clear through the alphabet, to *Schlag-wasser*, which means bilge-water, and including *Schlag-mutter*, which means mother-in-law.

Just the same with *Zug*. Strictly speaking, Zug means Pull, Tug, Draught, Procession, March, Progress, Flight, Direction, Expedition, Train, Caravan, Passage, Stroke, Touch, Line, Flourish, Trait of Character, Feature, Lineament, Chess-move, Organ-stop, Team, Whiff, Bias, Drawer, Propensity, Inhalation, Disposition; but that thing which it does *not* mean, when all its legitimate pendants have been hung on, has not been discovered yet.

One cannot over-estimate the usefulness of Schlag and Zug. Armed just with these two, and the word *Also*, what cannot the foreigner on German soil accomplish? The German word *Also* is the equivalent of the English phrase 'You know,' and does not mean anything at all—in *talk*, though it sometimes does in print. Every time a German opens his mouth an *Also* falls out; and every time he shuts it he bites one in two that was trying to *get* out.

Now, the foreigner, equipped with these three noble words, is master of the situation. Let him talk right along, fearlessly; let him pour his indifferent German forth, and when he lacks for a word, let him heave a *Schlag* into the vacuum: all the chances are, that it fits it

like a plug; but if it doesn't, let him promptly heave a *Zug* after it; the
two together can hardly fail to bung the hole; but if, by a miracle, they
should fail, let him simply say *Also!* and this will give him a moment's
chance to think of the needful word. In Germany when you load your
conversational gun it is always best to throw in a *Schlag* or two and a
Zug or two; because it doesn't make any difference how much the rest
of the charge may scatter, you are bound to bag something with *them*.
Then you blandly say *Also* and load up again. Nothing gives such an
air of grace and elegance and unconstraint to a German or an English
conversation as to scatter it full of 'Also's' or 'You knows.'
   In my note-book I find this entry:—

July 1.—In the hospital, yesterday, a word of thirteen syllables was
successfully removed from a patient—a North-German from near Hamburg;
but as most unfortunately the surgeons had opened him in the wrong place,
under the impression that he contained a panorama, he died. The sad event
has cast a gloom over the whole community.

That paragraph furnishes a text for a few remarks about one of the
most curious and notable features of my subject—the length of
German words. Some German words are so long that they have a
perspective. Observe these examples:—
   Freundschaftsbezeigungen.
   Dilletantenaufdringlichkeiten.
   Stadtverordnetenversammlungen.
   These things are not words, they are alphabetical processions. And
they are not rare; one can open a German newspaper any time and see
them marching majestically across the page—and if he has any
imagination he can see the banners and hear the music, too. They
impart a martial thrill to the meekest subject. I take a great interest in
these curiosities. Whenever I come across a good one. I stuff it and
put it in my museum. In this way I have made quite a valuable
collection. When I get duplicates, I exchange with other collectors,
and thus increase the variety of my stock. Here are some specimens
which I lately bought at an auction sale of the effects of a bankrupt bric-
à-brac hunter:—
   GENERALSTAATSVERORDNETENVERSAMMLUNGEN.
   ALTERTHUMSWISSENSCHAFTEN.
   KINDERBEWAHRUNGSANSTALTEN.
   UNABHAENGIGKEITSERKLAERUNGEN.
   WIEDERHERSTELLUNGSBESTREBUNGEN.
   WAFFENSTILLSTANDSUNTERHANDLUNGEN.
Of course when one of these grand mountain ranges goes stretching

across the printed page, it adorns and ennobles that literary landscape—but at the same time it is a great distress to the new student, for it blocks up his way; he cannot crawl under it, or climb over it, or tunnel through it. So he resorts to the dictionary for help; but there is no help there. The dictionary must draw the line somewhere—so it leaves this sort of words out. And it is right, because these long things are hardly legitimate words, but are rather combinations of words, and the inventor of them ought to have been killed. They are compound words, with the hyphens left out. The various words used in building them are in the dictionary, but in a very scattered condition so you can hunt the materials out, one by one, and get at the meaning at last, but it is a tedious and harassing business. I have tried this process upon some of the above examples. 'Freundschaftsbezeigungen' seems to be 'Friendshipdemonstrations,' which is only a foolish and clumsy way of saying 'demonstrations of friendship.' 'Unabhaengigkeitserklaerungen' seems to be 'Independencedeclarations,' which is no improvement upon 'Declarations of Independence,' as far as I can see. 'Generalstaatsverordnetenversammlungen' seems to be 'Generalstatesrepresentatives-meetings,' as nearly as I can get at it—a mere rhythmical, gushy euphuism for 'meeting of the legislature,' I judge. We used to have a good deal of this sort of crime in our literature, but it has gone out now. We used to speak of a thing as a 'never-to-be-forgotten' circumstance, instead of cramping it into the simple and sufficient word 'memorable,' and then going calmly about our business as if nothing had happened. In those days we were not content to embalm the thing and bury it decently, we wanted to build a monument over it.

But in our newspapers the compounding-disease lingers a little to the present day, but with the hyphens left out, in the German fashion. This is the shape it takes: instead of saying 'Mr. Simmons, clerk of the county and district courts, was in town yesterday,' the new form puts it thus: 'Clerk of the County and District Court Simmons was in town yesterday.' This saves neither time nor ink, and has an awkward sound besides. One often sees a remark like this in our papers: '*Mrs.* Assistant District Attorney Johnson returned to her city residence yesterday for the season.' That is a case of really unjustifiable compounding; because it not only saves no time or trouble, but confers a title on Mrs. Johnson which she has no right to. But these little instances are trifles indeed, contrasted with the ponderous and dismal German system of piling jumbled compounds together. I wish to submit the following local item, from a Mannheim journal, by way of illustration:—

'In the daybeforeyesterdayshortlyaftereleveno'clock Night, the inthistownstandingtavern called "The Waggoner" was downburnt. When the fire to the onthedownburninghouseresting Stork's Nest reached, flew the parent Storks away. But when the bytheraging, fire-surrounded Nest *itself* caught Fire, straighway plunged the quick-returning Mother-Stork into the Flames and died, her Wings over her young ones outspread.'

Even the cumbersome German construction is not able to take the pathos out of that picture—indeed it somehow seems to strengthen it. This item is dated away back yonder months ago. I could have used it sooner, but I was waiting to hear from the Father-Stork. I am still waiting.

'*Also!*' If I have not shown that the German is a difficult language, I have at least intended to do it. I have heard of an American student who was asked how he was getting along with his German, and who answered promptly: 'I am not getting along at all. I have worked at it hard for three level months, and all I have got to show for it is one solitary German phrase—"*Zwei glas*" ' (two glasses of beer). He paused a moment, reflectively, then added with feeling, 'But I have got that *solid*!'

And if I have not also shown that German is a harassing and infuriating study, my execution has been at fault, and not my intent. I heard lately of a worn and sorely tried American student who used to fly to a certain German word for relief when he could bear up under his aggravations no longer—the only word in the whole language whose sound was sweet and precious to his ear and healing to his lacerated spirit. This was the word *Damit*. It was only the *sound* that helped him, not the meaning;[1] and so, at last, when he learned that the emphasis was not on the first syllable, his only stay and support was gone, and he faded away and died.

I think that a description of any loud, stirring, tumultuous episode must be tamer in German than in English. Our descriptive words of this character have such a deep, strong, resonant sound, while their German equivalents do seem so thin and mild and energyless. Boom, burst, crash, roar, storm, bellow, blow, thunder, explosion; howl, cry, shout, yell, groan; battle, hell. These are magnificent words; they have a force and magnitude of sound befitting the things which they describe. But their German equivalents would be ever so nice to sing the children to sleep with, or else my awe-inspiring ears were made for display and not for superior usefulness in analysing sounds. Would

---

[1] It merely means, in its general sense, '*herewith*.'

any man want to die in a battle which was called by so tame a term as a *Schlacht*? Or would not a consumptive feel too much bundled up, who was about to go out, in a shirt collar and a seal ring, into a storm which the bird-song word *Gewitter* was employed to describe? And observe the strongest of the several German equivalents for explosion—*Ausbruch*. Our word Toothbrush is more powerful than that. It seems to me that the Germans could do worse than import it into their language to describe particularly tremendous explosions with. The German word for hell—Hölle—sounds more like *helly* than anything else; therefore, how necessarily chipper, frivolous, and unimpressive it is. If a man were told in German to go there, could he really rise to the dignity of feeling insulted?

Having now pointed out, in detail, the several vices of this language, I now come to the brief and pleasant task of pointing out its virtues. The capitalising of the nouns I have already mentioned. But far before this virtue stands another—that of spelling a word according to the sound of it. After one short lesson in the alphabet, the student can tell how any German word is pronounced, without having to ask; whereas in our language if a student should inquire of us 'What does B, O, W, spell?' we should be obliged to reply, 'Nobody can tell what it spells, when you set it off by itself—you can only tell by referring to the context and finding out what it signifies—whether it is a thing to shoot arrows with, or a nod of one's head, or the forward end of a boat.'

There are some German words which are singularly and powerfully effective. For instance, those which describe lowly, peaceful, and affectionate home life; those which deal with love, in any and all forms, from mere kindly feeling and honest good will toward the passing stranger, clear up to courtship; those which deal with outdoor Nature, in its softest and loveliest aspects—with meadows and forests, and birds and flowers, the fragrance and sunshine of summer, and the moonlight of peaceful winter nights; in a word, those which deal with any and all forms of rest, repose, and peace; those also which deal with the creatures and marvels of fairyland; and lastly and chiefly, in those words which express pathos, is the language surpassingly rich and effective. There are German songs which can make a stranger to the language cry. That shows that the *sound* of the words is correct—it interprets the meanings with truth and with exactness; and so the ear is informed, and through the ear, the heart.

The Germans do not seem to be afraid to repeat a word when it is the right one. They repeat it several times, if they choose. That is wise. But in English when we have used a word a couple of times in a paragraph, we imagine we are growing tautological, and so we are weak enough to exchange it for some other word which only approximates exactness, to escape what we wrongly fancy is a greater blemish. Repetition may be bad, but surely inexactness is worse.

There are people in the world who will take a great deal of trouble to point out the faults in a religion or a language, and then go gladly about their business without suggesting any remedy. I am not that kind of a person. I have shown that the German language needs reforming. Very well, I am ready to reform it. At least I am ready to make the proper suggestions. Such a course as this might be immodest in another; but I have devoted upwards of nine full weeks, first and last, to a careful and critical study of this tongue, and thus have acquired a confidence in my ability to reform it which no mere superficial culture could have conferred upon me.

In the first place, I would leave out the Dative Case. It confuses the plurals; and besides, nobody ever knows when he is in the Dative Case, except he discover it by accident—and then he does not know when or where it was that he got into it, or how long he has been in it, or how he is ever going to get out of it again. The Dative Case is but an ornamental folly—it is better to discard it.

In the next place, I would move the Verb further up to the front. You may load up with ever so good a Verb, but I notice that you never really bring down a subject with it at the present German range—you only cripple it. So I insist that this important part of speech should be brought forward to a position where it may be easily seen with the naked eye.

Thirdly, I would import some strong words from the English tongue—to swear with, and also to use in describing all sorts of vigorous things in a vigorous way.[1]

Fourthly, I would reorganise the sexes, and distribute them

---

[1] '*Verdammt,*' and its variations and enlargements, are words which have plenty of meaning, but the *sounds* are so mild and ineffectual that German ladies can use them without sin. German ladies who could not be induced to commit a sin by any persuasion or compulsion, promptly rip out one of these harmless little words when they tear their dresses or don't like the soup. It sounds about as wicked as our 'My gracious!' German ladies are constantly saying, 'Ach! Gott!' 'Mein Gott!' 'Gott in Himmel!' 'Herr Gott!' 'Der Herr Jesus!' etc. They think our ladies have the same custom perhaps, for I once heard a gentle and lovely old German lady say to a sweet young American girl, 'The two languages are so alike—how pleasant that is; we say, "Ach! Gott!" you say, "*Goddam.*" '

according to the will of the Creator. This as a tribute of respect, if nothing else.

Fifthly, I would do away with those great long compounded words; or require the speaker to deliver them in sections, with intermissions for refreshments. To wholly do away with them would be best, for ideas are more easily received and digested when they come one at a time than when they come in bulk. Intellectual food is like any other; it is pleasanter and more beneficial to take it with a spoon than with a shovel.

Sixthly, I would require a speaker to stop when he is done, and not hang a string of those useless 'haben sind gewesen gehabt haben geworden seins' to the end of his oration. This sort of gew-gaws undignify a speech, instead of adding a grace. They are therefore an offence, and should be discarded.

Seventhly, I would discard the Parenthesis. Also the re-Parenthesis, the re-re-parenthesis, and the re-re-re-re-re-re-parenthesis, and likewise the final wide-reaching all-enclosing King-parenthesis. I would require every individual, be he high or low, to unfold a plain straightforward tale, or else coil it and sit on it and hold his peace. Infractions of this law should be punishable with death.

And eighthly and lastly, I would retain *Zug* and *Schlag* with their pendants, and discard the rest of the vocabulary. This would simplify the language.

I have now named what I regard as the most necessary and important changes. These are perhaps all I could be expected to name for nothing; but there are other suggestions which I can and will make in case my proposed application shall result in my being formally employed by the government in the work of reforming the language.

My philological studies have satisfied me that a gifted person ought to learn English (barring spelling and pronouncing) in 30 hours, French in 30 days, and German in 30 years. It seems manifest, then, that the latter tongue ought to be trimmed down and repaired. If it is to remain as it is, it ought to be gently and reverently set aside among the dead languages, for only the dead have time to learn it.

A FOURTH OF JULY ORATION IN THE GERMAN TONGUE, DELIVERED AT A BANQUET OF THE ANGLO-AMERICAN CLUB OF STUDENTS BY THE AUTHOR OF THIS BOOK.

GENTLEMEN: Since I arrived, a month ago, in this old wonderland, this vast garden of Germany, my English tongue has so often proved a useless piece of baggage to me, and so troublesome to carry around, in a country where they haven't the checking system for luggage, that I finally set to work, last week, and learned the German language. Also! Es freut mich dass dies so ist, denn es muss, in ein hauptsächlich degree, höflich sein, dass man auf ein occasion like this, sein Rede in die Sprache des Landes worin he boards, aussprechen soll. Dafür habe ich, aus reinische Verlegenheit—no, Vergangenheit—no, I mean Höflichkeit—aus reinische Höflichkeit have ich resolved to tackle this business in the German language, um Gottes willen! Also! Sie müssen so freundlich sein, und verzeih mich die interlarding von ein oder zwei Englischer Worte, hie und da, denn ich finde dass die deutsche is not a very copius language, and so when you've really got anything to say, you've got to draw on a language that can stand the strain.

Wenn aber man kann nicht meinem Rede verstehen, so werde ich ihm später dasselbe übersetz, wenn er solche Dienst verlangen wolien haben werden sollen sein hätte. (I don't know what wollen haben werden sollen sein hätte means, but I notice they always put it at the end of a German sentence—merely for general literary gorgeousness, I suppose.)

This is a great and justly honoured day—a day which is worthy of the veneration in which it is held by the true patriots of all climes and nationalities—a day which offers a fruitful theme for thought and speech; und meinem Freunde—no, mei*nen* Freund*en*—mei*nes* Freund*es*—well, take your choice, they're all the same price; I don't know which one is right—also! ich have gehabt haben worden gewesen sein, as Goethe says, in his Paradise Lost—ich—ich—that is to say—ich—but let us change cars.

Also! Die Anblick so viele Grossbrittanischer und Amerikanischer hier zusammengetroffen in Bruderliche concord, ist zwar a welcome and inspiriting spectacle. And what has moved you to it? Can the terse German tongue rise to the expression of this impulse? Is it Freundschafts-bezeigungenstadtverordnetenversammlungenfamilien-eigenthümlichkeitem? Nein, o nein! This is a crisp and noble word, but it fails to pierce the marrow of the impulse which has gathered this friendly meeting and produced diese Anblick—eine Anblick welche ist gut zu sehen—gut für die Augen in a foreign land and a far country— eine Anblick solche als in die gewönliche Heidelberger phrase nennt man ein 'schönes Aussicht!' Ja, freilich natürlich wahrscheinlich ebensowohl! Also! Die Aussicht auf dem Königstuhl mehr grösserer ist, aber geistlische sprechend nicht so schön, lob' Gott! Because sie sind hier zusammengetroffen, in Bruderlichem concord, ein grossen

Tag zu feiern, whose high benefits were not for one land and one locality only, but have conferred a measure of good upon all lands that know liberty to-day, and love it. Hundert Jahre vorüber, waren die Engländer und die Amerikaner Feinde; aber heute sind sie herzlichen Freunde, Gott sei Dank! May this good fellowship endure; may these banners here blended in amity, so remain; may they never any more wave over opposing hosts, or be stained with blood which was kindred, is kindred, and always will be kindred, until a line drawn upon a map shall be able to say, '*This* bars the ancestral blood from flowing in the veins of the descendant!'

APPENDIX E

Legend of the Castles

CALLED THE 'SWALLOW'S NEST' AND 'THE BROTHER,' AS CONDENSED FROM THE CAPTAIN'S TALE

In the neighbourhood of three hundred years ago the Swallow's Nest and the larger castle between it and Neckarsteinach were owned and occupied by two old knights who were twin brothers, and bachelors. They had no relatives. They were very rich. They had fought through the wars and retired to private life—covered with honourable scars. They were honest, honourable men in their dealings, but the people had given them a couple of nicknames which were very suggestive—Herr Givenaught and Herr Heartless. The old knights were so proud of these names that if a burgher called them by their right ones they would correct him.

The most renowned scholar in Europe, at that time, was the Herr Doctor Franz Reikmann, who lived in Heidelberg. All Germany was proud of the venerable scholar, who lived in the simplest way, for great scholars are always poor. He was poor, as to money, but very rich in his sweet young daughter Hildegarde and his library. He had been all his life collecting his library, book by book, and he loved it as a miser loves his hoarded gold. He said the two strings of his heart were rooted, the one in his daughter, the other in his books; and that if either were severed he must die. Now in an evil hour, hoping to win a marriage portion for his child, this simple old man had entrusted his small savings to a sharper to be ventured in a glittering speculation. But that was not the worst of it: he signed a paper—without reading it. That is the way with poets and scholars, they always sign without reading. The result was, that one night he found himself in debt to the sharper eight thousand pieces of gold!—an amount so prodigious that it simply stupefied him to think of it. It was a night of woe in that house.

'I must part with my library—I have nothing else. So perishes one heartstring,' said the old man.

'What will it bring, father?' asked the girl.

'Nothing! It is worth seven hundred pieces of gold; but by auction it will go for little or nothing.'

'Then you will have parted with the half of your heart and the joy of your life to no purpose, since so mighty a burden of debt will remain behind.'

'There is no help for it, my child. Our darlings must pass under the hammer. We must pay what we can.'

'My father, I have a feeling that the dear Virgin will come to our help. Let us not lose heart.'

'She cannot devise a miracle that will turn *nothing* into eight thousand gold pieces, and lesser help will bring us little peace.'

'She can do even greater things, my father. She will save us, I know she will.'

Toward morning, while the old man sat exhausted and asleep in his chair where he had been sitting before his books as one who watches by his beloved dead and prints the features on his memory for a solace in the aftertime of empty desolation, his daughter sprang into the room and gently woke him, saying—

'My presentiment was true! She will save us. Three times has she appeared to me in my dreams, and said, "Go to the Herr Givenaught, go to the Herr Heartless, ask them to come and bid." There, did I not tell you she would save us, the thrice blessed Virgin!'

Sad as the old man was, he was obliged to laugh.

'Thou mightest as well appeal to the rocks their castles stand upon as to the harder ones that lie in those men's breasts, my child. *They* bid on books writ in the legend tongues!—they can scarce read their own.'

But Hildegarde's faith was in no wise shaken. Bright and early she was on her way up the Neckar road, as joyous as a bird.

Meantime Herr Givenaught and Herr Heartless were having an early breakfast in the former's castle—the Sparrow's Nest—and flavouring it with a quarrel; for although these twins bore a love for each other which almost amounted to worship, there was one subject upon which they could not touch without calling each other hard names—and yet it was the subject which they oftenest touched upon.

'I tell you,' said Givenaught, 'you will beggar yourself yet, with your insane squanderings of money upon what you choose to consider poor and worthy objects. All these years I have implored you to stop this foolish custom and husband your means, but all in vain. You are always lying to me about these secret benevolences, but you never have managed to deceive me yet. Every time a poor devil has been set upon his feet I have detected your hand in it—incorrigible ass!'

'Every time you didn't set him on his feet yourself, you mean. Where I give one unfortunate a little private lift, you do the same for a dozen. The idea of *your* swelling around the country and petting yourself with the nickname of Givenaught—intolerable humbug! Before I would be such a fraud as that, I would cut my right hand off. Your life is a continual lie. But go on, I have tried *my* best to save you from beggaring yourself by your riotous charities—now for the thousandth time I wash my hands of the consequences. A maundering old fool! that's what you are.'

'And you a blethering old idiot!' roared Givenaught, springing up.

'I won't stay in the presence of a man who has no more delicacy than to call me such names. Mannerless swine!'

So saying, Herr Heartless sprang up, in a passion. But some lucky accident intervened, as usual, to change the subject, and the daily quarrel ended in the customary daily loving reconciliation. The grey-headed old eccentrics parted, and Herr Heartless walked off to his own castle.

Half an hour later, Hildegarde was standing in the presence of Herr Givenaught. He heard her story, and said:—

'I am sorry for you, my child, but I am very poor; I care nothing for bookish rubbish, I shall not be there.'

He said the hard words kindly, but they nearly broke poor Hildegarde's heart, nevertheless. When she was gone the old heart-breaker muttered, rubbing his hands,—

'It was a good stroke. I have saved my brother's pocket this time in spite of him. Nothing else would have prevented his rushing off to rescue the old scholar, the pride of Germany, from his troubles. The poor child won't venture near *him* after the rebuff she has received from his brother, the Givenaught.'

But he was mistaken. The Virgin had commanded, and Hildegarde would obey. She went to Herr Heartless and told her story. But he said coldly,—

'I am very poor, my child, and books are nothing to me. I wish you well, but I shall not come.'

When Hildegarde was gone, he chuckled and said,—

'How my fool of a soft-headed soft-hearted brother would rage if he knew how cunningly I have saved his pocket. How he would have flown to the old man's rescue! But the girl won't venture near him now.'

When Hildegarde reached home, her father asked her how she had prospered. She said,—

'The Virgin has promised, and she will keep her word; but not in the way I thought. She knows her own ways, and they are best.'

The old man patted her on the head, and smiled a doubting smile, but he honoured her for her brave faith, nevertheless.

II

Next day the people assembled in the great hall of the Ritter tavern, to witness the auction—for the proprietor had said the treasure of Germany's most honoured son should be bartered away in no meaner place. Hildegarde and her father sat close to the books, silent and sorrowful, and holding each other's hands. There was a great crowd of people present. The bidding began:—

'How much for this precious library, just as it stands, all complete?' called the auctioneer.

'Fifty pieces of gold!'

'A hundred!'

'Two hundred!'

'Three!'

'Four!'

'Five hundred!'

'Five twenty-five!'

A brief pause.

'Five forty!'

A longer pause, while the auctioneer redoubled his persuasions.

'Five forty-five!'

A heavy drag—the auctioneer persuaded, pleaded, implored—it was useless, everybody remained silent:—

'Well, then—going, going—one—two—'

'Five hundred and fifty!'

This in a shrill voice, from a bent old man, all hung with rags, and with a green patch over his left eye. Everybody in the vicinity turned and gazed at him. It was Givenaught in disguise. He was using a disguised voice, too.

'Good!' cried the auctioneer. 'Going, going—one—two,'

'Five hundred and sixty!'

This in a deep harsh voice, from the midst of the crowd at the other end of the room. The people near by turned, and saw an old man, in a strange costume, supporting himself on crutches. He wore a long white beard, and blue spectacles. It was Herr Heartless, in disguise, and using a disguised voice.

'Good again! Going, going—one—'

'Six hundred!'

Sensation. The crowd raised a cheer, and some one cried out, 'Go it, Green-patch!' This tickled the audience and a score of voices shouted, 'Go it, Green-patch!'

'Gling—going—going—third and last call—one, two—'

'Seven hundred!'

'Huzzah!—well done, Crutches!' cried a voice. The crowd took it up, and shouted all together, 'Well done, Crutches!'

'Splendid, gentlemen! you are doing magnificently. Going, going—'

'A thousand!'

'Three cheers for Green-patch! Up and at him, Crutches!'

'Going—going—'

'Two thousand!'

And while the people cheered and shouted, 'Crutches' muttered, 'Who can this devil be, that is fighting so to get these useless books?—But no matter, he shan't have them. The pride of Germany shall have his books if it beggars me to buy them for him.'

'Going, going, going—'

'Three thousand!'

'Come, everybody—give a rouser for Green-patch!'

And while they did it, Green-patch muttered, 'This cripple is plainly a lunatic; but the old scholar shall have his books, nevertheless, though my pocket sweat for it.'

'Going—going—'

'Four thousand!'

'Huzza!'

'Five thousand!'

'Huzza!'

'Six thousand!'

'Huzza!'

'Seven thousand!'

'Huzza!'

'*Eight* thousand!'

'We are saved, father! I told you the Holy Virgin would keep her word!' 'Blessed be her sacred name!' said the old scholar, with emotion. The crowd roared, 'Huzza, huzza, huzza—at him again Green-patch!'

'Going—going—'

'TEN thousand!' As Givenaught shouted this, his excitement was so great that he forgot himself and used his natural voice. His brother recognised it, and muttered, under cover of the storm of cheers—

'Aha, you are there, are you, besotted old fool? Take the books, I know what you'll do with them.'

So saying, he slipped out of the place, and the auction was at an end. Givenaught shouldered his way to Hildegarde, whispered a word in her ear, and then he, also, vanished. The old scholar and his daughter embraced, and the former said, 'Truly the Holy Mother has done more than she promised, child, for she has given you a splendid marriage portion—think of it, two thousand pieces of gold!'

'And more still,' cried Hildegarde, 'for she has given you back your books; the stranger whispered me that he would none of them—"the honoured son of Germany must keep them," so he said. I would I might have asked his name and kissed his hand and begged his blessing; but he was Our Lady's angel, and it is not meet that we of earth should venture speech with them that dwell above.'

APPENDIX F

German Journals

The daily journals of Hamburg, Frankfort, Baden, Munich, and Augsburg, are all constructed on the same general plan. I speak of these because I am more familiar with them than with any other German papers. They contain no 'editorials' whatever; no 'personals'—and this is rather a merit than a demerit, perhaps; no funny-paragraph column; no police court reports; no reports of proceedings of higher courts; no information about prize fights or other dog fights, horse races, walking matches, yachting contests, rifle matches, or other sporting matters of any sort; no reports of banquet speeches; no department of curious odds and ends of floating fact and gossip; no 'rumours' about anything or anybody; no prognostications or prophecies about anything or anybody; no lists of patents granted or sought, or any reference to such things; no abuse of public officials, big or little, or complaints against them, or praises of them; no religious column Saturdays, no re-hash of cold semons Mondays; no 'weather indications;' no 'local item' unveilings of what is happening in town—nothing of a local nature, indeed, is mentioned, beyond the movements of some prince or the proposed meeting of some deliberative body.

After so formidable a list of what one can't find in a German daily, the question may well be asked, What *can* be found in it? It is easily answered: A child's handful of telegrams, mainly about European national and international political movements; letter-correspondence about the same things; market reports. There you have it. That is what a German daily is made of. A German daily is the slowest and saddest and dreariest of the inventions of man. Our own dailies infuriate the reader pretty often; the German daily only stupefies him. Once a week the German daily of the highest class lightens up its heavy columns—that is, it thinks it lightens them up—with a profound, an abysmal, book criticism; a criticism which carries you down, down, down, into the scientific bowels of the subject—for the German critic is nothing if not scientific—and when you come up at last and scent the fresh air and see the bonny daylight once more, you resolve without a dissenting voice that a book-criticism is a mistaken way to lighten up a German daily. Sometimes, in place of the criticism, the first-class daily gives you what it thinks is a gay and chipper essay—about ancient Grecian funeral customs, or the ancient Egyptian method of tarring a mummy, or the reasons for believing that some of the peoples who existed before the flood did not approve of cats. These are not unpleasant subjects; they are not uninteresting subjects; they are even exciting subjects—until one of these massive scientists gets hold of them. He soon convinces you that even these matters can be handled in such a way as to make a person low-spirited.

As I have said, the average German daily is made up solely of correspondence—a trifle of it by telegraph, the rest of it by mail. Every paragraph has the side-head, 'London,' 'Vienna,' or some other town, and a date. And always, before the name of the town, is placed a letter or a sign, to indicate who the correspondent is, so that the authorities can find him when they want to hang him. Stars, crosses, triangles, squares, half-moons, suns—such are some of the signs used by correspondents.

Some of the dailies move too fast, others too slowly. For instance, my Heidelberg daily was always twenty-four hours old when it arrived at the hotel; but one of my Munich evening papers used to come a full twenty-four hours before it was due.

Some of the less important dailies give one a tablespoonful of a continued story every day; it is strung across the bottom of the page, in the French fashion. By subscribing for the paper for five years I judge that a man might succeed in getting pretty much all of the story.

If you ask a citizen of Munich which is the best Munich daily journal he will always tell you that there is only one good Munich daily, and that it is published in Augsburg, forty or fifty miles away. It is like saying that the best daily paper in New York is published out in New Jersey somewhere. Yes, the Augsburg 'Allgemeine Zeitung' is 'the best Munich paper,' and it is the one I had in my mind when I was describing a 'first-class German daily' above. The entire paper, opened out, is not quite as large as a single page of the 'New York Herald.' It is printed on both sides of course; but in such large type that its entire contents could be put, in 'Herald' type, upon a single page of the 'Herald'—and there would still be room enough on the page for the 'Zeitung's' Supplement and some portion of the 'Zeitung's' next day's contents.

Such is the first-class daily. The dailies actually printed in Munich are all called second-class by the public. If you ask which is the best of these second-class papers they say there is no difference, one is as good as another. I have preserved a copy of one of them; it is called the 'Münchener Tages-Anzeiger,' and bears date January 25, 1879. Comparisons are odious, but they need not be malicious; and without any malice I wish to compare this journal, published in a German city of 170,000 inhabitants, with journals of other countries. I know of no other way to enable the reader to 'size' the thing.

A column of an average daily paper in America contains from 1,800 to 2,500 words; the reading matter in a single issue consists of from 25,000 to 50,000 words. The reading matter in my copy of the Munich journal consists of a total of 1,654 words—for I counted them. That would be nearly a column of one of our dailies. A single issue of the bulkiest daily newspaper in the world—the London 'Times'—often contains 100,000 words of reading matter. Considering that the 'Daily Anzeiger' issues the usual twenty-six numbers per month, the reading matter in a single number of the London 'Times' would keep it in 'copy' two months and a half!

The 'Anzeiger' is an eight-page paper; its page is one inch wider and one inch longer than a foolscap page; that is to say, the dimensions of its page are somewhere between those of a schoolboy's slate and a lady's pocket-handkerchief. One fourth of the first page is taken up with the heading of the journal; this gives it a rather topheavy appearance; the rest of the first page is reading matter; all of the second page is reading matter; the other six pages are devoted to advertisements.

The reading matter is compressed into two hundred and five small-pica lines, and is lighted up with eight pica head-lines. The bill of fare is as follows: First, under a pica head-line to enforce attention and respect, is a four-line sermon urging mankind to remember that although they are pilgrims here below, they are yet heirs of heaven; and that 'When they depart from earth they soar to heaven.' Perhaps a four-line sermon in a Saturday paper is the sufficient German equivalent of the eight or ten columns of sermons which the New Yorkers get in their Monday morning papers. The latest news (two days old) follows the four-line sermon, under the pica head-line 'Telegrams'—these are 'telegraphed' with a pair of scissors out of the

'Augsburger Zeitung' of the day before. These telegrams consist of fourteen and two-thirds lines from Berlin, fifteen lines from Vienna, and two and five-eighths lines from Calcutta. Thirty-three small pica lines of telegraphic news in a daily journal in a King's Capital of 170,000 inhabitants, is surely not an overdose. Next, we have the pica heading, 'News of the Day,' under which the following facts are set forth: Prince Leopold is going on a visit to Vienna, six lines; Prince Arnulph is coming back from Russia, two lines; the Landtag will meet at ten o'clock in the morning and consider an election law, three lines and one word over; a city government item, five and one half lines; prices of tickets to the proposed grand Charity Ball, twenty-three lines—for this one item occupies almost one fourth of the entire first page; there is to be a wonderful Wagner concert in Frankfort-on-the-Main, with an orchestra of one hundred and eight instruments, seven and one half lines. That concludes the first page. Eighty-five lines altogether, on that page, including three head-lines. About fifty of those lines, as one perceives, deal with local matters; so the reporters are not overworked.

Exactly one half of the second page is occupied with an opera criticism, fifty-three lines (three of them being head-lines), and 'Death Notices,' ten lines.

The other half of the second page is made up of two paragraphs under the head of 'Miscellaneous News.' One of these paragraphs tells about a quarrel between the Czar of Russia and his eldest son, twenty-one and a half lines; and the other tells about the atrocious destruction of a peasant child by its parents, forty lines, or one-fifth of the total of the reading matter contained in the paper.

Consider what a fifth part of the reading matter of an American daily paper issued in a city of 170,000 inhabitants amounts to; think what a mass it is. Would anyone suppose I could so snugly tuck away such a mass in a chapter of this book that it would be difficult to find it again if the reader lost his place? Surely not. I will translate that child-murder word for word to give the reader a realising sense of what a fifth part of the reading matter of a Munich daily actually is when it comes under measurement of the eye:—

'From Oberkreuzberg, January 21, the "Donau Zeitung" receives a long account of a crime, which we shorten as follows: In Rametuach, a village near Eppenschlag, lived a young married couple with two children, one of which, a boy aged five, was born three years before the marriage. For this reason, and also because a relative at Iggensbach had bequeathed 400 marks (100 dollars) to the boy, the heartless father considered him in the way; so the unnatural parents

determined to sacrifice him in the cruelest possible manner. They
proceeded to starve him slowly to death, meantime frightfully
maltreating him—as the village people now make known, when it is
too late. The boy was hut up in a hole, and when people passed by he
cried, and implored them to give him bread. His long continued
tortures and deprivations destroyed him at last, on the 3rd of January.
The sudden (*sic*) death of the child created suspicion, the more so as
the body was immediately clothed and laid upon the bier. Therefore,
the coroner gave notice, and an inquest was held on the 6th. What a
pitiful spectacle was disclosed then! The body was a complete
skeleton. The stomach and intestines were utterly empty—they
contained nothing whatever. The flesh on the corpse was not as thick
as the back of a knife, and incisions in it brought not a drop of blood.
There was not a piece of sound skin the size of a dollar on the whole
body; wounds, scars, bruises, discoloured extravasated blood,
everywhere—even on the soles of the feet there were wounds. The
cruel parents asserted that the boy had been so bad that they had been
obliged to use severe punishments, and that he finally fell over a bench
and broke his neck. However, they were arrested two weeks after the
inquest, and put in the prison at Deggendorf.'

Yes, they were arrested 'two weeks after the inquest.' What a home-
sound that has. That kind of police briskness rather more reminds me
of my native land than German journalism does.

I think a German daily journal doesn't do any good to speak of,
but, at the same time, it doesn't do any harm. That is a very large
merit, and should not be lightly weighed, nor lightly thought of.

The German humorous papers are beautifully printed upon fine
paper, and the illustrations are finely drawn, finely engraved, and are
not vapidly funny, but deliciously so. So, also, generally speaking, are
the two or three terse sentences which accompany the pictures. I
remember one of these pictures—a most dilapidated tramp is ruefully
contemplating some coins which lie in his open palm; he says, 'Well,
begging is getting played out. Only about 5 marks (1.25 dollars) for
the whole day; many an official makes more!' And I call to mind a
picture of a commercial traveller, who is about to unroll his
samples:—

'*Merchant* (pettishly). No, don't. I don't want to buy anything.

'*Drummer.* If you please, I was only going to show you—

'*Merchant.* But I don't wish to see them!

'*Drummer* (after a pause, pleadingly). But do you mind letting *me*
look at them? I haven't seen them for three weeks.!'